The Bushes are Red

Carole McKee

authorHOUSE®

AuthorHouse™
1663 Liberty Drive, Suite 200
Bloomington, IN 47403
www.authorhouse.com
Phone: 1-800-839-8640

First published by AuthorHouse 3/11/2009

ISBN: 978-1-4389-6076-0 (sc)

Library of Congress Control Number: 2009901957

Printed in the United States of America
Bloomington, Indiana

This book is printed on acid-free paper.

To my kids, Terra and Eric

1

LINDY DECELLI OPENED her eyes and looked at the alarm clock on the nightstand near her side of the bed. Two-ten in the morning. A noise. There. There it was again. She sat up in bed and swung her legs over the side. Ricky stirred beside her.

"What's wrong?" His voice was muffled with sleep.

"I think Sammie fell out of bed."

"Want me to go?"

"No....that's okay. I got it. Go back to sleep."

"Um....hmmm." Ricky mumbled as he rolled over and went back into a deep sleep.

Lindy stood up and started toward their daughter's room, without putting on a robe or slippers. It would only take a moment to pick her up and put her back into bed and cover her up. Luckily, the bed was low to the floor and the area rugs on both sides of the bed were made of thick faux fur—huge, pink faux fur bunnies fashioned after bear-skin rugs, to be exact. The heads on the bunnies were actually soft pillows. Samantha loved them. Lindy thought she would probably see Samantha lying with her

1

head on one of those pillow-headed rabbits when she went into the room. She turned the door knob to open the door and noticed a chill in the room. It was early March. March nights in Pennsylvania were *never* warm. Walking swiftly to the bed, she didn't notice the open window, nor did she see Sammie lying on the floor. She quickly went to the other side of the bed. No Sammie. Even more quickly, she moved to the wall switch and flicked on the overhead light. Her piercing scream brought Ricky up out of their bed instantly as he hit the floor running. Horrified, Lindy was staring at the open window. Ricky sailed past her and vaulted out of the window in his bare feet and boxer shorts.

"Call nine-one-one. Go! Lindy, do it now!"

Lindy ran down the hall to the kitchen, grabbed up the telephone, and dialed nine-one-one.

A voice came on the line instantly. *"Nine-one-one.... what's your emergency?"*

Lindy's throat was constricted. She tried to force words out of her mouth but only short gasps escaped her lips.

"Hello? Nine-one-one. Do you need help?"

Lindy found her voice. "My baby.....my daughter....is missing. She's not in her room and.....and the window.... is open. My husband....went out the window to look for her."

"Ma'am....how old is your daughter?"

"Five...she's five."

"Verify your address for me. Stay calm, ma'am. A car is on the way."

"Two-forty-four Carlisle. Please.....she's only five." Lindy hung up.

Lindy's breathing was labored. Michael. He was crying for her. She staggered down the hall to the room across from Samantha's and opened the door. Michael was standing in his crib, looking very frightened when Lindy scooped him up and hugged him to her.

"I scared, Mommy." He said as he wrapped his chubby three-year-old arms around her neck.

"I know, Baby. Come on in the kitchen with me."

She heard Ricky coming back through the window and she stopped and waited for him. As soon as she saw his face, she knew he had failed to find her. She jumped when the doorbell sounded. Ricky quickly responded to it. Two police officers entered the living room and furtively looked around. Lindy, tears streaming down her face, held Michael in her arms and stared at the officers. Ricky took charge.

"Our daughter. We put her to bed around nine. My wife woke up around two because she thought she heard Samantha fall out of bed. When she went into the room, Sammie was gone and the window was standing open. I ran out through the window to see if I could see anything, but...."

"Show us the room."

The officers started down the hallway without waiting for an invitation. One quickly went to the open window and the other went to the bed.

"You didn't touch anything in here? Since you discovered her missing, I mean?" The question came from the older man whose name tag read Joseph Lang.

"Only when I went out the window. I touched the frame, I'm sure."

"The latch on this window is broken. Was it before?"

"No." The reply came from both Lindy and Ricky.

"Well, somebody broke it…looks like from the outside. There are some scrapes on the outside frame….probably from a tool of some sort. Screwdriver, I'd guess."

The full impact of what he was saying hit Lindy hard.

"Are you saying…..someone broke in….and…and…. *took* our daughter?"

"It looks like it, Ma'am."

"Kidnapped? Sammie's been kidnapped?"

Her voice was steadily becoming higher in pitch and shakier with every word. Ricky sensed that she was becoming hysterical and quickly moved toward her. In a fluid movement he took Michael from her arms and wrapped one of his arms around her, holding onto her tightly. Her body trembled and as he held onto her he felt the quaking intensify. Lindy was losing control.

"What do we do? Officers? Please….help us. My wife and I…..we'll go crazy if anything happens to her. Lindy's losing it now. I have to call someone……okay?"

"Yeah, sure. Go ahead." Officer Lang glanced at him sympathetically.

Ricky led Lindy down the hall to the kitchen and sat her down on a chair. He reached for the phone and dialed his Uncle Nick's number. Nick answered on the second ring.

"Yeah…." His sleep laden voice hissed into the phone.

"Uncle Nick….we need you. Samantha's been kidnapped. Lindy's losing it."

Jolted fully awake, Nick spoke into the phone. "Rick? What did you say?"

"Sammie....Uncle Nick....someone broke in and took her."

"We'll be right there." He was already climbing out of bed and nudging Liz before he replaced the receiver onto the cradle.

"Nick....what's wrong?"

"That was Ricky. Samantha's been kidnapped."

Liz gasped and immediately jumped out of bed, throwing on clothes as she headed toward the stairs. She stopped in Nick's den and grabbed her medical bag as an afterthought, just knowing that she was going to have to calm Lindy and probably Ricky, too.

Although Ricky was hesitant to do it, he dialed his mother's number next. She would be useless, but Ron Shultz was a detective. He could help search for Samantha, maybe. Ron answered the phone.

"Shultz...."

"Ron.....Ricky."

"What's wrong? I can hear it in your voice. What's wrong?"

"Ron....somebody broke in here tonight and took Sammie."

"What? Jesus....I'm on my way."

Ricky held onto Lindy and she clung to him tightly with one arm, and the other wrapped protectively around Michael.

"I can't stop shaking, Ricky. Our beautiful little girl.... why? Who? Oh God, Ricky.....Oh God....."

Ricky could feel her going to pieces, and he hoped that Liz and Nick would hurry and get there. They were going to need all the help and support they could get. Lindy was becoming a basket-case by the minute and it was only a matter of time before he totally lost it, too. His wife and kids were his whole world.

Married since they were eighteen, Lindy and Ricky would be celebrating their fifteenth anniversary next month, and were still very much in love. Together they finished high school, and then college, both obtaining a Master's degree in their fields. Ricky had gone on to become a chemist, working for a large national company that developed household cleaning products, and Lindy taught second grade until she became pregnant with Samantha. She returned to work after she gave birth to Samantha, only to go on maternity leave again when she became pregnant with Michael. After Michael was born, she and Ricky decided that until the children were both of school age, Lindy would become a stay-at-home mom. It was a decision that worked out well for the four-part nucleus that made up their happy family. Lindy and Ricky still felt that jolt of electricity when their eyes connected, and still melted into each other's arms when they touched. They adored each other and they adored their children. No two children were ever more secure in knowing that they were loved than Samantha and Michael. During the weekdays, Ricky went to work while Lindy took care of the household responsibilities, but on weekends and evenings, they focused on their children. Ricky and Lindy reveled in the happy smiles on their children's faces when they executed planned weekend outings for the four of them. As parents, they couldn't be faulted in any way.

Liz and Nick were the first to arrive. Liz immediately went to them and took Michael out of their arms. She ran down to the master bedroom and grabbed Lindy's robe for her, urging her to put it on when she returned to the kitchen. Ricky turned Lindy over to Nick's arms and started a pot of coffee. The number of police in the house increased after the original two made calls to get federal crime scene investigators there to comb through Samantha's room for clues. Ron Shultz and Angie appeared right after the crime scene investigators got there. Two more men in suits showed up, and introduced themselves as FBI. Ricky surveyed their badges briefly and then handed them back. They wanted to interview both Lindy and Ricky to get some facts and details. While the coffee was brewing Ricky went back to Lindy's side and just held her. Nick showed the two from the FBI into the family room where they agreed they would be comfortable. They went about setting up phone equipment and asked that Ricky and Lindy come into the family room to talk. Angie was getting coffee cups out of the cupboard while Ron followed Ricky and Lindy into the family room.

The two men who were setting up equipment gestured for Ricky and Lindy to sit down, but stared at Ron Shultz, quizzically.

"I'm Ron Shultz. I'm a local detective....and a family member."

"Okay, Detective Shultz....how are you related?"

"I married Ricky's mother."

"Oh....well, this is the Bureau's jurisdiction."

"I know. I'm only here to support any way I can."

The agent nodded his acceptance of Ron's explanation, and then turned to Ricky and Lindy.

"Now....I'm Agent Tom Morrow and this is my partner, Jack Daily. We need to ask some questions...some of them may sound...probing...but believe me, we have done this before….so bear with us. We know what we're doing. Understood?"

His unwavering stare waited for their response. They both nodded.

"Now who was the first to go to your daughter's room?"

"Lindy….my wife."

"Okay….Missus….."

"DeCelli. Lindy and Ricky DeCelli."

"Missus DeCelli….I'll need to interview you first. Mister DeCelli can wait out there." His gesture indicated that Ricky was to go back to the kitchen. "Detective, you can remain here if you like, but I'm going to ask that you don't interfere with our interviews or with the investigation."

Ron nodded his agreement.

"Now….Missus DeCelli….what woke you up?"

"I-I'm not sure. I know I heard a noise, but…."

Lindy's voice was quivering from the constant tremors seizing her body. Ron reached over and took her hand, and looked up for the agent's approval.

"May I?" He asked the agent.

Agent Morrow nodded then began again. "Try to think…..think hard. What was the noise?"

Lindy concentrated on remembering the sound that awakened her. She closed her eyes and rubbed her forehead in an attempt to remember.

"It was…sort of a scraping sound….I think. I thought I heard Sammie cry out right after it. I thought I heard her say 'mommy'. That's when I sat up in bed."

"The scraping sound….could it have been the window being pulled open? Metal against metal?"

Lindy thought for a moment. "Y-yes. It could have been. I don't know. I think that I, like most mothers, have a built-in alarm system that awakens us when…something's not right with the children."

Morrow's normally stoic face smiled slightly. "Not all mothers have that….just the good ones. So then what happened?"

Lindy proceeded. "I got out of bed and went down to her room, and opened the door."

"Was the door completely shut?"

"Yes. We shut their doors but keep ours partially open so we can hear them if they call out to us."

"So you opened the door and….?"

"I noticed the chill in the room, but I was focusing on Sammie's bed. I-I c-could see she w-wasn't in it, nor was she on the f-floor. I….went around to the….other side of the…bed….and….and she…wasn't there. That's when I went over and….switched the light on….and…saw the window….o-open…." Lindy was gasping for air. "Oh…. oh, *God!* Please……find her….*please!*"

Lindy couldn't go on. Her body was overtaken by uncontrollable sobs as she seemed to crumble before the agent's eyes.

"Okay….that's all for now. You can go ahead and…we can talk later. I'll talk to your husband now."

Morrow nodded to Ron indicating that he should escort Lindy out of the family room. "Bring the husband in, if you would, please. Make sure someone is with *her*, though."

Ron nodded and helped Lindy out of the chair. He held her tightly for a moment, stroking her hair. A lump was forming in his own throat as he soothed her, and he thought about what he had said so many years ago. 'She could still melt the heart of a granite statue...even now,' he thought.

Lindy had gone from an adorable teenager to a beautiful woman, but she had somehow managed to stay as sweet as she had been then, in her teenage years. The whole family loved her and they all had an uncontrollable urge to protect her all the time. Ron handed her off to Angie and told Ricky that the agents wanted to talk to him. After making sure that Lindy was going to be all right, he followed Ron into the family room, where the two agents were still working at setting up equipment. They nodded to Ricky when he entered.

"We have technicians coming to do the rest of this, but we wanted to get some of it started. Time is of the greatest importance in these....cases. Sit down."

Ricky complied by sitting in the chair Lindy had occupied, while Ron returned to the chair he had sat in moments ago while they spoke with Lindy. At the moment, Lindy was seated at the kitchen table with a cup of coffee in front of her and Angie's arm around her shoulders. Liz, seated on the other side of her, was handing her tissues, while Nick held Michael who was almost back to sleep.

When Michael was totally asleep, Nick took him into his room and laid him down in his crib. As an afterthought, he went over to the windows and checked them to make sure they were locked. Satisfied that they were secure, he returned to the kitchen.

The agent studied Ricky for a few minutes. It was obvious to him that Ricky was putting up a brave front, probably for his wife. In dealing with so many of these cases, he could tell which parents were taking it the hardest, and in this case, he would have to say that both of them were taking it equally hard. The wife cried and crumbled, and he could see that this guy was close to it, but held on for his wife's sake. Agent Morrow concluded that there was a lot of love in this house. He began his interview.

"Mister DeCelli....what do you do for a living?"

"I'm a chemist. I do a lot of research and testing... always trying to improve a product...or ensure that it's safe."

"Any friction at work? Anybody pissed at you about anything?"

"No, not that I know of. We all get along. We all have a common goal."

"What about in your personal life? Have any problems with anybody?"

"No...Lindy and I do almost everything together... with the kids. Most of our social life is taken up by things the kids enjoy. We....wouldn't have it any other way."

The agent came close to a half smile again. He sat in thought for a moment, rubbing his chin.

"Okay....I can't help noticing that you...both of you... are pretty good looking. Any chance of...say, a jealous ex...either of you?"

Ricky smiled a little. "We've been together since we were sixteen. We'll both be thirty-three next month. That would be a long time for an ex to harbor any kind of jealousy...and besides, neither one of us actually really had anybody else before we met each other. We just knew from the day we met that we both had found what we needed. There was never a need to go anywhere else."

The agent nodded and looked thoughtful once again,

continuing to stroke his chin. He brightened a moment, before he spoke.

"Any money?"

"What? What do you mean?"

"Well….for starters…do either of you owe anybody any money?"

"No…not really. We have credit cards and stuff like that, but…no…we don't owe anybody."

"Okay…well…do you *have* any money? I mean…. enough that would make you a target for ransom?"

"Well….yeah. There's money. Lindy's grandfather was William Stockwell. He owned everything around here at one time. But that money is all in trust. She gets a nice allowance from it every month, but the estate cannot be broken. Most of the time she invests her allowance back into something, so *that* is growing into something. But I don't think we have enough money that would make us….appealing to a kidnapper looking for a big ransom. I mean…the Stockwell estate is huge…but most people don't know about it, nor do they even remember who he was or how much money Stockwell had."

The agent seemed satisfied with Ricky's answer. He jotted down a few notes as he had when Lindy sat in that same chair.

"Okay…so can you tell me what you heard and saw tonight?"

"Yeah…well, Lindy heard something. She has that radar when it comes to the kids. I felt her sit up in bed and I asked her what was wrong. She said she thought Samantha fell out of bed. I offered to go, but she said it was okay…she would go. I rolled over and went back to sleep. A few seconds later, probably no more than a minute and a half…I heard Lindy scream. I ran and immediately saw the open window. I jumped out the window and ran up to the street….but I didn't see anything. It's pretty dark around here at night. Very few street lights."

"We will have the area scoured as soon as it gets to be daylight. We may find something. There's always something."

He gave Ricky a reassuring look and Ricky nodded and smiled weakly at him.

"Can I bring you guys coffee or something?"

"Yeah….coffee would be great. Oh, and we get an allowance…food allowance…so we'll help out with food here. We're going to be your house guests for the duration."

Ricky seemed relieved by that information. He didn't want any of them to go away until they had their precious Samantha back home again.

"If you get a chance to sleep…these two chairs open up into beds. Just thought you'd like to know that. I'll bring some bedding in for you to use if necessary."

"Thanks." Agent Morrow watched Ricky walk out of the family room, almost forgetting that Ron Shultz was still seated in the chair. He jumped when Ron spoke.

"They're good people. Both of them. Devoted to each other, and to their kids. You don't see that real often now-a-days."

"No…you don't. But when you do see it….it makes it all the more tragic. Bad things happen to good people." Agent Morrow shrugged and then turned back to the equipment in front of him, only looking up when Ricky set a cup of coffee down in front of him.

"If you need anything….just help yourself. There is an

extra refrigerator back here….we keep a lot of stuff in it."
Ricky offered. He was about to walk back out to Lindy but
suddenly changed his mind. "Sir? What are we supposed
to do? I mean…is there something we are supposed to do
right now?"

"No. Let us do our job….that's all. You have to be here
in case the abductor calls…but that's all. You and your wife
and son can watch Disney movies all day if you want…or
sleep….or whatever. You just have to be available to answer
the phone. After all, this is the contact point. If there is to
be contact, it will be here at this phone number."

"What do you mean *if* there is to be contact?"

"Mister DeCelli…do you know of anybody who would
want to kidnap your daughter?"

"Yeah….everybody. Have you seen her? Picture my
wife's face under a very dark brown, nearly black, wig. She
has Lindy's face and eyes and my hair."

"Yes, and we will need pictures of her, by the way."

"We already have a bunch of them out on the table in
the kitchen. We knew you would. Take what you need."

Ricky went back to the kitchen and found Lindy
crying, holding her face between her hands. He went
around to the back of her chair, bent down and wrapped
his arms around her shoulders. He gently kissed her hair
and laid his cheek on top of her head. She reached for his
hand and stroked it.

"Call…Chris….and my dad."

"Okay, Baby. Just let me hold you for a minute.
Okay?"

Ricky needed to hold her. He needed to draw strength
from her. That's how it was with them. They drew strength
from each other by holding on to one another. Like the

time when Michael had gotten sick—so sick that they had to take him to the emergency room. Both Lindy and Ricky were falling apart until they grabbed on to each other. Together they emerged strong and were able to deal with the situation at hand. Of course, Michael recovered from a bout of pneumonia, for which they were grateful and relieved, but they knew then that the strength they needed to deal with crises came from each other.

Ricky reached for the phone and called Chris first, just knowing that he would be awakening him. It was only six AM on a Saturday. Chris answered the phone after four rings.

"This better be life or death…" He mumbled.

"It is. Samantha's been kidnapped."

Chris shot up out of bed fully awake and alert. "*What? When?*"

"At around two this morning. Right out of her bed."

"And you're just calling me *now?* What the *fuck*, Rick?"

"Well, we called the police first, and then they came and the FBI came and questioned us. We've been busy with them. This is the first chance we got. Coming over?"

"I already have my clothes on. On my way." He abruptly hung up.

Lindy's brother, Chris was Samantha's Godfather and he took the responsibility seriously. He never forgot her birthday and he was good to her on Christmas, without ever slighting Michael. He loved both his niece and his nephew and never tired of showering them with attention and affection. Samantha always got a little extra since she was his Godchild. Cindy, Ron Shultz's daughter and one of Lindy and Ricky's best friends, was the Godmother, and she was equally generous with her love and affection. Ricky made a quick call to her, awakening her as well. He could hear Cindy panicking and gasping for air, as she said she would be right there.

The next call was to Ray Riley, Lindy's father. This call was the hardest to make. It was only after Samantha was born did Lindy concede to seeing her father again. It took a lot of coercion from Ricky to make Lindy agree to it. By telling Lindy that Samantha had a right to know her grandfather, Ricky was able to break the barrier that kept father and daughter estranged for all those years. Upon that first meeting, seeing each other after eight years, all the animosity from Lindy melted away into a tearful reunion. Lindy no longer held baby Nicholas' death against Ray, since she accepted that the shooting had been an accident. Ricky described to Lindy the shock on Ray's face when the gun went off and Lindy fell to the floor. He also told her about Ray's remorse when he came to the hospital while Lindy was in surgery. Of course, the time that Ricky shared a jail cell with Ray just reinforced how much Ray was emotionally suffering over what he had done. Ricky had described over and over how miserable Ray felt. The renewed relationship after the first meeting, was formal and distant at first, but Lindy was warming up to Ray, and she seriously liked Diane, Ray's wife who he married after he got out of prison nine years after shooting Lindy and four months before Samantha was born.

Since the reunion, Ray had become a devoted grandfather, and Diane a loving grandmother. Both Samantha and Michael took to them and were excited when they were going to see them. Lindy agreed to give Michael the middle name of Raymond after her father, and Ray could not have been a happier or a prouder man over it. Ricky remembered all of this as he dialed Ray and Diane's number.

"Hullo....?"

"Diane? Ricky."

"Ricky. Ricky?" Diane sat up in bed. "What's wrong?"

"Sammie's been kidnapped. Can you come over? We need all the love and support we can get right now."

Diane shook Ray by the shoulder while she was hanging up the phone.

"Wake up! Ray....wake up. We have to go."

"Go....where? Are you crazy? It's six-fifteen.... Saturday morning. Not even a work day."

"Samantha's been kidnapped. Ricky just called. He said they need....all of us."

Diane was reaching for her clothes as she headed toward the bathroom. Ray flung away the blankets and stood up.

"Jesus. Did he say when?" Ray raised his voice to be heard over the running water in the bathroom as he made his way there.

"No. It must have happened while we were sleeping.... while they were sleeping. My God, Ray. Lindy must be out of her mind by now."

2

CHRIS ARRIVED AT the house as the police were taping off the area on the side where Samantha's bedroom window was located. He stopped and looked only momentarily and then bounded into the house. He felt the pressure of a hand on his chest even before his eyes adjusted to the light inside the house.

"I'm Officer Brownley. I need to check to see if your name is on the visitor's list before I can let you pass. Standard procedure until we get used to the regular visitors."

"Sure. Christopher Riley....Lindy is my sister."

The officer nodded and told him to pass through. Chris spied Lindy and immediately went to her and put his arms around her trembling shoulders.

"My God, Pumpkin....my God." He couldn't say anything more. Tears were glistening in his eyes as he held onto his sister. Pumpkin had always been his nickname for Lindy, and even though she was an adult, Chris still called her that.

"Thanks for coming, Chris." Ricky spoke as he stood beside Lindy.

"Rick....what can I do? I'll do....whatever....just tell me."

"The Feds said not to do anything....let them do their jobs. We just have to be here to answer the phone. You all are here for support for us. As you can see, we're pretty useless right now. Neither of us can think, function, cook, eat, clean....nothing. We just need those who love us to give us a hand with things. Michael will be needing attention when he wakes up. He was up with us most of the night, so he's in bed right now...."

Chris lured Ricky into the hallway to ask what took place before he called him. Ricky told him of how Lindy heard a noise and assumed Sammie had fallen out of bed, and how she went in and found her gone, the window standing open.

"No note? Or anything like that?"

"No....nothing. Chris, I'm trying to keep it together.... but it's getting harder by the minute. Lindy needs me to be strong right now....but I'm not sure I can keep it up. You know how I feel about my wife and kids."

"Yeah....I do. I'll try to pick up the slack. Rick, nobody expects you to be iron man here...okay?"

"There's your dad and Diane. Looks like they brought something. Bagels...good. Gotta feed the cops."

Ray and Diane carried in bags of bagels, enough to feed everybody, police included. After passing the sentry at the door, they brought them to the kitchen and set them down on the counter and immediately went to Lindy. Upon seeing them, new tears fell from Lindy's tear ducts and a sound not too much different from a wounded animal was coming from her lips. Diane pulled her close and cried with her, rocking her in a soothing manner.

"What can we do? Lindy?" Ray asked her quietly.

"Nothing....pray....that's all."

Cindy parked behind a squad car and got out of her car. A curious neighbor walking her dog, stopped her to ask what happened, since there were by now, four squad cars, two unmarked cars, a crime scene investigation van, and the one that the FBI came in. Television stations were beginning to arrive as well.

Cindy told the neighbor lady that Samantha was kidnapped and the woman paled in shock.

"I'm Alicia Weston. I live next door. I wonder if those noises I heard last night had anything to do with it. Around two, maybe?"

"Maybe. You need to see one of these cops. Wait... there's my dad. He's a detective. Dad!"

"Hey, Cindy. God, this is terrible. Lindy's a mess. Glad you're here."

"Dad, this lady heard something last night. She lives in this house which is right next to Sammie's room."

"Ma'am....can you come with me?"

"Sure."

"Thanks, Cin. See what you can do for Lindy and Ricky, Honey. This is terrible for them."

Cindy nodded as she was on the cell phone calling Lukas and Shawna. Ron led the neighbor woman, dog included, into the family room to meet with the agents. Two technicians had been added to the roster, and they were working diligently setting up recording devices and speakers.

"Agent Morrow, this is the neighbor. She says she heard something around two this morning."

"Please…sit down. You are?"

"I'm Alicia Weston. I live in the house next to this one. Around two this morning, I heard something. Sounded like metal being dragged against metal. Then I heard someone say 'Shhh'. Not two minutes later I heard Lindy scream and then I heard Ricky running the length of the house."

"You heard someone….go 'Shhh'?"

"Yes." She sat poised with her dog on her lap.

"Could you tell if it was a man? Or a woman? More than one person?"

"I think it was a man…I don't know why….but I think it may have been a man."

"Okay…if you think of anything else….please let us know. Thank you for your cooperation. You're free to go after you write down your name, address, and phone number." Morrow handed her a notebook and pen.

Alicia Weston left the house and took it upon herself to notify the neighbors of the situation in the DeCelli home. Nobody else heard anything, but they were all more than happy to send over dishes of food to help out. The first arrived at noon. Missus Kaminski across the street put together a huge casserole dish of stuffed cabbage, cooked them, and sent them over with her husband. Many dishes began arriving after that. Just past noon, Lukas and his wife Michelle pulled up with four pizzas and their three year old in tow. Lindy was grateful that Michael would have someone to play with for awhile, and especially because Michael and little Lukas always played well together. Shawna and her partner Ally came in, bringing cases of soft drinks and iced tea. With each new arrival came new tears from Lindy. Liz, Angie, and Diane had taken over the kitchen, keeping coffee in the pot, food on the counter, and the dirty dishes to a minimum. Liz urged Lindy to lie down for awhile but she refused, thinking she would miss a call from the kidnappers if she did. Liz was worried because Lindy looked deathly pale.

Agent Morrow called for Lindy and Ricky to come into the family room.

"Okay. This system is ready. Now....you have to answer the phone in here when it rings. Got that? Don't answer it anywhere else. Oh, and the television news cameras are ready for you. Think about what you're going to say. Got that eight-by-ten of Samantha ready? Let's go outside."

The cameras were set up. Four local news stations and CNN were standing by. Those watching television across the country were about to experience an interruption in their current programming. Every station's interruption began the same way: *"We interrupt regular programming to bring you a special news bulletin."* Each station's reporter filled their audience in on the details while Ricky and Lindy waited in the background for their chance to plead for their daughter. The cameras focused on Ricky and Lindy, all microphones poised and pointed toward them. Ricky held onto Lindy as he spoke into the microphones.

"Whoever you are....don't hurt our little girl. We'll give you whatever you want....just don't hurt her."

It was Lindy's turn. The pain and suffering was clear in her face. She spoke almost breathlessly.

"Please....she's only five years old. Please. Please. Give her back to us. *Please.* My husband and I will see to it

23

that you get whatever you want. Just please return our daughter."

Lindy couldn't go on. She crumbled in Ricky's arms and the cameras momentarily focused on it. She and Ricky were whisked inside and the cameras stopped rolling, but only after they focused on the picture of Samantha. The reporters concluded and wrapped up the bulletin report.

Several miles away, a man sat in a sparsely furnished living room and chuckled at the scene on the television.

"Of course you can have her back. Untouched and unharmed when you give me five million dollars."

He glanced over at Samantha who was still out cold, and worried that maybe he had given her too much of that stuff to make her sleep. She hadn't moved since he brought her in and laid her down. He supposed he should check on her, but he kind of liked it that she wasn't a bother to him right now.

3

INSIDE THEIR HOUSE, Ricky and Lindy clung to each other. Lindy cried hysterically while Ricky held her, choking back his own tears. He walked Lindy into their bedroom, shutting the door behind them, and lifted her onto the bed. He lay down beside her and wrapped her in his arms, holding her tightly, and waited for her to calm down. When her breathing became even, he leaned over to see if she were sleeping. He saw that her eyes were closed but he didn't think she was sleeping. She proved his thinking to be correct when she opened her teary blue eyes and stared up at him.

"Talk to me, Ricky. Say things....things that will help me get a grip. I know....I'm losing it. I'm sorry. This is hurting you, too....I know that. So just say things to me that will give me strength."

"I love you, Lindy. I love you with all my heart and soul. I always have. I love Sammie and I love Michael. We're a family...a good family. We will be a family forever. We'll get her back, Baby...she'll come back. Whatever the bastards want, they can have it. *But we will get her back. We will do whatever it takes to get her back.*"

Ricky stroked Lindy's hair as he spoke, feeling her slowly calming down. They dozed off for about fifteen minutes, and awoke feeling slightly refreshed. They walked out, arm in arm, to spend time with the family and friends who had gathered there for the duration of this ordeal.

Lukas and Michelle said their good-nights even though it was relatively early, and promised to be back tomorrow. They were the first to leave.

"Do you need anything? Want us to bring anything over?"

"No…just having Lukas here to play with Michael is help enough. It's keeping him occupied. He doesn't know about Sammie. He wouldn't understand anyway."

Lindy lifted Michael into her arms and encouraged him to say goodnight to Lukas. Suddenly fiercely protective, she was reluctant to put Michael down. She smiled at him and kissed his cheek.

"Are you hungry, Honey? Let's get you something to eat."

"Sammie? Her eat, too?" He stared at Lindy through his innocent brown eyes.

"Not right now." Lindy answered him as she felt her chest constrict.

Liz heard Michael's question and immediately diverted his attention by asking him if he saw something on the counter that he wanted to eat. Lindy carried Michael over to look at the foods spread across the counter.

"Dat!" His chubby index finger was pointed at a casserole dish full of macaroni and cheese. "And dat!"

He swung his arm over to point at a yellow layer cake with chocolate frosting. Two pieces had been cut out of it.

"And how about some of dat?" Lindy asked as she pointed at a bowl of green beans. She watched Michael's face, and not waiting for a decision, asked. "A little bit?"

Michael nodded.

Satisfied that he would eat enough she sat him in his booster seat while Liz warmed up the macaroni and green beans on Michael's special Disney plate, with Eyore the donkey on it. Lindy sat down with him while he maneuvered the small fork that had been purchased just for him. He looked up at Lindy with his most endearing smile, and Lindy's heart melted as it always did. She smiled back with love in her eyes.

"I love you," she whispered to him as she kissed his chubby left hand.

"I yuv you, too," he grinned back at her, macaroni falling out of his mouth.

Lindy never ceased to marvel at the features her children had. Samantha had her face and eyes, but her hair was almost as black as Ricky's, and Michael had Ricky's face and eyes, and hair almost as blonde as Lindy's. She once said to Ricky that it was like they went through a time machine together and the hair got mixed up at the other end. She thought about that as she watched Michael devour the food on his plate. When all but a couple of green beans were gone from the plate, Michael set the fork down.

"All done! Cake now?" He looked expectantly at Lindy.

"Lindy?" Liz waited for her approval before she set the cake in front of Michael.

"Okay....cake now," she smiled at him. "You ate it *all*!"

Michael responded by vigorously nodding his head up and down and grinning. He made a mess of the cake, getting more on the table than into him, but Lindy felt that was probably good—the less cake the better. Ricky joined them as Michael was finished making his mess.

"Shawna and Ally are getting ready to leave, Babe. I'll take Michael in to bathe him....why don't you spend a couple of minutes with them before they go?"

"Okay....I've been a terrible hostess today.....I know."

"Hey...you've been a champ. Nobody is expecting you to be Emily Post today. Let's go, Frosting Face...ready to go deep tub diving?"

Ricky scooped Michael up and tucked him under his arm like a sack of potatoes, causing Michael to squeal with delight. Lindy favored Ricky with a weak smile and got up from the table to go talk to Shawna and Ally. She embraced them, one on each side of her, and thanked them for being there. Tears were coming along with the gratitude, and Shawna hugged Lindy tighter.

"I haven't been very good company, guys; I'm sorry. I'm *so* glad you're both here though...honest."

"We know, Lin. We're going to go now, but we *will* be back tomorrow....you know....for moral support. You know we love you and Ricky and the kids. You're family."

"Thanks...we love you, too. Thanks *so much* for being here."

"We wouldn't want to be anywhere else right now. Night, Lin...love you."

"Night....love you, too."

Lindy watched them walk out the front door, holding

hands, and wondered if Angie noticed. Angie still couldn't fathom same sex relationships, and her wide-eyed shock was almost comical when she encountered such a relationship.

Lindy quietly sat down on the loveseat next to her father. He had been sitting there quietly with his elbows resting on his thighs and his face resting in his hands. He looked up when Lindy sat down.

"How you holding up, Honey?"

"By a thread, Dad....by a thread. I think I'm about to go mad. I don't know...what do we do? I...can't just sit here....I feel like I have to go look for her....but where? I have no idea where to look...."

Lindy dropped her face into her hands and spread her fingers out across her forehead, massaging her temples with her thumbs. Ray studied her for a moment, and then slowly moved his arms until they were wrapped around her, pulling her toward him. When she was close enough, he kissed her hair. Lindy dropped her hands and stared at him for just a moment before the waterworks began again. She fell against Rays' chest and sobbed, while Ray pulled her tighter. Diane's eyes were wet as she watched. 'Too bad you didn't think of doing this years ago, Ray. A lot of pain could have been spared,' she thought to herself.

Angie and Ron planned on staying all night and taking turns getting catnaps on the couch and loveseat, with Nick and Liz, who had no intention of going anywhere. Chris also had nowhere he wanted to be but there with Ricky and Lindy, so he suggested to Ray and Diane that they stay at his place since it was closer to them. They reluctantly agreed, but said they would be back early in the morning. Cindy wanted to stay but Ron urged her to go get some sleep and come back in the morning. He stealthily handed her a fifty dollar bill and told her to bring breakfast with her when she came back in the morning.

Ricky came out of the bathroom with a squeaky-clean Michael dressed in his Winnie the Pooh pajamas and sitting on Ricky's shoulders. It was time for everyone to settle down for the night, so Lindy took Michael's hand to put him to bed, while Ricky grabbed the other hand. They walked down the hall and Michael stopped short in front of Samantha's room, trying to peer around the door.

"Sammie?" He spoke her name in the form of a question.

Lindy froze and looked at Ricky. Closing her eyes she quickly recovered for Michael's sake and walked the rest of the way to Michael's bed with him in tow. After the goodnight kisses, Ricky agreed to stay and read a story to Michael while Lindy went to see if the FBI agents needed anything. It was unnecessary, since Cindy had already handled it before she left. Both agents had plates of food and fresh coffee in front of them. There wasn't much for Lindy to do but join the family in the living room. Liz was by her side instantly, holding a fresh cup of coffee out for her. The room was strangely quiet considering the number of people present. Lindy turned to Nick.

"When do you think....the kidnappers...will call?"

"I don't know. I'm guessing they're going to let you stew for awhile...make you desperate....that way....you're more willing to go along with....what they want....whatever that is...."

"Oh, God.....you don't think.....they'll hurt her? Do you?"

"Honey...she's their bargaining tool. No....they won't hurt her." And he prayed silently that he was right.

Ray and Diane got up to leave. Lindy felt a little disappointed but knew there would be no room for everyone to sleep there. She went to them and hugged them as they promised to be back very early in the morning. Ricky came from Michael's room in time to say goodnight to them, and, at the same time, to assure Lindy that Michael was fast asleep. He walked Ray and Diane to the door, and Diane hugged him.

"Make sure you both get some sleep....okay?"

Ricky nodded his promise and then returned to the rest of the family. Nick grabbed up the remote control and flipped on the television. His eyes were met by a picture of Samantha, as big as life, on the screen. The unseen commentator was ordering anyone who had any information as to the whereabouts of Samantha Renee DeCelli to call the FBI phone number that was stationary across the bottom of the screen. Nick stole a glance at Lindy and spotted the tears on her cheeks. He immediately draped his arm across her shoulders. Lindy looked down at her clothes and realized that she had managed to get out of her nightclothes at some point during the day, but she didn't even remember doing that.

"Ricky...." Lindy quietly got his attention. "Why don't we sleep on the sofa in the family room? Those two agents can each have those chairs to get some rest. Then somebody can use our bed."

"Oh, Lindy....you look exhausted." Liz told her. "You should get a good night's sleep in bed."

"But...if the....kidnappers try to call....Ricky and I

will be all the way on the other side of the house. This way if the phone rings, we'll be right there to answer it."

"She has a point." Ricky responded. "We can do that….it's not all that uncomfortable. Just let me check with the Feds."

Ricky was in and out of the family room within a minute.

"They think that's wise….so…one of you couples can take our bed."

It was settled. Nick and Liz slept in the master bedroom while Ron took the sofa and Angie curled up on the love seat. Curled up with Ricky on the sofa in the family room, Lindy managed to fall asleep, listening to the steady rhythm of Agent Daily's light snoring.

The first call came at six on Sunday morning.

4

SAMANTHA SLEPT MOST of the day on Saturday, which pleased him. She awoke around four in the afternoon asking for her mommy.

"Forget about your mommy for right now, kid. How about something to eat? You hungry?"

"Yes.....but my mommy will make me dinner."

"Kid...your mommy's not here. It's just you and me."

"I want to go home!"

"Yeah...well, you can't...not yet. Your mommy has to do what I tell her if she wants you back. And if she doesn't....well, I guess she doesn't want you back."

Samantha started to cry.

"Yes, she does! Mommy loves me! Daddy does, too!"

"Yeah....well, we'll see. Don't start giving me trouble. I don't like kids to begin with...but cry-baby brats really make me mad.....so just shut up."

Samantha shivered and tried to control her sobs, but it sounded like she was hiccupping. The man went to the refrigerator, got out a small bottle of juice, and handed it to her. He suddenly remembered that she probably couldn't open it, so he grabbed it back and twisted the cap for her.

"There...something to drink. Now....how about a grilled cheese?"

Samantha stared at him without answering, and he treated her actions as a go-ahead sign. He stood up and walked to the small stove where he started preparing the grilled cheese sandwiches as he watched her from the corner of his eye. She was certainly a beauty. Those big blue eyes and dimples looked adorable under that mop of thick, rich almost-black hair. He stopped what he was doing, moved over in front of the television, and popped in a Disney movie, unmindful of which one it was. It turned out to be *Cinderella,* one of Samantha's favorites, so to the delight of her kidnapper she was quiet and occupied while he made the cheese sandwiches. Since she was the key to his future he decided he would try to make friends with her. He put the sandwich on a plate and added some potato chips to it, and then carried it over to the loveseat she occupied and set the plate down in front of her. He congratulated himself on buying those Disney movies; they were going to keep the peace, he felt sure.

"So which one is Cinderella?" He tried to draw her into a relaxed conversation.

"The pretty one." She answered.

"Then....that would be....you. You're prettier than all of those ladies."

That brought a smile to her face. 'This is easy,' he thought.

"My mom's the prettiest," she responded.

"You don't say." He answered back.

"Can I go to the bathroom?"

"Yeah...sure. Come on."

"You don't have to go with me....I can, by myself."

"Well.....I have to show you where it is. Come on."

He didn't worry about her escaping since the only window in the bathroom was protected by a steel grate attached to the outside of the house, not to mention that there was nowhere for her to go. Finding this perfect hiding spot was a stroke of luck. There were no other houses around except the one next door where the old lady lived and the only way in and out of the place was a narrow unpaved driveway. Nobody could see or hear anything from outside of the house. If the days were nice, and *if* he felt charitable, he might consider taking her for a walk in the woods. Kids liked that sort of thing. When *Cinderella* ended he rewound it and asked her to choose the next one.

"Mommy says I can only see one movie a night."

"But...see....mommy is not *here!* You're on *vacation!* So if you want to see two movies....or three....you can. Let's watch this one."

He extracted the movie *"Babe"* from its cover and plopped it into the VCR. Samantha watched with interest, taking a cookie from the plate he had set down in front of her. He watched her from the corner of his eye again and marveled at how well behaved she was. 'Her mother must spend a lot of time with her' he thought to himself. He actually enjoyed the movie, and she apparently loved it. She didn't appear to be sleepy so he surprised her with a coloring book and a box of crayons. She actually smiled at him, and that smile brought back a flood of memories. Finally, she fell asleep, holding the stuffed dog he carried out of her room when he took her. He covered her and tuned in to the local news station. No further developments in the kidnapping case of Samantha Renee DeCelli—good. He fell asleep and awoke at five-thirty in the morning. He made coffee, settled into the recliner with a fresh cup, picked up the prepaid disposable phone and dialed the DeCelli telephone number.

5

THE TINNY SOUND of the telephone brought both Lindy
and Ricky to the surface of the deep sleep they had been
weighted under. They had only slept a couple of hours,
but those hours were spent in a sound, fitful sleep. Agent
Morrow was awake immediately. On the third ring he told
Ricky to answer it.

"Hello?"

"I have your kid," the disguised muffled voice came
over the line.

"What do you want? Name it...just let us have her
back." Ricky answered, unconsciously pulling Lindy close
to him.

"Not so fast...."

"Hey, I don't even want to bargain. Whatever you
want, you can have."

"We'll get to that."

"Is our daughter okay? Please let me speak to her."

"It's six AM! Your daughter is sleeping....what kind
of a parent are you? You can talk to her later.....when I
call you back."

"No! Don't hang up! Just tell me what you want.....
I'll get it."

"Later."

He hung up. 'Kid, you don't have any room for
bargaining, anyhow,' he thought. He removed the voice-
changing device from the phone and slipped both items
into his pocket. With a self-satisfied sigh he drifted back
to sleep.

Lindy was on the verge of hysteria again. The agents
were busy with the phone equipment while Ricky held
onto Lindy, trying to soothe her.

Agent Morrow looked up at Ricky.

"I think he's using a prepaid phone....can't track those.
At least not this way, with this equipment. He wasn't on
the phone long enough for anything anyway. You have to
try to keep him on as long as possible."

"He's the one hanging up." Ricky retorted.

"I know. But...that was the first call. They'll get more
in depth.....then.....he'll make a mistake. They always
do."

Agent Morrow stared at Lindy and Ricky with an air
of confidence. Ricky stood up and wrapped the blanket
they had used around Lindy.

"I'm going to go make coffee. Be right back."

He kissed Lindy's forehead and strode out to the
kitchen. Agent Daily saw the pain in Ricky's eyes as he
passed by him. He knew he would be in the kitchen trying
to regain his composure while he made the coffee. 'What
a guy...putting up a front like that so he can appear strong
for his wife. He's hurting just as badly as she is. So...
unselfish...that's what he is.' Daily was lost in thought as
he ran his hand through his hair.

This was day two. Cindy arrived with donuts and pastries, and immediately began cooking the eggs and bacon she had picked up before she got there. Angie awoke and heard Michael calling for Lindy. She went into his room and lifted him out of his crib and put him down on the floor. He padded out to the kitchen and was delighted that Cindy was there.

"Hi, Aunt Cindy. Where mommy?"

"In the family room, Sweetie. Go see her, and then come out here so I can give you a donut...okay?"

Michael grinned and nodded and then ran toward the family room to see Lindy and Ricky. He hesitated when he saw the two men sitting there with them, but his desire to get to Lindy and Ricky quickly overcame any fears he may have had. He climbed up on the sofa right into Lindy's lap, and she embraced him with both arms. He pointed at Agents Morrow and Daily.

"Mans," he declared.

"Men," Lindy corrected.

"Men."

"Right. FBI men."

"F...B...I men," Michael mimicked.

Morrow chuckled. He could see what wonderful parents these two were. The kids were bright, well cared for, and obviously loved. He hoped, when this was all over, that they still had two children to lavish their love on. Cindy appeared at the family room door.

"Michael...coming? Donuts!"

Michael scrambled off of Lindy's lap and waddled toward the kitchen, calling to Cindy. Lindy smiled after him, a melancholy look in her eyes. Ricky stood up and followed.

"When do you think he'll call back?" She asked.

"Don't know. He said later....but....can't say for sure. He'll toy with you for awhile. Make you more anxious to give him what he wants.....and willing to disobey our command in the meantime. See, most kidnappers think that if they can get the parents to break off with the law enforcement things will go easier. And that's true...in some cases....but we never stop hunting them. We'll get this guy, Missus DeCelli....don't worry."

"Lindy."

"What?"

"Please....my name is Lindy. Please call us Lindy and Ricky."

"Okay...fine with us. We have to wait until you ask first before we assume we can call you by your first name."

"I know. That's why I just asked."

The household came alive with everyone awakening and heading toward the kitchen. Lindy stood up.

"Let me bring you guys some breakfast," she offered as she made her way to the kitchen.

Morrow's eyes followed her. He was thinking that Ricky was a very lucky guy.

The day wore on with more people showing up, including Chris's ex. They hadn't seen each other in months but when she heard the news she knew she had to be there. She loved Lindy and Ricky. In fact, she got along better with them than she ever had with Chris. She and Chris met on campus when he enrolled at the college after he got out of the army. They went to dinner, ended up in bed almost immediately after dinner, and were married within three months. It was a mistake for both of them. They were too different in their ways, their thinking, and their goals. Chris wanted to settle down and raise a family while Katie wanted to travel, see Africa, climb Mount Everest, and surf the Pacific. Although they loved each other, and even liked each other, they were not compatible. After giving it their best shot, they got out of the marriage before they actually got out of college, but they remained friends—friends at a distance. They were cordial and friendly when they saw each other, but they didn't go out of their way to do that. Since the divorce, Chris dated occasionally, but nothing serious. Lindy and Ricky secretly hoped that a spark would start between Chris and Cindy. They got along well, and had the same sense of humor. Cindy was still unattached and had gotten cuter since high school. She still kept her dark ash blonde hair cut short in a pixie style, but she had slimmed down quite a bit, and the hairstyle was very becoming on her. She had lovely grey eyes that turned gorgeous when she wore make-up, and a cute turned-up nose. After college, Cindy took a job teaching high school algebra while Chris taught geometry and trigonometry—even their careers were compatible. Every chance they got, Lindy and Ricky placed Cindy and Chris together, and they could see by the look on Cindy's face when Katie walked in that, at least on Cindy's side, their scheme was working.

The chatter Sunday morning and afternoon concerned the phone call.

"At least he made contact." Nick pointed out.

"That's an indication that he wants to negotiate." Liz agreed.

The two of them were on their way home to shower, change, and stop to pick up a newspaper, or three of them, when Ray and Diane passed their car on the way to Lindy and Ricky's.

"What can I do for my daughter, Diane? I want to show her how much I love her. Can you think of something special?"

"Just…be there, Ray. She needs you…she needs all of us. Just be there for her. You don't even have to speak… your presence is all she needs."

Sunday was spent in a subdued trance for everybody— everybody except Michael. He asked twice about Sammie, and appeared to be confused that she wasn't there. Two more agents showed up, just as a support team for the original two. They relieved them so they could go get a shower and clean clothes, and have a lunch break. The crime scene investigating team was finishing up the job of collecting whatever it was they collected, and were heading back to the department. The discussion turned to where the ransom money was going to come from. There were a couple of possibilities, but they still had no idea how much the ransom would be.

Ricky's boss called him on his cell phone. After expressing his shock and sympathy, he told Ricky not to worry about work—to just stay home until things were back to normal. Tom Siverson called Nick and Liz and told them the same thing, extending that to Angie as well. Ray called his boss and told him what was going on, and he was told the same thing—stay home, don't worry about work—worry about getting the granddaughter back.

Lukas and Michelle showed up with little Lukas. Michael was delighted to see him again.

"Lindy, would you mind if we took Michael with us for the afternoon? The daycare center where Lukas goes is having a bazaar today. Things for kids all day, including pony rides. What do you think?"

"I-I guess...it would be okay. I know he would be in good hands, but that awful...fear of never seeing him again....something I never even imagined I'd have to fear...."

"We'll watch him like hawks. It would give you a little break....come on, what'd ya say?" Lukas smiled at her.

Lindy turned to Ricky. "What do *you* think?"

"I think we should let him go, Babe. Let him have some fun."

"You're right...okay, he can go."

"We'll call you on Ricky's cell phone if we decide to take them both out to dinner."

"Thanks, guys." Lindy smiled gratefully at them, as she hurried into Michael's room to dress Michael for the outing.

The late afternoon brought another reporter to the house. She introduced herself as Jill Toms, a feature writer for a newspaper distributed in central Pennsylvania. She wanted to interview the parents and get their heart-rending reaction to their daughter being kidnapped. Miss Toms sat down at the kitchen table with a cup of coffee—compliments of Cindy—readied her tape recorder, and sat with a pen poised in her hand.

"Let's begin. Missus DeCelli....can you describe how it feels to have your daughter taken from you by an unknown...person or persons?"

Lindy's breathing began to quicken as she stared at this woman.

"It feels......it feels....like...someone....reached in....

43

into my body….and tore….out…all…of…my….organs. I…oh, *God*!!! I can't *do* this!"

Ricky intercepted Lindy's body as she began to slide out of her chair onto the floor. He turned to the reporter and stared at her, his face showing dark contempt.

"Do you want to know how it feels?" His voice was thick with emotion as he held tightly onto Lindy. "First of all, how do you *think* it feels? You can print this verbatim. It feels like hell. It feels like all of my flesh was burned off of my body and my nerve endings are exposed to the air. With every tiny breeze, the pain is acute and when there is no breeze, there is a dull ache. It's pain…all the time. Emotional and physical pain. Then there is the feeling of the fist in my chest…pressing hard….making it hard to breathe. Do you get the idea? Lady, I know you have a job to do…but don't do it at our expense. Now get the fuck out."

Ricky looked beyond where Jill Toms stood and saw that Ray had the door standing open waiting for her to leave. Her eyes followed in the direction of Ricky's vision and she quickly gathered up her belongings and retreated from the house. Ricky held Lindy and absently stroked her hair as he watched the reporter go. Chris and Cindy overflowed with emotion as they corralled Lindy and Ricky and hugged them tightly. Their tear-filled eyes connected as they held onto these two people they loved so much.

The family quietly sat in the living room, exchanging dialogue in low tones. Nobody felt like talking. Liz made eye contact with Nick.

"Has Lindy or Ricky eaten anything….at all?" She whispered.

"Lindy hasn't. I saw Ricky eat a piece of bacon this

morning. No....Lindy hasn't eaten since....God knows when."

Liz let out a short sigh. "She *has* to eat something. I think I'll go out there and make her something. Something nourishing but easy to eat. I'm sure her stomach is in knots."

After surveying the refrigerator and the freezer, Liz opted to make milkshakes for both Lindy and Ricky. It was something they could swallow and it had some nutritional value. They both sipped the shakes and by the time they were finished with them, the shakes were warmer than room temperature. Their eyes met and they both recognized the pain that was visible all the way through from their eyes to their souls. Lindy closed her eyes and stifled her sobs as she clung to Ricky at the kitchen table. Chris nodded to Cindy indicating that she was to follow him. They disappeared into the family room where the agents sat ready for action—should there be any.

"Hi," Chris greeted them. "Listen....besides sitting here watching the telephone is there anything else being done to find Sammie? I mean...is there anybody out there looking for her?"

"You're Chris Riley....right?" Agent Morrow began.

Chris nodded.

"Well, listen....Mr. Riley...we *do* have some experience in these matters. The bureau is quite capable of handling things like this."

"Well...you say that, but....how many kids are never found? Never brought back?"

"Put it this way...more are returned than not. Now.... in answer to your question....it's hard to look for a child that's been abducted. It's like a needle in a haystack....

45

but....every law enforcement officer gets a copy of the child's picture. They keep a look out for them. And.... they pay attention to all leads....follow up on them. Any unusual activity is investigated. Kidnapped kids are our number one priority. Believe me....we're doing all that we can. We're doing the *best* we can."

"But....what if your best isn't good enough?"

Agent Morrow sighed. "Let's not talk like that... especially in front of those two parents."

Again, Chris nodded, sighed, and then stood up to join the crowd in the living room. Cindy followed; glad that Chris's ex-wife hadn't stuck around. Diane and Angie were back in the kitchen preparing food. More offerings had been dropped off, including a chicken noodle casserole from Marie Siverson. Tom delivered it right at five o'clock, right after the reporter made tracks back to Central Pennsylvania. Tom stayed a few moments, talking to Nick and Liz.

"How are they holding up?" His head jerked toward Lindy and Ricky.

"As well as can be expected, I guess." Liz raised her eyebrows and shrugged.

"They have certainly had their share...wouldn't you say?"

"Yeah...I'd say," Liz responded.

"Have you heard from....?"

"The kidnappers? Yes......six o'clock this morning they made contact. They haven't made any demands yet.... so we still don't know what they want."

"Well, let me know. If it's money maybe I can help."

"Thanks, Tom....we'll keep you informed."

Nick and Liz watched him walk out and were surprised

when his figure was replaced by a man in uniform. They both jumped up and went to the door.

"Hi....I'm Officer Jack Downing....I'd like to see Mister and Missus DeCelli....along with the agents assigned to the case."

"Come in." Nick invited as he held the door. "Uh, the agents are in the family room. I'll show you in."

"Thanks. I need to see the DeCelli's, too."

"Yeah, I'll send them in." Nick noticed a yellow envelope in his hand.

Liz went to the kitchen to tell Lindy and Ricky that a police officer wanted to see them in the family room. She saw the apprehension and terror in their eyes as they got up to go into the family room. Liz absently grabbed Angie's hand as she watched them go.

"Sit down, Mister and Missus DeCelli.....please."

Lindy and Ricky looked at each other as they held each other. Lindy's body began to shiver again. Her body was trembling but this time Ricky didn't notice it because his body tremors matched hers. Their hands were clutched tightly together as they stared at the officer who obviously had something to tell them.

"I need to know if any of these items are you daughter's," he began as he opened the envelope he held.

He emptied the contents out onto the table and leaned back so they could see them. A couple of ponytail holders, an earring, and a small pink elephant barrette fell out of the envelope. Lindy and Ricky stared at the items. Lindy let out a wail as she reached for the pink barrette. Agent Morrow stopped her from picking it up.

"She....she....had that in her.....hair. I wanted to take it out....but she begged me to leave it in her hair..."

47

Lindy's speech was becoming incoherent and her sobs were like hiccups.

"Oh......oh......oh....*God*! *Please*! Oh, God.....please bring her back. *Please*!"

Ricky held Lindy tightly, his face turned away from the officer.

"Okay.....look.....this is actually a good piece of evidence. See....this stuff we found on this street east of your house....but this pink thing....we found to the west of your house. This indicates that the kidnapper took your child and went west. It gives us a direction to go in."

Lindy attempted to calm down. She stared at the officer with large tears rolling down her face. It was almost too much for him. 'Tears coming from her eyes could just about break anybody's heart,' he thought.

"See if they can get anything off of that. DNA, print.... anything." Morrow ordered him.

"Right." Officer Downing left swiftly, just glad to get away from those beautiful blue haunted eyes with the large tears coming from them.

Agent Daily quietly and furtively went out to see Liz.

"Can you give her something? You're a doctor.... right?"

"Yes."

"She needs to be....sedated. I'm not sure how much more her nervous system can take."

"So.....what was that all about? Or can't you say?"

"Yeah...I can say. They found a barrette that belongs to the little girl. At least we know that the guy headed west after he left here."

Liz expelled air from her lungs. "God! I was really scared when he came in here."

"Yeah…I know. He could have used a little more tact. Anyway….do you have anything you can give her?"

"Yeah, I'll get it. I'll probably have to disguise it in a drink though."

Liz poured water into the kettle and began heating it for tea. She emptied out a capsule into the cup and added a teabag, sugar and lemon. When the water boiled she lifted the kettle and poured the water into the cup. As an after-thought she got a cup ready for Ricky—minus the capsule contents. She carried the tea into the family room and set the cups in front of them. 'Hopefully Lindy will fall asleep for awhile,' she thought to herself as she joined Nick in the living room.

"I wish they would call!"

Ricky's voice sounded agitated. He felt as though his nerves were raw hamburger being seared by hot coals.

"Is it normal to wait this long?"

"Yes….very normal. I told you….the more anxious they make you feel the easier you'll go along with what they want."

Agent Morrow glanced at Lindy for a moment and then nodded toward her as he stared at Ricky. Lindy was falling asleep. 'Good,' Tom Morrow thought. 'She needs to.'

Ricky gently lifted Lindy into his arms and carried her toward the master bedroom. When he passed the living room with her in his arms, he could see alarm on all the faces but Liz's. He knew she had put something in that tea for her, and for that he was grateful. He laid her down on their bed, covered her with a quilt, and kissed her forehead, brushing her hair back first. He studied her sleeping face for a moment and all the love he felt for her rushed forward. She was the love of his life, always was, and always would be. Straightening up and squaring his shoulders back, he forced back the emotions that were dangerously close to the surface. He shut the bedroom door and went back to the family room to sit with the FBI for awhile.

6

"WHEN IS MY vacation over?" Samantha's blue eyes stared at the man.

"Oh….not for awhile. But….we're going to have fun…. if it's nice outside…tomorrow."

"What kind of fun? What are we going to do?"

"Well, I know where there are some baby birds in a nest. We can go see them if you are really quiet. If you're not, you'll scare them off."

"Really? We can see baby birds?"

"Yep."

"My mommy takes us to the zoo. Not the big zoo, but the little zoo. When we go to the big zoo we wait for daddy to be off work…..then we all go."

"So then….you would like to see the baby birds?"

"Uh-huh. Can we go now?"

"No….it's getting dark. Tomorrow…if it's not raining. Okay? Now…how about hot dogs for dinner? Then we can watch 'Shrek' …..okay?"

"Can we call my mommy?"

"No….not today. She's not home right now. We'll call her tomorrow."

"Okay." Samantha smiled up at him, her eyes full of warmth and trust.

He waited for her reaction and was relieved that she didn't start wailing about wanting to see her mother. He couldn't stand that. She did that when she first woke up this morning. It took all his strength to keep from shutting her up because he knew that would be a bad move. It was better to keep her trusting him than to have her terrified and crying for her mother. Besides, she wasn't all that bad to have around. He remembered the closet full of diversions that he had managed to acquire while planning his little money-making scheme. He got up and went to the closet, unlocked it and found a doll he had bought the week before. There was a box full of new toys to give her as she became bored with each new item he presented to her. He walked over and set the doll down beside her.

"Is that for me?"

"Yep….do you like her?"

"Uh-huh. Did you get Michael any presents?"

"Oh, yeah…we have presents for Michael….and when your vacation is over you can take them to him….okay?"

"Okay."

She smiled at him, and once again the memories flooded back into his brain. He didn't want to think about that right now. He couldn't. He needed to focus on the present and the future. Forget the past Five million dollars would certainly help him forget the past, and would certainly provide a bright future. The DeCelli's could get that much together, and he knew they would, too. What choice would they have? He had one of their most treasured possessions. He was pulled from his thoughts by the sound of the five year old voice.

"Mister?   Excuse me...when can we call my mommy?"

He looked at his watch and sighed.

"Tomorrow morning....okay? And you can call me.... John....okay?"

"John? That's your name?"

"Yep. So how about it, cutie-pie? Call me John?"

"Okay."

"How about some cookies and milk?"

Samantha vigorously shook her head and smiled in anticipation of the promised treat. The man was relieved and happy that things were going well. Hopefully, all he had to do was keep up a good front, keep the kid happy for maybe a week, and then get his money and get the hell out of the country. Life, from that point, would be easy. He dreamed of buying a boat—a small yacht, maybe—and just traveling from port to port, soaking up sun, picking up women, using them and discarding them when he grew tired of them, and just doing whatever the hell he pleased— forever. One more week of this tedious baby-sitting. He felt sure he could do it since she was such a good little girl. He set the small plate of cookies down, handed her a glass of milk, and smiled at her. She returned the smile, and then they settled down to watch the movie.

She was asleep. Her abductor stared at her as she lay on the love seat with her eyes closed, her long, thick lashes resting on her delicate cheeks. She had the face of an angel. When she was awake and smiling, her big blue eyes sparkled and her perfect tiny mouth was drawn up to create big dimples in each cheek. The almost black hair enhanced her eyes, making them look even bluer than her mother's. He stared at her profile for a moment. 'What perfect delicate bone structure she has,' he thought silently. 'She's going to break a lot of hearts when she grows up.'

After removing the video from the VCR, he switched to the news, keeping the volume down so as not to awaken her. There was another plea for Samantha's safe return being aired. Ricky was on the television begging the kidnappers to please return his daughter. The kidnapper spoke to the television.

"Don't get your panties in a bunch, kid. Just start looking for five million dollars. I have no desire to hurt your kid. I just need to get out of the country."

7

RICKY SAT ON the sofa chatting to Agents Morrow and Daily. Lindy had been sleeping for almost an hour now, and Ricky was relieved that she was finally resting. He had sent the family out of the house for awhile, explaining that Lindy needed to sleep and she wouldn't be able to if she knew they were sitting there. He suggested that they go have dinner and go home and rest. Lukas called and asked if they could keep Michael overnight, and Ricky agreed to it. He felt that a night with just the two of them and the FBI would be good for both Lindy and him. The family told him they would return in the morning, if that was okay. He let them know that it was more than okay—he expected it. Kissing and hugging all of them he held the door as they left, and then watched them all drive away. So here he sat with the two men who hopefully would be instrumental in bringing his daughter back home.

"So you two have been married fifteen years, huh?"

"Yeah, fifteen years next month." Ricky smiled quickly. "God, it's been great. Every minute of it."

"But you waited to have kids….."

Ricky found himself telling them about Nicholas.

"He was our first. We were seventeen when we had him. We got married the following April when we turned eighteen."

"So...her father shot her? And that's why the baby didn't live?"

"Yeah....that's all water under the bridge now. It was a crazy thing....he suffered for it. Lindy didn't speak to him for over nine years. I told Lindy that Samantha had a right to know her grandfather, and that's when Lindy relented."

"So why did he shoot her?"

"Well....it was supposed to be me. Lindy was pregnant and he was going to....not shoot....but scare me into staying away from her. He pointed the gun at me and Lindy pushed me out of the way....the gun went off...hit her....and....well, I almost lost her as well as Nicholas. She was in surgery for hours. They had to take the baby because he started struggling and Lindy had two wars going on in her body....her own fight for life and Nicholas' fight for life."

"Gees....that's an almost unbelievable story. If *you* weren't the one telling it, I don't think I *would* believe it." Morrow commented.

Ricky laughed lightly. His thoughts seemed to wander far away as he sat there staring at nothing. He told them the story of Carrie, and how she tormented Lindy in school all the time, and how he was accused of her murder. After he finished the entire story, Agent Daily cocked his head and stared at him.

"You two have been through it....haven't you? Yet... you seem so normal....no, more than normal. I've never seen so much love under one roof before. Whatever it takes, you two got it."

Ricky raised his eyes and stared at Daily.

"You know…..my heart has always been so full of love for Lindy…when we were going to have Samantha I worried that I wouldn't have any room in my heart to love Samantha. I don't know…..maybe my heart got bigger, but when I looked down at her that day she was born…..I found that I had more than enough love for her. I teased Lindy, telling her that I didn't know what I was going to do now that I was in love with two girls. Anyway….then Michael came along….and my heart grew again." Ricky shook his head slightly. "You know…they are everything to me. I love Lindy more than I did when we got married, and believe me, I didn't think that could be possible. Then…. the kids….my love for them….well, I love Lindy even more for having them."

There was silence in the room for several minutes. Tom Morrow shifted his weight to his other hip and Jack Daily sat straight up in an upright position and cleared his throat.

"That's a beautiful story. Seeing love like this is something…well, it's something we don't see a lot of. You're both very fortunate."

"I know."

Ricky glanced at the clock near the fireplace. It was almost nine o'clock. Day two was coming to a close and they still had no idea what to expect. Ricky stared at the phone willing it to ring.

"Listen….Ricky…why don't you join your wife? You look like you could use some sleep. We'll come get you if the phone should ring. Go ahead."

"Maybe…yeah, maybe I will. Help yourself, if you want anything."

Ricky turned out most of the lights in the living room, leaving a small nightlight on, and then checked to see if the coffee pot was off before heading down the hall. He stopped in front of Samantha's bedroom and peeked inside. Slowly he walked into the room and sat down on the bed. Samantha's stuffed bear was lying at the foot of the bed where they had left it when they said goodnight to her on Friday night. He raised the bear up and stared into its face before he brought it to his chest. Like a dam breaking, the tears began to fall. He hugged the bear fiercely as the non-stop tears raced down his face onto the bear's head. He felt a sob catch in his throat and then release into the silence of the room. Another sob came. He sat in the dark on his daughter's bed and cried—cried his heart out.

•••

Lindy slid out from under the quilt and stood up slowly, still groggy. Looking around and listening for noises she realized that there were none. Quietly, she opened the bedroom door and tiptoed out into the hall. A noise coming from Samantha's room stopped her. She stood quietly for a moment and recognized the sound she heard. Sobbing. Ricky. Ricky was crying. She slipped into the room and went to him.

"Oh…Ricky," she spoke past the lump forming in her own throat.

Lindy put her arms around him and held him, running her fingers through his hair.

"I'm sorry, Lindy. I didn't want you to see me like this."

"Why? She's your daughter, too. I *know* this is killing you…I *know* how much you love her…love all of us. You don't have to be strong now, Ricky. We have FBI agents for that. It's okay to cry. Come on….let's go lie down for awhile."

Lindy took Ricky's hand and led him to their bedroom, and unbuttoned his shirt for him. After he slid his jeans off, he lay down beside Lindy, who was already undressed. In the darkness, they reached for each other with the intention of holding each other to reinforce their strength. Lindy kissed Ricky's cheek and tasted his salty tears, and then she reached up and ran her fingers through his hair. Ricky stared down into her face, barely making out her features in the dark, and lightly kissed her lips. Her hand came up into his hair again and she pulled his face down, kissing him again, her lips parting this time. Their usual passion began to surface as they kissed again. Ricky ran his hands down her body and she quivered with desire. Slowly, Ricky trailed his lips down to her breasts and he kissed each of them lightly, and then circled each nipple with his tongue. His hand found her panties and he slowly slid them down. When her legs slightly parted, he caressed her there. One of his fingers entered her and she quietly gasped with pleasure. Slowly, he moved his finger in and out of her until she was dizzy from wanting him. She tugged at his boxers and he helped her by yanking them off. He rolled on top of her and entered her slowly, and very slowly began to move in and out. She moved with him, slowly, keeping her mouth on his. Ricky slid his arm around Lindy's back and he claimed her breast in his hand, teasing the nipple to bring it to a hard bud. He held her face with his other hand as he kept his mouth over hers. He felt the beginning of her shudders, and matched them with his own. In perfect timing they exploded simultaneously, their bodies racked with electric jolts. After several quiet and still moments, Ricky lifted himself off of Lindy and cradled her in his arms, kissing her cheeks first.

"Should we not have done that?" He whispered.

"No….we should have. We need each other. We need to reinforce our strength. It's okay, Ricky. We *are* husband and wife. We have to get through this together any way we can." She twisted a little to see his profile, and then she ran the back of her hand over his cheek. "Besides….it sure felt good…didn't it?"

"Yeah," he admitted as he laughed through his nose.

They fell asleep together wrapped in each other's arms, and awoke just before daybreak. Lindy slid out of bed and went into the shower and Ricky went into the kitchen to make coffee. When she returned to the bedroom to dress he went to take his shower. The day seemed almost normal until they both realized that nothing had changed since yesterday. Dressed and sitting at the table with coffee cups in front of them, they debated whether to see if the FBI agents were awake. They decided not to check and just have the quiet time together alone. That time was short-lived. Tom Morrow smelled the coffee and came out of the family room to get a cup. He poured one for himself and one for Jack Daily. He couldn't help but notice how much better Lindy and Ricky looked after a night's sleep. Lindy got up from her chair and went down the hall and quickly ran back in a panic.

"Where's Michael? MICHAEL!"

"Lindy, relax…..he stayed at Luke's all night. They

called while you were sleeping and asked if he could stay. I said okay. Honey....calm down."

"Oh, God, Ricky....I'm turning into a hysterical shrew....like one of those women I can't stand."

Lindy started crying and Ricky reached for her.

"No, you're not, Baby. I'm sorry...I should have told you earlier. Hey...this is as tough as it gets....and you're hanging in there...just fine."

He rubbed his cheek against her temple and kissed her forehead. His arms tightened around her before they loosened up.

"Somebody's pulling up. I think it's Uncle Nick and Aunt Liz. How about some breakfast? You haven't eaten since Friday evening....and it's Monday morning."

Ricky looked at the clock on the wall. Seven-twenty. He sighed and stood up, reaching for the refrigerator door. Liz and Nick came in without knocking, carrying a brown grocery bag.

"We brought eggs, ham, bacon, coffee, cream, and potatoes for home fries. Lindy, you look so much better." Liz added as she kissed Lindy's cheek.

"You drugged me....didn't you?" Lindy smiled at her.

"Me? Of course not! Ricky....sit, please. I'm cooking."

Ricky started to protest as the phone rang. He and Lindy jumped and started running toward the family room. They stopped at the door, both having trouble breathing. Slowly they entered the family room and walked gingerly toward the ringing phone.

"Answer it, Ricky." Morrow ordered.

Ricky picked up the receiver and spoke.

"Hello?"

"Your kid wants to say hi."

Ricky's heart lurched and skipped a beat. He sucked in his breath and waited.

"Daddy? I miss you."

"I miss you, too, sweetheart. Are you okay?"

"Uh-huh. I'm on *vacation!* John says we're going to have fun today. Is mommy there?"

Ricky handed Lindy the telephone, no longer trying to hide his tears.

"Sammie? Baby? Are you all right? Where are you, honey?"

"I'm on vacation, Mommy!"

Lindy heard a voice in the background. "That's enough. Tell mommy bye, and that you want to talk to daddy."

"I love you, Sweetheart…"

"I love you, too, Mommy. Bye!"

Lindy handed Ricky the phone, her hand shaking. Tears overflowed from her eyes as she stared at the telephone. Ricky took the receiver and waited.

"Are you there?" The muffled disguised voice came through the receiver.

"Yes….I'm here."

"Good. Got a pen and paper?"

"Yeah." Ricky grabbed the pen and tablet sitting near the phone. "So go."

"I want five million dollars. You want your child back?"

"Yes, I do."

"And I want five million dollars. Even trade. Little Samantha here for five big ones. Worth it to you?"

"Yeah. Where and when?"

"I'll let you know. Keep the pen and paper handy."

The call ended abruptly.

"Ricky? Five million dollars, did he say?"

Ricky stared into Lindy's eyes for a moment and then closed his. He took Lindy by the arms and then hugged her to him.

"Yeah, he wants five million dollars. Samantha....she sounded okay....didn't she?"

"Yes...she sounded okay. Five million dollars! Where are we going to get that?"

Morrow interrupted them. "I'll put a call in. We'll get that money. Once again, he didn't stay on the phone long enough. Longer than last time though. If each time gets longer we may get lucky....but then again it will be hard since he's using a prepaid. We're going to have to get all the cell phone companies to give us a schematic diagram of all of their towers. We may be able to trace which tower his phone waves are bouncing off, and then come up with a geometric equation to see where he is. It's sort of like this."

The agent drew a circle and an arrow into the circle, and then he drew an arrow away from the circle into a square.

"See? Tower....your house....the waves are coming to the tower from somewhere over here." He retraced the first arrow with the pen. "Then we could get an idea where he is." He drew a circle at the other end of the first arrow.

"So...are you going to do that, then? Get the diagrams of all the towers?"

"Of course. That's being done right now. Now.... if he moves around a lot....then it becomes even more complicated....but we're banking on him staying put in one place. Another problem might be if he's using more than one prepaid phone."

Ricky sighed and sat down. Unconsciously he slid his arm around Lindy, and he could feel her tremors starting again. He rested his head on top of hers.

"Let's go out and get some breakfast. We'll bring yours in here....unless you would like to join us at the table...."

"Thanks....can't....we have work to do. But you two go eat something."

"We'll send breakfast in to you then."

When they were out of earshot, Morrow commented to Jack Daily.

"This house is like a fairytale...almost too good to be true."

"I was thinking the same thing."

"You don't think? No....they're both too earnest. I think we can safely rule out that they had anything to do with the kidnapping."

"Yeah, I agree. It's a shame that we think like that.... you know...that they can't be for real. I guess this job has jaded us pretty bad."

Liz entered with a tray of eggs, bacon, ham, home fries, and toast. Nick followed with the plates and silverware.

"Enjoy it, guys. Lindy and Ricky will be out in the kitchen....hopefully eating breakfast. Well, maybe Ricky will...Lindy will just push the food around her plate."

"They're a beautiful couple," Jack Daily responded.

"Yes....they are. Better known as Romeo and Juliet to their friends. Everybody loves them...wants to be them."

"Why do you think that is?" Morrow asked.

"I don't know, exactly. I think, though....it's because they have always been so confident of each other's love, and they know they love each other. They have never been jealous and they have never questioned whether one loves the other. They know. They just know."

Agent Morrow smiled at Liz and she noticed the sadness in his eyes.

"Ma'am...I would have given anything for something like that. My wife and I fought when we were married. If I was gone all night....which I am...a lot...she accused me of being with other women. Victims or informants would call me...she would think it was another woman. Sometimes it was a woman....but it was never *like* that. But...when she had had enough...she began seeing other men....it was over. That was ten years ago. Since then I have managed to just stay single. I see those two and...well, it's hard to accept that they are for real."

Liz stared at the agent for a moment, not quite sure what to make out of what he just said.

"They're for real. Believe me....they are for *real*."

She turned and walked out of the room, feeling just a little edgy.

AT EIGHT-THIRTY MICHAEL burst through the door.

"Mommy! Mommy! I rode a horse!"

"You did?"

Lindy scooped Michael up into her arms and smiled up at Michelle and little Lukas in her arms.

"Thanks so much for all you did. Do you have time for coffee, Chelle?"

"Yeah, I do. Have you heard from anybody?"

"He called again. We talked to Sammie."

"Wha…? Is she all right? How did she sound?"

"She…sounds okay. She said she was on vacation….I guess that's what he told her. She called him John. I don't know if that's his real name but that's what she called him. She also said they were going to have fun today…..God, I'm not sure what that means…I just hope it's good."

"Did he say what he wanted yet?"

"Five million dollars…."

"Oh my *God*! Where can you get *that* kind of money?"

"The FBI agent said they would get it for us."

"So….did he say anything else? Like when and where?"

"No…he hung up."

Michelle sighed and stared at Lindy.

"This has got to be just awful for you."

"It is. Were you here when that reporter came here yesterday?"

"No, I don't think so."

"Ricky threw her out. She starting asking questions and….it was so painful…"

"Good for Ricky. Where is he anyway?"

"He and Aunt Liz and Uncle Nick are in the family room with the FBI agents. Aunt Liz got the impression that they think we had something to do with the kidnapping."

"That's ridiculous!"

"Yeah…well, that's what Aunt Liz told them….now they're in there with them asking them why they would think something so horrible about us."

"I think it's the job. They think everybody is bad because they see so many bad people….know what I mean?"

"Yeah….and you're probably right."

"Well, listen I have to get going. Thanks for the coffee."

"No….thank you! Thank you for taking Michael and showing him a good time….and keeping him overnight. Thanks so much….we appreciate it."

"No problem….any time. We'll stop by later. Keep the faith."

Lindy watched Michelle leave with Lukas in her arms. 'She and Luke are such good friends,' she thought as she smiled to herself. As she looked down at the cold food on her plate, she watched Michael pick it up and eat it. She hugged him to her.

"Are you hungry, Sweetheart?"

"No….me ate pancakes….Uncle Yuke made them."

"Really? So tell me all about the horse you rode."

"He was big….and he was brown and white. Me rode him two times!"

"I…..I rode him two times."

"You did, too?"

In spite of the dire situation, Lindy laughed. She hugged Michael again and kissed the top of his head.

"Where daddy?"

"In there." Lindy pointed toward the family room.

"Wiff those men?"

"With…..*with* those men."

"*With*…..wiff those men."

Lindy laughed again as she helped Michael down to the floor. He ran toward the family room to see Ricky. Lindy got up and began clearing the table, rinsing dishes and loading the dishwasher. She listened as Michael entered the family room and heard Ricky greet him. Today was day three.

The front door opened again and this time it was Diane and Ray. Diane held the door for Ray as he carried in boxes of pastries.

"Lindy, I brought your favorite. At least it used to be your favorite."

"What is that?"

"Blueberry cheese Danish."

"Still is….thanks, Dad. Coffee?"

Diane assisted Lindy by getting clean cups out of the

cupboard, while Lindy got out the cream she had just put away. She decided she liked being busy.

"He called again."

"Yeah? What'd he say?" Ray asked as he studied her face.

"He wants five million dollars."

"Shit! So….now what?"

"We give it to him. We get it and give it to him."

"But from where? I mean….yeah, you have your grandfather's money, but…I don't think there is that much cash. The trust can't be broken."

"There isn't. The agent said he'd make a call and get it for us."

Ray breathed a sigh of relief. "Wow…they do that?"

"That's what he said."

"So…when and where?" Diane asked.

"We don't know yet."

Liz came out of the family room holding Michael in her arms. She spoke to Ray and Diane before she put Michael down. He went from the floor into Ray's lap. Ray hugged him and kissed his cheek.

"Michael, we brought donuts. Want one?" Ray asked him.

Michael nodded and smiled at Ray.

"Sammie, too? Sammie get one?"

Everyone remained still. Liz glanced at Lindy and saw her begin to crumble again. Diane quickly sat down beside her and reached for her hand while Liz handed her a tissue. Lindy fought the urge to just sink into the emotional bog that had claimed her the past two days. She had to be strong and brave for Michael's sake. She dried her tears and smiled across the table at Michael.

"When Sammie comes home, she can have one, too."

Michael seemed satisfied with that answer, and then turned to Liz.

"Aunt Yiz….I rode a horse….a big one."

"Tell Aunt Yiz what the horse's name was." Liz laughed as she always did when he said her name.

"I don't know. It was brown and white."

"So I guess its name wasn't Blackie then."

"No."

Diane and Lindy exchanged glances and smiled at one another. Lindy reflected for a minute on what a good friend Diane had become. Even though no one could ever replace Lindy's mother, Stacey, Diane had become like a mother to her as well as a friend. Lindy had told Ricky once that her dad had really good taste in women.

Ricky and Nick came out of the family room and Ricky immediately went to Lindy and hugged her as he stood behind her chair. Nick poured them coffee and set Ricky's down in front of him.

"The nerve of those guys…." Nick muttered.

"Uncle Nick….it's the job. They see so much bad that they just can't believe somebody is good. I didn't take offense….not really. They said this house is like a fairytale? Well, that's because they think love is a fairytale. That's *sad*, really. I mean…Ricky and I wish everybody had what we have….but few do. That's why they think we're not for real. It's okay. Remember what you said a long time ago, Ricky? It doesn't matter what anybody thinks…we know the way it is. And that's the truth."

Nick smiled at Lindy. He loved his nephew's wife like she was his own daughter. At thirty-two she still had that angelic quality that everybody seemed to notice when she was a teenager. He watched Ricky and Lindy exchange glances, their eyes full of love for one another. They were the paragon of matrimonial bliss. Ricky's mother was sure it wouldn't last when they came home from South Carolina as husband and wife. He knew it would. He saw the bond they had and he knew that their marriage would be a good one—a lasting one. He recognized their determination to succeed and accomplish their goals together and he knew that they could. He could see that they were strong—strong as long as they were together. He was the cog and she was the gear—or vise versa, it didn't matter. All he knew was that one couldn't function completely without the other. He remembered every event of their lives and how with every accomplishment, every joy, and every sorrow their bond strengthened. Ron Shultz once said that they were like both ends of a shoelace—one didn't work right without the other, but together they tied the shoe. One thing puzzled Nick—how did they know at sixteen that they were meant for each other? 'Maybe if we all met the one that was meant for us at that age there would be no games, no hurt, and no divorces,' he reasoned silently.

Angie and Ron arrived, their arms loaded down with bags and packages. Since it was not even ten o'clock, Nick assumed that they had been to the all-night Wal-Mart, where a person could buy anything from eggs to tires and furniture.

"Lindy?" Angie called to her. She couldn't see her sitting at the table on the other side of Ricky.

"I'm here, Mom."

"Oh...there you are. I brought ingredients to make stuffed shells...the ones you like the best. And....

I also brought something for Michael. Where is he? MICHAEL?"

"Nana! Nana Angie! I here! Wiff Aunt Yiz!"

Angie opened a bag and produced two new books and a frog game of some sort. Michael seemed to be delighted by it. Ray got up from his chair and stooped down to where Michael was hunched down inspecting the game.

"Want Poppa Ray to help you play it?"

Michael nodded vigorously.

"Okay...let's take it into the living room and figure it out."

Ray took Michael's hand and grabbed the game and they walked together to the coffee table and started laying out the pieces of the game, Ray reading the instructions to Michael. Angie quietly disappeared for a few minutes and Lindy knew where she went. Angie never bought something for one child without getting something for the other. Lindy knew she had gone to Samantha's room to put something in there for her. She did it without letting either her or Ricky see it because she wouldn't want to upset either of them. In spite of all Angie's quirks and insensitivity, Lindy loved her. She knew she meant well even if it didn't come off that way. Lindy also knew that Angie planned on making the stuffed shells because she thought that it would entice Lindy to eat. Her heart was in the right place even when her mouth wasn't.

Chris showed up around ten AM.

"Chris....don't you have classes to teach?" Lindy questioned him.

"Well, I did, but....one of the kids in my second period class mentioned the kidnapping....and....and...he said... that he heard...they found Samantha....her body. I broke down and starting crying....right there in the classroom. The kid felt like shit when I told him that Samantha was my niece. I had to leave the room and...well...I couldn't get a grip after that....they brought in a substitute....and told me to go home."

Chris stared hard at Lindy.

"It's not true....is it?"

"No....it's not true. The agents already told us we would hear stuff like that. People like sensationalism...not to mention that some people are merely sadistic. It's not true, Chris. We spoke to Samantha this morning."

Chris jerked his head back and he felt his heart skip a beat.

"What'd she say? Is she okay?"

"She thinks she's on vacation....she said that she and *John* were going to have fun today."

"John? That's the kidnapper's name?"

"That's what she called him. The point is....he's apparently not hurting her. She...she seems okay."

"Those...agents....are they searching the database for possible suspects named John?"

"Of course they are.....and they are tracking them down, one by one. Remember, it may not be his real name."

The conversational buzz in the kitchen was interrupted by Ricky's cell phone ringing. He read the number before he answered it.

"Shawna," he assured everybody.

"Hey, Shawna....what's up?"

"Are you guys okay? Do you need me?"

"Well, we *always* need you...but why?"

"I heard that they found....Sammie's body...."

"It's a hoax. Nobody found anything. We spoke to Sammie this morning..."

"Is she okay?"

"Yeah....she thinks she's on a vacation. He must have told her that."

"Did he....make any demands yet?"

"Yeah....five million dollars. Break open your piggy bank."

"Gees.....hey, I'll stop after work....if that's okay."

"Of course it is. See ya then."

Ricky snapped the cell phone shut and told all present that Shawna heard the same rumor that Chris had heard.

"What's *wrong* with people?" Nick's temper flared for a moment.

Liz covered Nick's hand with hers.

"People just want to be part of the act, I think. They make that stuff up to let others think they are in the know."

"Yeah? Well, they found Sammie's pink barrette.... how is it that nobody is telling that?"

"Because they don't know about it."

"My point....they don't know that a body was found either. Sick....sick bastards."

A knock at the door turned all heads toward it. A gentleman in a navy blue suit was standing there holding something in his hand. Nick jumped up, ran toward the door, and flung it open. He stood glaring at the man without speaking. Liz came up behind Nick and spoke to the man.

"Can I help you?"

"Uh, hi….my name is Howard Helms….I'm the editor of the *Central Pennsylvanian*…."

"Nobody's doing an interview. Can't you understand how these people are suffering?"

"Yes, sir….I can. My son was kidnapped several years ago….so I know exactly how they are feeling. I came here today to apologize for the insensitivity my reporter showed when she came here for an interview. I personally reprimanded her and oversaw the article before it was printed. I brought a copy of it with me today. I just hope…. this meets with the parents' approval."

"Come on in. Sorry I jumped on you like that. We have about had it….you can imagine. We just heard a rumor that they found her…body."

"Don't listen to stuff like that. We heard that all the time when my son was gone. Did the kidnappers make contact or anything yet? Oh, never mind….I know you can't say. Anyway, here is the article that I permitted to be printed."

He handed Nick the newspaper that he had been holding. It was already turned to the article. The article stated Ricky's words almost verbatim, except for the expletive, and told of how Lindy and crumbled before the reporter's eyes. The article went on to say that the media should not use their journalism to exploit people who are suffering as much as the DeCelli's are suffering, and she gave a heartfelt apology for coming to the house. She wished the family well and promised to pray for the safe return of Samantha DeCelli.

"I think Lindy and Ricky will approve of this. It's very tastefully done."

"Thank you." Mister Helms replied.

"Tell me…did you ever get your son back?"

Howard Helms peered inside the house to see if there was anyone within earshot. Satisfied that he couldn't be heard, he answered.

"Yes….minus two fingers and an ear."

"Come on in for coffee….but don't repeat that."

Helms nodded as a sign of agreement.

"I can tell you if he's asking for money, that's just plain lucky. My son….the exchange was to be that the Pittsburgh Plate Glass building be blown up. When that happened, I would get my son back. It would have been easier to settle for a few million, I think."

"Well, since the building wasn't blown up I'm assuming they found the kidnappers first."

"Yeah….we got lucky because the kidnappers made a big mistake. That was before cell phones and prepaids… they accidentally didn't hang the telephone up properly. Left it off the hook long enough for the Feds to get a location. That should have been in the *stupid criminal* section of that men's magazine."

Nick laughed and agreed. He took Howard Helms in to introduce him to Lindy and Ricky and everyone else. He handed Ricky the article before he reached for a clean cup for their guest. Ricky slipped his arm around Lindy as he read it. He looked up and nodded his approval at Mister Helms.

9

He HUNG UP and turned to Samantha.

"Your mommy and daddy said for you to have a good time and that they would see you soon."

Samantha beamed.

"And….for being such a good little girl….we are going to go see those baby birds. We may even see bunnies if we're quiet."

Her little face lit up with excitement and anticipation.

"But….breakfast first. How about Fruity Pebbles?"

"Okay."

'Such an agreeable child,' he remarked silently.

While she was eating the cereal he disappeared back into his bedroom. There were new clothes in the bags he had placed on the bed before he brought her here. She would need a bath first, but at least she would be cleaned up. He pulled out a pair of jeans and hoped they fit her. He held them up and studied them. Yes, they should fit. He pulled out a polo shirt with pink and white stripes and a little pink bow at the neckline. There were sneakers in a shoebox in one of the bags. Socks and underwear, too.

He had talked with his cell mate a lot while he was in prison. The guy had a kid at home just waiting for him to get freed. He let the guy ramble on about what it costs to raise a kid. He acted curious when he asked what all a kid required. He wouldn't let the guy stop at clothes, but wanted details about what kind of clothes and the cost of them. The cell mate had a daughter about Samantha's age, so he drilled him on things concerning what a five year old girl needed. He shopped a little at a time, in different stores so as not to attract attention to himself. One nosy cashier asked him if the underwear was for his granddaughter. He told her that the child was staying with him and his wife for a few days and her mother forgot to pack underwear for her. The clerk seemed to buy it, or at least she shut up about it. That was weeks ago. He bought clothes at Wal-Mart and K-Mart where there were hundreds of people in and out all day, and too many cashiers to keep track of. The toys came from those places, too. Another cashier mentioned the crayons, reminding him that they had bigger boxes for almost the same price. He said he would come back and get them at another time, but his Godchild's birthday party was in an hour. She suggested wrapping paper and he informed her that he already had it in the car, along with ribbon, scotch tape, and scissors. She seemed satisfied with his answer. If he were ever caught, which wasn't going to happen, and they asked him why he bought clothes for the child, he would tell them the truth—he couldn't stand dirty kids.

"Samantha....are you done eating?"

"Yes, sir."

"Sir? What is my name?"

"John."

"That's right....John. Now....how about a bath? Can you take a bath by yourself? I have these new clothes for you."

He held them up for her to see.

"I can take my own bath. That shirt is pretty. Pink is my favorite color."

"I know that. Your mommy told me before she let you go on vacation with me."

The gullible child smiled at him, looking so happy that mommy thought to tell him that. He let her go into the bathroom after he drew water into the bathtub for a bath. He added bubble bath soap to the running water so she would enjoy it more. He would listen to make sure she was okay in there, but he quickly stepped outside for a cigarette. He didn't smoke often, but once in awhile he enjoyed one. He finished his cigarette and went back inside, down the hall to see if she was okay.

"Samantha? Are you okay?"

No response.

"Samantha!"

Still nothing. He burst in through the bathroom door and ran to the tub. She was submerged under water. He grabbed her and brought her up fast, causing her to cough and sputter.

"What the hell were you doing?" He yelled.

She started to cry.

"Don't cry! What were you doing?"

"Washing my hair."

He expelled air from his lungs and sat back, covering his face with his hand.

"Oh....I'm sorry. You scared the heck out of me! Don't cry. I didn't mean to yell."

She was trembling a little and her bottom lip was still quivering, but she was recovering.

"Okay....you almost done with your bath?"

He glanced up at her and almost burst out laughing. She was sitting in the tub covering her would-be breasts with her hands. He quickly averted his eyes so as not to embarrass her any further.

"Okay....get out of the tub and dry off. Your clothes are here."

He patted the toilet seat as he reached for a towel for her. He swiftly walked out to the living room, and a thought occurred to him. He knew how to put terror into her parents' minds. He looked toward the bathroom and saw that the door was still shut, so he grabbed the phone and the voice changer and dialed the DeCelli number. He asked to speak to the mommy, and waited until she got on the line. He all but whispered into the phone.

"I've seen your daughter naked." And then he hung up, chuckling to himself.

Samantha came out of the bathroom all dressed in the new clothes. He congratulated himself on the perfect fit, except the shoes which were a little too big. He tested them and they didn't seem like they would fall off, so he left them on her.

"Ready to go see the baby birds?" He asked her.

"Yes," she answered, smiling.

He took her hand and they walked out into the bright sunlight. She looked around in wonder.

"What's the matter?'

"All the bushes. The bushes are *red*."

"Well, I'll be darned. I never noticed that before. I wonder what kind of bushes they are. Come on....we'll go up this way."

The afternoon was pleasant and Samantha was awed by the birds and the rabbits. There were squirrels running up and down trees, all for Samantha's delight. He walked with her holding her hand, listening to her chatter and her laugh. He thoroughly enjoyed the day; he had to admit to himself. Maybe—maybe he should have had a child. With the right woman, it might have been fun. Judging from this child's behavior, Missus DeCelli would have been the right one.

10

LINDY AND RICKY had heard the phone ring and they ran for it. Ricky answered, but the kidnapper had asked to speak to the mommy. Ricky handed Lindy the phone. When she heard those terrible words, she screamed and threw the phone down like it had burned her. Gasping for air, she screamed. The agents heard an explosion as she screamed and their heads swiveled toward the sound. Ricky had punched a hole in the wall. They turned back to Lindy. Her face was dangerously scarlet as she still gasped for air.

Jack Daily ran out and yelled for help.

"We need one of you doctors in here.....*now!*"

Liz dropped the cup she was holding and ran into the family room. She could see Agent Morrow trying to get Lindy to lie down, her scarlet face now turning purple. Liz heard rumbling coming from behind her and turned to see Ricky slamming his fists on the wall, putting holes into it. His face was almost as red as Lindy's.

"Call nine-one-one," she ordered, as she looked up at Agent Morrow. "NICK! Get in here....*hurry!*"

Nick, Chris, and Ray burst into the room. Chris and Ray grabbed Ricky and tried to pull him into a chair, while Nick ran to assist Liz. Nick held her down while Liz breathed into her mouth. Lindy gasped for air.

"I can't breathe!" She choked out.

"Shhh….don't….just try to breathe….don't talk."

Lindy's body was convulsing as paramedics rushed into the room. Liz and Nick moved out of their way and let them take over. Liz watched while Nick looked over toward Ricky. His face was covered with his blood streaked hands and he was sobbing—sobbing hard. Nick rose from his knees and ran to embrace Ricky. He held him until the sobs seemed to be subsiding. Looking over his shoulder, he could see that Lindy's face wasn't purple any more, but she was still flushed. The paramedics were about to put her on the portable gurney when she began to protest.

"No! No! You can't take me out of this house! I have to *be* here!"

One of the paramedics looked around the room for support, and spied the telephone equipment.

"These are the people whose daughter is missing, right?" He whispered to Liz.

"Yes…..you can't take her. If the kidnapper calls and asks to speak to her again and she's not here….well…we don't know what he'll do. Can you look at Ricky's hands? He put those holes in the wall…."

"Yeah….okay….let me call my supervisor and see what I should do….about *her*, I mean."

Angie stood in the doorway of the family room holding Michael who was crying and looking terrified.

She watched as Ron spoke to the two agents and waited to hear what happened. All those who were not present in the room when the phone call came, did not know what had happened and they feared the worst. Ron walked over to the group and told them what the kidnapper had said to Lindy.

"Oh, God....no wonder." Diane spoke in a whisper.

She glanced at Ricky and saw that one of the paramedics was looking at his hand, and the other still had Lindy lying flat on the floor. She looked back toward Ricky and listened to the exchange of words. Ricky was staring straight ahead like a blind man.

"Sir? I think your hand may be broken."

"I don't care."

"I think you need an x-ray."

No response from Ricky.

"Sir....did you hear me?"

Ricky began to get up.

"Yeah...I heard you. Let me tend to my wife."

The other paramedic was helping Lindy into a sitting position when Ricky dropped down beside her. He reached for her but winced in pain. He thought maybe his hand might be broken. Stupid. Now what? He reached for Lindy's face with his good hand and stroked her cheek, and then lifted her face by holding his hand under her chin. He stared into her eyes, and their eyes locked and held for several moments. Nobody else in the room spoke. Nobody moved. They were mesmerized by what was taking place. Still holding her face, Ricky pressed his forehead against hers, and then pressed his cheek against her cheek and held it there. They didn't speak to each other, but they breathed as one. As every moment passed their breathing became calmer, until it was back to normal. Ricky moved his face away from her and stared into her eyes.

"I think that was to make us flip out. It worked."

Lindy nodded.

Ricky kissed her swollen eyelids and pulled her face into the crook of his neck and shoulder.

"Ricky?"

"What, Baby?"

"Go get x-rays."

Ricky pulled away from her and just stared at her for a moment.

"Please? He won't call back for awhile."

Agent Morrow heard the exchange and told Ricky that they would treat it as a priority, since he had to get back here. Another agent was on the way over now to see that it happened that way.

"Will you be okay?"

"Yeah, I'll be fine. Take Uncle Nick with you and everybody else can stay here with me. Okay?"

Ricky nodded, and with a smile, said, "Yes, Dear."

Ricky was escorted by Nick and another Federal Agent to the emergency room for x-rays. The hand was not broken, but badly cut and bruised. The emergency room doctor bandaged and disinfected it and told him to keep ice on it

"Thanks. Let's go." He nodded at the two men with him and headed toward the huge double doors.

"Who did you hit, by the way?"

"The wall. Ready to go, Uncle Nick?"

The doctor shook his head. "Now what could make someone that mad?"

Nick stared at him for a moment. "You have no idea." He responded.

.

11

Samantha and the kidnapper walked down the natural path from the woods and into the small yard in front of the little cottage. She stopped to stare at the bushes again.

"The red bushes are pretty...aren't they, John?"

"Yep. Sure are. Now guess what! We're going to have a very special treat for dinner."

"What? What is it?" She asked enthusiastically.

"McDonald's! How does that sound?"

"Yeah! That sounds good!"

"Does mommy take you to McDonald's?"

"Sometimes."

"What do you like from there?"

"Chicken McNuggets happy meal!"

"Well, then…...that's what you're going to get. Oh, wait….I almost forgot. Another present."

He reached into the hall closet and retrieved a pair of pink sunglasses shaped like hearts.

"How about these?"

Samantha grinned one of those rare grins that could melt a heart. He felt a quickening in his pulse as he

91

remembered a grin like that long ago. He put her into the back seat of the car and fastened the seatbelt. He went around to the front and got in, started the engine, and put the car in gear.

"Ready? Here we go!"

He drove the speed limit to the McDonald's six miles from the cottage. There were few cars in the parking lot and the drive-thru was empty. Good. He whizzed through, placed their order, paid, and picked it up and they were on their way back to the cottage. It went without a hitch. Nobody noticed the tiny five-year-old in his car. Inside the cottage he placed the food on the coffee table and got extra napkins out for her. He needn't have bothered; she was a neat, meticulous child—the product of obvious good upbringing. Silently, he commended the DeCelli's. He laughed to himself when he thought about his last phone call. He knew what that did to them. He could almost see the anguish in her eyes and the anger in his, but at least now, he knew they would hasten to get him the five million. He had everything worked out, except for the place to leave Samantha. He didn't want to leave her at the cottage, since he knew the Feds would be all over the place looking for anything that could lead them to him. Hell, the toilet seat, the refrigerator, the tables, chairs, all of it would have his DNA all over, not to mention finger prints. Maybe he could just drop her off at a McDonald's—a crowded one. He had to think on that for awhile. Maybe—maybe he could take her with him! She could be his child. If you're going to have a kid, why not have a good one? No. He didn't want to be saddled down. On the other hand, women liked that sort of thing. A widower raising his little daughter could stir up all sorts of motherly instincts, getting him laid all the while. His thoughts were interrupted by Samantha.

"John? When is my vacation over?"

"In four more days. Why? Don't you like being with me?"

"Yes....but I miss my mommy and daddy....and Michael. Did they say I should come home sooner?"

"No....they didn't. They want you to have a long vacation, just like grown-ups."

That really didn't make any sense to him, but she seemed to buy it. He watched her gather up her trash from the happy meal and take it into the kitchen to dispose of it. Yeah, she would definitely be a chick-magnet.

"Samantha, I was thinking maybe if you wanted to stay longer, I would take you on an airplane ride. Would you like that?"

"Yes, but we would have to ask mommy and daddy first."

"Of course."

He sat back and smiled at her. Maybe taking her with him was the solution. He still needed to think it through. 'Maybe after she was through the stage of being the chick-magnet she would be on her own,' he pondered that thought, and then laughed lightly. 'Taking her with me is an absurd idea,' he realized. It was the only part of his plan he hadn't finalized yet. He had four days to figure that one out.

"What movie do you want tonight? How about *One-hundred-and-one Dalmatians*?"

"Yes! I love that one!"

"Good....because I have never seen it."

"You will like it," she assured him with a smile.

He actually did enjoy the movie. There was something about these kids' movies that made them appealing to adults as well. He never knew it until now. He had four more to go, so he would be enjoying four more evenings of entertaining movies. He reflected on their walk today. She was such a good pupil. She listened when he explained things and she asked questions without interrupting. Again, he commended the DeCelli's.

She fell asleep right after the movie. He covered her up and tuned in to regular programming. No updates or bulletins on the DeCelli kidnapping. He found the station that carried the Monday night sitcoms and watched them until the eleven o'clock news came on. Nothing he didn't already know concerning the kidnapping was being reported. He turned the television off and drifted off to sleep. Another phone call in the morning should have a few nerve endings raw. He smiled as he thought about it.

Yesterday, he had a screaming contest going with Samantha. He told her it was to see who could scream the loudest. The winner got ice cream. He taped her screams.

12

Ricky and Lindy had a rough night's sleep. Ricky's hand throbbed with pain, and Lindy's chest and throat hurt. Nick and Liz spent the night and were both sleeping on the sofa when Ricky and Lindy got up. If either Liz or Nick had even entertained the thought of going back to their place and then going to work, the incident yesterday completely changed their minds. No way were they leaving Lindy and Ricky alone. Ricky hurt himself and Lindy could have died.

Ray and Diane took Michael home with them for the night. They would be back today but not until later. They wanted to spend some time with Michael first before bringing him back.

Angie and Ron went home, too. Angie's nerves were frayed and Ron thought it best that they spend a night in their own bed.

Chris and Cindy left together. As much as Lindy and Ricky would have liked to have seen that, they had no idea that it had occurred.

Lukas and Michelle and Shawna and Ally called on

Monday but did not make an appearance. They would all check in later in the week, Lindy and Ricky were sure.

Lindy sat at the table while Ricky got the coffee ready. It was not quite six o'clock yet.

"Does your hand feel any better today?" Lindy whispered.

"Somewhat, I guess." He shrugged.

"You should soak it...in Epsom Salts maybe. Can't hurt."

"No....I guess it can't."

Lindy looked up and smiled at him. It was a melancholy smile, but full of tenderness. She stood up and went to him, slipping her arms around him. She laid her head against him, and then turned her face toward him and kissed his chest. He wrapped his arm around her shoulders, and squeezed his eyes shut. He was very close to tears. Kissing the top of her head, he sighed raggedly and tightened his grip on her, using his good hand.

"This is a nightmare," he mumbled into her hair.

She nodded as she tightened her arms around his waist.

"You know....I feel like...I failed."

"What? How?"

"It's my job to protect my kids....my family. If I had been doing my job Sammie wouldn't be gone."

"Honey.......no.....don't do this to yourself. Ricky.... look at me.....please....look at me. You're the best. You're a wonderful father and a terrific husband. There was no way you could have seen this coming. And besides...when it comes to protecting the kids...I'm just as responsible as you are for protecting them. You've heard of a hen protecting her chicks? To the death. This isn't your fault....or mine.

I just know that I want the bastard who took Sammie to pay...*hurt*....I want him *hurt*....for a long time."

"Me, too, Baby....Me, too."

Ricky poured their coffee as she sat down at the table. Setting a cup in front of her and then taking a chair at the corner of the table facing her, he grasped her hand and held it tightly.

"I'm scared, Baby. I've never been this scared.....even when I was running around on the streets as a teenager, getting into trouble every night. If something happens to Samantha...."

Ricky covered his face and concentrated on breathing normally.

"I feel like such a coward...saying that. I should be..... I don't know...out there...looking.....finding him, whoever he is....and beating him to a pulp...."

"No! Ricky...*no! You shouldn't be!*" Lindy's sigh came out raggedly. "Look....this is not a macho thing. You can't....*we* can't....take a chance with our daughter's life. You are doing what you have to *do! Please....please...don't even think that you have to play hero here!*"

Ricky reached up and pushed a strand of her hair away from her eyes and sighed.

"Okay.....you're right. I just feel so helpless."

"You're doing what you can."

Their little tête-à-tête was interrupted by the telephone ringing. They ran to the family room where the two agents were trying to crawl out of the blankets they had wrapped themselves in.

"Answer...." Agent Morrow ordered, once again.

Nick and Liz stood at the doorway waiting for Ricky to answer the phone. The agent turned the volume up on the speaker part of the telephone device, and Ricky picked up the receiver. He didn't get a chance to even say hello because of the noise coming from the phone. Screaming. Sammie screaming. Lindy closed her eyes and wrapped her arms around herself. Her head dropped to her chest as she squeezed her eyes shut.

"Oh God!" Liz yelled as she ran to Lindy.

Nick fell against the door frame, his hand over his chest. He stared up at the ceiling just trying to keep from crying. He gave up and just let the tears flow.

The two agents stood in one spot, unable to move, mesmerized by the screaming.

Ricky reacted.

"YOU *BASTARD*!! YOU *SICK BASTARD*!! TELL US WHAT YOU *WANT*!! WHATEVER IT IS…. IT'S YOURS….JUST GIVE US OUR DAUGHTER BACK!"

The screaming stopped. The disguised voice came over the phone.

"Got the money?" The gravelly voice taunted.

"We'll have it today or tomorrow. Please….don't hurt her any more."

The call ended with a gravelly insane-sounding laugh.

Ricky turned to Lindy and saw that she was curled up in a fetal position, arms wound tightly around her, and her eyes tightly squeezed shut. Liz came around on the other side of her and helped pull her up into a sitting position. Nick abruptly left the room. As she watched him go, she understood why. Lindy started trembling, and then began to shake violently. Liz jumped up.

"Wait here," she spoke in a whisper.

Liz ran to get her bag. She quickly filled a syringe with the mild tranquilizer for which she had written a prescription the day before. She knew Lindy was going to need it before this was all over. She hated doing it, but Lindy's convulsions on Monday scared her. She quickly grabbed what she needed, ran back to the family room, and in a flash, before Lindy could protest; she injected the tranquilizer into her.

"Ricky...you need something, too. You're on a thin wire right now. Let me give you something."

"Aunt Liz, I don't want to pass out."

"How about a half of a sedative? You won't go to sleep but you'll stop shaking."

"Okay," he conceded.

While Liz went to get the sedative he stared down at Lindy as she leaned against his side. She had not spoken at all since the call.

"Are you all right?" Ricky asked her.

"I don't know. I don't know how much more I can take. Why is he tormenting us? We agree to whatever it is he wants. Why the torture?"

"He's sadistic. He knows what it's doing to us. He also knows we'll do anything to get our daughter back... including telling the FBI to take a hike."

"You don't want to do that," Agent Daily interjected.

"I know." Ricky agreed, as he accepted the half-pill and a glass of water from Liz. "But that's what he wants."

"You two want some coffee?" Liz asked the agents.

They both nodded. Liz got them coffee and brought a dish of pastries into them as well. After they thanked her, they began going over notes they had taken since they got involved with the kidnapping.

"You know…if he asks that…I'm going to agree to it. I don't expect you to go away, but I'm going to tell him I'll get rid of you."

"Fine….but you're right…we won't go away."

Ricky nudged Lindy.

"Come on….maybe you should lie down."

"I don't want to. Let's have a nice cup of coffee together…okay, Ricky? You and me and Aunt Liz and Uncle Nick."

Ricky looked over at Liz and waited for her response. When he saw her nod of approval he helped Lindy stand up on wobbly legs and he walked her out to the kitchen. After one cup of coffee, Lindy began to nod off at the table. She didn't resist when Ricky walked her into the bedroom to lie down. She was asleep before he pulled the quilt over her. Ricky dipped down and kissed her cheek, and then stood up and stared down at her face.

"I love you…so much, Lindy. I know this is killing you. I hope I get my shot at that bastard. I'll make him pay for every agonizing moment you've had to suffer. I promise."

Ricky left the bedroom door standing open about six inches just in case Lindy called out to him.

He thought about her current condition as he walked back down the hall.

'Lindy—always so full of life—full of energy. Her laugh, her easy smile, her quick wit—she was like sunshine all the time. Except now. Thanks to that bastard, she had two modes—hysterical or zombied-out. He or they, whoever he or they are, need to pay for this.

13

Liz and Nick were sitting at the kitchen table with fresh cups of coffee. Ricky helped himself to one and sat down with them. All three of them were subdued as they sat there staring into the coffee cups. Ricky noticed Nick's red-rimmed eyes and his heart went out to him. His uncle loved him, his wife, and his children more than anything, except Liz, of course. Nick was being torn apart by all of this. Ricky could tell by the dark circles under his eyes, just like his own. On the way back from the bedroom, Ricky stopped into the bathroom to rinse off his face. He barely recognized himself when he looked into the bathroom mirror. His face looked hollow; his eyes appeared to be sunken in, and his skin was pale.

He thought about those screams they listened to over the phone. His baby girl. What had been done to her to make her scream like that? Answers began to spring up in his mind, as he forced them back down again. No. He couldn't think about it. He had to stay strong. Strong for Lindy—God, she needed him. If he thought about what may have caused those screams he would go to pieces.

He was pulled from his thoughts by Nick's voice.
"Ricky?"

Ricky jerked his head up toward the sound of Nick's voice. He stared at him waiting for him to say something.

"The agents want to see you. They said it's okay to let Lindy sleep."

Without a word, Ricky rose out of the chair and followed Nick into the family room. Both agents were standing in front of the sofa, deep in conversation when Nick and Ricky walked in. Their conversation stopped and they directed their attention toward Ricky.

"We have the five million. It's coming within the next couple of hours. A secured courier will be bringing it. We will be adding a couple of more agents here because of all that cash. They'll be stationed around the perimeter of the house....you won't even know they are there. Now....we need a safe place to keep it."

"No problem. There is a wall safe here. Lindy's grandfather put one in when she was about Samantha's age."

"Good.....where is it?"

"This way."

Ricky led Agent Morrow to the wall that separated the family room from the living room, and moved a picture out of the way. Behind the picture was a metal door with a slide latch on it. Ricky slid the latch and the door popped open. Behind that was the combination lock of the safe.

"When Lindy wakes up we'll get the combination from her. She's the only one who has it. I don't need it. Lindy keeps all important papers in there, including birth certificates. Our college transcripts are in there, too."

Ricky dropped down into a living room chair and covered his face with his hands.

"Damn it...I'm trying so hard to be normal right now. Carry on a normal conversation about normal things. If I'm rambling, I'm sorry..."

"It's okay, Rick," Morrow soothed, placing his hand on Ricky's shoulder. "It's okay....I get it."

Morrow started back to the family room, but turned around again.

"Is she okay? Lindy, I mean?"

"She's sleeping off the drug my aunt gave her. No.... she's not all right. Lindy is an incredible mother. Our kids are happy, intelligent, well cared for kids. They know love. And Lindy....well, Lindy manages the house and the kids like a magician, but the kids are everything to her. Having one of them in jeopardy like this is just killing her. Hell, it's killing me, too. I don't know how long I can keep up being the strong one, because the kids are everything to me, too."

Ricky ran his hand over his face and through his hair, trying to keep his composure. He flexed his sore hand to feel the pain in order to give himself something else to concentrate on.

"Well, okay....let us know when the courier gets here. Oh....and by the way, we're buying dinner tonight. Hope you all like Chinese."

"Yeah...I think so. Thanks."

Ready for another fresh pot of coffee, Ricky stood up, stretched his arms, and walked to the kitchen to make another pot. He looked at the clock and saw that it was almost ten o'clock. Briefly he wondered what time Ray and

Diane would be bringing Michael back. He wanted very badly to hold one of his kids in his arms.

Lindy awoke feeling groggy. She sat up slowly to get her bearings and to get the cobwebs out of her head. Taking very deep breaths, she sat on the edge of the bed concentrating on coming out of the fog. When she was sure she could walk without falling over she stood up and stretched. Slowly she made her way out of the bedroom and down the hall. She stopped in front of Samantha's room and pushed open the door. She stared with contempt at the huge designer windows. She had loved those windows all her life. They were large and clear with no obstructing frames, and she always loved the sunlight they allowed into the room. Her mind drifted back to when she was younger—to a time when this was *her* room. She remembered the pink and orange sunrises she used to enjoy as the colors came through those windows. Briefly she thought about her seventeenth birthday. She had awoken just as the sun was rising that day. She was pregnant with Nicholas then and what she remembered was that it was the first morning since getting pregnant that she awoke without morning sickness.

She remembered how her mother loved those windows, since they were so easy to wash. To get to the outside portion of the window all she had to do was open them up, since they opened like doors and swung inward. She must have thanked Ray a thousand times for those windows. Who would have thought that something that made her and her mother so happy would be the very avenue that created the nightmare in which she was now walking?

Lindy walked into the room and went to the bed to straighten the coverlet. She picked up a stuffed cat and hugged it to her. Since she had never seen it before, she assumed that Angie bought it for Samantha when she took Michael shopping—yesterday, was it? She placed the cat back on the bed and walked around the room, just staring at everything, but not actually seeing anything. She ran her hand over the dresser, and then rearranged some of Samantha's hair ribbons and barrettes. She straightened the hairbrush and comb and reached for the door to her closet. 'No. Don't open that,' she reprimanded herself. Her hand dropped and she turned and hurried out of the room toward the kitchen. She felt her heart quickening and she began to consciously breathe deeply and slowly, in and out. She found Ricky sitting at the kitchen table with a cup of coffee in front of him, staring down at the pattern on the table. She helped herself to a cup and joined him at the table, resting her hand on his thigh. He smiled at her, and she returned his smile.

"I'm sorry I went to pieces."

"Aw, Baby.....don't. How could you help it?"

"Ricky....I thought about those screams. I hear them over and over again in my head."

"Baby....don't."

"No....wait....Ricky....listen. I know Sammie. That was not a scream of terror, nor a scream of pain. Somehow he got her to scream for the fun of it. I know our daughter. He must have taped her after somehow convincing her to scream. Maybe they had a screaming contest or something. I don't know, but those screams were harmless. He did that to....drive us over the edge. He just doesn't realize how well I know our kids."

"Let's go see Morrow. I think he needs to know this."

Holding onto each other's hand they went to the family room and told Agent Morrow what Lindy believed.

"Okay....I hope you're right, but don't let on that you believe that. That information might just give you a little bit of an edge. How do you think he got her to scream?"

"Well....first of all, she's a little girl. Little girls love to scream. All he had to do was encourage it...believe me.... she'd go for it....particularly if she thinks it's a game."

"I want to listen to that tape again." Morrow responded. "I want to dissect it to see if there are any hidden background noises. In fact, I'm sending copies of these first few tapes to an expert in the bureau. Someone who will be able to filter out sounds in order to hear other ones."

They nodded and then left the family room to talk to Liz and Nick. Nick was stretched out on the sofa and Liz was curled up on the love seat. Nick's arm rested over his eyes as he lay flat on his back, while Liz was curled on her side staring at the carpet. Ricky and Lindy sat down on the carpet next to Liz.

"Aunt Liz....those screams weren't real."

"What do you mean?"

She stared at them in surprise.

"I know my daughter. Those screams weren't from pain or fear. Somehow he talked her into screaming." Lindy smiled a little. "I'm sure of it."

Nick overheard the conversation and sat up and stared at Lindy.

"Honey, that's the best thing I've heard today. I sure hope you're right. Now...is anybody in this house hungry? My stomach is beginning to think my throat is cut. I'm *starving*."

Ricky stood up. "Okay...okay...I'll make everyone breakfast. And there's Diane and Ray pulling in with our son. Maybe they want breakfast, too."

Ricky went to the door and held it open for them, and then intercepted Michael out of Ray's arms. He hugged Michael tightly and rubbed noses with him, before he handed him off to Lindy. Diane followed Ricky into the kitchen and offered to help with what was now brunch. Ricky put her to work on toast detail while he started heating the frying pans for ham and eggs. While they worked, Ricky filled Diane in on what had happened in the morning. Diane told Ricky about their evening and morning with Michael.

"What exactly is a Ya-Yindy?" Diane asked him.

Ricky started to laugh, and then called to Lindy.

"Hey Lindy! Diane wants to know what a Ya-Yindy is."

Lindy actually smiled a true smile for the first time since Saturday. She went out to the kitchen to explain it to Diane.

"Did he want that for breakfast?"

"Yes....that's what he asked for."

Lindy actually laughed this time.

"Okay...I'll tell you what a Ya-Yindy is. When Ricky and I were in college we sometimes ran late in the morning, so I would make breakfast to go. I used croissants and made egg and bacon or egg and ham sandwiches on them. At first, I told Ricky they were McLindy breakfasts, but Ricky said the croissants made them French....that meant that they were LaLindies. So....that's what we always called them. We introduced them to the kids and they loved them….because they were like fast food breakfasts….but Michael pronounces his L's as Y's….thus….Ya-Yindy."

Diane covered her mouth and laughed behind her hand.

"We could not figure out what he was asking for."

"We better get some croissants in here because he'll want that again. It's their favorite breakfast. Maybe I'll call Ricky's mom and tell her to bring some with her."

Unconsciously, Lindy reached down and picked Michael up and placed him in her lap while she was talking. She nuzzled his ear and kissed his cheek and then asked him if he had fun with Poppa Ray and Gram Diane. He grinned at her and nodded.

"Mommy?"

"What, Honey?"

"When Sammie coming back?"

"Soon…I hope."

"Me, too. I miss Sammie."

"Me, too." Lindy assured him as she brushed his hair from his forehead.

Ricky and Diane set a plate of food in front of Lindy. The smell of Ricky's cooking made her regain her appetite, as she picked up a fork and started eating. Nick and Liz joined her, while Ray and Diane poured themselves coffee. They had taken Michael out to breakfast and since having eaten all the pancakes they could eat, they had no room for any more. Diane took Michael from Lindy's lap so she could enjoy her food. While they were eating, Chris came in through the front door, asking if there were any news. Ray filled him in on what he had learned when he and Diane got there. Helping himself to a cup of coffee, he joined them at the table.

Quietly and solemnly, they sat around the table eating, drinking coffee and staring down at nothing, each of them hurting in their own way. Silently they said their own prayers—praying for Samantha's safe return.

14

He was in a good mood. His little captive was taking a nap after their time together in the yard swinging on the swing he erected just for her. He looked at his watch. It was a little past two in the afternoon. It was time for another phone call. He took the phone and voice changer out of his pocket and dialed the DeCelli phone number.

Ricky answered.

"Got a pen and paper?"

"Wait….I'll get one."

"NO! Too late! Next time….be prepared."

He disconnected the call and slammed the phone down hard on the arm of the chair. He sat in silence for a moment and then recovered from his anger, as he smiled to himself. For once, he was in charge—he held the cards.

Never had he ever had the upper hand like he did right now. When he was married, his wife ran the show, telling him what to eat, what to wear, and what to do. Then before that, it was his mother—always calling him a moron. Then it was 'do this; do that, clean your room, you can't go out, stay away from that girl, stay away from all girls, they'll get you in trouble.' How he hated her! He was glad when she dropped dead, even if it meant going to a boys' home until he was eighteen. That was only for thirteen months. It was in the home that he learned to sell. He started by selling cigarettes, and then moved up to booze. He never imbibed, which made him even better at selling and making a profit. Since there was no chance of going to college, he started selling cars for a living, and he did quite well at it. Well enough to pay for college courses at night. From cars, he went into insurance, and then finally into high tech equipment. He made a more than decent living at it, but of course, not as much as his intelligent ex-wife. He had to admit that she never rubbed it in his nose, but her attitude showed it. She definitely thought she was superior to him, especially when she threw him out on the street with nowhere to go. Of course after that it was prison—no freedom, no choices, and nowhere to go.

But all that is over and it's different now. He is in charge. He makes the decisions, and damn it, they had better jump when he says jump.

His smile was turning into a grimace and he sat there thinking about his next move. A couple more phone calls, then call the private jet service to Brazil. He had a tentative date for the flight, having put the request in for the chartered flight almost two weeks ago.

The matter closer at hand was the drop-off point. This had better work or he was screwed. The money was to be put in a gym bag—the kind with the local high school logo on it, and put into locker Y-26 in the girls' locker room next to the gymnasium early Monday morning, before school started. He knew nobody used that locker. The good old janitor told him about it. The girls all said it smelled funny.

This was supposed to take place on Friday but his fake ID and passport weren't going to be ready until Friday, so he changed it to Monday. He would already be in the school waiting, dressed as a girl. He had already found the perfect hiding place. Then right before first period began, he would disburse a smoke bomb, and then pull the fire alarm in the locker room, and during the chaos, grab the gym bag and leave through the basement. He thought that would be the way it worked. He wasn't sure of the order in which things would go yet. The average person didn't even know about that basement, but he remembered from when he attended that school while living in the shelter. He used to sit down in the basement and play blackjack with the janitor. It was the janitor who showed him the secret entrance and exit when he got older. It was their way to contact each other. Nobody else ever used that exit except him and the janitor, and that janitor was now deceased.

No shots would be fired because of the school kids. Not even the Feds would take a chance on any of those kids getting hurt.

He calculated the distance between the locker room and the janitor's room. Twelve feet. He had to make it in five seconds or less. The Feds would be watching. He had to blend in and be fast. He would walk into the locker room right at first period with his own gym bag, and quickly striking up a conversation with a girl to make it look like he belonged there. He had to look good. For the past week he was using a cream hair remover on his face rather than shaving it. His face looked a lot smoother. He wouldn't be a pretty girl or a shapely one, but he could pass for a girl for a five minute period. It had to work. It *had* to! Then he would be home free.

The only problem was still Samantha. He didn't know what to do with her. He had grown fond of her over the past four days and didn't want to hurt her. He toyed more and more with the idea of just taking her.

He didn't know where the feelings were coming from. He never liked children—never wanted any—but she was different. He grew uncomfortable when he wondered why Samantha was so special.

Samantha's voice pulled him from his thoughts.

"John? I'm hungry."

"You are? Okay...well, now....tonight we are having.... *pizza*! I'll order it and then we'll go and pick it up. How does that sound?"

"Yummy! Can I get olives on it? The black ones?"

"Yeah, sure....you like black olives?"

"Uh-huh....mommy does, too."

"Yeah....I remember that. So....let me call the pizza place, and then we'll go get it when it's ready."

He ordered the pizza and they got ready to go pick it up. He parked in back of the building and locked Samantha in the car. He ran in, paid for the pizza, brought the hot pie out to the car, and placed the box on the back seat next to Samantha, who was still strapped into her seat belt.

"Careful! It's hot!"

"Okay." She smiled at him.

'Her smile can melt the heart, just like I remember someone else's did,' he thought.

After they finished the pizza he put in another movie for Samantha. This one was about a dog named 'Airbud'. Samantha liked dogs, she told him.

"Why don't your mommy and daddy get you one, then?" He asked her.

"They're going to. This summer, they said. A puppy. Mommy said we had to wait until we were both old enough to know not to hurt a puppy."

"Well, now....that will be nice, won't it? A puppy?"

"Yeah....I can't wait."

He decided to have some fun by asking a five year old some questions about her household.

"Do mommy and daddy ever fight?"

"No...never. They love each other."

"Do you and Michael ever fight?"

"Sometimes."

"Does mommy get mad when you do?"

"We get a time out....and then mommy tells us how important we are to each other, and we shouldn't waste our time fighting."

"Hmm....good point. Do you have two grandfathers?"

"Yeah....Poppa Ray and Pap Ron."

'Oh yeah....I remember Poppa Ray,' he thought to himself. He came back to Samantha with more questions.

"How about your grandmothers? How many of them do you have?"

"Two. Gram Diane and Nana."

"Have any aunts and uncles?"

"Uncle Chris...he's my Godfather....then Uncle Nick. Aunt Cindy, Aunt Shawna, Aunt Ally, Aunt Liz....oh, and there's Uncle Luke and Aunt Michelle."

"Who do you like the best?"

"I don't know. I like them all."

"Uncle Nick…..that's your daddy's uncle, isn't it?"

"Yeah….mine, too."

"Okay…yours, too. Do you ever see mommy and daddy kiss?"

"All the time. They always kiss and hug each other. Then they kiss us….and hug us."

"Do mommy and daddy take showers together?"

"I don't know. They have their own bathroom."

Samantha yawned on her last answer.

"Are you tired? Go ahead and lie down. I'll watch over you."

He got up from his chair and went over and covered her up, and then he leaned down and kissed her forehead. She smiled at him and closed her eyes. Within moments she was sound asleep.

15

THURSDAY MORNING. RICKY and Lindy awoke before five AM and decided to get up out of bed and have coffee together alone in the dark. It had always been a special time for them; awake before the kids, and long before they had to be anywhere. It was at these times they discussed future plans, trips, and surprises for the kids. Showered and dressed in sweatpants and tee-shirts, they sat at the corner of the kitchen table facing each other in silence, fingers linked together.

"Ricky....something's gnawing at me and I don't know what it is. It's like I'm missing....something...something I should know. You know how your subconscious picks up things and....they don't surface? There's something....I'm not...picking up on...and I don't know what it is."

"Baby, if it's important, it'll come to you. Relax your mind...let it drift. If it's not surfacing it's because your mind is cluttered with anxiety and torment."

Lindy's blue eyes shone as she looked into the dark eyes of her husband.

"You're *right*! Sometimes I forget how smart you are."

She smiled and reached up to run her fingers through his hair. She brought her hand down and touched his cheek, running her thumb across it.

"Kiss me," she whispered.

Ricky leaned forward and pressed his lips lightly on hers, and kissed her, very gently and tenderly. His lips lingered over hers, just touching them lightly before he pulled away.

"Thank you. That's just the way I wanted you to kiss me."

Ricky smiled.

"You know what I was thinking about last night?"

"What?"

"Our place. Remember? Remember our shelter that we built? Our rock?"

"Yeah. The first time we kissed was down there….that first day we went exploring." Lindy reminded him.

"I remember. But that wasn't the first time I wanted to kiss you. Remember I walked you home from school that day we met? We got to your door and I wanted to kiss you….so bad….but I was afraid you didn't want me to."

"I remember….waiting for you to kiss me….and you didn't. I thought maybe you really didn't like me all that much."

"I was crazy about you already….but I didn't know it yet."

"And when did you know it?"

"That night. That's when me and Uncle Nick went to the mall to get my cell phone. He was looking at clothes and I went to buy that colored tape to take with us."

"I remember that tape! It was red."

"Yeah....it was red. Anyway...after getting the tape I walked past the arcade and there were some wild looking chicks standing outside of it. They reminded me of the girls I knew in Chicago. Anyway, I went outside with them and smoked a couple of cigarettes. They were saying some pretty lewd things to me. One of them gave me her phone number. Anyway, the whole time I was there with them I was thinking about you. Then I realized I wasn't enjoying myself with those girls. That's when I realized that I was yours....and you were the only one for me."

"You never told me that story."

"I didn't think it was important. What was important was that I....only had eyes for you from the day I met you."

"Same here."

"Really? Only me? Not even the pizza delivery guy?"

Lindy smiled.

"Oh, gees.....remember him? He used to just stand at the door and stare at me."

"Oh, yeah....I remember him. I came real close to paying him a visit once...to tell him he better stop staring at you like you were a sideshow on his delivery route."

Lindy laughed lightly, and then her eyes dropped to her coffee cup.

"What's the matter?"

"We always use this time to discuss future events. Why are we suddenly talking about the past?"

Ricky sighed and reached for her, pulling her close.

"Maybe....maybe it's because the future is suddenly

very uncertain. Maybe because we can't face the future right now."

Gasping, Lindy pulled away from him. Her face looked stricken like he had slapped her.

"Oh, God….Ricky, *don't talk like that*! We'll get Samantha back….we *have* to!"

Lindy squeezed her eyelids shut and she swallowed hard. She placed her hand over her mouth to stop her lips from quivering. When she opened her eyes Ricky was staring at her, his eyes holding a look of sadness she had never seen before. Silently they watched each other, their eyes held together by a bond that could never be broken.

The phone was ringing.

Ricky and Lindy ran toward the family room where the two FBI agents were already in place for the call. Morrow pointed to Ricky indicating that he was to answer it.

"Hello?"

"Got that pen and paper?"

"Yes."

"Good. Quick learner. All right. Get a gym bag with the Washington High School logo on it. Wal-Mart sells them. I'll tell you later where the bag is to go. Now…let me talk to the mommy."

Ricky handed Lindy the phone.

"Yes?"

"Yes….my, how formal we sound. Your little girl is a baby doll, but I guess you know that already…don't you?"

"Look….what do you want? Stop torturing me like this, you bastard. I want my daughter back."

There was silence on the line, but Lindy could tell he hadn't hung up.

"Hello?"

"Just watch the name calling, Sweet cheeks.... remember I still have the little lamb chop here."

The line went dead.

A sudden awareness came into Lindy's eyes and she gasped for air. Again, she gasped for air.

"I can't breathe! I can't breathe!"

She was leaning over the arm of the chair trying to breathe.

"Lindy! Lie down! Let me get Aunt Liz!"

"NO! Ricky.....*I know who it is*! The kidnapper.....*I know who it is!*"

The two agents' heads jerked up toward Lindy.

Both of them, and Ricky asked, in unison, "Who?"

"Nelson....Nelson Sutter. Ricky....*Nelson Sutter has our sweet little girl!*

"Baby, he's in prison."

"It's him, Ricky.....I *know* it is!"

"What makes you so sure?"

"He just called me Sweet Cheeks, and referred to Sammie as the little lamb chop. He called me that once before....."

"But....Lindy....he's..."

"You say he's in jail......but...."

Lindy turned to the agents.

"Can you check? Nelson Sutter. Can you see if he is still in jail?"

"Who is he?"

Lindy's sobs were becoming out of control again as she was gasping for air even harder.

"It's *him*, Ricky....I *know* it!"

Liz rushed into the family room when she heard Lindy

crying. She ran to her and wrapped her arms around her, holding on to her tightly.

Agent Morrow appealed to Ricky again. "Who is this guy she's talking about?"

Ricky sighed.

"Lindy was put into a foster home....with a couple named Sutter. The wife was okay...but the guy....Nelson.... raped Lindy...more than once...every time the wife worked late. Lindy came to me and told me, and....we ran away. We left town and ended up in South Carolina...where we stayed for five months. Lindy left a trail of evidence for the police to deal with Sutter....and they did. But without Lindy to testify they released Sutter from jail."

Ricky stopped talking for a moment and rubbed Lindy's back while Liz held her. He sighed again.

"Well....anyway...Sutter found us in South Carolina. He had Lindy by the throat and he came in waving a gun at me. I remember that he said that after he killed me, he and Lindy were going to...get it on. Well, Lindy...that's all she had to hear....she flipped out.....and went wild on him. She fucked him up....all by herself. Sliced his arm with a putty knife she had in her pocket, kicked him in the balls when he released his grip on her, and the gun fell to the floor and went off. The bullet hit him in the ass. By this time the police were there. They took him away and Lindy called the police up here and said she would come back to testify. We came back, and she was ready to testify.... but he pled guilty and went to prison without a trial. He should still be there."

Agent Daily was at the other end of the family room talking on his cell phone. He glanced up at them a couple of times while he held the phone to his ear. He joined them when he ended his call.

"Nelson Sutter was released from the state prison a little more than a month ago. He got time off for waiving his right to a trial, time off for good behavior, and they paroled him."

Lindy's face was ashen. The terror in her eyes made them look black from a distance. She gasped for air, but no air was entering her lungs. Nick was already on the phone dialing the number he had been given if they needed the special ambulance service. Within seconds, the ambulance was on the way.

Liz pushed Lindy into the recliner and pushed the lever for the chair to recline.

"Breathe slowly, Lindy. Don't gasp for air."

The sirens got closer as Nick went to the door to let the paramedics in. They rushed past him and into the family room where they took over.

One paramedic took her vital signs while the other inserted an airway down her throat.

"She has a heartbeat but she's not breathing. Vital signs are dropping. Breathe for her, Rob."

Ricky heard them say she wasn't breathing and lunged forward, only to be pulled back by Agent Morrow.

"Let them do what they're trained to do."

"She's my wife! She's not breathing!"

"They can handle it, Rick! Stay back!"

Ricky watched as they inserted a needle into Lindy's arm, and then watched as they hooked up an IV to her other arm. He saw the blue airbag connected to the white plastic trachea that went in through her mouth, and he watched the paramedic squeezing the bag, trying to get air into Lindy's lungs. Liz and Nick found a place beside Ricky and flanked him on both sides. Liz was silently crying and Nick's face was contorted with concern. They both had an arm around Ricky's waist, and could feel the tension in his body as he watched. Liz glanced at his face and knew that he was silently praying for his wife, and willing her to breathe at the same time.

"There she goes!" The paramedic named Rob exclaimed.

"What?" Ricky's voice held alarm in it.

Rob looked up at Ricky and saw the naked fear in his eyes.

"She's breathing...on her own. She'll be okay...in a little while. I think we should take her in this time."

"Yes....go ahead. Aunt Liz....you'll go with her?"

"Of course. Nick....follow in the car...okay?"

Nick nodded, not trusting his voice to come out in a normal tone.

The gurney was lifted and they wheeled Lindy out to the waiting ambulance. Ricky called for them to stop before they lifted her into the back. He ran up and kissed her lightly on the cheek.

"I love you, Baby," he whispered.

He moved away from the gurney just as a tear dropped from his cheek to hers. He wiped his tears with the back of his hand as he watched the ambulance drive away. Agent Morrow was standing at the doorway watching when Nick pushed past him to get into his car.

"Dr. Bazario....what causes her to stop breathing like that?"

"Fear....intense fear. It's hysteria caused by that kind

of fear. Ever hear of being frightened to death? Well...you just witnessed something close to that. I gotta go."

Morrow nodded and watched him get into his car, start it, and drive away in the direction the ambulance had gone. He looked away when he felt Ricky standing beside him. Morrow went back into the family room while Ricky went to get Michael out of his crib. He had been calling for his mommy for a good five minutes already.

Ricky lifted him out, making a mental note that it was time for Michael to get a new bed. They had only kept him in the crib this long because he rolled a lot while he slept. It was obvious that the bed was getting too small for him now. He stood him up on the floor and watched him run to the bathroom. In spite of everything, Ricky laughed. Michael had that effect on people.

Ricky dressed Michael and carried him to the kitchen for breakfast.

"Want Ya-Yindies."

"But mommy makes Ya-Yindies and she's not here right now. Tomorrow...I promise. Ya-Yindies tomorrow for breakfast....okay, buddy?"

"Where mommy?"

"She'll be back in a little while. How about some waffles with strawberries and strawberry syrup?"

"Kay."

Ricky got the frozen waffles out of the freezer and then reached for the package of frozen strawberries. He put the plastic container into the microwave and pushed the button for them to thaw. He took two waffles out and placed them in the toaster but did not press the lever to make them drop down yet. When the strawberries were thawed he pressed the lever on the toaster to let them toast.

He got the strawberry syrup and the butter out of the refrigerator and set it on the counter to wait for the toasted waffles. When the toaster popped up he placed the waffles on Michael's Eyore plate and covered them with butter and then the strawberries. He covered the whole thing with syrup and then added a dab of cool whip. Michael was already in his booster seat when Ricky placed the plate in front of him.

"Tank you, Daddy."

Ricky smiled at him. "You're welcome, Buddy. Let me cut them up for you."

Ray and Diane walked in through the front door and immediately joined Ricky in the kitchen.

"Where's Lindy?" Ray asked.

Ricky hesitated and then looked down at Michael. He spelled it out.

"H-O-S-P-I-T-A-L."

"What? Why? What happened?"

"We know who the kidnapper is."

"WHO!"

The word came from both Ray and Diane.

"Nelson Sutter."

"Nel….oh, shit….isn't he in prison?"

"Released a month ago."

Ray ran his fingers through his hair, and sighed.

"Damn it! This is all my fault! If I had been a better father….oh, hell…if I had been a father at all….she would never have met that slime ball. When does it end? When in the hell does this end?"

"It ends this time. First my wife and now my daughter? It ends. I'll make it end. I'll have a shot at him….this time for sure. Last time I was afraid for Lindy. I didn't want to see him hurt her….but I'll make sure I have a shot at this bastard and nobody but he gets hurt."

"So what happened to Lindy that she's in the….?"

"She stopped breathing again….when she realized who it was that had our daughter. Paramedics came and got her breathing again, but they thought she should go in this time. I agreed. Aunt Liz and Uncle Nick are with her. I stayed back in case the phone rings."

"Is there anything we can do, Ricky?" Diane asked.

Ricky started to say no, but changed his mind.

"Yes…there is something you can do. Can one of you go to Wal-Mart and buy a gym bag with the Washington High School logo on it? He asked for that to put the money in. Get the biggest one. It has to hold five million dollars."

"Yes, of course. I'll go and take Michael, if I may."

"Michael, want to go to Wal-Mart with Gram Diane?"

Michael smiled and nodded.

"Okay…after you're done eating and we clean the strawberries off of you, you can go."

For the third time this morning, Ricky felt a burning sensation in his stomach accompanied by pain and nausea. He knew he was going to be sick. He excused himself from the kitchen and ran down the hall to the bathroom in the master bedroom. Getting there just in time, he began heaving into the toilet bowl, first the contents of his stomach, then bile, and then some pinkish colored blood. He stood staring down at it as he tried to catch his breath and remain calm.

"Great. This is *all* I need." He whispered to himself.

He knew he had to speak to Aunt Liz when she got

back. She could give him something to stop the burning and the blood as well, he was sure. He hoped so.

Ricky and Ray watched Diane take Michael by the hand and leave for Wal-Mart. It took a complete change of clothing to make Michael presentable to go shopping. The clothes Ricky had put on him were dotted with the red strawberry syrup and bits of strawberries. He vaguely wondered if he were a sloppy eater like that when he was three. He doubted that Lindy could have been.

Jack Daily came out of the family room and motioned to Ricky.

"We got a former address on him…probably where he used to live with his wife. A couple of men left to go there to talk to the wife right after we found the address. Hopefully they caught her before she left for work."

"That address would be on Bramble Bush Drive?"

"Yes."

"That's the house where Lindy lived with them."

"Well, apparently Missus Sutter still lives there. We may know something after they talk to her."

"What about his parole officer? Shouldn't he have a parole officer?"

"Yeah, the guy is on vacation…..up in Canada at some kind of festival. Won't be back until Monday. Because of the work overload, nobody got assigned his cases."

"Great…..so Sutter is basically free to do whatever he wants. Nice."

16

LORAINE SUTTER WAS almost ready to leave for the office when she heard someone knocking on the front door. She frowned as she wondered who it could be this early in the morning, just knowing that it was too early for any kind of sales pitch. She was surprised to see two very large men, both in suits, standing there with sober looks on their faces.

"Loraine Sutter?"

"Yes. And who might you be?"

"I'm Agent Ted Weber and this is Agent Frank Joyce. We're with the FBI. We would like to talk to you about your husband....Nelson Sutter?"

Loraine sighed. 'It figures,' she thought silently.

"Well, for starters....he's my *ex*-husband...and has been for quite a long time."

"We understand that. Sorry."

"So what is it that you think I can do for you?"

"Well, do you know where he is?"

"Come on in and sit down for a moment. I have to call

to say I'll be a little late. Not that I really have to, but I feel like I should. Give me a minute."

Loraine called her office and told her secretary that something came up and that she would be late, and then she sat down at the kitchen table, gesturing that the two agents do the same.

"Now...the question was...do I know where he is?"

"Yes, Ma'am."

"No....I don't. As long as he's not near me, I don't care where he is either."

"I see."

It was Agent Ted Weber who was asking the questions and doing all the talking. Loraine imagined he was the spokesperson while the other one watched body language— if that's the way it worked.

"What's he done now?"

"Well, Missus Sutter...."

"Loraine....please call me Loraine."

"Loraine...we believe he may be involved in a kidnapping."

"What? Nelson *hates* kids. Always has. Who do you think he kidnapped?"

"Little Samantha DeCelli....the five-year-old that's been missing since last Saturday. We understand that her mother used to live here as a foster child."

Loraine stared blankly at the two men, and then recognition came into her eyes.

"Lindy? That little beauty is Lindy's little girl? I never made the connection. Lindy's name was....Riley...I would not have known what her married name would be. I-I'm sorry....I don't get to watch television very often. I knew of the story but never really heard the details. But of course....that child looks just like Lindy....except she has very dark hair. Who did Lindy marry?"

"Ricky DeCelli."

Loraine smiled.

"Ricky. She married Ricky. I'm glad. She was so much in love with him."

"Ma'am...do you have any idea where your ex-husband is?"

"No....I don't. He came here the day after he was released from prison the first time. To get his things, he said. I opened the garage door up for him and told him to take his things and never set foot back here again. If he did I would get a restraining order."

"You must really hate him."

"Yes....I do. I took Lindy in as a foster child to give her a better life....and that...that slimy bastard....raped her.... not once....but every time I worked late."

Loraine stopped and reached for a tissue.

"I'm sorry. I was so fond of Lindy. She was sweet and gentle....and...I wanted to give her everything she deserved. She didn't deserve Nelson....doing that to her. He had her convinced that I would think she was the one who came on to him. Then of course, he threatened her if she told anybody."

Loraine had to stop again, reaching for a new tissue. She glanced at the coffee pot and saw that there was still quite a bit of coffee in it.

"Can I offer you two a cup of coffee? It's not too old.... just from about an hour ago."

"Sure....this seems sort of painful for you. Is it?"

Loraine stood up and got out three coffee mugs. She filled them and put the cream and sugar on the table. She needn't have bothered with that, since both agents drank it black like she did.

"It's painful…because I remember how sweet Lindy was. I cried when I found out about what he was doing to her….but I cried for her…not him. When I heard what he had done, I….was sickened."

"And how did you find out?"

"Well, Lindy left a trail. On the day she ran off she turned in a paper to her English teacher, describing the…. rapes….and where the evidence could be found. She put two pairs of her panties in her locker. They had his semen on them, one pair was torn. He was arrested. But then he was released when they couldn't find Lindy. *He* found Lindy….in South Carolina. He threatened her, held a gun on Ricky, and somehow she got the upper hand. Sliced his arm wide open….there's a big scar there on his right forearm…she kicked him where it hurts, and then the gun went off. The bullet hit him in his buttocks. That part was sort of funny. So….that's twice Lindy won over Nelson. Nelson hates to lose….at anything. He took Lindy's child for revenge."

"He also wants five million dollars for her return." Weber added.

"Ma'am, do you have any idea where he is living? When he came here….was he driving a vehicle?"

This time it was Agent Joyce asking the questions.

"Yes….yes, he was. It was gray…a gray Ford….I think. I believe it was a Ford Taurus….older model…..like around the early nineties."

"Can you tell us anything else?"

"Let me think. There's the scar on his arm….and a

slight limp. He limps a little now. Agent Weber.....how is Lindy? Do you know?"

"They had to rush her to the hospital today. When she discovered who had her child she stopped breathing. Paramedics revived her, but took her in for observation. She may be back home now...we don't know."

"Her last name is DeCelli?"

"Yes."

"I wish I could help you more...but like I mentioned.... I told Nelson never to come here again. Oh...wait a minute....maybe I can help you. Nelson had a couple of bank accounts of his own. Maybe had a few thousand dollars in them. He may have reactivated them to cover his expenses...."

"What bank?"

Agent Weber had a notebook opened and a pen poised in his hand. Loraine noticed that he was left handed—like Lindy.

"National Bank....the one at the corner of Main and Sixth. That's all I can help you with...but if I think of anything...."

"Here is my card.....if you think of anything, please call."

"I will."

She watched the agents walk down the walk and get into their car and drive away. Sadly, she thought of Lindy and what she must be going through right now. 'Sweet Lindy. Life just isn't fair sometimes,' she whispered to herself.

She shut off the coffee pot and made sure all the lights were off and then she left for work through the door from the kitchen to the garage. She used her automatic opener to lift the garage door and then closed it when she pulled out of the garage. If she drove the speed limit she would be at work only one hour behind her normal arrival time.

The two agents who had just left her place rode in silence for several minutes. Agent Weber finally spoke.

"Do you think she's telling us everything?"

"Yeah….everything she can think of, anyway. If she thinks of anything, she'll call."

"Why are you so sure?"

"It was obvious. She loved Missus DeCelli…when she knew her as a seventeen year old teenager. She was heartbroken over what her scumbag husband did to that girl. I think the lady has a lot of love, but also a lot of integrity. If she remembers anything she'll come forward.

Loraine sat down at her desk ready to start the day's work that had been forwarded to her, but she was finding it hard to concentrate. She read and reread several documents that required her signature, and she still didn't know what she had read. Leaning back in her chair, she recalled something important. She had a copy of Nelson's bank information in her desk here at work. She opened her bottom drawer and found the folder marked with the letters N S and leafed through it. Yes, here it is. She pulled the card that the FBI agent had given her out of her handbag and quickly dialed his number. He answered almost immediately.

"Weber."

"Agent Weber….this is Loraine Sutter."

"Yes, Ma'am. Did you remember something important?"

"Well, no…but I have the bank information for

Nelson. I can give you whatever you need off of this. His statements were coming to the house for awhile and I must have had a couple in my purse....that's why I would have created a folder for them here...at my office."

"Okay...so what information can you give me?"

"Bank account numbers....if you need them. I see that he had seven thousand dollars in one account and twenty-five hundred in another one while he was in prison. He may be using that money to live on now."

"Do you mind if we stop by and pick those up from you? It may or may not be helpful...I don't know."

"Sure. I work in the Walsh Building....I'm vice president of operations, on the fifth floor, suite five-oh-one. What time do you think you'll be here? In case I have a meeting or something."

"We'll swing by there now....if that's okay."

"Fine.....I'll be here."

Loraine hung up and resignedly got back to reading documents. She knew she wasn't going to stay at work all day, because there was something she simply had to do.

Right after the two agents came and claimed Nelson's bank information; Loraine wrapped up her day and let her secretary know that she was leaving for the day. The woman looked surprised but didn't say anything. Loraine never left work early, particularly since the problem with her husband. She knew all about Nelson and his antics, and she knew about the teenaged girl he raped. She believed it from the beginning since she knew that Nelson was a bit of a letch. He had made a pass at her at a Christmas party one year, which made her feel sorry for Loraine.

Loraine had been on edge since she came in late this morning. Something was going on, and if the secretary could bet on it she would bet that Nelson somehow was the source of it. How he and Loraine ended up together was a matter of speculation. Loraine was classy, intelligent, and ethical. Nelson was slime.

Loraine pulled out of the parking garage and made a left. At the light she made another left, and headed toward the next township, to Carlisle Street. After a right and then another left, Loraine found herself on Carlisle, and slowed down as she passed over the small bridge. She was not sure of the address, and hoped that there would be something that would indicate that it was Lindy's house. She wished she had looked up the address on the Internet or even in the phone book.

There. On the right. There were four cars in the driveway and an unmarked car with a government license plate sitting in front. Another car was partially parked on the lawn. It looked to be an unmarked police car—this had to be the place. She eased her car up behind the government car and put it in park. She left the car running as she sat there for a few minutes. She hadn't seen Lindy since she left town over fifteen years ago. How would Lindy react to her? Would she blame her for any of this? Would she refuse to see her? Loraine shut the car off and opened the car door. 'We will find out,' she murmured.

Liz answered the door when she heard the light taps on it. She looked at Loraine quizzically.

"Hi…is this…where Lindy lives?"

"Who are you?"

"Please….I have to see her."

"I don't want her upset….so if you're a reporter you can't see her."

"No....I'm not.....I'm....Loraine Sutter. Please....I really want to see her."

Liz nodded and stood aside to let Loraine pass.

"She's in the kitchen....uh, she's been in the hospital for a good part of the morning, so she's....weak. This has really taken its toll on her. She's a little bit....drugged....so...."

"I mean her no harm. I...love Lindy. What my husband....or ex-husband, I should say...did to her....... damn it, I hate him!"

Liz nodded again and stared at the floor for a moment.

"Go ahead and see her. I'm Liz Bazario, by the way.... their aunt."

"Oh....Aunt Liz....she told me about you....she really loves you."

"Well, the feeling has always been mutual." Liz smiled a little.

Loraine walked toward the kitchen and stopped just inside. She spied Lindy immediately, as she was sitting at the table holding her face in her hands, blotting out all light from the room. Loraine slowly walked to her chair and stood beside her.

"Hello, Lindy."

Lindy raised her head, focused on Loraine, and stared. Recognition and surprise were evident as she spoke.

"Loraine.....I-I'm glad you came. Please sit."

Loraine took a chair next to her and before she could say another word, the tears came.

"I'm sorry, Lindy.....I'm so...sorry."

"This isn't your fault, Loraine."

"No....not directly....but...."

Loraine stopped to try to get control of herself. She looked into Lindy's eyes and recognized the pain in them. She closed hers to block out that look of pain and misery, but it wasn't working.

"Lindy....when I took you in as a foster child I wanted to give you a better life....make a difference in your life.... help you achieve. That's all I wanted. I wanted to be able to some day say I helped that girl and look how far she went in life. I never.....never....ever wanted to see you hurt.....not in any way. I was sick when I found out about what Nelson did to you. I threw him out that night. He told you I wouldn't believe you? Well, he was wrong....I believed you from the moment I learned of it. You were not a liar or a trouble-maker, and I knew that. I cried, Lindy....I cried for you."

Loraine stopped to wipe her eyes and blow her nose. She halfway smiled at Lindy before she began again.

"I wish you would have come to me....but I understand why you didn't. By the way....that detective....Bruno, was it? He told me you asked about me. I was touched. Anyway....I prayed that you were safe and that one day you could come back and lead a normal life. From what I hear, you have done exactly that. I hear you married Ricky....I'm so glad. I....remember that first day you came to live with us....you were heartbroken that you had been taken away from him. You know...eventually I would have arranged for you to see him...I hope you know that. So you managed to live a decent, normal life until...Nelson.... that son of a bitch....came back into your life."

"Loraine.....I'm so glad you came here. You were wonderful to me...and I was always grateful for that. I did okay....by the way. Ricky and I came back after we got married....then we finished high school, and then went on to college together...we both got Master's degrees. We started a family after we were out of college. Until.... now...our life has been wonderful....."

Lindy stopped to grab a tissue. She felt Ricky's arm go around her shoulders as he slid into the chair next to her. Loraine looked past Lindy in time to see Ricky sit down.

"You must be Ricky."

He nodded as he stared at her.

"Ricky....this is Loraine....Loraine Sutter."

Loraine saw the muscle in Ricky's jaw twitch, but his eyes softened as he spoke to her.

"Lindy has always spoken very highly of you. Your ex-husband is garbage....but I'll bet you already know that."

"Yes, I do. Look.....I hope you don't think me forward but I *had* to see Lindy. I'm sick over the things that Nelson has done to her. I only wanted the best for her."

"Yeah, me too." Ricky smiled sadly as he looked down into Lindy's face.

"I'm glad I got a chance to meet you. I'm so glad you two ended up together."

"Thanks. But it couldn't have been any other way for either of us."

Liz set a cup of coffee in front of Loraine.

"The cream and sugar are there." Liz pointed at the edge of the table.

"She drinks it black."

Loraine smiled for the first time since she came in.

"You remembered that."

"Yeah.....I did." Lindy smiled weakly back at her.

Chris appeared with Michael on his shoulders. He had offered to give Michael his bath after he made sure Lindy was all right when she came home from the hospital. Chris had gotten to the house not long after Lindy was taken in the ambulance earlier in the day, and he was panic-stricken when he heard the latest. In order to help out as well as keep busy, he offered to do the honors of deep tub diving with Michael.

Lindy looked up and smiled at Michael.

"Loraine….this is Michael….our youngest."

"Oh….how handsome you are!"

"Me look like Daddy wiff Mommy's hair."

Loraine laughed.

"And your daughter looks like you with Ricky's hair."

"How did you find out about Samantha being kidnapped by Nelson?" Lindy asked after she introduced Loraine to Chris.

"Two FBI agents visited me this morning before I left for work. I had heard bits and pieces of the news story, but really didn't pay much attention. When they told me that Samantha was your daughter, I realized the resemblance. Your face and eyes and Ricky's hair. She's beautiful, Lindy."

"Thank you."

Lindy began to tear up again.

"Lindy….if you need anything…..please….I'm a phone call away. I'm so glad I got to see you. May I come back again?"

"Of course. Hopefully, you'll get to meet Samantha next time."

"I hope."

"Oh….Loraine? The FBI doesn't want Nelson to know that we know he's the one who has Sammie….so if he should contact you…."

"Oh, he won't....but don't worry....I wouldn't tell him anything if he did. I just hope he gets what's coming to him."

Loraine stood up before she bent down and kissed Lindy on the cheek.

"Remember....anything....just call. I'll be praying."

"Thanks, Loraine. I'm glad you came."

Lindy's smile was weak but genuine. She watched Loraine walk out of the kitchen and then out the door. Lindy felt sorry for her—sorry for her because she knew how Loraine was affected by what happened to her and now Samantha.

On the drive home Loraine smiled as tears rolled down her cheeks. Lindy had done well and that made Loraine very happy. It amazed Loraine that Lindy was still as adorable as ever, even though she was thirty-two years old now, and she still remained just as sweet. And Ricky—he certainly was a handsome man. They were a beautiful couple. Loraine wiped her tears with the back of her hand and sniffed. Quietly, she whispered, "I love you, Lindy. I love you like you were my own daughter."

17

NELSON COULD HAVE slapped himself. He knew he made a mistake when he called Lindy Sweet Cheeks. She didn't even flinch, so maybe—just maybe—she didn't catch it. Lindy had certainly become feisty over the years. She was no longer the timid little fawn she used to be.

"I'll bet a romp in the sack with her now would be a true delight," he muttered.

He only hoped that she was too distraught to pick up on the nickname. He stared over at the little one. She was still fast asleep, her chest rising and falling evenly, and her face held an angelic look. Nelson recognized that she was a smart child, but then again so had Lindy been. He wondered vaguely if either of the kids got Lindy's beautiful singing voice. He still had her CD. He had been listening to it in his car on the way home that day they discovered she was gone. He kept it with his belongings, and Loraine was never the wiser. She would have wanted it as a memento if she knew he had it. Maybe little Samantha would like to hear her mommy sing. That would put him in real solid with the kid. He heard her stirring over on the love seat and he raised his eyes to see her.

"Good morning, Munchkin."

He smiled and winked at her causing her to smile back.

"Want to take a walk today? See what else we can discover?"

"Yes."

She rolled out from under the blanket he had placed over her after she fell asleep and ran to the bathroom.

"I'll make breakfast…then we can go outside."

"Okay," she yelled back over her shoulder.

He had a breakfast of scrambled eggs and ham started when she came out of the bathroom.

"Umm….it smells *good!*"

"See? That's why I like you….you say nice things about my cooking."

Samantha giggled.

"And you know what? I have a big….really big…. surprise for you later."

"Really? What is it?" She asked him as she tried to contain her excitement.

"Now if I told you….it wouldn't be a surprise….now would it? You'll see."

Samantha giggled again as she climbed up onto a kitchen chair.

"Oh….so we're eating in here, are we? Are you trying to domesticate me?"

"What does that mean?"

"It means…..teach me good social etiquette."

"Oh….what does etiquette mean?"

"Uh…..proper manners."

Samantha laughed. "But….you're not a kid….so you already know that stuff."

"I guess you've never been in jail. If you had been you would know that hardly any of those grown-ups know that stuff."

"Were you in *jail?*"

Samantha stared at him wide-eyed, waiting for his answer.

'Careful, Nelson….careful. Tread lightly with this one,' he said to himself.

"Yeah….when I played cops and robbers with my friends when I was just a little bit older than you."

"Oh…..well, that's not real jail. That's pretend."

"Yeah….that's pretend."

He smiled at her and thought, *'you ain't just whistling Dixie, Honey…that's not real jail.'*

Nelson placed the breakfast dishes in the sink and turned to Samantha.

"Want to get dressed and go outside?"

She answered him with a happy grin, which suddenly turned sad.

"John…..I miss my mommy and daddy….and Michael. Can I see them soon? I mean…I like you, too….maybe you could go to my house with me….and stay there for awhile."

"Hey, yeah! Maybe I could do that sometime. When you go back home you can ask your mommy if that's okay."

"I will."

Nelson laughed hard at that one.

She put on the jacket he bought for her and reached for his hand as they went outside. They walked up the hill into the woods and found that the bird's nest was empty. Samantha was upset about it until Nelson explained to her that the birds grew up and flew away to make their own nests. As they walked, a rabbit ran across their path, causing Samantha to jump at first, and then jump up and down with delight. At the top of the hill they came to a clearing and could see farmland below.

"Look, Sam....see the sheep?"

Samantha watched them with interest, and then turned to Nelson.

"Do they get hot in the summer?"

"Well.....they would....but the farmer shaves them so they aren't. Then he sells the wool to make clothes."

Nelson was suddenly glad he grew up on a farm since it was obvious that Samantha was interested in animals. The farm he grew up on had over a hundred head of cattle, at least four pigs, about three dozen chickens, two horses, and four sheep. There were two goats as well. He realized that he could entertain her for hours with stories about the farm. This was valuable knowledge to him.

It appeared to be getting on toward noon and he was getting hungry. They started back down the hill, through the woods, and came out right next to the red bushes that bordered the small yard. They were walking very close to the bushes when Samantha let out a small yelp and reached down to grab her leg.

"What's wrong?"

Nelson knelt down beside her and lifted her pant leg a little. One of the bushes scraped her leg and broke the skin a little. She had a scratch of about an inch and a half long with just a trickle of blood coming from it.

"Oh....you got a little scratch. We'll see if we can find something to put on it. Maybe a band-aid, too."

She nodded as they continued toward the house. She pulled herself up onto a chair while he went to the bathroom to see if there was anything there to put on a cut. He found band-aids and a tube of something that claimed to be an antiseptic, and took it out to the kitchen. He wiped the cut off with a wet paper towel and applied a little of the contents from the tube onto the cut, and then applied a band-aid to cover it.

"There. Feel better?"

Samantha nodded and smiled tentatively.

"Okay....now....for lunch.....how about grilled cheese and tomato soup?'

Samantha nodded again as her smile got bigger.

"My mom's favorite."

"Yes....yes it is.....I remember that."

Nelson started making the grilled cheese and got a pan out to heat up tomato soup. He did indeed remember that the combination was Lindy's favorite meal. Lindy. She was the source of his demise.....but she was also going to be the source of his wealth. Five million dollars worth of wealth.

"Thanks, Sweet Cheeks," he muttered under his breath.

He placed the plates holding the grilled cheese on the table and then the bowls of soup beside the plates. He got out silverware and napkins and then called Samantha to the table.

"What do you want to drink? There's soda, and then there's milk."

"Milk, please."

He couldn't help but to smile. He loved her manners and her politeness. He ran down the hall to the bedroom and grabbed the CD player and Lindy's CD, brought it back to the kitchen, and plugged the player into the wall socket on the kitchen counter. Then he dropped the CD onto the designated place, hit the play button, and turned the volume up a little.

"Here's your surprise."

Samantha turned her head a little to listen, and a big smile spread across her face.

"That's mommy!"

"Yep, it is."

"Mommy sings so pretty!"

"Yep, she does."

Samantha smiled at Nelson once again, but her smile soon turned into a large grin. She was quiet through the rest of the lunchtime meal as she listened to her mother sing the songs she had recorded when she was sixteen. Samantha knew one of the songs, since Lindy still sang it once in awhile. Nelson watched her and saw how animated she became as she listened to the CD. For a fleeting moment he actually felt bad about taking her away from her mother. Besides the money, Nelson took Lindy's child to hurt Lindy. He really never thought about how he would be hurting the child. Taking her to Brazil with him would really hurt Lindy, but Samantha would suffer, too. Maybe in time she would forget about her parents, but it would take a long time. Lindy and her husband would hurt forever, however—and that is what appealed to him about it.

18

Friday morning. Lindy and Ricky once again awoke before dawn. Angie and Ron had taken Michael home with them the night before, since Lindy looked really pale and worn out. Liz and Nick decided it was time to go home, too. Lindy and Ricky were alone in the house except for the agents in the family room. Ricky put a filter into the pot and added the coffee grounds while Lindy filled the carafe with water. She filled the back of the coffee pot with the water and Ricky flipped the switch.

"Teamwork," Ricky commented.

"Yeah….we have always been good at that, huh?"

Ricky nodded and wrapped his arms around her waist. He leaned his head against hers and kissed her temple very softly. They stood together like that until the coffee pot stopped brewing. Lindy reached for the cups while Ricky got out the cream for Lindy's coffee. Together they sat down and waited for the next phone call, silently fearing what it would bring.

Although it was nice to be relatively alone for a change, Ricky worried that Lindy was going to need Liz again when the next phone call came in. He had taken Liz aside yesterday and told her about his problem, and she wrote a prescription for him, but urged him to get tests done just as soon as possible. He promised that as soon as this was all over, if his stomach was still bothering him, he would go for tests. Liz told him she was sure it was probably caused from stress, but that he may be developing an ulcer. She held on to the prescription and said she would get it filled for him and bring it the next day. They both agreed that it wouldn't be a good idea to tell Lindy about it, even though Ricky did not like keeping things from her.

Lindy stared up at the kitchen clock.

"It's almost seven and....he hasn't called yet."

"He will."

"I want to speak to Samantha."

"Yeah....I was thinking the same thing. I'm going to ask to speak to her."

"Good."

"If we don't speak to her....we're not playing any more. I'm going to tell him that."

"Oh, God....don't jeopardize Samantha's life, Ricky."

"Baby, he wants the money. Without it he can't go anywhere. He knows he'll have to leave the country now, and that five million is his only chance of doing that. He'll let us talk to her."

"I hope so."

Lindy jumped when the telephone rang. They both ran for the family room, almost colliding with Agent Morrow as he came out of the door to find them.

"Answer the phone...but remember...we don't want him to know that you know who he is."

Lindy and Ricky took only a moment to look at Morrow and nod in agreement. Ricky grabbed the receiver.

"Hello?"

"Good morning."

"When and where?"

"What? The drop?"

"Yeah."

"Patience…..be patient."

"Look….I just want to get it over with. We want our daughter back."

"I'm sure you do. But you see….I don't want the Feds to be waiting for me."

"I don't care about that. Just tell *me* when and where."

Nelson laughed harshly.

"I wasn't born yesterday."

"I want to speak to Samantha."

"*Do you?*"

"Yes….or no deal. I want to know that she's okay."

"She's fine."

"I want to *speak* with her….and so does her mother."

"Okay. I'll call back when she's awake."

The line went dead.

Ricky held the receiver in his hand, just staring at it, his anger welling up inside. He flung the phone across the room, causing it to break apart.

"That son of a bitch!"

Ricky's eyes were black with anger. He felt the burning in his stomach and he knew if he didn't get up and run he was going to be sick all over the family room sofa. He moved quickly and left the family room, running down the hallway to the bathroom. He heaved, bringing up bile and blood. He heard Lindy calling him. *'She can't find out!'* he silently reminded himself. He flushed the toilet and leaned against the door.

"Ricky! Are you okay?"

Tears stung his eyes.

"I'm okay, Baby.....I'm okay."

His muffled voice came through the door to her. He hoped Aunt Liz would get there soon with whatever it was she was going to pick up for him. His stomach felt like it was on fire. He rinsed his mouth with mouthwash and then listened at the door to see if Lindy was in the hall. He didn't hear her. Slowly he opened the door and almost ran into her as she came from their bedroom holding a telephone.

"We can hook this one up in the family room. The other one won't work now."

"No…I guess not. Sorry." He answered sheepishly.

Lindy linked her arm through his, as they walked toward the family room.

"It's okay….no problem. Did throwing it make you feel better?"

"Yes."

"Then maybe it was worth it."

Lindy stopped and smiled up at Ricky. She noted the haunted look in his eyes, and she knew he was suffering. She wrapped her arms around him and just held him tightly for a moment, releasing him after she kissed his chest. His lip twitched, offering her half of a smile as he touched her face with his fingers. Lindy grasped his fingers and kissed them as she stared into his eyes. He focused on her face and stared back. The jolt of electricity came, just as it always did. Wrapping his arms around her, he kissed her lightly, just barely touching her lips. His words went into her mouth.

"I love you, Missus DeCelli. I love you so much."

"And I love you, Mister DeCelli…..please don't tell my husband."

Ricky laughed through his nose and hugged her. They embraced and engaged in a long kiss, standing just outside the family room door. Ricky was the first to break it off. He smiled crookedly at his wife.

"I guess I have to go in and apologize now."

"It was *our* phone…." Lindy answered, shrugging her shoulders.

Ricky laughed a little as they went into the family room together.

"Sorry, guys….I guess I lost it there for a minute."

"It's okay, Rick…as long as you have a replacement phone," Jack Daily responded, lightly patting him on the shoulder.

Lindy handed Morrow the new phone. Immediately, he hooked it up to the bureau's equipment.

"Listen….Ricky….Lindy…..this is getting to you….I know it is. He's not going to call back for at least an hour. Take a walk….for at least twenty minutes. Just go outside and take a walk. It'll do you both good."

"Ricky….why don't we walk up to that little store where you used to get the Starbuck's knock-offs? I think we need one….what do you think?"

"Yeah, we can. Let's go right now, and then get back here for when he calls again. I know he'll call when Sammie wakes up."

Dressed in light jackets, they walked hand in hand up to the small convenience store that held so many good memories for them. They bought their lattes and strolled back home. The little walk was extremely therapeutic, putting them both in a better frame of mind by the time they got back to their house. They went directly to the family room when they returned.

"Thanks, Agent Morrow. It helped….it helped a lot."

Morrow noticed a change in their faces, as well as their coloring, and he knew he had advised them correctly.

"You're welcome. You both look a lot better. Now….. go do something other than stare into space or stare at each other. Play a game of gin, watch a movie….we see this all the time. Parents make themselves ill….forget that they started out loving each other first…stop living. I don't know how you feel….I couldn't know….but I can tell you that losing yourself in grief and terror isn't helping anybody….you or your child."

Lindy and Ricky mentally digested what Morrow said, and nodded.

"Gin?" Lindy asked Ricky.

"Be prepared to lose." Ricky responded.

They walked to the kitchen, poured themselves coffee, and pulled out a deck of cards from a kitchen drawer. Until the telephone rang again, they played gin at the kitchen table, thoroughly enjoying the game.

Liz and Nick showed up shortly after ten in the morning, and after getting themselves each a cup of coffee, sat in on a few hands of gin with Ricky and Lindy. When Lindy got up to use the bathroom, Liz slipped Ricky the prescription she had written and then picked up for him.

"Take one now. The sooner they get into your system, the sooner you'll start to feel better. Have you thrown up any more blood?"

"Yeah.....after the phone call this morning."

"What happened?"

"Well.......I asked to speak to Sammie....and he said I could...when she wakes up. Then he hung up. I got sorta...pissed....and threw the phone and broke it. Then I got sick again."

"It sounds like stress is causing the problem. Just take those and hopefully you'll feel better. Does....she know?"

Liz used her thumb to point toward the hallway.

"No. I don't want her to, either. She has enough going on."

Nick listened to the conversation quietly. Liz had already told him of Ricky's stomach problem, so he understood what they were talking about. He thought about how it could affect Lindy and he believed that Ricky shouldn't keep it from her. He felt that she needed to know in case the problem worsened, but also, he felt that Lindy would not go to pieces as easily if she thought that it was hurting Ricky. Nick knew that Lindy wouldn't hurt Ricky for the world, and if she found out later that every time she got hysterical, Ricky's condition worsened, she would feel guilty and blame herself. He was about to voice his opinion when Lindy walked back into the kitchen. He made a mental note to discuss it with Ricky later, as soon as he got the chance.

Lindy stood behind Ricky's chair and placed her hands on his shoulders. She leaned down and kissed his cheek, and whispered into his ear.

"Oh, love of my life.....the coffee pot is empty....oh, great coffee maker....."

All three of them laughed, and Ricky stood up to make more coffee.

"Well, he *does* make the best coffee," Lindy defended.

"Yes, he does. I have to agree. I'd like to know what he does differently." Liz added.

"Ancient DeCelli secret," Ricky responded with a smile and a wink.

'*Normal. It's like things are normal.*' Lindy thought. '*This is the way it has always been. The four of us playfully bantering back and forth. I just want us to be normal again.*' She glanced over at Ricky, caught his eye, and quickly winked at him. He rewarded her with a smile only she understood.

The moment was ruined by the ringing of the telephone. Lindy and Ricky made a bee-line toward the family room. Agent Morrow pointed toward Ricky and then toward the telephone. Ricky answered, sitting down as he said hello; Lindy quickly joined him.

"Daddy? It's me....Sammie."

"Hey, Sweetheart...how are you doing? Are you okay?"

"Yeah....I guess."

"Why, Princess? What's wrong?"

Lindy's face tightened and then turned white with alarm.

"I miss you. John says I can come home real soon."

"That's great, Princess.....'Cause I miss you, too."

Lindy's face relaxed a little.

"John and I are having fun. We saw cows and sheep."

"That's nice, Honey. Are you eating okay?"

"Yeah...John makes good eggs."

"I'm glad. Want to talk to mommy?"

"Yeah! Hi, Mommy!"

"Hi, Sweetheart."

Lindy tried to keep the quiver out of her voice. She bit down hard on her lip to keep from crying. She wanted to hold Samantha so badly that her heart was breaking all over again.

"You're really okay?"

"Well….I"

"What? What is it, Sweetheart?"

"I got scratched by the red bushes."

"The what? What happened?"

"The bushes…..the bushes are red….and I got scratched on them. John put some cream on it and then a band-aid. He says it will be fine. When can I come home, Mommy?"

"Why, Sweetheart? Are you scared?"

"No….I'm not scared….I just miss you."

Lindy had to squeeze her eyes shut tightly and swallow hard to keep her composure.

"I….miss…you, too….Sweetheart. Are you sure you're okay?"

"Yeah….except for the scratch. It hurts a little bit."

"Well, you be sure to tell…John…to check it…. okay?"

Lindy could hear him in the background telling Samantha it was time to go.

"Say bye and then we will go out and play on the swing." Lindy heard him say.

"John says I have to go…..bye, Mommy….See you soon."

"I hope so, Sweetie."

The line went dead.

Lindy put her head between her knees and placed her arms over the back of her head, trying to stay calm. She practiced breathing deeply and slowly until she could feel her heart slowing down a little. Ricky placed his hand on the small of her back and held it there, hoping that it would help. It did. Her breathing slowed and she was able to swallow. She carefully sat upright and turned to look at Ricky.

"She.....seems okay....doesn't she?"

"Yeah....she does, Baby. I....don't think he's hurting her."

"The bushes are red......Does that mean anything to you?"

"What bushes? What bushes are red?"

Agents Morrow and Daily were quietly standing beside the sofa, arms folded, heads down, staring at the carpet.

"The bushes are red....what bushes could be red?" Morrow said half to himself and the other half to Daily.

"Can we look it up? On the Internet, I mean?" Ricky suggested.

"Yeah....it could be a clue....to something. Some rare bush, maybe."

Ricky quickly trotted across the room to their computer, and turned it on. When it was ready to operate, he went to the Internet, picked a search engine, and typed in 'red bushes and shrubs' and waited. There were several options to choose from.

19

AFTER SAMANTHA GOT off of the telephone Nelson took her outside, just as he had promised. He was thinking that maybe Lindy hadn't caught the little pet name he used, so it was safe to assume that they still had no idea who had their daughter. Because he was on parole as a sex offender, his parole officer had an address on him. If it was discovered that he had Samantha, they would go check out the address he was registered under, but they didn't know about the cottage. At any rate, he would be in big trouble no matter what. He was not supposed to be around anybody under the age of eighteen, and he was not supposed to be anywhere but the address he was registered under.

"Sex offender," he muttered. *'I have no desire to hurt this little girl. Just because I....initiated sex with Lindy doesn't mean I'm a sex offender. I would not hurt Samantha that way. Lindy? Well, that was different. She was a beautiful teenaged girl. She was almost eighteen and just extremely desirable. Samantha is a child....who will grow up to be beautiful like Lindy one day.'*

Nelson's thoughts were keeping him so preoccupied that he didn't hear when Samantha called to him the first time.

"John!" she called again.

"So sorry, Samantha! What is it?"

"Can you push me?"

"Sure."

Nelson pushed her on the swing for awhile and then asked her if she wanted to go for another walk.

"No…..I'm tired. I want to lie down."

"Sure….if that's what you want to do. We can go back in and take a nap. Is that what you want?"

Samantha nodded vigorously. Nelson took her hand and led her into the cottage. She seemed unusually quiet.

"What's wrong?"

"I don't feel good."

"No? Maybe you're getting a cold."

Instinctively, Nelson placed his hand on her forehead. She felt warm.

"Maybe you should lie down for awhile. You'll feel better after a little nap."

Samantha crawled up onto the love seat and curled up. She was sleeping within moments. Nelson covered her with a blanket and sat down in his recliner. He was restless. Something told him that he should get her some antibiotics, but how? You had to see a doctor for those. He checked on her and realized that she was sleeping soundly. He decided to chance it and let her sleep while he ran to the drug store to get something for her. Children's Tylenol might be good. He would ask the pharmacist what to get for his grandson who was staying with him and his wife.

Moving quietly and quickly, he left the cottage and got in his car. He headed for the pharmacy which was only three miles away.

He was returning back to the cottage with remedies that the pharmacist had recommended. He hoped everything was okay at the cottage. He felt nervous about leaving her. Upon entering the cottage, he realized he needn't have worried. She was still sleeping. He leaned over the back of the love seat and felt her forehead. She was burning up. He got out two aspirin and poured water into a glass. Shaking her, he woke her up to take the aspirin. She obeyed when he told her to swallow the aspirin, but then went right back to sleep. Momentarily he worried about her.

"Kids get sick all the time," he rationalized. "She'll be fine by morning."

Nelson fell asleep and awoke when it was dark. He turned on a lamp and looked over at Samantha. She was still sleeping. He got up from the chair, went over to the love seat, and felt her forehead again. It felt hotter than it had before and her cheeks were flushed. Should he wake her and make her take more aspirin? Should he make her drink something cold? He didn't know. He reached down and untied her sneakers and pulled them off of her feet. The socks came off, too and that was when he saw it. The small scratch was now red and inflamed. He could see some pus surfacing from the tiny wound.

'Could this be making her sick?' He wondered.

He ran to the bathroom and searched the medicine cabinet for something—anything that would help fight infection. Peroxide—yes, that was good for infection. He took the bottle out to the living area and placed a towel under her leg before he poured the peroxide onto her scratch. It bubbled up instantly. He poured some on it again and the second dose bubbled up, too. Nelson sat back and expelled air from his lungs. This wasn't good. He made up his mind that he would pour peroxide on the wound every hour to see if that helped. He covered her again and went back to his recliner and fell back asleep.

An hour later he awoke to hear her crying. He got up from the chair, went over and dropped down on the love seat.

"What's the matter? Want something to drink? Juice?"

"My head hurts, and my throat hurts."

"Let me get you some juice."

Nelson reached into the refrigerator and pulled out a bottle of apple juice. He poured her a glass and took it to her, with another couple of Tylenol caplets.

"Here….this might help."

"Thank you, John."

Nelson still couldn't get over the manners the child possessed.

Samantha started crying again.

"I want my mommy. She knows what to do when I'm sick."

"If you're still sick in the morning, we'll call her…. okay?"

"Okay."

She handed him the glass which was still half-full and went back to sleep.

Nelson became restless and nervous. He was genuinely worried about his little captive. Not only had he become fond of her, but she was his ticket out of the country. She *had* to be well. If he decided to take her out of the country with him, she had to be *well*. If he left her behind, she damn well better be *fine*.

'Give it time. She has to be better in the morning,' he reminded himself.

Exhausted, he finally sat back down in the chair and fell asleep. He didn't open his eyes again until it was daylight.

20

AGENTS MORROW AND Daily were joined by two more agents in the late afternoon on Friday. The two new agents, John Darrow and Al Hamilton each carried in large briefcases. Jack Daily called for Ricky and Lindy to join them in the family room.

Tom Morrow began.

"Okay....Lindy and Ricky....This is Agent John Darrow and Agent Al Hamilton. They have been doing some research....just finding information that can be valuable to....this case. Now....Agent Darrow has worked up a profile on Nelson Sutter. Agent Hamilton has been working on trying to identify the red bushes your daughter talked about. I'm going to let Darrow start. He can tell you what he believes to be true from the information he has on Sutter."

John Darrow glanced from Lindy to Ricky and saw two terrified parents who were afraid of what they might hear him say. Their hands were clutched together, both showing white knuckles. He cleared his throat and began by speaking softly.

"Hey, don't look so….frightened. What I'm about to tell you isn't exactly terrible. Just Relax."

Lindy and Ricky continued to stare at him, both pairs of eyes looking like a deer's eyes caught in the headlights of a car.

"Okay….well, here goes. Nelson Sutter is neither a killer nor a kidnapper. He just doesn't fit the profile. What he is….is a bungler. A bungler who doesn't take responsibility for his own actions. He'll bungle this kidnapping….just like he bungled everything else he's attempted."

"You say he's not a kidnapper…..but he kidnapped our daughter…" Ricky reminded Agent Darrow.

"Yes….but for two reasons. He needed money and he needed revenge against your wife. See….even though he went to prison for a crime *he* committed….he sees it as going to jail because your wife told on him. His thinking is rather juvenile….I admit."

"Doesn't that make him dangerous?"

"Well…it would….if he were someone else. Let me give you some background on him…okay?"

Lindy and Ricky nodded and waited.

"Sutter grew up on a farm….a working farm. The kind that sells their products as well as survives on them. His parents worked on the farm…they didn't own it. His father was the foreman and his mother was like a resident midwife….for both the animals and humans. She delivered all the babies on that farm. She was a piece of work, though. Very abusive, from what we learned. She dropped dead a month after her husband, when Sutter was close to seventeen…..massive heart attack. Since the farmer and his wife wouldn't take the boy…said they had two teenaged daughters and didn't want an unrelated boy living under their roof....he ended up in a shelter until he was eighteen, and then he found himself out on the street with nowhere to go. He went to college after he left the shelter, but only for a brief period. He hated farming and he lacked the self-discipline to stick it out in college. He turned to sales, and he wasn't half bad at it. Made a good living at it. He met and married Loraine Carter while he was working as an insurance salesman. She was the successful one of the two of them. She graduated from college, second in her class, and became an executive with Walsh Industries. She's still there and is a vice president in the company. Sutter was always trying to compete with her. And....when he couldn't top her....he secretly punished her by sleeping with other women."

"But he didn't exactly sleep with *me*.....it was rape." Lindy interjected.

"Yes.....the rape. His wife loved you....wanted you for her daughter. *He'd show her!* From what we learned, you were a beautiful teenaged girl....and extremely sweet. Nelson saw it as stepping on a kitten....his wife's kitten. Spite. He did it for spite...to get even with his wife for loving you and once again, topping him, because you and she quickly developed a rapport. Does that make any sense?"

Lindy stared at the agent for a moment, and then shook her head.

"Not really." She admitted.

"Okay.....anyway.....Sutter wanted to appear.... successful. He lived large. Expensive cars....suits.....you name it....it had to be the best. The only way he could have all that was with Loraine....and he knew it. He

167

resented her for it. He resented her because he was also dependent on her. As long as they were married, he was trying to somehow prove that he was the superior one. He kept bank accounts that she didn't know about, accruing money in them for his own security. When he went to prison the statements were forwarded to the house from his company's office. That's how she found out about them. She turned all that over to our department this week. There wasn't all that much in them, but enough for him to live on for a couple of months….if he was conservative. Not Sutter's style, though. He couldn't find a job; he was living in a one-bedroom apartment…..and becoming more desperate by the day."

"You found his apartment?" Ricky asked, suddenly very interested.

"Oh, yeah…..well, that was on file with the state. He is still on parole….and he is classified as a sex offender."

"What about the apartment?"

"Well, he hasn't been there in a couple of weeks, according to the landlady. Told her he was going out of town to work. Said he would be back."

"So….where is he?"

"My guess is he rented another place somewhere…. secluded. And he has your daughter there with him."

He watched Lindy gasp for air and swallow hard. He could see that she was strained as tightly as she could be. He didn't want to push her any more than necessary, so he would have to watch his choice of words closely.

"So….you say….he is or he isn't dangerous? Which is it?"

Lindy stared at him hard, when she asked that question.

"Well....it's this way. As long as he thinks he has the upper hand....he'll get more and more brazen.....and then bungle the whole thing. See.....may I call you Lindy?"

Lindy nodded.

"Okay, thank you.....Lindy. Right now he thinks he has you and your husband backed into a corner. He's enjoying that. It makes him giddy. He'll get more and more brazen....take more chances. Then....he'll make a mistake. And we'll get him."

Lindy expelled air and visibly relaxed a little.

"What if you're wrong?" Ricky asked.

"It's my job *not* to be wrong. I'm good at what I do. I'm not wrong. You two just play it as you have been. Comply with his demands....don't let on you know who he is..... and he thinks he's already won."

"If he's not a killer, then why did he have a gun in his hand when he found us in South Carolina?"

"For leverage. He didn't use it, did he? If he were a killer he would have shot you....Ricky....when he walked through the door. But he didn't."

"What about Samantha? How much danger is she in?" Lindy asked.

"Well...not a lot....providing she can be resilient."

"What do you mean?"

"Sutter knows nothing about children. He may feed her something that might make her sick.....not intentionally, but because he doesn't know any better. Things like coming in out of the rain, wearing a jacket....he doesn't understand that sort of thing. But...because of his own narcissism, he'll keep clean clothes on her and keep her clean. So.... hopefully, she's not a sickly child."

"She's not. She's very healthy, just as Michael is very healthy. We take care of our children."

"I can see that. You both appear to be wonderful parents."

"So why do you refer to him as a bungler?"

"Because….anybody who wants something too fast, without working for it, has a tendency to….screw up. He doesn't think things through….he just acts…and then makes up the rules as he goes. I'll bet he didn't even have a drop plan for the money when he took your daughter. He's making that up as he goes. That's why it's taking him this long to tell you where to leave the money. Not that he isn't enjoying your suffering. Remember, he wants to hurt *you* as well as get out of the county."

Lindy and Ricky turned to each other, communicating silently as they often did. At that moment, both of them were thinking the same thing. Ricky took over the conversation.

"Agent Darrow….the way to hurt Lindy….both of us, actually….would be to keep us from ever having Samantha back."

"I've already told you….Sutter is not a killer. If he were, he would have killed you both in South Carolina. I told you that, too."

"But….then, how about taking Samantha with him? Making sure we never see her again."

"Well, first of all….what would he do with a kid? And secondly….we're not going to let it go that far. We'll get him before he gets out of the country."

Lindy had that look she always got when she couldn't breathe, and Ricky immediately became concerned. He reached over and grasped her hands between his and held them tightly. She voiced her fear aloud.

"He could sell her. *God......*she's so *beautiful!* He could sell her on some black market...."

"Missus DeCelli....Lindy.....stop. Just stop right there. That...is...not...going...to...happen. We are *not* going to *let* that happen. Please stay calm. We need you to be calm."

Lindy leaned against Ricky and tried to recover. She was so tired. She wished she could just go to sleep and wake up when it was all over, and Samantha was back in her own bed, safe and sound. Ricky put his arm around her shoulders, and held her there tightly. He knew it was time to shift the subject from Nelson to the next topic.

"What about the bushes?"

Agent Al Hamilton took over.

"Okay....the bushes. We found a couple. First, there is one called Coral Embers Willow, and then there is one called Coral Twig Dogwood, a flowering shrub. Also, one called Burning Bush, and then Photinia Red Tip Xfraseri. There is also the Burning Bush Aronia Brilliantissima Shrub. Now....this bush scratched her...right?"

"Yes.....that's what she said."

"Okay....now it could be the Coral Twig Dogwood..... the stems can be brittle and sharp."

"Why is this important?"

Ricky was becoming impatient.

"It's important because.....none of these bushes are actually native to Pennsylvania. The only way to get them here is to buy them and plant them. There is a nursery in Ohio that sells the Coral Twig Dogwood. The proprietor says that lots of people from the state of Pennsylvania actually buy them and plant them here."

"But why would Nelson do that? He isn't the garden variety kind of guy."

Lindy looked just as impatient as Ricky did when she asked that.

"No....of course not....but he may be living in a place where they have already been planted. Anyway....the guy got in trouble with the IRS once, so he keeps excellent records. He is searching through his records as we speak, trying to come up with someone in this area who may have purchased them for their own yard."

Lindy still looked skeptical.

"But what if it's not *that* bush?"

"He's going through them all.....and before you ask.... we're checking out anybody else who may sell them, as well. Believe it or not.....we really *do* know how to do our jobs."

"I'm sure you do......but Samantha doesn't mean to you what she means to us. She's our flesh and blood and we love her....so much. To you, she's a job—a case—but to us, she's the world, our life. She shares the spot with Michael....and neither of them can ever be replaced. You'll wrap it up here and go on to your next case. For us, there's no wrapping it up and going on....without Samantha."

"Very eloquently put....point taken."

Hamilton was impressed by the strong message that came with her words. He wondered if other families who lost their children to kidnappers felt the same way toward him and his colleagues. 'Maybe we need to adopt a softer side,' he thought.

"Agent Hamilton?"

Ricky waited for him to respond.

"Yes?"

"What about the banking information? The information that Loraine turned over. Did you find out anything from that?"

"Yeah....we did. He had to wait until they found his account....since it had been archived for years.....when they retrieved it, he cleaned it out. Oh....and another thing we're checking on. We figure he had to buy clothes for your daughter. He wouldn't let her run around in dirty pajamas.....not his style....so we're checking stores for any possible identification. He probably went to Wal-Mart or K-Mart....somewhere where there were lots of cashiers and shoppers, but we're showing his picture around anyway. He may have said or done something that attracted attention to himself.....anything. We're checking it out."

They digested what he said, and then they nodded, showing that they understood.

Lindy and Ricky were satisfied that the FBI was doing everything it could to get Samantha back. Lindy felt badly about her attitude toward the bureau, and she would certainly remember to apologize when it was all over.

The session was interrupted by the family room door opening. Michael came into the room, smiling.

"Mommy? Daddy? Nana and Pap Ron brought me home. They in the kitchen. They brought....stuff. Is Yukas coming over?"

"Yukas." Lindy repeated with a smile.

Lindy and Ricky laughed, while Michael climbed up on Lindy's lap. She hugged him to her and kissed his forehead, while Ricky ran his hand up and down his back.

"Did you have fun at Nana and Pap Ron's?"

"Uh-huh….we got ice cream."

"Oh, now…..Michael….you weren't supposed to tell." Angie interrupted.

She and Ron were standing at the door smiling at Michael.

"Oh, you know he's a blabbermouth." Ricky laughed.

"Lindy….I made the shells. They're in the kitchen. There's enough for all of you guys, too," she added, her eyes sweeping across the four agents.

"That's okay, Missus Shultz…."

"No….guys….you want to eat these. They're the best you've ever had." Lindy interjected.

"We'll bring you all plates of them…..unless some of you can eat in the kitchen with us….you're welcome."

"Morrow and Daily….why don't you go eat with them? We can stay here and watch things." Agent Hamilton suggested as he waved them out of the room.

"That's highly unusual, don't you think?" Darrow asked him.

"Yeah….it is. But I think it's important that Morrow and Daily understand the love in this family. I don't think they're coming across as two agents who care whether this child comes back. I mean….I *know* they do, but they're not coming off as personable. They care that they get their man….but do they care about how these people here feel about their child being gone? I don't think so. They need to humanize themselves a little."

"Okay….I get it. Anyway….check with Conrad to see if anybody has recognized Sutter's picture yet. I want to look over the papers we found at Sutter's apartment. Something here could be important."

Lindy and Angie brought in plates of stuffed shells for

both Darrow and Hamilton, along with silverware and napkins.

"What would you like to drink?" Angie asked them. "We have iced tea, beer, wine, and Pepsi, diet or regular."

Both chose iced tea, and Angie went to get the drinks.

As Lindy was setting down the silverware and napkins, she glanced at the papers sitting in front of Darrow, and gasped.

"What's wrong?"

"That name....Stacey Stockwell. That was my mother....before she married my father. Where did you get these papers?"

"Out of Sutter's apartment. It could be a coincidence... not that I believe in coincidences. He had a letter he had written to her.....back around nineteen-sixty-eight or nine....here it is. Apparently he was in love with your mother at one time. The letter says how he's going to make it big and prove to her that he is good enough for her. Now....I have a theory on it....ready?"

Lindy nodded, not at all sure that she was ready.

"I think.....without his knowing that you were Stacey Stockwell's daughter, he saw a resemblance. When he first saw you he had to be taken back. He had a high school picture of your mother....the resemblance is uncanny. It drew me in when I saw it. I thought it was you."

Darrow pulled out the picture of Stacey Stockwell and showed Lindy. Lindy had seen it before, in her mother's scrapbook. It was her senior picture.

"Now....we don't think he knows that you are her daughter....but he saw the resemblance between you and his high school love. When he raped you....well, he finally had the girl that was too good for him in high school. Do you understand that?"

"Sorta……I'm no psychology major….but I think I understand. God….Nelson Sutter and my mother. He was right…she was too good for him."

Lindy turned away and walked out of the family room, tears stinging her eyes. She stopped just outside the door to regain her composure. She was determined to have a nice dinner with the family and not have it ruined by this new hideous information. She would tell Ricky later. Nick and Liz had joined the crowd while Lindy was in the family room. She kissed them both, welcoming them. She took her place between Ricky and Agent Morrow and picked up her fork without saying a word. When she glanced at Ricky, he raised an eyebrow quizzically. He knew she knew something he didn't.

She tilted her face up and kissed his chin as she whispered, "Later."

He let it go, knowing that it was something she didn't want everybody else to know. He would have to wait quite awhile to hear what she knew. After dinner, Shawna, Ally, Lukas, Michelle and Little Lukas all popped in to see how everything was going. They brought snacks for everybody, as well as drinks. Chris and Cindy came in together, and Lindy was sure that wasn't a coincidence. She cornered Cindy in the kitchen and it was confirmed that they had come together, and would be leaving together.

"We're sorta seeing each other….I guess. He took me out to dinner a couple of nights ago, and then I went to his place last night and cooked dinner. We watched a movie and….I stayed the night."

Lindy's face lit up, almost the way it used to before the kidnapping.

"Yeah?"

"Yeah….you okay with it?"

"I'm ecstatic over it. You *know* Ricky and I have wanted that all along. We'll do something special with you two…. when this is all over. Agreed?"

"Of course. Oh….and by the way…..your dad is on his way over. He just called Chris on his cell phone."

Lindy nodded. She wondered if her father knew what Agent Darrow just told her. 'My mom, me, and now Samantha…..Nelson is a predator to three generations of Stockwell girls. The pig!' Lindy mentally spat out the word pig. She quickly finished cleaning up the kitchen and went to join the family in the living room. Although Liz and Angie had wanted to clean up for her, she insisted that she wanted to keep busy. It gave her time to think— think about what she had just learned. Maybe that was it. Maybe Nelson *had* raped her because she looked like Stacey Stockwell. He couldn't have known there was a relationship. Her name was Riley before it became DeCelli.

In the living room she looked for Ricky and didn't see him. She looked around as he was coming down the hall. Lindy realized he must have been in the bathroom. Their eyes connected from across the room and they held as he joined her.

"Are you okay?" He asked her.

"Yeah….you?"

"Y-yeah…..I'm okay. I think I saw a car pull up."

"My dad. Oh…..Chris and Cindy are going out now. We did it…..finally."

"That's great! We'll have to do something with them.... when this is over."

"That's exactly what I said! Once again, DeCelli...we think alike."

Ricky smiled at her and put his hand on the back of her neck, giving her neck a light squeeze. Chris opened the door to Diane and Ray, who were carrying more bags of food into the house.

Ricky shrugged. "At least nobody goes hungry around here," he whispered into Lindy's ear.

She couldn't have agreed more.

21

NELSON WAS PACING the length of the living room. The child was sick—very sick. What the hell should he do? He felt her forehead again. Her temperature must be at least one hundred and four. She felt so hot. He tried to awaken her, and she was all but unresponsive. He tried again.

"Samantha......Sammie....can you hear me?"

She nodded without opening her eyes. She was talking, but he couldn't hear her. He leaned down closer and put his ear next to her mouth.

"Want mommy," she was saying, barely audibly.

He got up and paced the floor some more, not knowing what to do.

"Jesus....I hadn't planned on this."

He went back to the love seat and pulled up her pant leg to check the scratch. It was still very inflamed. There was a red line coming from it and it was starting to travel up her leg. Nelson began to pace again. Think! He had to think! He could call Lindy and tell her to get him some antibiotics or else her kid was going to die. Or why not just rob a pharmacy? He already was way in deep shit.

Wait. Now he remembered. He had some antibiotics from when he cut himself in the prison kitchen. He ran into the bathroom and searched the medicine cabinet. Not there. Where? Where did he put them? He knew he didn't throw them out. Oh, wait—in the shaving kit. He tore into the leather case that held his razor and toiletries. They were there. He opened the bottle and counted them. Five. There were five of them. The bottle said five hundred milligrams. Was that too strong for a five year old? He decided to cut them in half. The label said twice a day, so he would cut them in half and give her two halves every day until they were gone. He would give her a whole one now. That's what he had to do—take a double dose the first time and then one tablet twice a day. He went back to the living area to awaken her.

"Samantha? Wake up, Honey. Mommy is on her way, but she said you have to take this pill before she gets here. Sit up for a minute."

He handed her the tablet and a glass of water. She swallowed the pill with difficulty, but at least she got it down.

"Mommy is coming?"

"Yes, Love...now go back to sleep until she gets here."

Satisfied that there was nothing more he could do, he sat down in the recliner, tilted it back and fell asleep. He awoke an hour later and got up to check on her. He felt her forehead. It was still hot, but he thought maybe it wasn't as hot as it had been. He hoped not, anyway. Feeling a deep attachment to her, he watched her as she slept. What was it about her that made him have these paternal feelings towards her? He actually felt love for her. He reached out and brushed her hair off of her forehead, and then tucked the blanket around her. Before he went back to the chair he once again checked the scratch on her leg. The red line was still there, but at least it hadn't moved any. He tucked her leg in and tucked the blanket around her again. Without thinking he leaned over and kissed her cheek.

He checked his watch. It was almost time for the eleven o'clock news. He turned the television on from his remote, keeping the volume down. There was nothing new concerning the DeCelli kidnapping. Good. They still didn't know who the kidnapper was. If they did, it would make big time news, dredging up the past. He didn't want that. He just wanted to get the hell out of the country and live out the rest of his life peacefully, and yes, he wanted to take Samantha with him. He fell asleep.

He was dreaming. In the dream, Samantha was free-falling into a dark, pitch-black cavern-like hole, her arms out at her sides like she was flying. He tried to grab her, but she slipped from his grasp. He heard a scream and he turned around. Lindy was standing there, tears streaming down her face. She was naked. She screamed at him. "You killed my child." Then she turned to the man beside her and simply said, "Kill him." The man pulled out a knife—a knife like the one Lindy used to cut him in South Carolina. The man advanced on him, swinging the short knife at him. He jumped back and toppled over the side toward the place where Samantha fell. He grabbed onto the ledge, clinging for dear life. Lindy was cutting his fingers off, one by one, as he clung to the edge. He lost his grip and fell.

He jerked awake, looking around to make sure he was alone, except for Samantha. It was just a dream. He expelled air from his lungs and lay in the chair without moving, just trying to calm his nerves. After a few moments, he got up and went to the kitchen to get something to drink and to wipe his forehead and the back of his neck with a paper towel. He drank down a Pepsi in three gulps, and then got himself another one. Samantha. He had to check on her. He walked over to the love seat and placed his hand on her forehead. Hopefully it wasn't his imagination, but she felt cooler. She was still hot, but not burning hot like earlier in the evening. Maybe the antibiotics would work. He hoped.

Carrying his Pepsi, he went back to the chair, sat down, and raised the foot stool on the recliner. He thought about Lindy. In his dream she was seventeen again, and naked. Did she still look that good, he wondered? Maybe not, after two more kids. But she still looked good, he was sure of that. There was something about her. He wanted her from the moment he saw her. Her beautiful face, her gorgeous eyes, and her perfect figure made him want her. He remembered her figure. The luscious curve of her hips, her flat stomach, perky breasts that stood at attention when she walked and her perfectly shaped legs made his mouth water. He thought about her husband. Ricky. The lucky bastard. He got that whenever he wanted it. He got to lie beside her every night, touch her, look into her eyes while he screwed her.

Nelson stopped abruptly.

"Jesus…why am I obsessed with her?" He wondered aloud. "Not to mention that I'm almost twice her age. Why her?"

He sat in the recliner in the dark, slowly drinking his Pepsi, and thought about anything but Lindy. His mind wondered toward his prison days, and then focused on

Loraine. He wronged her; he knew that. She was a good, decent woman, even if she *did* act superior toward him. Lindy. Stop thinking about her! He warned himself.

He fell back into a restless sleep, dreaming of Lindy. They were both nude and lying in each other's arms. In his dream he felt warm, happy, and content.

22

LINDY AWAKENED AT three AM. She was restless. Something was wrong, but she wasn't sure what it was. It was something other than Samantha being gone. She had a very strong feeling that Samantha was very ill, and she couldn't shake the feeling. Putting on her robe, she wandered out to the kitchen. Maybe a cup of tea would help her relax. She poured water into the kettle, set the kettle on the burner, and turned the burner knob on high. Michael had gone home with Aunt Liz and Uncle Nick, so it was Lindy, Ricky, and the FBI in the house. Lindy loved and loathed the quiet. Even though the quiet was peaceful it was also a reminder that her children were not with her. While she waited for the water to boil, she wandered through the living room and stopped in front of the family photo that hung on the wall next to the living room chair. She studied it and smiled as she remembered that day. It was right before Thanksgiving. The same picture had been used for their Christmas cards last year. They looked so happy. It was a perfect photo. Ricky, in his dark suit and red tie, Michael in his light suit and green Christmas tie,

Samantha wearing her white dress with red and green lace trim, and she, Lindy in a red dress.

She smiled as she remembered them all standing there waiting for her to come out of the bedroom, fully dressed in her red dress. Ricky loved it when she wore red. She replayed the scene in her mind. She remembered hearing Samantha asking if mommy was almost ready when she walked into the living room announcing that she was ready. She would never forget Ricky's reaction to her in the red dress.

"Here's mommy....and mommy is *HOT!*" Ricky had exclaimed.

"Yeah, mommy hot," Michael echoed.

Both Lindy and Ricky had to laugh at their little parrot, as they called him sometimes.

They spent the morning getting the pictures taken and then went to lunch at a family-style restaurant. The photographer complimented them on their well-behaved, beautiful children, as did the waitress at the restaurant. They were so proud of them! She remembered looking over at Ricky and how the love she felt for him overwhelmed her. They had made it. All the hard work, the patience, the sacrifices, and the goal-setting had paid off. They had achieved the perfect life, the American dream. And they were happy. In all the time they had been together, neither Ricky nor Lindy ever even thought about ever being with anyone else but each other. They were still very much in love, and still crazily attracted to each other. She remembered their conversation at lunch.

Michael and Samantha were quietly eating their lunch and Lindy and Ricky were talking about starting Sammie in Sunday school classes.

"Probably have to wait until next fall, Babe." Ricky had speculated.

"Yeah....but I was just hoping you would agree to let her go. I know you've never been a religious person.... but I think it's important that they have some religious teachings."

"I couldn't agree more. With all we have, and all we have accomplished....well, somebody up there wanted us to have a chance. We should let our kids learn about Him."

Lindy had smiled at Ricky. It was that special smile that was only for Ricky. It said 'I love you, I adore you, and I'll do anything for you.' Their eyes met and held as the familiar bolt of electricity surged through them. They turned their heads to watch their most prized possessions, Michael and Samantha.

Lindy's mind wandered through the past fifteen years. All the Christmases. She remembered the first Christmas after they came back from South Carolina. She and Ricky were looking around in the attic for decorations. She came across a box of angel figurines and showed them to Ricky. She remembered his reaction.

"The Lindy-doll collection," he said almost reverently.

"The what?"

"The Lindy-doll collection. They were you mother's. She collected them because they reminded her of you," he had told her.

"How do you know that?"

"Your dad told me about them. When we were in the cell together. He said that everybody always said you looked like an angel....so your mother started collecting them. But look at them....they *do* look like you. Let's use them as a Christmas display on our mantel....okay?"

Every year they brought out those angels and arranged them on the mantel along with garland and twinkle lights. Samantha loved them.

Lindy's mind ran through every holiday and event of the past fifteen years. All the love and happiness they had shared. She mentally embraced it all as her thoughts traveled across the memories.

The whistle on the teakettle sounded and Lindy ran to take it off of the burner before it awoke someone else. She pulled a mug out of the cupboard and dropped a teabag into it, and using her other hand, poured the boiling water into the cup. She reached for the sugar and got the milk out of the refrigerator. After stirring the contents of the cup with the spoon she pulled out of the drawer, she carried the cup into the living room with her. All the way on the other side of the room the moon was shining through the front windows. Lindy stared up at it, remembering how she always told her children she loved them.

'I love you all the way to the moon and the stars, and back,' she would say to them. She smiled as she remembered the time that Ricky told them he loved them *'this much,'* stretching the length of his arms out on each side of him. Samantha countered him by saying, *'Mommy loves us all the way to the moon and the stars, and back.'* She remembered Ricky's answer and silently laughed.

"That's because mommy can jump higher that I can." Ricky had told her.

"Mommy can jump higher than you?"

"Way higher," he had answered.

Both kids were awestruck over that. Lindy had laughed and whispered to him.

"*If they ever want me to prove that, you are in big trouble,*" she had threatened.

She moved away from the windows and stopped in front of their wedding picture. Somewhere before she got pregnant with Samantha and after they had graduated from college, Angie had talked them into having a formal wedding. They went along with it since it seemed to be so important to Angie. Although it wasn't their idea, they ended up being glad they had done it. The wedding picture itself made the whole thing worth it. What a beautiful bride and groom they were! Before she went back to the kitchen she stopped in front of the portrait of the kids. Ricky had painted it. Ricky's artwork was amazing. He had captured the kids' personalities perfectly. Lindy wiped a tear off of her cheek. All that she held precious and dear to her were portrayed on the walls of this room. She prayed silently.

'*Oh God....please bring her back to me. She's just a little girl....but she's my little girl. I've been a good mother, God.... and Ricky is a wonderful father. Please give us the chance to continue raising our precious baby girl. It's all I ask, God. Please.*'

Lindy rinsed her cup and set it on the rack to dry. She had a sudden strong urge to go to Ricky and wrap her arms around him. He was her rock—her strength—her assurance that everything would be all right. She pictured his face in her mind—his eyes so full of love when he looked at her—his lips on hers. Shivering from the chill in the house, she moved down the hall quickly and climbed beneath the blankets after she tossed her robe onto a chair.

Ricky felt her climb into bed, and automatically reached for her.

"You're cold, Babe."

"I know....I was out in the living room."

"Are you......?"

Ricky was about to ask her if she was okay but didn't get to finish his sentence as her lips pressed against his, cutting off his words. She kissed him softly at first, and then parted her lips as her kiss got firmer. Her tongue teased his lips and then entered his mouth as his tongue came up to meet it. Ricky was fully aroused as he ran his hand up her back. He broke the kiss off and moaned as he nuzzled her neck and took her earlobe lightly between his teeth.

"Oh, God, Baby.....I want you...so bad......I"

"Shhh.....just make love to me.....please."

Ricky slipped her nightgown over her head as she worked on sliding his shorts down. She planted a trail of kisses on his stomach down to his abdomen, and then lower. Parting her lips, she took him into her mouth and began to move her mouth up and down on him, holding him between her lips. He moaned softly again, found her breast and rolled her nipple between his thumb and forefinger. Releasing him from her lips, she held his eyes with her stare as she raised herself up on top of him. Eyes still locked, she lowered herself slowly down onto him until he was deep inside of her. Slowly she moved up and down, never taking her eyes from his. Ricky's breathing quickened as he reached for her. Putting his hands on her arms, he pulled her down onto his chest. He wrapped his arms around her, crushed her hair in his hands, and rolled her until he was on top. His mouth hungry for hers, he kissed her intensely and passionately, while he moved in the same slow rhythm she had. He felt her body quiver and as he felt her spasms he drove deep into her, causing her to suck in her breath in a gasp. His arms tightened around her as he neared his orgasm. It came like an eruption, hot lava spewing forth. He moaned.

"Oh, Baby.....my love.....I love you so much," he whispered breathlessly.

She tightened her arms and clung to him.

"Ricky, I need you to tell me everything will be okay. I need for you to say that."

"And I want to be able to say that. If I have anything to do with it...everything will be okay. I promise you that."

They lay together in that position for a long time, dozing off for a little while, and then coming awake again. Fully awake, Ricky continued to kiss her face and nuzzle her neck. Once again they were both aroused. Ricky started to move off of her but changed his mind and began to move in a slow rhythm. He penetrated her deeply and held it there, knowing that drove her wild. Slowly he moved, kissing her shoulders and throat lightly. As her body began to flood with desire and passion, she arched her back up, as he moved in an even rhythm, moving faster and faster. Simultaneously they exploded once again, Ricky wrapping his arms around her as his orgasm commenced. Once again they made no attempt to part. When they fell asleep Ricky was still on top of her and inside of her.

They awoke at six AM, feeling as contented and relaxed as they could be, under the circumstances. In the kitchen, while the coffee was brewing, Ricky pulled Lindy down onto his lap and kissed her neck.

"How about when this is all over we take a vacation......take the kids to Disney World. What do ya say?"

"I think the kids would love that." She whispered.

"And how about mommy? Would mommy love that?"

"Yes.....mommy would love that very much. And Daddy?"

"He would love it, too." Ricky responded.

"It's settled then." She sealed the deal with a kiss.

Lindy sighed and ran her hand through her hair. Ricky caught the frown on her face.

"What is it?"

"I don't know.....I feel something is wrong with Sammie. I can't shake the feeling that she's sick."

"Maybe....when he calls....we should ask. I mean... if she is and he realizes you sense it....it may scare him enough that he'll tell us how to find her."

"But...he could also just lie and say she's fine."

"Yeah....but don't you think he would start looking over his shoulder if he thought you could sense stuff like that?"

"Maybe....but it's Nelson....and he's not the sharpest tool in the shed."

"True," Ricky snickered.

"The bushes are red.....the bushes are red......Ricky, there is something about that.....something....I don't know what....but something."

"I agree. I feel it, too. Red bushes.....maybe......."

"Maybe what?"

"Maybe if there are a lot of them.....they could be seen from a helicopter.....or something."

Lindy straightened her back and raised her head to stare into Ricky's face.

"Something *exactly* like a helicopter.....Don't law enforcement agencies have them? Like the FBI, for example? Wouldn't they have a helicopter?"

"Yeah.....coffee's ready....let's take our resident lawmen a cup and find out."

Armed with cups of Coffee and a plate of breakfast pastries, Lindy and Ricky entered the family room. Morrow and Daily looked as though they had just awakened.

"Morning, guys....brought you breakfast and an idea."

"I think I'm ready for both," Morrow responded as he reached for a cup and the plate.

"What do ya got?" He stared at Ricky.

"Well, Samantha has mentioned the red bushes twice now. There must be a few of them or she wouldn't find them so important. How hard would it be to spot red bushes from a helicopter?"

Tom Morrow and Jack Daily looked at each other and smiled.

"You two have good heads. We are working on that....but first...we have to get an idea of where to send the helicopter. Either from a phone signal or if someone recognizes him. Now Lindy....is there anything you can tell us about Sutter that may give us a clue on where to look?"

"Like what? Other than he's slime, of course."

"Anything.....habits....preferences....."

"Well, I know he likes junk food. When Loraine worked late he always had junk food for dinner. Pizza.... Chinese take-out...and from the wrappers in his car, he must have eaten fast food burgers for lunch. Mickey Dee's or Burger King, usually. When Loraine was home she cooked nutritious meals, but he preferred those nights when he could junk out."

Morrow grabbed his cell phone, punched in a couple of numbers, and began to speak.

"Yeah, this is Morrow. I need every fast food joint in Western Pennsylvania checked out. Show a picture of Sutter and the little girl, and the car…..a gray Ford Taurus….older model."

Morrow's eyes narrowed momentarily.

"I really don't *care* how many there are. Get pictures out there. Somebody may have seen something."

Morrow paused.

"Yeah, well….I have it on good authority that the guy likes junk food…..so the sooner you start….the better."

He snapped his cell phone shut, and turned to Ricky and Lindy.

"Now…..if someone recognizes him…..we'll know in which area to send the chopper. It was our plan, but…. well, we didn't know where to go with it. We're not having any luck getting a signal from his phone."

Jack Daily cleared his throat, and then began speaking.

"Okay….once we can pinpoint an area he's been in, we can start looking. I'm getting a vibe that there is something else on your minds. Am I right?"

"Lindy thinks Sammie may be sick," Ricky revealed.

"Why do you think so?" Morrow looked from Ricky to Lindy.

"It's just a feeling….but it's a strong feeling. I can't

shake it. I just feel she is sick...I don't know why I feel it....
but I do. I guess it's mother's intuition....or something."

"She has that built-in radar...I told you that. She
predicts colds before there are symptoms....earaches....
all that stuff. One time when Michael was just two years
old...Lindy got up and ran to Michael's room. He was
sound asleep but Lindy watched him with a worried look
on her face. She wouldn't go back to bed because she knew
something was wrong. Michael had a cold....but Lindy
thought it was more than that. We ended up taking him
to emergency that night....he had pneumonia."

Ricky slid his arms around Lindy's shoulders.

"Lindy knows. She just always knows."

"So....what is it you want to do?" Morrow asked
pointedly.

"Lindy wants to ask him point blank if Sammie is sick.
It may throw him.....I mean...wondering how she could
know that. It might make him nervous....and then he'll
make a mistake."

Jack Daily sighed and looked down at the floor. He
looked up at the two of them before he spoke.

"That's a possibility....but it's also a possibility that
he'll panic....and we don't want him to do that. It's the
difference between a nervous bungler and a panic-stricken
fool. You really don't want to force him off the deep
end."

"Give us a minute to think about that....okay?"
Morrow interjected.

23

NELSON JERKED AWAKE suddenly. He had been dreaming about Lindy again, only in this dream she was angry— angry enough to kill him—again. Samantha. He jumped up and quickly moved over to the loveseat to check on her. She opened her eyes as he peered down at her.

"How do you feel, Munchkin?"

"Hot," she barely spoke.

He reached down and felt her head. Yes, she was hot, but not nearly as hot as she had been last night.

"Want something to drink?"

She nodded.

"Did mommy come?"

"Yes...yes, she did, Munchkin. You were sleeping so she didn't wake you up. She said she wants you to have the rest of your vacation. She gave me some medicine for you....so you have to take it....okay?"

Again, Samantha nodded. Nelson took her a glass of juice and a half of an antibiotic tablet. She took the half-tablet and swallowed it, chasing it down with the juice.

"You are such a good girl. I hope you feel better soon.

As soon as you are better, I'm taking you on an airplane ride. Would you like that?"

"Yes....but can mommy and daddy and Michael come, too?"

"We'll see. If I can get them tickets.....okay?"

"Okay." She smiled weakly at him.

Nelson watched her fall back asleep, assuring himself that sleep was the best medicine. He marveled at how much she trusted him. It made him feel good, but didn't Lindy know enough to teach her kids not to trust strangers? But he wasn't a stranger. He told Samantha that he was an old friend of her mommy's. That would automatically make Samantha trust him. After all, mommy was nice, so mommy would only have nice friends.

He looked at the clock. Only five-forty-five. He would call in a little while, but first he had to think about the drop off point. When to drop it off was even more important. He would have to call about the plane first, to make sure it would be available right after he picked up the money. Nelson fell back asleep.

The dream began with Lindy. She was crying and trying to run away. He held onto her as she tried to pull away. She was screaming 'I hate you!' at him. Along came Ricky. When did he get so big? Ricky balled up his fists and pulled back to hit him. Nelson screamed in the dream. He jerked awake again. It was eight o'clock. Samantha was still sleeping.

Nelson stood up and made a trip to the bathroom and then went to the kitchen to put on a pot of coffee. He opened the drawer that held the private plane information and pulled out the documents holding his new identification. He would need a passport for Samantha.

No problem. It would just take a phone call. The only thing good that came out of his time in prison was hooking up with this guy who could give him whatever it was he needed in document form. Passports, birth certificates, licenses—whatever—were all available to him for the right price. He would have to call to get the necessary extra paperwork today. His documents showed him as being John S. Nelson. Samantha was going to be Samantha Nelson—no middle name. His wife left them both for another man, and Samantha missed her mother terribly. Women would eat that up! After awhile, Samantha would stop talking about her mother. She would be his daughter. Lindy and Ricky would suffer long after Samantha stopped talking about them. 'They deserve to suffer!' he thought as he smiled to himself.

Reading from a slip of paper he pulled out of the drawer, he dialed the number written down on it. The phone at the other end was picked up immediately.

"I need more paperwork."

A pause and then a sigh came through the phone.

"Now what?"

"I need a passport and a birth certificate for a five year old female. Samantha Nelson. Black hair....blue eyes....born.....March eleventh....five years ago."

"Picture? I'll need a picture."

Nelson took his phone over to Samantha and snapped a picture. He was glad he decided to use the Virgin Mobile phone with the built-in camera.

"Picture is on its way. How soon?"

"Probably later today. I can start working on it as soon as I get the picture."

"Good."

"Who is the kid?"

"Never mind."

"Hey….wait a minute. I hope you're not talking about that little girl that has been missing. I'm not getting involved in a kidnapping…."

"Just shut up. She's my granddaughter…okay? She's going to go with me and we'll meet up with her mother later. The kid is a decoy. Nobody will be looking for a man with a kid. It was my daughter's idea."

The man on the other end of the phone hesitated. The money for doing this would be great, but he didn't want to get involved if the child had been kidnapped. That was big time jail, and he knew what they did to guys who harmed a child. He had a bad feeling about this. His thoughts were interrupted by Nelson's voice.

"Hey…look….are you going to deliver or not?"

He thought about it for a moment. 'I don't know who the child is…..and it's none of my business….I'm really not involved,' he justified silently.

"Yeah….by tonight. I'll call when ready."

Satisfied, Nelson hung up and poured himself a second cup of coffee. His next call was to check on the date and time for departure. He was paying plenty for a private jet flight to Brazil, but it would be worth it.

He placed his call and waited for someone to pick up on the other end of the line. After seven rings, someone picked up.

"Confirming flight for John Nelson…..jet to Brazil."

"Oh yeah….Tuesday. Flight leaves at five o'clock Tuesday."

"Tuesday! We agreed on Monday!"

Nelson scowled as he listened.

"Have to replace a part in the engine. Part will be delivered Monday afternoon. By the time we get it in, it will be too late to leave on Monday. Tuesday....five o'clock."

"Okay...I guess it has to be."

Nelson sighed. That was putting him at risk of being caught by another twenty-four hours. He would have to be extra careful with the phone calls. He knew the risk of calling on prepaid phones was not nearly as great as if he used a contract phone, but it was still a risk. Phone calls were going to have to be shorter.

He went into the living area to check on Samantha and found her sleeping peacefully. Her temperature seemed to have dropped a little, making him wish he had a thermometer to prove it.

24

SEVENTEEN-YEAR-OLD JENNIFER BOYD was about to take her break. She passed the picture taped to the wall in the kitchen of the McDonald's restaurant where she worked. She had seen it when she came in and there was something about it that kept drawing her back to it. She had seen that guy. Was it here? At McDonald's? Wait! Yes! She was working the drive-thru that night. He drove through. There were no other cars in line that night. What did he order? A Happy Meal! Chicken McNuggets. That was it. She remembered trying to see if there was a child in the car. There was a child in the back seat. She didn't know if it was a boy or a girl, though. The car? It was gray, but she had no idea what kind. It was *old*. Jennifer made up her mind. She had to call the number on the poster.

The result of her call came to Agent Morrow an hour later. It came in right after a brief call from the kidnapper.

When the house phone rang, Lindy was instructed to answer it. Nelson almost choked when he heard her voice.

"Where's your husband?"

"He's here."

"Put him on."

"John…is my daughter sick?"

"Put your husband on!"

Lindy handed the phone to Ricky, glad that she had remembered to call him John instead of Nelson.

"Yes?" Ricky's voice came over the line.

"Have the money in the gym bag and ready. There won't be much time between giving the instructions and getting the money there. You got that?"

"Yeah, I got it. My wife wants to know if our daughter is sick."

"Yes….she is."

Nelson hung up without another word. Ricky clutched the receiver tightly in lieu of throwing it. Lindy collapsed against him.

"I *knew* it. I just *knew* it! I could feel it. Oh God…..I wonder what's wrong?"

Lindy began to cry. Ricky slowly slid the telephone receiver onto its cradle, as he stared at the floor. Absently, he placed his arm around Lindy and pulled her to him, running his hand up and down her arm. No one spoke.

When Agent Morrow's cell phone rang, both Ricky and Lindy jumped. Tom Morrow answered it on the first ring.

"Morrow."

He listened intently to what the caller was saying and then answered abruptly.

"Go. Get someone out there now."

He hung up and turned to Lindy and Ricky.

"The bureau got a call from a girl….works at

McDonald's....said she thinks she saw Sutter come in through the drive-thru. Said he ordered a big burger and fries for himself and a Happy Meal. Said it was Chicken McNuggets."

"That's what Sammie always gets!"

Lindy sat up and stared at Ricky. For the first time in a week, Ricky saw a little bit of hope in Lindy's eyes.

"The girl also said she was sure there was a child in the back seat, but she didn't know if it were a girl or a boy. Someone is on his way out there now to interview her."

"Which McDonald's was it?" Lindy asked.

"It's the one near Hickory. That's a fairly rural town about thirty miles from here. Let's wait until we hear from the agent who went out there. We'll know more then."

"So now....what about getting a helicopter?" Ricky asked Morrow.

"Let's just wait until we hear back from the interviewer."

"Agent Morrow.....our daughter is sick. We know that now. Don't you think it's important to start searching right now?"

Lindy was getting frustrated and it showed.

"Lindy....an hour isn't going to make much difference. We want to make sure we are going in the right direction before we send a chopper up. It's better the pilot knows where to look than to randomly search and waste more time. I think I hear someone at the door. Do you want me to get it?"

"No.....I'll get it."

Ricky stood up and went to answer the door. Lindy stared at the two agents for a moment and then followed Ricky.

Morrow looked at Daily and shook his head.

"I know this has to be tough on them, but when are they going to realize that we know how to do our job?"

"Would you entrust your child's life to two big guys who show no emotions? I sure as hell wouldn't." Jack responded.

Liz and Nick were at the door. Liz embraced both Lindy and Ricky while Nick carried two bags to the kitchen and set them down on the counter.

"Anything new?" Liz asked.

Lindy briefed her about the girl at McDonald's.

"Oh....I hope it's a good lead."

"Aunt Liz....where is Michael?"

"Oh, he's coming. Chris and Cindy pulled up behind us and Michael wanted to see his Uncle Chris. They're outside. Chris has something for him."

Before Lindy could answer she heard Michael laughing as he came in on Chris's shoulders. Chris had to duck down to keep him from hitting the door frame.

"Mommy! Yook what Uncle Chris gave me!"

Michael was holding an unopened kite in his hands.

"He going to open it and we going to fry it!"

"Oh, boy! That will be fun!"

"I show Sammie!"

Michael ran toward Samantha's room when Chris put him down on the floor. Michael came back looking very disappointed.

"Sammie not here yet?"

"No, Sweetheart....Sammie isn't here yet."

Lindy stared at Michael and saw the concern in his face. *'He's only three and yet he knows this is not normal. He knows something is wrong,'* Lindy thought silently.

"Uh....Lindy....Michael hasn't had breakfast yet. He insisted on Ya Yindies for breakfast."

Lindy smiled at Liz as she started toward the kitchen.

"Ya Yindies coming right up, Michael.....okay?"

"Kay, Mommy. I come wiff you."

Michael grabbed Lindy's hand and walked her to the kitchen. She picked him up and hugged him to her. After kissing his cheek she sat him down at the table in his booster seat. Ricky joined them and sat down next to Michael.

"Can I have a Ya Yindy, too?"

"Absolutely, you may."

Lindy smiled at Ricky as she reached into the bags Nick had carried to the kitchen. Liz and Nick had remembered to bring croissants for the Ya Yindies. Lindy quickly got out a frying pan, added butter and sliced ham into it. While the ham was slowly frying, she lined up the opened croissants in the toaster oven and turned the knob on the oven to broil. At the first sign of browning, she turned off the oven and brought the croissants out and lined them up on the counter. She buttered them and then she removed the warmed ham from the pan. Adding more butter, she added four eggs to the pan. While the eggs were frying she placed pieces of ham on top of the croissants. Just as the eggs were done, Lindy placed slices of cheese over each egg and covered the pan for thirty seconds. She took the cover off of the pan, and using a spatula, she placed an egg on each croissant on top of the ham. She closed each croissant, and put each one on a plate, putting Michael's in front of him first. Ricky got his next, and then she called Liz and Nick to come get their Ya Yindies. Ricky had started a fresh pot of coffee while Lindy was cooking the eggs.

"Aunt Liz….Uncle Nick….you are about to taste your first Ya Yindy." Ricky announced. "We should have a drum roll or something."

Nick laughed as he sat down.

"Lindy…..where is yours?"

"Oh….I….I'm not really hungry."

Nick didn't say anything else but it disturbed him that Lindy wasn't eating.

"Lindy….I wish you would eat," Liz pleaded.

"I think I'm going to make one for those two….and maybe I'll make one for myself."

Satisfied with that, Liz smiled at her. Lindy quickly made three more Ya Yindies, and took two into Morrow and Daily. Liz helped her carry fresh coffee into them, and then she and Lindy went back to the kitchen to finish their breakfast.

"So….what do you think of the Ya Yindies?" Ricky asked his aunt and uncle.

"They're great! No wonder the kids love them." Liz responded.

"Not exactly cholesterol-free or low-cal, though," Lindy reminded them.

"No….the tasty things never are. Once in a while it doesn't hurt to break the rules," Liz added.

Their conversation was interrupted by Tom Morrow.

"May I join you out here?"

"Of course," Ricky answered.

"Okay……Agent Darrow spoke to that girl. He believes that it was Sutter she saw. The car matches and she said he looked like his picture. So….we are going to get a chopper to survey the area. We're going to use a military chopper so as not to spook him with the FBI logo on the side. If.....and that's a big word....if...we spot something...we'll send ours in for a closer look."

They were silent for a moment, and then Lindy spoke.

"How soon? How soon will the....chopper be up there?"

"The arrangements are being made right now. Please be a little more patient with us. As soon as we know anything we will let you know."

Lindy and Ricky had to be satisfied with his answer. At least he was giving them some hope of finding Samantha soon.

"Samantha is sick, Aunt Liz. I sensed it and we asked Nelson when he called. He said she was sick, but then hung up."

"Are you sure he's not just toying with you?"

"No....I feel it. I know she's sick."

"What could be wrong with her?"

"I don't know.....but if anything happens...."

It was as far as Lindy could go before she choked on a sob. Ricky was right there holding her. Michael climbed out of his seat and put his little arms around Lindy.

"Don't cry, mommy. I yuv you."

Lindy's tears turned to a smile and then a laugh as she hugged her son to her. Chris and Cindy wandered into the kitchen and quietly watched the scene. Cindy wiped her cheek with the back of her hand and glanced at Chris. He didn't bother to wipe his tears away.

25

AGENT MORROW RECEIVED another call on his cell phone. He listened intently and then briskly walked back out to the kitchen.

"Uh….excuse me for interrupting you again…but the FBI just got another call. A pizza shop owner said he thinks he saw Sutter come in his place of business during the week. Seemed to be in a big hurry. Ordered over the phone and picked it up."

"What toppings did he get on it?" Lindy wanted to know.

She knew what Samantha liked but she also remembered from years ago what Nelson liked on his pizza.

"The guy didn't say…but we have someone going over there right now. I'll call him and remind him to ask that."

Morrow disappeared into the family room once again.

Lindy and Ricky stared at each other, their eyes full of hope.

"It *has* to be him. The junk food business increased in that area."

"I'm thinking the same thing. Why was he in such a hurry? Was Samantha in the car? Or did he leave her alone somewhere?"

"I don't know....but the girl at McDonald's said he had a child in the back seat. Maybe he left her in the car and ran in."

"I wonder if the chopper is in the air yet."

Lindy shrugged.

Laden with grocery bags, Ray and Diane arrived at the house at a little past noon. They found Michael and Chris on the living room floor, Chris assembling the kite and Michael watching. Ray set the bags down on the kitchen counter and went back to supervise the kite assembly project in the living room. Diane began taking items out of the bags and putting them away. While she worked, Lindy and Ricky caught her up on the latest information.

"This is all good...except for Sammie being sick.... right?"

"I guess. I just wonder how sick she is....and why."

Diane helped herself to a cup of coffee and sat down across from Lindy.

"And how are you two doing?"

"Still....the same. We just want this all over with and Sammie back home."

"I'm sure. Anything I can do for you right now? Lindy, anything need done? I'm sure you can't concentrate on much of anything."

"Thanks, Diane.....but I don't think so. Aunt Liz has done quite a bit around here....including the laundry. She's been a Godsend."

"Can we take Michael with us today? We'll take him to dinner and then rent a kid's movie tonight. Would that be okay?"

"Sure….I guess. He's going to be so spoiled when this is all over."

Diane smiled and nodded.

"But we love doing it. And, by the way….we plan on making it up to Sammie when she comes back. We owe her lots of stay-overs and dinners and special treatment."

"Oh, Diane…..just to hold her again. I ache. My body aches."

"I know you hurt, Honey."

"She has been gone a week……a *week*! Diane, I feel like I'm dying but I know I'm not because of the pain in my heart."

Lindy stopped talking. Tears were starting to roll down her cheeks and she wiped them away with the heels of her hands.

"I would think there wouldn't be any more tears. I thought it was impossible to cry this much. My kids and my husband are my life, Diane. Sure, I love other people besides them….but they are the reasons I breathe."

"I know. You are a wonderful mother and wife. Ricky is a terrific father and husband. The love in this house just….oh, I don't know….oozes. It's everywhere. It's in every crack and crevice, every corner, every room. When anyone walks in here they feel enveloped by the love. And that's why so many people love you and Ricky. You two are like a generator pumping out radio active molecules, but instead of radio activity…it's love molecules…and they effect everybody."

Diane stopped when she heard Nick laugh.

"Unusually put…but very well described. I agree….
that's exactly the way it is here."

He bent down and kissed Lindy's cheek.

"How are ya holding up? Can I do anything for
you?"

"No, Uncle Nick….thanks. Grab some coffee and join
us."

Nick did as Lindy suggested and made small talk with
Diane while he watched Lindy for signs of too much strain.
He watched her face light up when Michael ran into the
kitchen, Chris following.

"Kite all done, Mommy! We fry it now!"

Lindy picked him up and hugged him. She brushed
his hair off his forehead and kissed his cheek.

"It's ready to fly?"

"Uh-huh! Uncle Chris made it."

Lindy laughed and kissed Michael again.

"Pumpkin, can the guys all go to the park? It's a guys'
thing."

"Sure….who all is going?"

"Me! And Uncle Chris!"

Chris intervened.

"Hold on there, partner……Pap Ron, Poppa Ray,
Uncle Nick….all the guys."

"Can daddy go?"

Lindy and Ricky sought each other out with their
eyes.

"If daddy wants. Why don't you, Honey? You've been
cooped up here and you haven't really spent any quality
time with Michael."

"You're okay with it?"

"Yeah....go on.   It will be good for you.....and Michael."

"We'll probably only be gone an hour or so, Rick."

"Well....if you're sure you don't mind, Lindy.....I really haven't done anything with Michael."

"I know....so go."

"You'll be okay?"

"Yeah, I'll be okay. I have all my generals here."

Lindy raised her arms and held them out, encompassing the group around the table.

All the women laughed. Ricky crossed the kitchen and swooped down to kiss Lindy.

"Thanks, Babe.....I love you."

"I know," she answered him with a smile, as she ran her hand across his waist.

Cindy popped into the kitchen, with a look of anticipation.

"Are we ready?"

"Whoa! You can't go, Cin! Guys only!"

"Yeah, Cin....I guess you're stuck with us old hags." Lindy said with a smirk.

"Oh...all right!" She pouted for a moment and then reached for a cup out of the cupboard.

Chris sidled up to her and kissed her cheek.

"That's my girl. See ya in about an hour. Besides....you haven't spent any time with Lindy at all." He whispered into her ear. Cindy nodded in agreement.

All the women gathered around the kitchen table with fresh cups of the coffee that Ricky so graciously made before he left. Angie had been somewhere in the house when they left, and Lindy just imagined she was cleaning something—probably the bathroom. She was beginning to feel guilty about not doing any of her own housework, but she simply just couldn't bring herself to do any of those chores she had prided herself on doing so well over the past fifteen years. Ricky had always helped out around the house, but Lindy had always been meticulous about how the house looked and how it smelled. Now she couldn't seem to get up enough motivation to do anything. Thank goodness for Angie, Liz, and Diane. They seemed to be keeping the house clean for her. She would think of some way to thank them when this was all over. She was pulled from her thoughts by the conversation between Angie and Cindy.

"So....it's serious between you and Chris?"

"I think so."

"Cindy! What have you *not* been telling me?" Lindy interrupted the conversation.

"Well, I was going to tell you after....Samantha came home....but Chris and I are talking about marriage."

"Oh....Cin....I....I....don't know what to say."

"But you're okay with it.....right?"

"Yes....of course. But....Cindy....don't move too fast. You're one of my best friends and Chris is my brother. I don't want to have to choose between the two of you some day. Make sure it's for real and....forever."

"I promise....nothing until I'm sure it's something.... okay?"

"But.....if it's the real thing.....I'm *thrilled!*"

The men had been gone about an hour and twenty minutes, when Lindy heard the front door opening. She heard Michael first.

"Mommy! Mommy! I frew the kite! All by myself! It went way high!"

"It did! Wow! Was it fun?"

"Uh-*huh*!"

Michael ran into the kitchen and jumped onto Lindy's lap, his cheeks flushed from the outdoors, the exercise, and the sunshine. Chris and Ricky followed him into the kitchen, both of them grinning. It was good to see Ricky grinning like that. Lindy noticed an improvement in his coloring as well as Michael's. He leaned down and kissed her cheek, and then picked Michael up and carried him down the hall to wash his face and hands. When they returned to the kitchen, Lindy could see that Michael was still excited, but he was also ready for a nap. She poured a cup of coffee for Ricky and he sat down with Michael on his lap. Within minutes, Michael's eyelids were heavy and he was having a hard time keeping his head up. Ricky put Michael's head down on his shoulder and carried him into his bed for an afternoon nap. He went right to sleep.

26

NELSON PACED THE floor. Was this going to work? It had to! Okay. Nobody but he and the old janitor at the high school knew about the tunnel that went past the boiler into the storm drain. It came out by the creek about a quarter of a mile away from the school. He knew where to park his car so that it wouldn't be seen from the school. He could slip into the drain before daylight and wait in the janitor's room until the school filled with students. The gymnasium was visible from the janitor's room so he could see the drop-off person enter the gym and leave again. When the students started their classes, he would follow the first group into the girl's locker room, dressed as a girl, of course. Then get to the locker with the gym bag in it, grab it, throw the smoke bombs, hit the fire alarm on the way out, and get lost in the chaos. Slip into the janitor's room slippery quick, and then down the stairs, past the boiler, out the storm drain, and home free. Timing and speed. These two things were the key. It was Saturday afternoon. Maybe on Monday he would take a quick trial run to see how it worked. He wasn't worried about the storm drain being passable. He knew where the key was hidden if the gates were locked.

He silently thanked the janitor. He had shown Nelson that passage for travel when they had conducted business together just before Nelson had gone to prison. It seemed that the old janitor had a fondness for teen porn and Nelson always had new videos on hand. It was an amicable business relationship, with Nelson putting money into an account for himself and the old janitor drooling over the newest videos.

Pulling out a kitchen chair, Nelson eased into it and began looking over his checklist of things to do. The passport and birth certificate for Samantha should be ready in a couple of hours. He believed he had everything done and under control. The drop would be Tuesday morning, and then home to pack everything up, and head to the airport. He was feeling good about the plan. Only one snag was bothering him. Samantha was really sick. Her fever seemed to have gone down a little but she was still listless and sleepy. She had only gotten up once since this morning and that was to go to the bathroom. It worried him.

Samantha stirred and cried out in her sleep. Nelson quickly moved to the love seat, taking long strides and found that the blanket he had wrapped around her was on the floor. He picked it up and tucked it around her again, and then felt her forehead. She was warm. Frowning, Nelson stared down into her darling face. Her skin was pale except for two red spots on each of her delicate cheeks. As he stared at her, she opened her eyes and smiled weakly at him. Her blue eyes looked glassy.

"Hey, Munchkin….how about taking another pill?

They are helping a little. Your head isn't as hot as it was before. Okay?"

Samantha nodded weakly. Nelson retrieved the orange juice from the refrigerator and poured some into a glass, and then took her the juice along with another half tablet of the antibiotic. He smiled at her as he watched her swallow the pill and drink the juice.

"You're such a good girl, Munchkin. I really hope you get well soon so we can have more fun…..and then….take our airplane ride."

"Did you get tickets for mommy and daddy and Michael yet?" She spoke in a whisper.

"No…..but I'm still working on it. I hope I can so they can go, too."

Nelson found the lying part to be fun as well as necessary. It kept her happy. Samantha seemed to approve of Nelson, and he liked that. She looked up to him and trusted him. Loraine never did. Loraine thought that she was above him. Superior to him. Lindy? Lindy found him repulsive, but she also feared him. Maybe he had moved too soon with Lindy. Maybe he should have waited until they knew each other better; developed a rapport with her. Maybe he could have charmed her into loving him and then made love to her. He still didn't know why he moved on her so fast. There was something about her when he first saw her. Stacey. Yeah, that was it! She looked a lot like Stacey Stockwell, his first love. Stacey was too good for him. He wondered what had ever happened to her. Probably married some rich guy, living in a mansion somewhere. Maybe she spent her vacations in Europe— Paris, maybe. If he knew who she married he could try to look up her telephone number.

"I wonder if five million would be enough for you, Stacey-baby. Do ya think you would be willing to run off with me?"

"What?" Samantha asked.

"Oh…..nothing, Munchkin. I was just thinking about someone. Are you hungry?"

Samantha nodded.

"You are? Well, that's a good sign. What do you want? How about chicken noodle soup? And some toast?"

"Okay."

"You wait right here. I'll heat it up for you…okay?"

Samantha nodded again and then pushed herself up into a sitting position. Nelson was encouraged by that. It was the first time she had sat up since yesterday morning. He got the saucepan out of the cabinet, opened the can of soup, and poured it into the pot, adding a can of water with it. After putting the burner on low he got out two slices of bread, the butter, and the toaster. Dropping the bread into the slots on the toaster, he pressed the lever for the toast to fall down into the wells and returned to the burner to stir the soup. He got out a tray and arranged the soup bowl, a small plate, a glass, a spoon, a napkin, and another smaller bowl for saltine crackers. When the tray was ready he took it into the living area and set it down on the table in front of the love seat. Samantha was still awake.

"Can you eat by yourself or do you want me to help you?"

"I can…..I'm not a baby."

"I know….but you're sick. I just want to help you."

"Oh…"

Samantha accepted his answer with a smile.

"I can. I don't feel as sick as I did. I wish mommy would come back."

"I'll try to call her....maybe tomorrow. Okay?"

"Okay. Aren't you having any soup?"

"Do you want me to have soup with you?"

"Uh-huh. You have to eat, too....or you'll get sick, too."

'Of course,' Nelson thought. 'She wouldn't have any idea that her fever was from the scratch. She probably thinks it's from a flu bug, or something.'

"Okay.....I'll eat with you."

Nelson went back to the kitchen area and poured the rest of the soup into a bowl and joined Samantha on the love seat. They ate the soup together, as Samantha handed him a couple of the saltine crackers.

'This is what it's like to be a part of a family, I guess.' He thought silently.

After Samantha finished her food and drank the juice he poured for her, she took another half of one of the antibiotic caplets. She looked like she was getting tired again.

"Want a movie? You can lie here and watch it."

"Okay....can we see Cinderella again?"

"Of course......you like that one, don't you?"

Samantha nodded.

"Cinderella reminds me of my mommy."

"And is daddy Prince Charming?"

"Uh-huh."

"And so you and Michael are the mice that bring the coach?"

"NO!"

"You're not? Well, who are you then?"

223

"We're their kids!"

Nelson laughed. He couldn't help it. He laughed hard, out loud.

"Oh..." was all he said. He turned on the television and the VCR and placed the Cinderella movie into the slot. The movie started. Samantha was sound asleep before the step-sisters left for the ball.

27

AGENT MORROW FOUND Lindy and Ricky sitting in the kitchen with their families.

"Can I see you two a moment?"

"Sure," Ricky responded.

The two of them got up and followed Morrow into the family room, glancing at each other with a question in their eyes. They huddled together on the sofa and waited for Morrow to proceed.

"Okay....The pizza shop owner identified Sutter. He ordered a pizza with three quarters of it with everything on it and one quarter with black olives."

"That's Samantha." Lindy confirmed.

"Now.....we got lucky...twice....with cashiers at Wal-Mart. One lady said that she remembers Sutter coming through her line. He was purchasing a doll, and a package of little girls' underwear."

Lindy gasped. Morrow held up his hand indicating that she should not react to that information.

"He told the cashier that his granddaughter was staying with him and his wife and the mother forgot to pack underwear. He said the other items were because he loved spoiling his granddaughter."

"A true wolf in sheep's clothing...." Lindy commented.

'Anyway....another cashier recognized him.....buying some clothes and more toys. Said they were presents for his Godchild and he was going to her birthday party."

Lindy and Ricky stared at each other, relief showing in both pairs of eyes. Ricky was the first to speak.

"It seems as though he really wants her to feel comfortable. I mean....giving her toys and things. At least it seems that he's not abusing her in any way. I guess that's a little bit of a relief."

"Yeah....I guess that's good to know." Lindy agreed.

"Now.....we sent a chopper up today and found nothing. We plan on sending it back tomorrow. Hopefully we will have a sunny day. I think it would be better to spot any red bushes in sunshine. It was overcast today. Visibility was poor."

Lindy and Ricky couldn't hide their disappointment.

"Hey...the chopper is a shot in the dark, anyway. For all we know these bushes are hidden by trees, or they're not really red."

"The bushes are red. Samantha wouldn't get that wrong. She's pretty sharp."

"I understand, but they may look red to her but may not appear to be red from the sky. I'm hoping that's not the case. Anyway....that's all I have for you.....but it's more than I had an hour ago."

Lindy and Ricky nodded and glanced at each other before they left the family room to hurry back to the kitchen. Morrow looked over at Daily.

"What is it about those two? Sometimes they're almost spooky. It's like they communicate with each other without saying a word.....and I always get the impression that they think we're dolts, or something."

Jack Daily laughed. He knew what Morrow meant, but he wasn't fazed by it like Tom was. After all, the DeCelli's had been together for more than half of their lifetimes. They would certainly be able to communicate without speaking. By now they probably shared the same brain wave frequencies.

"I think you're just envious.....you know it would be nice to have something like that. *We can't*, but it would be nice."

"Yeah, maybe. My dad wanted me to be a dentist.... like him. Maybe I should have been. After office hours, I could be going home to a home-cooked meal, a warm, loving wife, and a couple of kids that would be glad to see me. Even a family dog. But.....I chose this life. Loneliness, lawlessness, and bitterness. Why aren't we happy....if it was our choice, I mean?"

"I don't know.....maybe it's because we watched too much television.....where the FBI is almost glamorous. They all seem to have wives at home....but they go home after the set shuts down for the night. They're actors....they don't have to worry about their families being wiped out by some asshole carrying a grudge, or their wives leaving them because they can't stand the long hours and the suspense of wondering whether their husband even comes home again. Some of the guys *are* married. Hamilton is."

"Yeah.....and he worries every day that his wife will still be alive and well when he goes home. Or that she hasn't packed up and left him like mine did. I choose not to have that worry again. Hey....I can retire in another ten years. I'll be forty-five. I think I can still have all that.... only a little later in life."

"Yeah.....when you're too old to get it up. Sure." Daily scoffed.

...

Lindy and Ricky returned to the kitchen and filled everyone in on what Agent Morrow had told them.

"Ricky and I are both relieved that he seems to be taking care of her.....and not hurting her. At least he thought enough about her to buy her something to play with."

"I suppose we have to be grateful for that," Liz agreed.

"You look tired, Lindy." Diane observed.

"Just stressed...I think. I just want our life back to normal...with Samantha in her bed and Michael in his. I want us to be a normal family again."

"I know, Honey.....I know."

Diane observed Lindy long after she had empathized with her. She could see that the emotional pain Lindy was going through was really taking its toll on her. Lindy was suffering much worse than she let on. What a bastard that Nelson guy must be. Cold, heartless bastard. Couldn't he understand that a mother like Lindy lives for her kids? Probably not....after all, he never even had any kids.

While they were all enjoying another cup of coffee from a new pot that Ricky had made, Ricky's cell phone rang, causing both Lindy and Ricky to jump. Ricky answered it as Lindy looked on, wondering who would be calling.

"Hi."

After a long pause, Lindy heard Ricky filling the caller in on some of the details of the nightmare they were going through.

"Yeah....Sutter. Remember the name?"

(Another long pause.)

"Thanks....just pray. That's all anybody can do.... really. Yeah, Lindy's trying to hang in there. It's really hard for her. Yeah....she's right here. Just a minute...."

Ricky handed his cell phone to Lindy.

"It's Sam and Renee. They were away in Puerto Rico and just got back. They saw the news and called right away."

"Hello? Sam? Renee? Hi...."

"Oh, Lindy....Should we come up?" Renee was speaking.

"If you want. You know we'd love to have you. I don't know how much company we would be. We're both pretty messed up. Praying can help....."

Lindy had to stop to try to compose herself. She was losing the battle. The tears began again and her chest heaved up and down with sobs.

"Renee....I....."

Ricky took the phone away from her.

"Hey....Renee.....she's....well, you know."

Ricky slipped his arm around Lindy and pressed her to him and held her tightly.

"Yeah....Ricky I *do* know. Listen....keep us posted. If you want we can be there. Anything you need....just ask. We love you guys...you know that."

"Yeah...and we love you"

"We know that, too. Otherwise you wouldn't have named your first-born after us. Call us if you hear anything.....or if anything changes. Day or night....it doesn't matter. Promise?"

"Yeah...promise," Ricky answered.

"Tell Lindy we love her. Love you, too..."

"And we love you back. Bye, Renee."

Ricky snapped his cell phone shut, set it on the table and wrapped his other arm around Lindy, surrounding her with both of them.

"They're really good friends....aren't they, Baby?"

Lindy couldn't speak but she nodded in agreement.

• • •

Renee hung up and turned to Sam.

"Do you think we should go up there?"

"Yeah....let's get unpacked and then packed and then leave in the morning."

Sam and Renee were like surrogate parents to Lindy and Ricky. They had helped them tremendously when Lindy and Ricky fled to South Carolina so Lindy could get away from Nelson Sutter and his brutal rapes. They had allowed Lindy and Ricky to stay in their beach motel the first night they arrived, and then allowed them to stay in return for dog-sitting while they visited their family in Ohio for the holidays. When they returned, Sam had asked Ricky to stay on and help with motel repairs. They stayed until they were married in April, having Sam and Renee stand up for them at the ceremony. They would always have love for Sam and Renee and the feelings were mutual.

Whenever Lindy and Ricky got a break in school they returned to South Carolina to spend time with Sam and Renee. The last time they had been there was when

Samantha was two and Lindy was pregnant with Michael. Lindy remembered their reaction to having a namesake. They had shown up after dark and had surprised them. Sam was just finishing the day's receipts when Ricky and Lindy entered the office, Ricky carrying Samantha. Jokingly, Ricky asked for the second room on the second floor.

"That room is taken," Sam had answered before he looked up.

He raised his head and saw them standing there and a wide grin spread across his face. He called for Renee and she joined him, the two of them grinning and then hugging Ricky and Lindy.

"And who is this?" Sam inquired as he pointed to Samantha.

"Tell them your name…" Ricky had told her.

"Sammie…..I'm Sammie."

"What's your whole name?" Ricky encouraged.

"Samantha Renee DeCelli."

Sam and Renee got the connection immediately.

"You named her after us?" Renee confirmed, with tears in her eyes.

Both Ricky and Lindy nodded.

"OH….WOW! I don't know what to say…..I'm honored," she had said.

And they both were. They felt honored and proud. Lindy and Ricky knew it was the best thing they could have done for them, but they also believed that it was well deserved. Sam and Renee had given them their start as a newly married couple, and what's more, they believed in them and in their love for each other.

Lindy remembered how Sam teased Samantha after that. He patted his chest as he spoke to her.

"*I'M* Sam!"

"NO….I Sam!" Sammie had responded.

"But that's my name!"

"Well….it's mine, too." Samantha had answered.

"Can we share the name?" Sam had asked.

Little Samantha smiled at him and nodded vigorously.

"It can be *our* name," she had conceded.

Sam grinned and reached for her. Samantha went willingly from Ricky's arms into Sam's. Sam explained that he was Uncle Sam and that his wife was Aunt Renee.

"So you have both our names….and I think that's really special."

"Me, too," Sammie had agreed.

They hadn't been back to South Carolina in over three years, so Sam and Renee had not met Michael yet. They had fallen in love with Samantha, both Sam and Renee commenting on how she had Lindy's face and eyes and Ricky's hair. They would find it amusing that Michael was just the opposite, having Ricky's eyes and features and Lindy's hair. They had gotten pictures of the kids, but nothing was like seeing them in person, where the resemblance was most prominent.

Lindy longed to see them. She and Ricky had been so happy with Sam and Renee. Not only did they approve of them, but they also believed in them. When everyone was silently taking bets on how long their marriage would last, Sam and Renee were so sure they were going to make it. They had been right. Lindy and Ricky were still as much in love as they had been the day they got married, and maybe even more so.

Lindy realized that she had quit crying as she leaned into the curve of Ricky's shoulder. He held her gently as she wiped her tears with the backs of her hands. She looked up at him and smiled.

"Sorry," was all she said to him. He understood.

Liz and Nick were the first to get ready to leave. It was close to nine o'clock when they put their jackets on to go home. Liz had made a large, delicious chicken pot pie that everyone seemed to enjoy, including Michael who ate a large bowl of it when he got up from his nap. Angie and Diane were finishing the dishes when Liz and Nick got ready to leave. Chris had been playing with Michael in his room since dinner ended, and he appeared with Michael on his shoulders.

"Pumpkin, can I take Michael home with me tonight?"

"Oh, Chris....I don't know...."

"Please? I'm the only one here who hasn't gotten a chance to take him for the night. Please?"

Lindy looked over at Ricky for his opinion. He shrugged.

"Well, I guess. Ask Michael if he wants to first."

"Michael....want to go home with Uncle Chris?"

"Uh-huh! We fry kite again?"

"When it's daylight. This time Aunt Cindy can go.... okay?"

"Yep! We go now?"

Lindy and Ricky laughed.

"So much for loyalty, I guess." Ricky concluded.

Lindy went to Michael's room and got out some clean

pajamas and clean clothes for him to wear the next day. She grabbed his toothbrush and comb out of the bathroom and his favorite stuffed animal, a worn-out gray cat, and tucked it into the small overnight bag she packed for him. She walked with Michael, Chris and Cindy to the front door and hugged Michael. She kissed his cheek and hugged him tightly once again, and then kissed Chris and Cindy each on their cheeks. Chris hugged Lindy and kissed her cheek.

"Pumpkin, this will all be over soon. It's going to turn out all right." He soothed.

"I hope so, Chris. Take care of my baby tonight. No scary movies!"

"No…..we got a Disney flick for us to watch. Goodnight."

"Goodnight, you three. Be good."

Liz and Nick were still in the kitchen saying their goodnights when she went back inside. Ron and Angie were getting ready to go home, too. Diane and Ray followed suit. They all walked out together, with Ricky and Lindy following them out. They said their goodnights and passed out the hugs and kisses before they all left for the night. All promised to be back in the morning.

Ricky and Lindy stood outside; arms around each other, watching them all pull away in their vehicles.

"It's a nice night, isn't it?" Ricky commented.

"It's going to snow. I can feel it. It's always balmy like this before it starts."

"You're probably right…but it's actually kind of warm and pleasant tonight."

Ricky broke away from Lindy and put his hands on her shoulders.

"Wait here....okay?"

He ran into the house and was back outside in moments, holding two blankets. He took one over to the wrought iron bench that sat in the front yard, and spread it out on the seat. He sat down and pulled Lindy down beside him, and draped the other blanket over them.

"Just for a change of pace....okay?"

He smiled at her as he draped an arm around her shoulders and brought the other arm across her chest, lacing his fingers together at her shoulder. She sighed and snuggled closer to him, resting her head on his shoulder. He breathed in the scent of her shampoo. Coconut—the fragrance was so Lindy. Over the years, Lindy had changed her hair style from the long tresses she always wore to a stylish shoulder length cut that just turned under at the ends. Ricky loved the look on her. He thought she looked sophisticated and adorable at the same time. She still wore very little make-up, opting only for a little eye shadow when they went out for an evening. In Ricky's mind, she still had the face of an angel.

"Thank you....for today."

"For what?" She wanted to know.

"I really needed to go out with Michael....I miss Samantha so much....but I've been neglecting Michael. It was great being outside with him today."

"Honey, I think we're both neglecting him right now. I feel bad, too, but I don't want him to feel the strain we're going through."

"No....me neither. You know...you never told me what you had to tell me."

"What do you mean?"

"Well...when we were eating the shells at dinner. I

knew you knew something that I didn't. When I looked at you....you said later."

"Oh....yeah."

"So.....are you going to tell me?"

"Yeah. Nelson was in love with my mother."

"What?"

"It's true. One of the agents found her picture and a letter he had written to her back in the sixties or seventies, I guess. The agent said it was back then. He was in love with her, but he wasn't good enough for her. In his letter he said he was going to make it big and then come back for her. Maybe then he would be good enough for her. He never mailed the letter."

"Did he know you were her daughter?"

"No....but the agent thinks that's why he raped me. Because I looked so much like Stacey Stockwell, the love of his life. He couldn't have her so he forced himself on me. The agent said that he finally had Stacey through me...her look-alike. But he has no idea that I'm her daughter."

"Wow....Stacey, her daughter, and now her granddaughter. Three generations."

"That's exactly what I said. I also said that Nelson was right about one thing....he wasn't good enough for my mother."

"Agreed."

Ricky kissed Lindy's forehead and rested his head on top of hers.

"Are you cold?"

"No.....I'm never cold when I'm with you."

Ricky laughed. They both turned when they heard the front door open. Agent Morrow came out of the house and stood on the front walk, lighting a cigarette.

"I didn't know you smoked." Lindy commented.

He seemed surprised that they were there.

"Oh....not very often. Just once in awhile. Enjoying this balmy weather?"

"Yeah. Lindy thinks it's going to snow."

"Might. Hope we don't get a blizzard. Helicopters don't fly in blizzards. But if the ground is covered, we might be able to spot those red bushes easier."

"I'm counting on it." Lindy admitted.

Lindy and Ricky watched Agent Morrow walk back inside after he ground out his cigarette in the grass, and then picked it up to carry back inside the house. Lindy hoped he would flush the butt down the toilet rather than toss it in a trash can. She would be able to smell it if he did that, and she did not like the smell of tobacco. Ricky waited until the door closed before he commented.

"Do you think they ever take their suits off?"

Lindy sniggered.

"I think they probably even have sex in them....if they have sex, that is."

"Why would you think they didn't?"

"Well.......they have been sleeping here for a week.... and I imagine they do this a lot. When would they have time for it?"

"Good point. Just checking....are you cold?"

"No."

"Good. You hair smells so good....like coconut."

"Thanks. Ricky, do you remember when I was pregnant with Sammie? I craved coconut...remember?"

"Yeah....I do. I remember going out at midnight trying to find a store that sold Mounds bars, coconut cream pie..... anything with coconut."

"Sorry," Lindy responded sheepishly.

"Don't be. I would do it all again if I had to. God, you were so beautiful when you were pregnant."

"Oh…..yeah…right," she added skeptically.

"You *were*! I melted every time I looked at you. With all three pregnancies. I can remember telling you how sexy you were when you were pregnant with Nicholas. You were, too. There was something about you. Drew me in like a magnet."

"Are you serious?"

"Yeah…..dead serious. You were so *beautiful*, Baby. Honest."

Ricky held up his right hand to prove his sincerity.

"I love you. I really love you, Ricky. When I met you life became so beautiful….maybe that was what you saw."

"I saw *you*….and *you* are the most beautiful woman in the world to me."

"And I hope *you* never get eyeglasses." She smiled up at him and kissed his chin.

"Ready to go in?" He asked.

In answer to his question, Lindy stood up. They walked into the house still wrapped in the blankets, arms around each other, locked the door, turned out the lights, and went into their bedroom. Within minutes, both Lindy and Ricky were sound asleep, wrapped in each other's arms.

28

Nelson awoke at three AM and walked over to check on Samantha. She was still warm and it was beginning to scare him. Couldn't kids get brain damage from prolonged high fevers? He thought he had heard that once. But didn't applying cool washcloths to their foreheads bring fevers down? He thought he had heard that one time, too. He decided that when she was awake he would try that. Not too cold—just a cool damp washcloth on her forehead. It might help.

He knew he wouldn't be able to fall back to sleep for awhile, so he decided to make a half a pot of coffee. He put the coffee on and went down the hall to the bathroom while the coffee maker brewed the coffee. When he returned to the kitchen the coffee was just about finished. Reaching into the cupboard, he pulled out a mug and dispensed the freshly brewed hot coffee into it. He sat down and went over his plan again, trying to find a flaw in it. He could find none. Leaning back in the chair, his thoughts turned to Lindy. He pictured her big blue eyes with tears coming from her ducts. He imagined big droplets running down her cheeks and dripping onto her breasts. He wondered how many tears she had shed already. Millions? And how many more will she shed when she realizes she will not be getting her precious daughter back?

His thoughts drifted back to that first day she came into his life. She had cried that day. Loraine had cried, too. Later that night, Loraine had told him that it broke her heart to see that sweet girl cry like that. Loraine. Classy lady. Attractive, too. She should have been enough for him, and she would have been, too, if she didn't have that snooty attitude. She was a college graduate, she had a career, she came from a normal family—yeah, yeah, yeah. Lucky her.

Samantha's voice pulled him from his thoughts.

"John? Where are you?" She was calling him.

"Right here, Munchkin. What's the matter?"

"I woke up to go to the bathroom. I just wondered where you were….that's all."

"I'm right here. Go ahead….go to the bathroom."

He listened to her get up from the love seat and pad down the hall to the bathroom and close the door. He waited and listened for her to flush the toilet and come back down the hall. She came into the kitchen area, cocked her head to one side, and stared at him.

"Why are you sitting in the dark?"

"Well, because…..I didn't want the light to wake you…. and well, sometimes….grown-ups like to sit in the dark."

"Oh," she responded, and then stared at a place somewhere over his head like she was trying to understand that.

"Want something to drink? Or something to eat?"

"Drink. Can I have something to drink?"

"Yes….of course."

He got up from the chair and went to the refrigerator to see what he could offer her.

"Well…..we have grape juice, water, orange juice, soda…..and that's about it. Except for milk…which you shouldn't have with a fever."

She chose the grape juice, and Nelson got a glass out for her. He poured the grape juice into the glass and set it down on the table.

"Want to sit in here with me for awhile? You seem like you're feeling a little better. Those pills must be working, huh?"

Samantha nodded, and Nelson was relieved. He was still concerned about the red line on her leg. It seemed to have moved about an inch further up her leg, but it could be his imagination at work.

"Does your leg still hurt?"

"Yeah….it does. That must really be a *bad scratch*. It still really *hurts*."

"Do you want a cookie?"

"N-no. I'm not hungry."

"They're Oreos…"

"Maybe tomorrow…..not now….okay?"

"Sure….okay."

Nelson studied her. He never knew a kid to turn down a cookie—but then he knew very few kids. Maybe they all did. He never would have turned down a cookie, but then again, he was rarely offered one.

"Does mommy always have cookies for you to eat?"

"Yeah….most of the time. For snacks she cuts up fruit and puts it on a plate with the cookies. Me and Michael eat all of it."

"What kind of fruit do you like?"

"Oh…..apples, bananas, pears, oranges…..sometimes mommy has watermelon."

"What about peaches? Do you like them?"

"Oh, yeah! Aunt Shawna brings those from her tree sometimes in the summer."

"Who is Aunt Shawna?"

"Mommy and daddy's good friend. She comes to visit with her friend, Ally."

"And who else visits you?"

"Oh….lots of people. Uncle Luke and Aunt Michelle…. and little Lukas….Aunt Cindy…..Uncle Chris…..Aunt Liz…….Michael calls her Aunt Yiz……Uncle Nick. Nana and Pap Ron come. Poppa Ray and Gram Diane come over a lot, too."

"Wow….that's a lot of people."

"Yeah….it is. But they all love us."

"Well…that's certainly good to know."

Samantha nodded in agreement.

Nelson picked out the name Ray. He knew that was Lindy's father. He must have remarried—Lindy's mother was dead as he recalled. Nana must be Ricky's mother. Pap Ron—why not grandfather or some short form of it?

"Who is Pap Ron?"

"He's a detective…..and Nana's husband."

'*Oh great,*' Nelson groaned silently. He wondered how involved the detective was getting in this. 'Maybe….not at all….with the FBI in on it. They don't like interference.'

"Do you like Pap Ron?" He asked Samantha.

"Uh-huh…daddy says Pap Ron mellowed Nana out."

Taken back by that statement, Nelson laughed.

"Did daddy tell you that?"

"No....he told Uncle Nick that. John....I'm getting sleepy again. Can I go back and lie down?"

"Sure, Munchkin."

"I don't want you to be sad and lonely out here. You could come and sit in your chair....."

"Okay.....I'll do that."

He picked up his coffee cup and followed her into the living area. After setting his cup down beside his chair he went over to the love seat and covered her up. On impulse, he leaned down and kissed her forehead.

"Sleep tight, Munchkin," he whispered in her ear.

She was asleep within moments.

Nelson watched for a few moments, thinking about what she had said to him. She didn't want him to be sad and lonely in the kitchen all by himself. Nobody had ever cared if he was lonely or sad. Samantha does. Samantha cares about him. She may be only five, but he felt that she genuinely cared about him and that she liked him. She is the first person who ever cared about him. He just had to take her with him.

29

LINDY WAS AWAKE at four-forty-five AM. She turned toward Ricky and was about to wrap her arms around him when she noticed the pained look on his face. Not moving a muscle, she quietly watched his face as he slept. She watched until she saw the single tear slide from his tear duct to his cheek, and travel down along his jaw line. She moved close to him and cradled his head in the curve of her arm and shoulder, where she held him gently. She felt an involuntary shudder come from him as he released a sob from his lips. He was crying in his sleep. Lindy tightened her grip on him and ran her fingers through his hair. She kissed his forehead, and then his temple.

"It's okay, Ricky......It's okay," she crooned into his ear.

She realized that as she soothed him that she was crying, too. Burying her face in his hair, she tried to regain control. He needed *her* now, and it was *her* turn to be strong, even if it was only for a few moments.

Lindy dozed off for a little while. When she awoke, Ricky was still cradled in the curve of her arm and shoulder, but now he was awake. She looked down into his face and smiled slightly as she kissed his forehead.

"Hey, handsome....are you okay?"

"Yeah...boy I had some rough dreams. We don't have a dog...do we?"

"Not yet....but we will have one...or two. When Sammie is back here with us I plan on getting two Dobermans....one for each kid's room."

Ricky laughed lightly. He knew that Lindy would definitely consider a dog for protection even though she had already ordered an installation of a home security system. The installers were coming on Monday.

"So why did you ask if we have one?"

"Because.....I had some really bad dreams....and there was a dog involved in one of them."

"I know you were having some rough dreams. That's why you woke up where you did. I was holding you."

"Wow....that's a switch. I must have really been acting out."

"You were."

"Sorry."

"No need to be. I owe you a few. You're always there for me."

"What time is it?"

"Five-forty. Are we ready to get up?"

"Yeah.....I think so. I'll go make the coffee if you want to get a shower first."

"Meet ya in the kitchen."

Lindy slid out of bed and into the bathroom for a shower, while Ricky headed down the hall into the kitchen to start the coffee. It was day eight of their nightmare.

Dressed in heather gray running pants and a black and

gray sweatshirt, Lindy met Ricky in the kitchen where she breathed in the aroma of Ricky's delicious coffee. Ricky had the frying pan out and was frying strips of bacon in it. Lindy's weakness was bacon. She loved it. Ricky's plan was to entice her to eat a good breakfast, because she was steadily losing weight since Samantha was kidnapped. Lindy's weight never went above a hundred and eight pounds anyway, but it was obvious that she was down to around an even hundred or less. It worried Ricky. Liz, too, was concerned. She had mentioned it to Ricky the night before and he had seen the worry in her face. This morning, Ricky was hoping to make a breakfast that Lindy wouldn't be able to resist.

"Ricky, I was thinking. A dog would be nice. A loyal one….one that would protect the kids and yet be fun for them to play with."

"It's got my vote. What kind were you thinking about?"

"Baxter. One like Baxter."

"That has my vote, too. Remember how much fun we had with him?"

"Yeah….I sure do. He was a Yellow Lab. Any kind of a retriever would be great. A yellow Lab….or a black one. I hear they're all really cool like Baxter."

Baxter was Sam and Renee's dog. Lindy and Ricky had dog-sat Baxter right after they got to South Carolina so Sam and Renee could go visit their family in Ohio. They had loved playing with Baxter and they both always said that if they ever got a dog, it would be like him.

"How about after we come back from Disney World we look into getting a dog?"

"Again….it has my vote. I don't know why we don't already have one."

"We don't have a dog because I wanted the kids to be old enough to be good to a dog and not hurt it. No ear pulling or tail pulling, jumping on its rib cage….that kind of stuff. That's how kids lose their faces. Little kids jump on top of the dog and the dog reacts to it. The dog ends up on the bad side of that. I think maybe our kids are old enough to respect a dog. Do you think?"

"Yeah….they are, I think. So….we can get one when we come back from Disney?"

"Yeah…..count on it."

Ricky's grin couldn't have gotten any bigger. He always wanted a dog and could never have one. He had asked Lindy about it once before and she declined the idea, saying that the kids were still too little. Ricky had to admit that she had a valid point, and now that the kids were older, he understood her reasoning a lot better. His grin stayed on his face as he set a plate down on the table in front of Lindy.

"For you, my lady….breakfast fit for a queen."

Lindy grinned up at him.

"Is this a bribe to make me eat?"

"No….it's an offering of gratitude for finally saying we can get a dog."

"Okay….I guess I can force it down."

Ricky set his plate down and sat down next to her.

"It smells wonderful. You know I married you for your cooking….right?"

"Yeah….so? I married you for the great sex."

He winked at her, forcing her to try to keep a straight face.

"I have to admit....you outdid yourself with this breakfast. Everything is done perfectly. I wonder if our resident cops are up yet. If they are, we should make them breakfast...don't you think?"

"Yeah, I guess....but I just want to have breakfast with my wife for now. I'll make them something when we're done. I just want to sit here and eat breakfast with you and think about our almost-dog."

Lindy burst out laughing.

"Oh, and by the way, Babe....you were right. There are about four inches of snow out there. It's not too deep, so maybe if the helicopter goes up they will be able to spot those bushes."

"Hope so. Ricky, I keep getting this terrible thought, and I don't know where it's coming from."

"What is it?"

"I just have a very strong feeling that Nelson doesn't plan on giving Samantha back."

"Why? Why would he not want to?"

"For spite. To hurt me. I just have this feeling."

"Well, if the feeling is that strong, we had better tell five-oh in the other room. By now they should know that your intuition is accurate. We have to be extra-careful and there can be no mistakes. We have to find him and get him before we lose our daughter forever."

Lindy got a chill that ran through her when Ricky said that. Forever was she and Ricky together, forever was the age of the Earth, forever couldn't have anything to do with Samantha not coming back.

Ricky touched her face.

"Stop thinking like that. I can see what's going on in

your head. Please…..don't think we aren't going to get her back. We *will*. We *have* to."

Lindy squeezed her eyes shut and nodded. She felt her breathing begin to quicken, and she concentrated on slowing it down. Ricky was right. He had to be right. She couldn't lose another child. Nicholas hadn't had a chance. He was born too soon and under traumatic circumstances. Samantha, on the other hand, was born healthy; and she had grown and matured for the past five years. She had a chance to become a lovely young woman some day. They just *had* to see that *happen*.

"Are you okay, Baby?"

"Yeah…..I think. I'm trying to control my breathing. Every time I think about that slime touching our daughter I get….frantic."

"Honey….I don't think he's doing anything like that to her. We would be able to tell it in Sammie's voice."

"I know…..but just touching her hand….anything…. makes me sick to think about it. Oh, Ricky….I still remember when he put his hands on me. I get nauseous when I think about it."

"Shhh….Shhh…..I know. I remember how it was for you. The nightmares, crying in your sleep, the screams. Many nights I held you as I cried, too. I wanted to kill him for what he did to you."

Ricky felt Lindy's tremors begin. He immediately put his arms around her and then tightened his grip on her, planting kisses all across her forehead and then on her cheeks.

"Take it easy, Baby. Come on. The bastard will be calling shortly. You don't want to be all in pieces, do you? Come on…..get a grip."

Lindy forced air into her lungs as she held on to Ricky. Slowly, she began to breathe, in and out. Ricky was right. He would be calling and she had to keep her wits about her.

"Help me make breakfast for the FBI. You're on toast and tray detail."

Grateful that she had something to do to calm her; she set about putting toast in the toaster and then got the butter and jelly out of the refrigerator. When breakfast was ready Ricky carried the tray into the family room. Morrow and Daily were awake and appeared to be working on something.

"Brought you guys breakfast. What's going on?"

"We're just setting it up for the chopper today. Now we checked back with the people who own all the nurseries in Ohio. None of them have sold any red bushes to anyone in the past seven years. So that means that the bushes may be older than seven years. Mature bushes are usually fairly big....so we may get lucky."

Agent Morrow paused to take a forkful of egg and home fries into his mouth. Daily was eating as he talked on his cell phone.

"Great breakfast," Agent Daily complimented. "You should have been a chef."

"It wouldn't be as enjoyable to cook. I do it now because I like to."

Before Morrow picked up another forkful, he used his napkin and sipped his coffee, and then spoke.

"Thank you for breakfast, by the way. Thank you for all of the meals we have had here. You and Lindy and the rest of your family have worked very hard to spoil two FBI agents. We'll have to see if that is illegal somewhere in the law books."

"Well, if it is, I'm sure we can come up with a bill for you to pay," Ricky retorted.

Both Morrow and Daily chuckled as they continued eating. Daily, still on his phone, appeared to be holding for someone

"By the way, guys....there are about four inches of snow out there right now. It quit snowing and there doesn't seem to be any wind."

"Good......perfect helicopter weather."

Agent Daily hung up as Morrow mentioned the helicopter. He had some news to share with them

"Ricky....Lindy.....do either of you know a man by the name of Juan Juarez?"

"No....never heard of him. You, Lindy?"

"No.....why?"

"Well....there was an accident on Route Sixty last night."

Morrow and Daily watched their faces tighten anticipating the terrible news Daily was about the tell them.

"It was a fatal accident. Mister Juarez is dead. Anyway....the state police found evidence in the car that leads to Samantha."

"Samantha? Like what kind of evidence?" Ricky asked as he automatically tightened his grip on Lindy.

"Well, he had a picture of her in the car.....and copies of documents....a fraudulent birth certificate with her name listed as Samantha Nelson. The police think they were just copies...and that the fraudulent documents must have been delivered. We think this guy knew Sutter. He probably had him make a fake passport and other identification for himself, and then…..it looks like he may have gotten I-D for Samantha. Juarez was a known counterfeiter. Spent time in prison for it."

"Oh my God……Ricky….I knew it."

Lindy's eyes looked like pinwheels as she began to back out of the room. Ricky recognized the signs of hysteria that he had seen twice over the past week. He ran after her.

"Lindy…….Lindy!" He called to her.

He caught up to her, led her toward the kitchen, and reached for the pill bottle sitting on the counter.

"Here…..take one of these….okay? Lindy? Take one now."

"*NO! I don't want to be a zombie! I want my baby back! Oh, God!! I want my baby back!! Damn him!! I hope he burns in hell for this!!*"

She began screaming and pounding her fists on the wall, putting a crack in the plaster board. Ricky grabbed her by the shoulders.

"Lindy! *STOP! STOP! Please*…..please."

Ricky's eyes were pleading with her.

"*Please*," he begged once more, but this time quietly.

Lindy stared up at him for a moment and saw the tears welling up in the corners of his eyes. As she tried to control her breathing, a sound that was somewhat between a moan and a whimper—much like the sound of an injured animal—was coming from her throat, and it was breaking Ricky's heart. He gathered her to him, feeling her tremors, and he could no longer hold back the tears. He lifted her into his arms, carried her into the bedroom, and gently laid her down on top of the comforter. Her chest was heaving as small hiccup-like sobs escaped her lips. She stared at Ricky through blurred vision, and watched his tears roll down his checks.

"Baby.....please....try to calm down. I'm so afraid.... that you'll stop breathing again....and I can't take that again. I just can't. Twice now....Lindy....when you stop breathing like that...you look.....dead.....and....I can't see you like that again. I love you so much."

Ricky stopped to wipe away tears with the backs of his hands, and stared down at her to see if what he was saying was getting through to her. She was staring back at him, appearing to comprehend, and he was satisfied. He sighed. He figured it was time to tell her the rest of it.

"Baby....I didn't want to have to tell you this....but I think you should know. The first time you stopped breathing I began throwing up blood."

Lindy gasped.

"I've been having problems ever since. I try to be strong for you....but the truth is....I'm like jelly on the inside. I know what all this is doing to you....because it's doing it to me, too. You know how I love you and the kids. Samantha....God...I want her home again! I miss her....I miss her *so much*! But I also want you here. Losing you.... I can't even begin to tell you what that would do to me."

Ricky was in a full cry now, and he covered his eyes with his hand. Lindy stared at him, watching, and then slowly reached for him and pulled him down beside her. She wrapped her arms around his shoulders and held him, as she slowly steadied her breathing. Quietly, they lay together, trying to soothe and calm each other.

"Ricky....why don't we go look for her?"

He turned his heard toward her, meeting her eyes.

Their eyes locked and they felt their strength returning. He stared at her for a moment, sat up, and then nodded.

"Yeah....we can do that. Come on.....get ready, wash your face...or whatever it is you do before we go out. No reason why we can't look.....at least for red bushes. I'm going to let the guards know."

He quickly rinsed his face and eyes, grabbed a pair of sneakers, and went into the family room.

"Uh....I'm taking Lindy out of here for awhile. She needs to get out. We'll be gone a couple of hours....is that okay?"

"Rick.....you're not going to do anything stupid....are you?"

"Stupid.....like what?"

"Well, let us do the police work here. *We* are the experts in this field."

"But you haven't found her yet...." He let his voice trail off.

"But we will....Rick, don't put Samantha in any jeopardy....or your wife, either."

"Look....we're just going to go look.....maybe for red bushes. Samantha said the bushes are red....there are some red bushes out there somewhere, and Samantha is nearby."

"The scout in the helicopter didn't find anything...."

"When?"

"It landed about ten minutes ago. He looked but found nothing."

"And maybe we won't either. But we can't sit here and not try....we can't do that any more. Look....I...just.... well, you don't know what our life...my life...is like. The last thing I see when I leave for work every morning is my beautiful wife smiling up at me and kissing me. When I come home, my beautiful kids are smiling and happy to see me....my wife greets me with a smile and a kiss.....the house is spotless, the kids are clean and adorable, there are good smells coming from the kitchen, and I love every moment of it. Our weekends are spent together...happily. We have fun and we love one another. I've been living in a utopia.....and I want it back. I want my life...our life.... back."

"We're doing the best we can, Rick."

"But you don't love her." Lindy's voice came behind Ricky. "You've never heard her laugh....or cry. You've never heard her sing, or talk. You have never seen how her smile lights up a room. We love her. We...I think we.... will look harder than you. We are both suffering so bad.... we can't sit around and do nothing. Can you understand that?"

Agent Morrow stared at the naked agony on Lindy's face. He could hear the tremors in her voice and he knew she was trying hard to keep it together. He could also see that she was at the end of her rope. Ricky, too. The strain was suddenly more noticeable in his face.

"All right....look...do this for us. Take my cell phone number with you. If you see anything that might be a lead....call me immediately. I'll get someone there with you right away. Will you do that?"

Ricky looked at Lindy before he answered. She nodded.

"Okay....write your number down. If we see anything.... we'll call you. If we don't, at least we will be satisfied that we at least tried."

Morrow nodded. He didn't like it, but he knew he

was not going to be able to stop them from going. He saw the pain and desperation in their eyes. He wondered if it was like this for all parents who lost their children, or was it really harder on Lindy and Ricky than on other parents. He could see how much they loved their kids. It showed in little Michael. As he heard them go out the front door, he began wandering around the family room, just observing the pictures on the walls and on the tables and shelves. There were many. Some were paintings and some were photographs. There was a painting of Lindy wearing a flower in her hair, and a long flowing yellow dress that fell off of her shoulder. Morrow stared at it for a few moments. Daily joined him.

"Good work.....isn't it?" Daily offered.

"Good subject. She's beautiful, isn't she?"

"Yeah."

Morrow followed the contour of the walls and found some attractive photos of Lindy and Ricky together, and then some of the children—together and separate. There were a couple photos of Lindy with the children and then Ricky with the children. They all looked so happy in every picture. In every picture they had smiles on their faces and love in their eyes. 'This must be what true happiness is,' Morrow pondered. He wondered how you found it, or did it find you?

As Agent Morrow wandered back to the sofa, it dawned on him that Sutter hadn't called this morning.

30

Nelson had let Juan out through the kitchen door and had watched him get into his car. As Nelson stood there watching, Juan started his car and put the lights on. The beam of the headlights captured the heavy, wet falling snow as Nelson watched the car back out of the driveway.

"Asshole," Nelson muttered under his breath.

Juan Juarez had produced the necessary documents but the price had gone up considerably. Juarez knew who Samantha was and he certainly did capitalize on it by charging twice as much. 'So be it,' Nelson thought. He would be gone from here after Tuesday, and little Samantha would be right there with him. He smiled and stared over at her sleeping form under the blanket. He was glad that she hadn't awoken while Juarez was in the house. He didn't want to have to explain who he was, even though he would have told her a lie anyway. Besides, Juan was scary-looking, and some things are better left unseen and unsaid. Once again he turned toward the door and stared out at the snow.

"I won't miss this stuff," he said aloud. "End of March and still snowing."

It happened in March sometimes. In Pennsylvania and surrounding states, March was always unpredictable. The weather could be mild and sunny one day, but turn cloudy, blustery, and frigid the day after. Usually a snowfall like this one—heavy and wet—turned out to be the last one of the season. Nelson stood at the door until he could not see Juarez's vehicle any more, and then closed the door, poured himself another cup of hot coffee, and returned to his recliner in the living area. He dozed off.

...

Juarez slowly made his way up the small grade that began just past Nelson's cottage. The roads were slick and Juarez was worried. He had never driven in winter weather and he knew he wasn't doing very well. All he hoped for was that the main roads and the highway were clearer than this one. His windshield was frosting up so he put on his defrosters in lieu of heat. His feet were numb from the cold and he could barely feel them. He made a mental note to buy a pair of boots for next year, if he was going to remain in this part of the country. As he approached the stop sign, he stepped on the brake and felt the rear end of the car begin to shift forward. Immediately, he removed his foot from the brake and the car righted itself. 'Neutral,' he hissed under his breath. He remembered what his neighbor had told him. 'Put the car in neutral. That way you're taking one of the driving forces away. The go and stop together make your car go into a spin. Take the go away, and you only have stop,' he remembered him saying. Juan tested the theory and found that it worked.

He breathed a sigh of relief as the car came to a tentative halt at the stop sign. After sitting behind the wheel of the running car for a full minute, he edged the car forward toward the main road. That was relatively clear and he regained his confidence. The highway was just up ahead and he hoped that it had been cleared. He turned left onto the on-ramp and was happy to see that the highway just looked wet. The car picked up speed as he accelerated onto the highway and he began to feel comfortable and confident behind the wheel. He turned up the sound on the radio and sat back in a relaxed position. He sat up quickly as he noticed a car up ahead begin to slide. Checking his speedometer, he became alarmed. The speed of his car had climbed to seventy-five miles per hour. Keeping an eye on the car in front, he tapped the brake. Juan's car shot off to the side and went into a spin. He quickly dropped the gear shift into the neutral slot, but it was too late. What Juan had believed to be wet roads was actually what people call black ice—a thin covering of ice that is very hard to detect, but is extremely slippery. Many have said that it is like driving on grease. Juan began to panic as he fought the wheel attempting to straighten the car out. Swerving to the right and going into a tailspin, the car's tires began to scream on the iced pavement. Juan cut the wheel to the left and it was the last mistake he would ever make. The car shot over the median and flipped onto its side, slid across the highway, through the guardrails on the other side of the road, and over the embankment. Juan did not have the seatbelt fastened and on the impact with the median, his body was thrown forward and his head was forced through the windshield. The impact with the guardrails caused the windshield to almost sever his head from his body, and Juan Juarez was no more. The state troopers found his wrecked car and his body at the bottom of the ravine. Part of his scalp was found along the side of the road. It was when they pulled the car up out of the ravine and were searching the car looking for identification, that they found the papers concerning Samantha DeCelli. As soon as a trooper could get a free moment, he notified the FBI of his find.

Although the information was important, it still didn't tell them where Sutter was. They might have a better idea of a location if they knew exactly where Juarez had gotten onto the highway.

One piece of evidence that was of interest was that Juan Juarez and Nelson Sutter had done time together, thus making it a clear connection. The other piece that was of interest was that Lindy have been right—Sutter was planning to take Samantha out of the country with him.

31

RICKY CAREFULLY DROVE past the state troopers' cars and the flatbed tow truck that was holding the wrecked vehicle. It looked like the emergency vehicles were getting ready to clear the scene.

"Ricky, that must be the car....the one that had Samantha's picture in it. Did you notice the mud on the tires and on the back of the car? Do you think some of that may have come from the roads he had been on before the accident?"

"Maybe. Maybe we're looking for an unpaved or dirt road. I'm getting off at the next exit. I just have a feeling."

"Okay."

Lindy glanced at him appreciatively.

"Thank you.....for this."

"For what?"

"For going along with this."

Ricky reached for her hand and brought it to his lips and kissed the back of it. He smiled at her.

"You know I'd do anything for you. Besides.....I don't think this is all that bad of an idea."

"You don't?"

"No.....I don't. You have that radar going for you. I just have a feeling that if we are near Samantha, you will know it."

"I hope so."

"But, Baby....we are not going to do something stupid...okay? If we find anything...anything at all...we are calling Morrow. Okay? I'm not going to put you or Samantha in danger."

"I know....okay."

Lindy relaxed and began to survey the land alongside of the road. Ricky eased off the gas pedal and signaled to turn right off of the highway. They stopped at the stop sign and stared in both directions at the secondary road that led away from the stop sign.

"Which way, my little beagle?"

A short laugh expelled from Lindy's lips as she sat pondering on which direction to go.

"Right. Go right."

Ricky signaled a right and took his foot off of the brake and eased it onto the gas pedal. Slowly he started to the right.

"I'm glad we decided to take the SUV. I don't know how well your Toyota drives on icy roads like this."

"It's fine on snow and ice. I drive it all the time.... remember?"

"Yeah....but I feel safer in this."

They were silent for a few minutes, both studying the sides of the road. Ricky slowed and then stopped for another stop sign. Lindy indicated that they should turn right, and Ricky signaled. They rode in silence for what seemed like miles.

"How far have we come from the highway? Any idea?"

"Six miles. I've been keeping track." Ricky assured her.

"You're so smart.....and I love you for it." She answered him.

"So it wasn't my cooking? It was my brain you married me for?"

"Maybe....does it make a difference?"

"No.....but for me it still was the great sex."

He grinned like a Cheshire cat as he grabbed her hand.

"Liar," she retorted.

Lindy looked out of the front and side window and surveyed the land up ahead. She froze momentarily.

"Ricky.....look."

Ricky's eyes followed her gaze. A group of houses stood off to the side, not too far away. Every house had bushes in the yard, and the bushes were *red*. Both Lindy and Ricky felt their hearts jump as they focused on the upcoming scenery. Ricky glanced over at Lindy and saw that her eyes were a kaleidoscope of sparkling blues.

"She's near here....somewhere. Ricky, I feel it......I just feel it."

"What do we do?" He asked, giving her the lead.

"Let's just drive around, past these houses and see if there are more."

Nodding in agreement, Ricky accelerated a little so as not to draw suspicion from anyone who may be inside and looking out from any of the houses. As they stopped at another stop sign, Lindy indicated that they should drive forward rather than turn. The road that went left at the stop sign appeared to be surrounded by woods, and the road that went to the right seemed to go through farmland. Forward held more promise, so forward they went. Lindy was right. There were more houses and many more red bushes. Again, they rode in silence until Lindy spoke up.

"Now how could the helicopter miss this? There are so many red shrubs!"

"Maybe because of the tree covered hills. This hill behind these houses is pretty high. Maybe the helicopter couldn't see them because of it."

Lindy noticed that the houses on this road were not as big or as well-kept as those they had seen at first. These were more like cottages. She could feel the blood coursing through her veins as she stared at the small houses as the car passed each of them. Samantha was nearby somewhere.

"Ricky......our daughter is near here......somewhere. I can feel it. I feel it here more than when we saw the first houses."

Ricky nodded and reached for her hand as he drove downhill and around a bend.

"I feel it, too."

They rounded the bend and discovered that the road went back to the main road after passing several pastures.

"Ricky....Sammie talked about seeing cows and sheep. Do you think that is what might be kept in these pastures?"

Ricky found a clearing in the road, pulled over, and punched in Morrow's cell phone number. Morrow answered almost immediately.

"Yeah, Rick….what's up?"

"We think we may have found the location where Nelson is keeping Sammie."

"Where are you?"

"Somewhere….off of….sixty….I think. We're coming back. I can show someone the way after we get back."

"Ricky….we can't just *go*! She's *here*…..I *know* it."

"Baby, we can't go door-to-door looking for her. I believe she's here, too, but I'm not going to do anything that will get you or her hurt. Sutter may not be a killer, but he *is* unpredictable. That makes him *dangerous*. Believe me…..*believe me* when I tell you that I would like nothing more than to break down his door and beat him to near death….but I can't. Let's go back and let the feds figure it out. They *have* to be good for something."

Reluctantly, Lindy agreed to return to their house. All the way back she felt her pulse racing and heard a rushing sound in her head. She felt frightened, frustrated, and exhilarated all at the same time. She knew where her daughter was. She was in one of those houses. Samantha was right. *The bushes are red.*

Ricky pulled into the driveway, turned the key to off, and stepped out. He vowed to himself at that moment that he would definitely get a shot at Sutter before this was all over. Lindy got out of the passenger side and found that she could barely walk; her legs were trembling so badly. She kept her breath shallow as they entered the house and went directly to the family room. Another agent was waiting for them so he could be shown to the area they found. After much cajoling, Lindy agreed to stay behind while Ricky left with the agent. Liz and Nick, Angie and Ron, and Diane and Ray were already at the house when they had

267

returned. Lindy agreed to stay behind if Ron agreed to go with Ricky and the new agent, whose name was Ralph Gaines. Ron was more than happy to go along.

Lindy filled the family in on what she and Ricky had discovered.

"She's there….somewhere. I know it."

Her eyes were brimming with tears, as Liz held one of her hands and Ray held the other. Angie set a cup of steaming coffee down in front of her, and she looked up at her appreciatively. Nick hadn't spoken yet. He sat there taking it all in for a few minutes before he spoke.

"Lindy…..you're going to get her back. Now we know where to go to get her back. Just let the feds do their job. Relax a little."

Lindy told them all about the accident and the papers proving that Nelson was not planning on giving Samantha back.

"We have to get to him before he leaves the country. I know that's what he is planning on doing. Leaving the country and taking our daughter with him. Then when he gets tired of having a child around…he'll discard her."

"Why would he want to take her, Honey?" Diane asked her.

"For two reasons….one is because he wants to really hurt me, and I just figured the other one out. Sammie is probably the only person who treats him like he's awesome. She acts like she approves of him….and he doesn't get that very often. He knows he is a major screw-up. Sammie is only five….she doesn't know any better."

Lindy couldn't have been more correct.

32

SAMANTHA SAT UP and looked around for Nelson. He was sleeping in his chair. She got up off of the loveseat and limped down to the bathroom and quickly returned to the living area. He felt her presence as she stood staring at him, debating whether to awaken him or not. He opened his eyes and looked over at her.

"Hi, Munchkin," he greeted.

"John....my leg really hurts."

"I know....and right after we get off of our plane, I'm going to take you to a doctor so he can fix it and make it better."

"Will I have to get a shot?"

"I don't know. Don't you want one?"

"No."

"Come here so I can feel your forehead."

Samantha walked over and stood beside his chair, and he reached out and felt her forehead. She was still very warm, but at least she seemed to be functioning better.

"Are you hungry?"

"A little bit....but you don't have to get up yet. I can wait."

"Well now....aren't you just so sweet? That deserves a special breakfast."

"What kind of special breakfast?"

"How about.....some....pancakes with...peaches and Cool Whip on top?"

"Do we have that?"

"We sure do."

The *we* part did not escape Nelson, and he liked the sound of it. He had been saving the special pancake treat for the day they left, but today seemed like a good day. Samantha appeared to be getting better. He only had two more antibiotic halves left, and he hoped they would be sufficient. If nothing else, they were keeping her well enough to get on the plane. He regretted that he was going to have to sedate her while he went out to collect the ransom money, but he didn't know how else to keep her there alone while he was gone. It was Sunday morning. He had no intention of calling the DeCelli's today. Let them stew for a little bit.

Looking outside, he discovered that the snow had stopped, but there looked to be several inches on the ground—and that appeared to be melting. He was glad he decided to keep the car in the garage every day. At least he wouldn't have to clean snow and ice off the windows if he decided to go anywhere.

Nelson readied the coffee pot to make some fresh coffee, and then ran to the bathroom. Samantha had settled back onto the loveseat and turned the television to the cartoon channel, using the remote. Had either of them been standing in the kitchen looking out of the window, they would not have missed Lindy and Ricky driving past the cottage.

Nelson prepared the special pancakes and then called Samantha to the table. She smiled at him as she climbed up onto the kitchen chair.

"These look good! And smell good, too!"

"Well….let's see how they taste, then." He encouraged her.

"Ummm! They're really good, John!"

"Well, thank you…my special little lady! I'm glad you think so"

She smiled at him again, and he rewarded her with a smile of his own. She was, indeed, a very special little girl. The DeCelli's were going to miss her a lot. There was so much he wanted to do with her. He planned on teaching her to sail when she was older, and then teaching her how to drive a car. He planned on buying her a pony as soon as they found a place to live in Brazil. Maybe they would get a dog. They were going to grow their own vegetables—as a learning experience for her. And she was going to love him and look up to him. He would be her super-hero for the rest of his life. Nobody had ever appreciated him like little Samantha did. She was special—very special.

'When did I start loving her?' he mused silently. And he realized that he *did*. For the first time ever in his life he loved another human being for no other reason than to just love. He walked away from many people and never looked back and never even thought about them again. This was different. He knew he could not just walk away from his little munchkin. She was all that was special in his life—the only thing that was special.

33

Ricky, Ron and the agent returned back to the house. Lindy could see that Ricky was pumped up.

"They're going to set up surveillance in the area. But they have to do it so they don't look suspicious. There isn't a lot of traffic out that way. They are thinking about sending someone door-to-door....posing as a salesman or a bible thumper. They have to single out which house he is staying in. But we're going to get her back, Baby.....we're going to get her back."

Lindy clung to Ricky and cried tears of relief. He stroked her hair as he held her, tears stinging his own eyes.

"It's almost over, Babe....it's almost over."

Angie put a cup of coffee down in front of Ricky, as a whirlwind of activity at the door drew everyone's attention. A squealing and laughing Michael came in with Chris and Cindy behind him.

"Mommy! Daddy!" He called to them.

"In the kitchen, Michael!" Lindy called.

He came in and bounded onto Lindy's lap. His nose

was red from the cold and his cheeks were flushed, but the grin on his face said it all.

"Well, I guess you had fun, huh?"

"Yeah! The kite went way high! Uncle Chris was running and he fell in the snow, and Aunt Cindy was yaffing at him, and then we threw snowballs at him! He threw one at Aunt Cindy and hit her in the face, and then he threw one at me! I was yaffing and yaffing!"

And now Lindy was laughing, too. She looked up to see her brother standing in the doorway smiling sheepishly. He was watching her with Michael and marveling over how much like their mother she was. Stacey always clung to every word they said like they were saying something profound every time they opened their mouths. Lindy was exactly the same.

"We kind of over-did it, I think. He's going to sleep well today. So what's going on? What's new?"

Lindy and Ricky filled him in on what had been discovered. They noticed the look of relief cross Chris's face.

"So.....when are they going to start the surveillance?"

"Apparently it was started before we even got back here. There are agents out there now putting a plan into action."

Tears sprang into the corners of Chris's eyes as he sat down and hugged Lindy.

"Almost over, Pumpkin. Our Sammie will be back here soon."

He tightened his grip on her and just held her there for a moment as he tried to get a grip on his own composure.

The front door sprung open again, this time bringing Lukas, Michelle, and little Lukas. Lukas was carrying a large electric roasting pan and it looked like it was heavy. Ricky moved to give him a hand with it.

"Ribs! Millions of them in here!" He told Ricky.

"Millions?"

"Well, maybe not millions....but a lot of them. Enough to feed everybody here. Shell has two quarts of potato salad and a green salad as well. We feel guilty that we have been neglecting you all week. Shawna and Ally are on their way over, too. They have more peace offerings. Desserts."

"We understand. Everybody had things to do.....but we'll take the food. Come on in....we have news." Ricky led Lukas to the kitchen, each holding an end of the roaster.

"Uncle Yukas! Is Yukas here?"

"In the living room, Buddy!"

Michael jumped off of Lindy's lap and ran to the living room, shouting for Little Lukas. Lindy had to laugh as she got up to get Michelle and Lukas each a cup of coffee. Ricky filled them in on the latest developments.

"Lindy....don't you just want to go out there door-to-door yourself? And then just rip your daughter away from that creep?" Michelle asked her.

"Yes....but nobody will let me."

"Because it's a risk....to Samantha and to you, Lin. We can't let that happen. Not now that we are so close. Be patient, my little Beagle." Ricky told her.

"What is the beagle part about?" Lukas asked.

"Long story," Ricky responded as he winked at Lindy.

Shawna and Ally arrived with oval dessert trays consisting of cheesecake, a chocolate fudge cake, and a couple dozen chocolate chip cookies. Once they were brought up to date with the newest developments, Ricky set about putting on a fresh pot of coffee.

Ray, Chris, Ron, and Nick went to the family room to shoot some pool, turning the kitchen table over to the newcomers. Angie was rearranging the food on the counter.

"Lindy.....what do you say we change the sheets on Samantha's bed and get it ready for her?" Angie asked.

Lindy's eyes shimmered with tears as she smiled at Angie.

"Good idea, Mom. Let's go do it."

Liz and Diane got up to help.

"We'll dust and vacuum." Liz offered.

Angie stared at Lindy for a moment. She thought she looked frail and fragile, and about ready to fall over.

"Lindy, Honey....stay here and entertain your guests. We three can handle it. Just tell me which sheets you want on the bed."

"Her Cinderella sheets. They are her favorites."

"Okay....you got it. Just relax and enjoy the company out here."

Lindy looked at those remaining around the table and shrugged.

"I must look pathetic to her," she explained.

"Hey, Girlfriend....you're doing okay. This has got to be the worst experience you and Ricky have ever been through," Shawna held Lindy's hand as she spoke. "I'm sorry Ally and I deserted you for a few days. We had some stuff going on...but we're back."

"And I'm so glad you are," Lindy assured them.

The doorbell rang, causing Lindy to jump. Ricky and Lukas were already at the door when Lindy stood up. She heard Ricky call to her, so she made her way to living room. Sam and Renee were standing in the doorway! Lindy ran to them, throwing her arms around both of them and crying. She clung to them as she and Renee cried together.

"Thank you for coming. How did you *find* us?"

"It really wasn't hard, since everybody knows you right now," Sam offered.

"Come on in….we'll fill you in on everything….and introduce you to everybody," Ricky invited.

Arms wrapped tightly around Lindy, Sam and Renee followed Ricky to the kitchen for hot coffee. Ricky started to introduce them to people but they stopped him.

"Let us see if we can figure out who everyone is," Renee suggested. "We've heard so much about everybody….let us tell you who these people are."

"Okay," Lindy and Ricky agreed.

Renee started with Shawna and Ally. She knew their names and that they both had hearts of gold, she told them. As Lindy and Ricky's family and friends made their way to the kitchen, Renee identified each of them accurately. Liz offered Sam and Renee each a hug, telling them how much she and Nick appreciated all they had done for Lindy and Ricky fifteen years ago, when they first met. Renee reciprocated by telling Liz how much Lindy loved her and Nick and how fondly she always spoke of them. Liz seemed pleased, even though she knew that she and Lindy had a special bond from the moment they met. Renee almost laughed when she met Angie. She was exactly as Ricky had described her, even though over the years Angie had mellowed.

Angie loved *Lindy* in spite of their rough beginning.

Once she realized that Ricky and Lindy had a good solid marriage that was not going to dissolve, she began to build a loving and affectionate relationship with Lindy. Angie saw how good Lindy was for Ricky, and that she was good to him. She also saw that Lindy was an excellent mother. Angie couldn't fault her on any count so she began to love her like a daughter. Renee was pleased to see that it showed.

Lindy and Ricky sat together at the kitchen table just chatting with everyone. Renee noticed that they always touched—Ricky's hand on Lindy's arm, or their little fingers linked together—always in some way. Renee knew—she just knew—that it was their way of staying strong. After all, she and Sam had always done the same thing. As she studied their faces, she saw the strain they were under, but she also saw the determined strength to get through this. Renee thought they were remarkable, and she was glad that she and Sam decided to come up here in support of them.

The day was dwindling fast. Lukas and Michelle, along with little Lukas were the first to leave for the day. Chris and Cindy left next. Shawna was holding Michael on her lap while Sam talked to him. This was the first meeting between Michael and Sam and Renee. They were delighted with him and he seemed to like them, too. Michael had a way of making people laugh and Sam was not immune to it. He seemed to be laughing at everything Michael said.

When Shawna got up to leave, she asked Lindy if she could take Michael home with her and Ally.

"Shawna, he is going to be so *spoiled!*" Lindy protested.

"Yeah.....so? Come on, let us have him. We bought special stuff for him. Goodies and things. And we bought a tent we are going to put up in the living room for him. *Please?*"

"Ricky? What do ya think?" Lindy turned to Ricky.

"Yeah.....why not? If he gets too bad we can start beating his....rear."

Ricky winked and smiled at Lindy when he said it. They both knew that would never happen. Shawna bristled.

"Over my dead body!" She snarled at Ricky.

"That can be arranged, too."

Ricky laughed and ruffled Shawna's hair.

"You know I would never......and yes....go ahead and spoil him some more."

"I guess I better pack another bag for him."

Lindy started to get up, but Ally stood up first.

"I'll do it, Lindy. I know where everything is."

Lindy shrugged. "I haven't done a thing in over a week." She admitted to Renee.

"You have enough to do with just the worry alone. Let it go. Everybody obviously loves you and they want to help. Let them. I'm sure you'll think of a way to repay them all once this is all over."

Renee smiled at her and reached over and squeezed her hand.

"By the way....I'm so glad to see that your dad is back in your life."

"Yeah...me, too," she answered as she smiled back at Renee.

Liz sidled up to them and sat down, eager to get to know both Renee and Sam. She had heard such good things about them from Ricky and Lindy. Ricky set a cup of coffee in front of her. Liz started right into the conversation.

"Renee, where are you and Sam staying tonight? Usually these two use the family room as a guest room but the FBI took it over. Never mind….I'm asking you to stay with me and Nick. We have two extra bedrooms and we would love to have you. What do ya say?"

"Well…."

Nick jumped in.

"Please…..it would be our pleasure. We heard all about what you did for Lindy and Ricky. We are grateful, even to this day."

"Okay….if it's not an imposition."

"Oh hell, no! We have two extra bedrooms and an extra bathroom. We'd love the company."

Renee looked at Lindy and Lindy shrugged.

"It's okay with everybody?" Renee asked.

"Sure. We'll be back here in the morning for one of Ricky's wonderful breakfasts…..right, Rick?"

"Sure."

"It's settled, then. We can stay here for another cup of coffee and then go get a good night's sleep. I have a feeling things are going to change tomorrow."

Nick glanced at everyone as he spoke.

"I know you two can't wait to get Samantha back. Do you have any big plans after she's back?" Diane asked.

"Well, after we're sure she's okay we plan on taking them to Disney World." Lindy answered.

"And when we get back, Babe? Tell them about when we get back."

"What are you talking about, Ricky?"

"What are we getting? Come on….say it. What are we going to get?"

Lindy winked at Diane slyly.

"New curtains?"

"No….come on….say it. You said we were going to get…..come on, *say* it."

"I haven't any idea what you are talking about."

She winked at Nick this time.

Ricky dropped the subject, looking disappointed. Lindy winked at Nick again.

"Unless you're talking about the *dog* we're going to get."

Ricky's face lit up into a big grin.

"Yeah……that's exactly what I'm talking about. The *dog* we're going to get. You tortured me on purpose!"

Everyone in the room laughed as Ricky hugged Lindy.

"But Honey…..I was thinking….we may just get two."

"That's better yet."

Ricky kissed her temple.

34

NELSON AWAKENED BEFORE dawn as was his usual pattern. On the way back from the bathroom he checked on Samantha. She felt hot this morning. He worried as he made the coffee. He had to keep her relatively well until they got to Brazil. He would find a doctor immediately and get her treatment. Could something like a scratch cause her to die? He didn't know, but it worried him. What would Lindy do right now? There probably wouldn't be a *now* situation. Lindy would have already had her to a doctor, he was sure of that. He knew that he should have done that, too. But how? By the time she got the scratch, her face had been on every television station and in every newspaper in the country, and probably Canada, too. As soon as the coffee was done brewing he poured himself a cup and sat down at the kitchen table. He had to think. How could he get her some more antibiotics? What he had given her seemed to help for awhile. Maybe something stronger or a different kind.

"Think, Nelson…..think. What can you do here?" He spoke under his breath.

Suddenly it dawned on him exactly what he could do. He looked at the clock and saw that it was five-forty-five. He would wait another half an hour. He sat back and enjoyed his coffee, and then poured another one.

"Nelson...sometimes you're such a genius that you scare me," he chuckled under his breath.

With his second cup of coffee in front of him, he worked out his plan. When the clock on the wall pointed to six-fifteen he reached for the telephone and the voice changing device.

Ricky answered the phone.

"Put your wife on," Nelson demanded.

After a brief pause he heard Lindy's voice.

"Hello?"

"Here is the way it is. Your daughter is sick. She may be very sick...I don't know. She needs antibiotics. It's up to you to get them to her."

"How? How did she get sick? What exactly is wrong? I have to know to get the right antibiotics."

"I think it's the scratch on her leg. I think it's infected. There's a red line going from it up her leg. She has a high fever......enough information for you?"

"Yes. Can't you just give her back? Take the money? I don't care about it. Can't you just give her back? Please? *Please?*"

Nelson gave out a short, harsh laugh.

"Do you think I'm that stupid? Huh? Sure! Just make the exchange. Kid for cash. Then what? The FBI all over my ass. Think again, little lady. Get the antibiotics. I'll call tomorrow with drop-off instructions for the money. Make sure that the antibiotics are in with the money."

"But.....I thought if you got the money....we would

get Samantha *back*! We can take care of her! She needs a hospital. That kind of infection can be deadly. *Please....* we'll take care of her. Just let us have her. After you get the money, that is."

"You wait for my call. Get the antibiotics; put them into the bag with the money. By the time I let you know where she is the antibiotics will already be working. Got it?"

"Yes......uh, John....can I speak to her?"

"She's sleeping. Wait for my call."

He hung up.

Lindy covered her face with her hands and began to weep. Ricky was at her side instantly.

"Ricky....he said the scratch on her leg is infected. That's why she's sick. Oh, God.....Ricky."

"Come on, Lindy. We need to think."

Ricky led Lindy back out to the kitchen and sat her in a chair. He reached for the pill bottle and a glass, and filled the glass half-full with water. Lindy took the pill without hesitation, and swallowed it with the water. Her hands were shaking violently. After Ricky took the glass from her, he sat down and held onto her hands, trying to steady them. He sighed.

"Okay....Aunt Liz will get us the antibiotics.....I'm not worried about that. But...." He trailed off.

"But what?"

"Sammie must be pretty sick...."

Ricky couldn't say any more. The lump in his throat seemed to be growing by the second. He suddenly couldn't swallow. He felt the bile gorging up into his throat and he ran for the bathroom, heaving as he got inside the bathroom door. Lindy sprang into action. She had to run to Ricky. She rinsed a washcloth at the sink and cooled the back of his neck with it. He took it from her and wiped his mouth, still kneeling in front of the toilet. Lindy pressed his face to her and held him, her hand entwined through his hair. After a moment, she spoke to him.

"Are you okay?" She stared down at him with a look of deep concern on her face.

"Yeah…..I guess. Sorry."

"Oh, Honey….."

Tears sprang into her eyes as she knelt down beside him and wrapped her arms around him. She saw the tears begin to form in the corners of his eyes and she tightened her grip on him and pressed her face against his shoulder.

"I love you," she whispered.

"I know. Why else would you be sitting here holding me in front a bowl full of puke?"

Lindy laughed. In spite of everything, she laughed.

"I see where Michael gets it," she noted, her voice shaking.

"Michael. He's a character….isn't he?"

"Yeah. He makes me yaff."

"Me, too," Ricky answered with a short laugh.

They helped each other up and Lindy returned to the kitchen, leaving Ricky behind to clean up. Liz, Nick, Sam, and Renee would be coming in any minute, and he had promised them breakfast. Lindy began setting the table for breakfast, and Ricky returned to the kitchen and got out the ingredients he would need for the omelets he planned on making. Lindy already knew she was on toast detail, since she usually was when Ricky made breakfast.

Ricky had the omelet ready to go into the large frying pan when they heard the car doors outside in the driveway.

"Just in time," he announced.

"Let's not say anything until after they've had breakfast. We don't want to ruin it for them."

"Okay...but we have to ask Aunt Liz for the antibiotics."

"After they all eat."

Ricky nodded in agreement. Lindy went to answer the door while he continued making the omelets.

Liz and Nick and Sam and Renee ate ravenously, complimenting Ricky on the delicious breakfast. Lindy and Ricky were quiet throughout the meal, and it didn't go unnoticed. Nick silently watched them as he ate, just knowing that there was something else wrong. When his plate was empty he set the fork down, used his napkin, took a sip of his coffee, and asked the question.

"So when are you two going to tell us what happened? I know something new has happened. I know you both too well."

Lindy and Ricky stared at each other. Ricky reached for her hand as her eyes welled up with tears. Ricky sighed.

"Sammie is very sick. Asshole says it's from the scratch on her leg. He says it's infected and there's a red line starting up her leg. She has a high fever."

"Oh, no! So what is he going to do about it?" Liz asked.

Ricky and Lindy both turned their eyes to Liz.

"He wants a prescription of antibiotics......and he wants them put into the bag with the money. Lindy begged him to just give Samantha back and just take the money. He refused. Says he knows the FBI would be all over his ass if he did that. Also.....he says he wants Samantha to get the antibiotics into her as soon as possible....so they would be working when he gave her back.....he said. I think he's full of shit. He doesn't want to give her back."

"Aunt Liz, how serious is it when there is a red line going up the leg?"

"It can be *very* serious, Lindy. I'm not sure what I can write without knowing what caused the scratch."

"It's from the red bushes."

"Well, that's a help, anyway."

Liz reached into her bag and pulled out a prescription pad and began to write. After tearing off one of the slips from the pad, she began to write again. By the time she was finished she had written out four slips from the prescription pad—two for Samantha, and one each for Lindy and Ricky. She could see that their emotional state was deteriorating. She handed the prescriptions to Nick.

"I'll get these filled in a little while. What can I do around here to help you two out? You both look like death warmed over," Nick added.

Lindy's eyes filled with tears again.

"Uncle Nick....I.....don't.....I don't think I can take much more. I....."

She broke down before she could say any more. Nick got up, came around the table, and sat down beside her. He pulled her close to him and kissed her hair. Tears welled up in his own eyes as he held her. He glanced over at Ricky who had his back to the table as he rinsed dishes and stacked them in the dishwasher. Nick could tell by Ricky's stance that he was choking back tears, too. Liz reached for tissues and handed some to Renee and then to

Lindy, keeping a few for herself. Nobody spoke. Nobody had to. Sam was the first to break the silence. He spoke to Liz in a low tone.

"How serious is it when a scratch gets infected?" His voice was barely more than a whisper.

"It can be very serious. Bacterial infections can be lethal, depending on what type of bacteria it is," She answered him.

"Oh, God," he whispered.

Liz nodded. She knew what he was thinking. She had been thinking the same thing. Nick looked up when he saw movement from the corner of his eye. Agent Morrow was standing in the doorway. All eyes rested on him waiting for him to speak.

"Coffee?" Liz offered.

He waved off the offer.

"Okay…we checked out every house out there that had red bushes in the yard. Sutter wasn't in any of them. He's not there. It's a dead lead."

He watched their reactions, one by one, not wanting to focus on Lindy.

"NO! NO! YOU'RE *WRONG*! SHE'S *THERE*! I *KNOW* SHE IS!!" Lindy screamed. **"SHE IS *THERE*! I *FELT* HER! *RICKY* FELT HER!! YOU'RE MISSING SOMETHING! THE FBI OVERLOOKED SOMETHING! SHE IS OUT THERE! SHE IS IN ONE OF THOSE HOUSES!!!"**

Lindy felt all hope slipping away and she began to crumble. Sobbing, she turned toward Ricky.

"Ricky….she's there. You know it and I know it. *How can they say she isn't there? She is! She is **there**!*

Lindy jumped as she heard what sounded like an

explosion as Ricky slammed his fists against the cabinet doors, shattering the wood. Splinters flew onto the counter.

"Lindy…..shut up!!"

All eyes quickly focused on Ricky. All mouths dropped open in shock. Lindy quietly got up and ran down the hall to their bedroom. Wrapping her arms around herself, she sank down into a chair. Liz and Renee quickly joined her.

"He…didn't mean it, Honey. He's under a great strain." Liz soothed.

"He….has never talked to me like that. God….that hurt."

"I know it did."

Liz put her arm across Lindy's shoulders and held her. Renee held her hand. They sat like that while Lindy cried. All three women held heavy hearts in their chests.

35

Morrow had backed out of the room and retreated to the family room. It was the reaction he had been afraid of—Lindy getting hysterical again. The bureau had sent a couple of people out there. They knocked on every door and questioned neighbors of those who weren't home. Only two homes were unoccupied. One of the houses belonged to an unmarried woman of around fifty. Her neighbor said that the woman was in Florida and due back at the end of April. She had a key to the house and checked on things over there regularly. The other house was part of an estate owned by a family named Heiser. Mister Heiser was elderly and his two sons did the upkeep on the property. They brought him out there a couple times a year just to relax and enjoy the place. The neighbor lady, Missus Bentley told the agent that the oldest son had been there a couple of days ago. When the agent asked if she were sure it was the son, she nodded and said that she had spoken to him. The agent seemed satisfied with that. He looked over at the house and noted that there seemed to be nothing indicating that there was any life around the place. The walk hadn't been shoveled nor had the driveway been cleared.

The actual facts were that the elderly Missus Bentley had seen someone on the property and just assumed that it was a young Heiser. It was Nelson she had seen, and when she waved and said "Hello, James," Nelson had waved back and returned the greeting. With Missus Bentley's eyesight not being what it used to be, she had no way of knowing that it was not James Heiser she had spoken to, but Nelson Sutter, alias John Nelson. Missus Bentley told the agent that James Heiser told her he would be bringing his father out to the cottage as soon as the weather turned warm. The fact was that Missus Bentley asked Nelson if he would be bringing Mister Heiser out soon, and Nelson said he would be—real soon. The agent was satisfied with Missus Bentley's assurance that she had spoken to a young James Heiser, so he wrapped up his search and left for the day, never bothering to check to see if there was anybody in the house. Lindy and Ricky were not wrong.

Agent Tom Morrow stood inside the family room door, leaning against the wall, staring at the floor. He had heard Ricky's outburst and debated on going out there again. No. Let them handle it. He knew it was emotions running high that caused it, although he was a little surprised at the way Ricky shouted at Lindy. He was always so loving and tender with her. Morrow ran his hand through his hair. Jack Daily watched him.

"Something on your mind, Tom?"

"Yeah....sorta."

"What is it?"

"Well, you heard what just took place out there. Jack,

the hell of it is....I believe Lindy. She says she feels her daughter is out there and....I kinda think she's right."

"Why?"

"I don't know why. I just do. Gut....gut instinct. She's got intuition....we have gut instinct."

Jack stared at Morrow, knowing in his heart that Tom was right. He decided to go out into the kitchen and get a cup of coffee to see what the atmosphere was like.

Ricky held himself up by his hands pressing down on the counter, leaning over and staring down at nothing, while Nick stood beside him, his hand on the small of Ricky's back. Sam watched from a chair at the kitchen table. The three men appeared to be frozen in time. Daily got his coffee and made a beeline back to the family room, nodding at Sam as he passed by him. Ricky was the first to break the silence.

"I shouldn't have talked to her that way. I've *never* talked to her like that. I need to go apologize."

"Calm down first. Hey....you're only human," Nick advised.

"Uncle Nick, I......"

Ricky sighed and ran his hand over his face. He turned and looked at Nick, tears welling up in his eyes.

"I'm angry...I'm sad....I'm scared. I'm scared that I'll never see my daughter again. I'm frustrated.....because I know Lindy and I are right. *What the hell do we have the FBI here for if they can't follow a simple lead? Lindy is right...they missed something. I have to go back out there. I have to!*"

"Just think it through, Rick. That's all I ask."

"Before I do anything I have to go apologize to my best friend."

Nick nodded, showing his approval by a thin weak smile. Ricky straightened and walked out of the kitchen, patting Sam's shoulder as he walked past him.

Liz looked up at the doorway and saw Ricky standing in it. She signaled to Renee with her eyes and they both stood up quietly and quickly and slid out of the bedroom. Ricky approached Lindy and knelt down in front of her. He saw the pain in her eyes and he felt the tears begin to well up in his eyes. He reached for her hand and held onto it.

"I'm sorry. I'm so…so…..sorry."

"I know," Lindy nodded slightly as she answered him.

She touched his cheek with the back of her finder tips and wiped a tear away. Leaning forward, she gently placed a kiss on his lips.

"Do you trust me?" He asked her.

"Yes….of course….more than I trust anyone."

"Okay……now listen to me….okay?"

Staring at him with tears and pain in her eyes, she waited to hear what he had to say.

"I'm going back out there. Me and Uncle Nick. We're going to go out there and have another look. You have to be here in case he calls. If he asks for me….tell him…..I don't know….tell him something. If he calls….have Aunt Liz call me on my cell……I'll come right back."

"Okay….you'll be careful?"

"Of course. Samantha's life depends on it."

Ricky stopped and stared at the oval rug Lindy's feet were on.

"What's wrong?" She asked him.

"I still can't believe I talked to you that way. I feel….

terrible about it. You're my best friend....the love of my life. I'm so sorry."

"Shhh....it's over and done with. Tell me you love me and I'll forgive you."

"With all my heart....I love you."

They stood up and walked back to the kitchen arm in arm. Those sitting around the table were relieved. Ricky took them all in with his eyes.

"I apologize for.....I just lost it. I'm sorry. I can't let that bastard get to me any more. I can't let him tear us apart. Uncle Nick....let's take a ride."

36

NELSON PRESSED HIS hand against Samantha's forehead and pulled it back quickly. She was very hot. Turning her head toward him, she opened her eyes and smiled weakly.

"John...I don't feel good. Call mommy....please. She can make me better...then we can go on our airplane ride."

Her voice was barely audible and her eyes appeared to be glassy. Nelson assumed that was because of the fever.

"Want some juice, Munchkin?"

Samantha nodded. In the kitchen, Nelson poured some cherry flavored juice into a small glass and dropped an ice cube into it. He carried it into the living area and sat down beside her. Samantha struggled to sit up and although she managed it, Nelson could see that she was becoming very weak. She drank half of the liquid, shivered, and handed Nelson the glass.

"You don't want any more?"

Samantha shook her head, indicating that she didn't.

"Well, I'll leave it right here….if you want some later…. it's here. Want to watch TV?"

Samantha nodded.

"Video? How about the one hundred and one Dalmatians?"

Again, Samantha nodded. Nelson turned the television on and placed the video into the VCR and leaned back to watch the movie with her. She was sound asleep five minutes into the movie. Nelson turned it off and began to pace. He went back into the bedroom and in order to keep busy he began packing his things. He had a little pink suitcase for Samantha to put her things into. It had been purchased at Wal-Mart when he made his last buying trip there. Since he had purchased some new clothes for her, he bought the little suitcase to put the clothes into when he returned her back to her parents. He had no intention of taking her with him at the time, but now he was glad he had bought the suitcase. He pulled it out of the plastic store bag and began putting her things into it. He had saved a new outfit for her to wear onto the plane, so he got that out and hung it up. He would call the DeCelli's at seven tomorrow morning. That would give them a half hour to get to the school and put the bag with the money and antibiotics in place. He would call them tonight and make sure they had the antibiotics and that the money was ready in the bag for delivery. Tomorrow. Tomorrow at five he and Samantha would be on the plane ready for take-off. He got out the paperwork for the chartered flight and carried it to the kitchen table where he sat down to peruse it. Once again, he checked the passports and birth certificates for authenticity. They looked good. No one would look twice at them. He tucked them into his valise that was just big enough to carry them and one-fourth of the five million dollars.

Nelson looked at the clock. It was well past noon and he hadn't eaten anything all day. He was hungry and he wondered if Samantha might be. She needed to eat something since she hadn't eaten anything at all since yesterday, he decided. Looking into the refrigerator and then the cupboards, he decided to make her grilled cheese and tomato soup again. She seemed to like that meal when he made it a couple of days ago. It was Lindy's favorite so it wasn't unusual that her daughter would be fond of it.

He prepared the lunch and took it in to Samantha, waking her after he set it down on the table. She whimpered a little but sat up anyway.

"Come on…..a couple of bites, Sweetheart. You haven't eaten since yesterday. You have to eat to get strong. It will help you get well. Okay?"

Samantha nodded and took a small bite of the sandwich. She chewed and swallowed like it hurt her. Nelson held the spoon for her to taste the soup and it seemed as though she could swallow that a lot easier.

"That's a girl….just a little bit at a time."

Samantha finished the soup and ate a little more of the grilled cheese but appeared not to be hungry. Nelson got her some juice to drink and she drank an entire glass and asked for more. That worried him. Was she dehydrating? He brought her more juice, a glass of water, and a couple pretzels to munch on, thinking the salt would help keep her hydrated. He had very little medical insight.

Samantha was staring up at him, her eyes still appeared glassy.

"Feeling any better, Sweetheart?"

"No......John.....I need mommy. I'm real sick.....and I need my mommy. Can you call her? I need to go home *now*," she whispered.

Nelson felt the perspiration form on the back of his neck and under his arms. He wiped the beaded sweat off of his forehead. He was becoming extremely nervous. If she was really this sick maybe he should call Lindy and let her have Samantha back. But then...there would be no five million dollars to start a new life, and he would fall right into the hands of the feds and sentenced to hard time. No, he had not hurt Samantha, but kidnapping was kidnapping. He would have to take his chances on her making it to Brazil. He wanted her to get well. There were good medical facilities in Brazil, he heard.

"Mommy and daddy will be on the plane tomorrow. Is that good?"

"Yes. Michael, too?"

"Yes, Michael, too. Think you can hold out until then?"

Samantha nodded. Her eyes fluttered and she appeared to be falling asleep. Nelson covered her up with the blanket and kissed her cheek. He whispered to her.

"Munchkin, I didn't plan on this happening. I didn't plan on you getting sick, nor did I plan on falling in love with you. You're an angel like your mother."

Samantha's eyes fluttered open again. She stared at Nelson for a moment, and then smiled and closed her eyes. She fell asleep.

Nelson showered while Samantha slept. As he was getting out of the shower, he glanced into the mirror and was surprised by the look he saw on his face. Worry. He never had that look before. Fear, frustration, anger, lust, contentment—yes, he had had all those looks before—but never worry. He stared into the mirror for another few moments and then quietly spoke to himself through it.

"If she dies you killed her. You'll be called a murderer and you'll be hunted."

Nelson shook his head to clear it.

"No....I never wanted to hurt her. I want her to get better. I don't want her to die."

('She might, Nelson....and it's your fault.')

"**NO!** I....can't let her die........."

He dressed quickly and went back to the living area to check on Samantha. She was warm and sleeping heavily. He covered her and then sat down at the kitchen table to think. Running his fingers through his still-damp hair, he frowned, trying to remember something—something important. Wait—what was it his mother had done when Richard was so sick with the flu? He had a high fever—and—she—what? What did she do? 'Think, Nelson... what did that old bitch do?' He asked himself. Then it hit him—alcohol bath! He ran down the short hallway to the bathroom and opened the medicine cabinet. There it was—alcohol. He found a small washbasin under the sink and turned the tap on until the water was tepid. He filled the basin one-fourth of the way and added half the bottle of alcohol, and then got a washcloth out. He carried the basin out to the living area and set it down on the table and began to unbutton Samantha's pajama top. She stirred but didn't protest. Wringing the washcloth a little to keep it from spilling all over her, he quickly began wiping her body down with it. When he was satisfied that he had done what he could, he buttoned her top and covered her. He decided to take a nap before he called the DeCelli's house, so he stretched out in his recliner and fell asleep, making sure all the lights were off first.

If any of the lights had been left on, Ricky and Nick may have spotted them. When they drove past that house it looked as though it was uninhabited.

37

AGENT TOM MORROW paced the length of the family room. Something was gnawing at him—something he knew he should be looking into. In his mind he was going over the report from the agent they had sent out to check on the houses with the red bushes. The agent was young—a rookie. He could have missed something. Morrow stopped pacing and picked up the written report and stared at it. He sat down in one of the chairs and began reading it. He snapped his fingers and stood back up again.

"What? What is it?" Daily raised his eyebrows quizzically.

"These people….the Heisers. We need to speak to them."

"Why?"

"Well, for starters…why would we take the word of a….." He stopped and checked the report. "A ninety-year-old woman? How do we know that it was really a man named Heiser? And….maybe….just maybe…a man named Heiser rented out the cottage."

"We don't know that…" Daily retorted.

"No…we don't….no more than we know he didn't. We need to speak to him. Is there a phone book here? I'll call every Heiser in the phone book until I find one who is related to the owner of that cottage."

Morrow opened a cabinet and found the white pages telephone book. He took it over to the sofa and sat down, thumbing through it until he came to the letter H. Running his finger down through the name Heiser, he stopped at James Heiser first. Good—there were only eight of them. He'd start there.

After speaking to the eighth James Heiser, Morrow, looking discouraged, snapped his cell phone shut and set it down on the table. No luck. He called the bureau and asked to be connected to the computer search room. Adele Sethner came on the line.

"Adele…..I need you to look something up for me. I don't have all the information but I know I'm talking to the best……"

"And flattery will get you everywhere. What do you need, Tom?"

"I need you to find me a name, address, and phone number of the owner and heirs of this address. It's a cottage."

Morrow gave her the address of the cottage that the young agent marked as vacant and then added his cell phone number.

"Call me back as soon as you have something."

"Got it, Tom…..you'll hear from me."

Jack Daily stared at Morrow as he hung up.

"You really have a gut feeling about that vacant cottage, don't you?"

"Yeah.....something about Lindy's reaction tells me she's not wrong....you know? Ricky, too. He's been the rational one so far....but not this time. The guy lost it in the kitchen. Did you see the cabinet doors? Gees! The wall in here, and then Lindy smashed the wall in the kitchen, now the cabinet doors. Between the two of them, they're destroying the house. They both have a strong feeling that their daughter is out there near those cottages. I intend to go with that feeling. I'll wait and see what Adele digs up for me."

Morrow went out to the kitchen to help himself to another cup of coffee. Lindy and a few others were sitting at the table. All of them looked calm, but drained. Ricky and his uncle were not around, and Morrow wondered about that. Maybe the uncle took Ricky somewhere to calm him down. He stared at Lindy for a moment, drawing her attention to him.

"Are you okay?" he asked.

She nodded, and he left it at that.

"Mind if I sit here with you awhile?" He stood at the edge of the table and waited expectantly.

"No....sit down. Is there something new? Did you find out anything?"

"No....I just wanted to see how you're doing...and also...to tell you that I'm doing something about your feeling. I have somebody at the bureau working on something for me right now. Lindy, I believe you....okay? I really believe that your feeling is....right. I'm going to do all I can to follow through....okay?"

Lindy stared at him and nodded. Morrow looked back into her watery china-blue eyes and saw the gratitude shining in them. She took her bottom lip between her teeth and gently bit at it before she thanked him. Morrow stood up abruptly and quickly retreated to the family room where he collapsed into a chair. He was sweating as he breathed a sigh of relief. *'Wow....she didn't do anything out of the ordinary....but....wow! I almost lost my mind and went to kiss her! Jesus! I need to stay away from her like that! I didn't know I felt that for her.'* He ran his hand through his hair and breathed deeply. *'It has to be the loneliness.'* He thought. *'I've never come close to doing anything like that before. But it's her, too. She has that...thing....that quality.... that makes you want to grab her and crush her to you, and kiss her, and kiss her, and kiss her. I can't wait to get out of here! I'm falling in love with another man's wife....who I'm supposed to be...helping.'*

Tom Morrow sat in the chair and stared at the ceiling for a long time. He had to get a grip on himself, and above all, he had to keep his distance from Lindy. That feeling he got while sitting next to her in the kitchen must not happen again. He heard his cell phone ring and he focused on the call.

"Tom....I found the owner of that address. The old man is in a nursing home and the sons take care of the estate. Here is the address and phone number for James and the other brother, Julius. They're twin sons, forty-nine years old. Julius is married and has four kids; James is not married, but lives with a woman. Her name is.....Rebecca Willis. The phone is listed under her name."

Morrow jotted down the information into his notebook.

"Thanks, Adele....I owe you. Dinner maybe...next time I'm there. Okay?"

"Hey....yeah! That would be great! I'll hold you to that."

Morrow smiled and hung up. "Sure, why not?" He whispered under his breath. He had no idea what he had just gotten himself into, since he had never even seen Adele. *'Desperate measures for a desperate man,'* he winced to himself.

"Jack, I'll be back. I'm going to go check this out personally. Make sure one of them is nearby in case Sutter calls."

Morrow grabbed the keys and left out through the front door. He headed in the direction of the first address, which was Julius Heiser's address. He pulled up in front of a good-sized white colonial house in a high income neighborhood. There were two cars in the driveway which was a good indication that both the Mister and Missus were at home. He got out of the car, went up the walk, and rang the bell. A man answered the door.

"Are you Julius Heiser?" Morrow started right in when the man opened the door.

"Yes....I am."

A man who was about six feet tall, with light brown hair, showing some gray in it, stood in the doorway. He had very gray eyes that held a sharp look. Intelligent, was Morrow's first impression. Morrow showed him his badge, and the man immediately stepped aside and let him in.

"What can I do for you? Is this some sort of official business? I don't think I've broken any laws....."

"Well, I hope not...." Morrow attempted a smile. "I'm here about the cottage your family owns....out past Route Sixty."

Julius looked alarmed.

"Why? Has something happened to it?"

"No…..I just wondered if anybody from your family has been out there within the last couple of weeks."

Julius stared at the floor pensively for a moment before he answered. He looked back up at Morrow.

"No….I don't think so. We take my dad out there around June. He stays a week or so, and then goes back to the nursing home. We take him back out in July and then August. We usually go air the place out about a week before we take him. Usually around Memorial Day weekend."

"So you or your brother weren't out there….say…. about a week ago?"

"Well, you can check with my brother….but I don't think so. I know Jim went out there in January to check on the pipes….just to make sure nothing was broken. Everything seemed fine. We keep them heat-wrapped all winter."

"Do you or your brother ever rent the place out?"

"Oh, no…..dad would have a fit. Besides, the estate doesn't permit it."

"Well, thank you for your time. I'm going to need to speak to your brother."

"Yeah, well he's at his office. Here….one of his business cards with the office address on it." Julius added as he reached into his wallet and pulled out a card.

Morrow took the card and asked Julius one more question.

"Are you and your brother identical twins? I don't want any surprises when I see him."

Julius Heiser laughed. "Yes…we are. You'll think he's

me when you see him. One difference. He's left-handed. Agent? Why the interest?"

"I was wondering when you would get around to asking. We're investigating a kidnapping. The little girl told her mother over the phone that the bushes were red. We're investigating any place with red bushes. The neighbor woman told our agent that your brother was out there last week."

"Oh….well….maybe he was. I doubt it. If it was that elderly lady next door she probably has the dates confused. She probably saw Jim out there in January."

Morrow nodded, shook Julius Heiser's hand, and climbed into the sedan and drove to the office of James Heiser. He walked into the building and read the marquis. He quickly found James Heiser's name, plus the words *financial planner* alongside of it. He took the elevator up to the third floor and walked into the plush-looking office. A pretty, slender brunette behind a glass topped desk looked up at him.

"May I help you?"

"I want to see James Heiser."

"Do you have an appointment?"

"Yes….right here." Morrow showed her his badge.

Stricken, she quickly got up and went through the door behind her desk. She returned promptly and told Morrow that Mister Heiser would see him now.

James Heiser, a replica of his brother Julius, stood behind a mahogany and glass desk, twice the size of the one in the front office. He immediately extended his hand to Morrow and needlessly introduced himself.

"What can I do for you….Agent….?"

"Morrow. Agent Tom Morrow. I'll get right to the

point. Have you been out to your family cottage within the past two weeks?"

"N-no......yes. I was. I went there to make sure the furnace was working. Why? Any laws broken?"

Morrow instinctively did not like this brother. There was something shady about him.

"No.....hopefully not. We're investigating a kidnapping and we have reason to believe the little girl may have been taken to that area. The neighbor said she saw you out there....and we were just making sure it was you she saw."

Morrow saw something flicker in Heiser's eye, but was not sure what it was.

"So why investigate our family's cottage?"

"It's not the cottage...it's those red bushes. The little girl mentioned them to her mother in one of the phone calls."

"Oh.....those things are everywhere out there. I remember when everybody bought them. Some guy in a horse-drawn cart went around selling them. If you bought them, he came back and planted them for you. I was about ten at the time. So....Agent Morrow....if there is nothing else....I have work to do."

He opened up a folder that was sitting on the middle of his desk, giving Morrow the signal that he was dismissed. Morrow hesitated long enough to set his card on the desk.

"The little girl....got scratched on those bushes. The kidnapper says it's infected. She's very sick....and could die. If that happens.....I'll take the kidnapper and anybody who is an accessory....down. Make sure they all go away for a long time. Have a nice day."

Morrow nodded and left the office of James Heiser. He stopped and smiled at the receptionist on his way out, handing her his card. In the car, Morrow stared straight ahead. "I wonder why he is lying....." he said into the rear view mirror.

38

NICK AND RICKY were frustrated and disappointed as they pulled into the driveway on Carlisle Street.

"What is it that we're missing?" Ricky asked Nick.

"I don't know….but it's something. She's there, Rick…. I feel it, too."

"But where? Nothing jumped out at me. We should have taken the blood-hound…Lindy, I mean."

"We can't risk it. She's too emotional. That can be dangerous."

"Yeah….I guess. But she would know, Uncle Nick. She would find her."

Nick sighed.

"Let's just go in. I don't think it would be a good idea to take her out there again. Her emotions are too fragile right now. You're not doing too well either. I'm starving…. how about you?"

"Yeah….I could eat something. We have plenty of food in the fridge. Let's heat some up."

They walked into a house full of cooking aromas. Liz,

Angie, Diane, and Renee were all cooking food. Lindy was lying down, they told Ricky.

"I would suggest you go join her before you fall down. You look exhausted." Liz observed aloud.

"Yeah....maybe I will," Ricky conceded. "Call me when the food is ready. I'm hungry."

Lindy was sound asleep when Ricky went into the bedroom. He kicked his shoes off and curled up beside her, draping an arm over her. She didn't stir, and he quickly fell asleep.

They slept fitfully for another half hour, awakening at the same time. Lindy stared deeply into Ricky's eyes.

"Nothing?"

"Nothing. I know we're all missing something.....but what?"

Lindy stared at the ceiling for a moment before she answered.

"I don't know. We need to clear our minds and let them drift. We'll get it if we do."

"Yeah, tonight when we go to bed....let's try it. Are you hungry at all? Because I'm starving."

"Let's get up then. I think I just heard someone come in the front door."

Morrow returned from his investigation just as Lindy and Ricky awakened. He went directly to the family room and consulted with his partner.

"Jack, that James Heiser is lying about something."

"What do you think he's lying about?"

"I don't know. Julius, the other brother was straight up with me, but James....I don't know....I didn't get good vibes from him. There's something he's not telling. It's the gut talking again."

"So you think he knows something about Sutter?"

"Yeah...but what?"

"It'll come to you. Clear your mind."

Ricky and Lindy entered the family room in time to hear Daily tell him that. When they woke up and went to the kitchen Nick told them that Morrow had been out and had just returned, so they immediately went to see what he had been up to. They stared at Morrow, silently questioning him.

"I can't tell you anything yet....but give me some time. My gut instinct is working just like your intuition, Lindy. Like I told you before.....I know you're right. Give me some time to sort it out....okay?"

Lindy nodded, and she and Ricky turned resignedly toward the doorway.

"We'll bring you some dinner in a minute." Lindy said over her shoulder.

When they were out of earshot, she turned to Ricky and whispered to him.

"He believes us. He just has to find the right.... whatever...to prove us right. He can't go busting in through any doors unless he has concrete evidence that Nelson Sutter is behind one of them. The important thing is that he believes us."

"Yeah, maybe....but there's still something....something we're not getting. We're overlooking something.....and we have to figure out what it is. Getting Sammie back may depend on it."

"Let's try to remember everything....from the start of this...up until now. We can do that tonight when we're alone."

They joined everyone at the table for dinner.

Throughout the meal Lindy and Ricky were relatively quiet, concentrating on what it was they had to remember. Lindy pushed her food around her plate and occasionally put a forkful to her mouth, but then set the fork back down again. Liz watched her as she sat there, vowing to make her another milkshake after dinner.

"Where's Michael, Ricky?" Lindy asked.

"Shawna has him in his room. She's playing some game with him."

"Oh….has he eaten?"

"Yeah, Honey…..Renee and I fed him earlier. He's been bathed and he's ready for bed," Liz told her.

"God…..I'm being such a terrible mother to him."

"Honey….you can't help it…..and besides, do you want him to feel your anxiety?"

"No….I guess not…..but I need to see him."

"I'll go get him for you. Stay right there."

Liz was gone and back in seconds with Michael in her arms. She handed him to Lindy.

"Mommy missed you, Sweetheart." Lindy kissed his cheek.

"I miss-ed you too, Mommy." Michael smiled and wrapped his arms around her neck.

"Did you have fun with Aunt Shawna and Aunt Ally?"

"Yeah! We slept in a tent! And we ate cookies and drank stuff."

"What kind of stuff?"

"Tell her beer," Shawna interjected.

"Beer."

"No you didn't…..what did you drink?"

"Cherry soda."

"Okay." Lindy smiled at him and hugged him tighter. "I love you all the way to the moon and the stars.....and back."

Michael smiled and then spotted Ricky standing at the doorway.

"Daddy! Mommy loves me.......say it, mommy."

"You say it with me....okay?"

"I..."

"I..." Michael repeated.

"Love you...."

"Yuv you..."

"All the way..."

"All da way..."

"To the.........."

"Moon...." Michael answered.

"And the...."

"Tars...." He quoted.

"And...." Lindy led.

"Back," Michael finished with a smile.

Lindy hugged him as everybody applauded. Tears sprang into Lindy's eyes as she hugged him. Ricky saw them and reacted quickly.

"Don't I get to hug my little guy?" He asked as he reached for Michael.

"You have to say it, too, daddy."

"Okay.....I love you all the way to the moon and the stars and back.....and I love Sammie that much....and mommy that much, too. Did I do good?"

"Uh-huh. I yuv you, daddy."

Ricky shook his head and blinked his eyes a couple of times. He looked at Liz and smiled.

317

"Do you know how beautiful those words are to me?" He asked her.

"Yes….I do." Liz smiled at him. "I see it in your eyes."

"So….Lindy….what makes you think I didn't feed Michael beer?" Shawna teased.

"Because….I may be little….but you know that if you did….I would beat your…*ass*." She mouthed the last word so Michael didn't hear it.

Shawna burst out laughing

"You know, girl friend….I think you would when it comes to your kids."

Everyone chuckled over Shawna's remark, but nobody doubted it. Lindy would go to any length to protect her children.

Silence came with the ringing of the telephone. Lindy and Ricky ran to the family room to answer. Morrow sat poised and told Ricky to answer it. When Ricky said his greeting Sutter started right in.

"You have everything together? The money and the antibiotics?"

"Yes."

"Is everything in the gym bag?"

"Yes."

"All five million dollars fit into it?"

"We got the biggest one and filled it and then tucked the rest into the side pockets of it."

"You know I'm going to count it all out before you get Samantha back, don't you?"

"I figured as much."

"Good. We understand each other."

"Not really."

"Doesn't matter. Just be ready. You may have your daughter back tomorrow night.....if you do as you're told and everything works out. Understood?"

"Yes."

"Good. Tomorrow."

Nelson hung up abruptly, and Ricky let the air out of his lungs. Running his hand over his face and into his hair, he stared over at Lindy. He saw the hope in her eyes again and he reached for her hand and held it.

"Damn it...it was so hard to be that polite to him. I just didn't....want to....you know...piss him off and have him say forget it.....you know what I mean?"

"Yes....I do. It's the same reason why I haven't yelled into the phone, 'Nelson, you bastard'.

Ricky started laughing and hugged Lindy.

"I love it when my wife uses profanity. It's so....cute." He said to both agents.

"I take it she doesn't use language like that."

"Never did. Right, Babe?"

Lindy just smiled and nodded. Morrow stared at both of them for a moment.

"It sounds like he's planning the drop tomorrow. Are you ready?"

"I think....except we don't know who he wants to make the drop and where or when."

"Just be ready...like he said. Get a good night's sleep and get up early and be ready. The bag is all ready to go...you just need to grab it and go. See you both in the morning."

Morrow smiled at them reassuringly before they walked out of the family room. In the kitchen everyone was quiet and subdued, just waiting to hear about the call.

"It sounds like it happens tomorrow," Ricky informed everyone.

All eyes darted back and forth, not knowing if this was good news or should they be even more frightened than they already were. The air was thick with apprehension. Ricky snapped open his cell phone, walked into the living room, and called Lindy's brother, Chris.

"Chris, I know you have school tomorrow....but I think we're going to need you."

"No problem, Rick....let me call my principal and tell him....tell him what?"

"The drop is tomorrow. I think I want you with me tomorrow.....and Chris...."

Ricky walked to the furthest point of the room and lowered his voice. "Bring all your military training with you."

"You got it, Rick. How about I come over after I talk to my principal and maybe stay all night?"

"Good idea."

Ricky returned to the kitchen and informed everyone that Chris was coming over to spend the night.

39

Lindy and Ricky tried to sleep, but both of them tossed and turned all night long. They finally gave up and got up at four o'clock and went to the kitchen to make tea. Chris was sitting in the dark at the kitchen table.

"Couldn't sleep?"

"No….we tried, but….."

"Yeah, me too."

"So Rick….what's the plan?"

"Don't know yet. We don't know what he's planning. But I can tell you this…."

Ricky looked over at the family room door to see that it was closed before he continued.

"We're acting…okay? Fuck caution….we're going after my daughter. As soon as we're positive that she is in one of those houses we're going for it. The FBI hasn't done shit."

"How are you going to know if she is in one of the houses?"

"Lindy and I are missing something. We're trying to

think about what it is. As soon as we figure it out we'll know."

"So....how do you figure it out?"

"We have to go over every phone call. There is a clue in there somewhere. We have to remember everything that was said, and then we have to remember our drive out there. Something has to stand out. Our emotions and our nerves have been rubbed raw....that's why we can't remember. We're going to concentrate on everything right after we have a cup of tea. Stand by."

"Okay....ready and waiting. I'd love to have a piece of that son-of-a-bitch."

"Sorry, Chris....but if there's a chance, he's all mine."

"Understood."

"Ricky, don't do anything that's going to...hurt us. You know what I mean."

"Don't worry...I just want him to remember why he shouldn't have fucked with us....that's all."

While they were talking the kettle started to whistle. Ricky got up and poured water into their cups that already held teabags. He got out the cream for Lindy's tea and the sugar, and added them to their cups, setting Lindy's in front of her. Before sitting down he made sure Chris didn't want any.

"No....I'm good with this stale coffee. I like strong, stale coffee. Anyway.....I'm always so in awe of how you know exactly how to fix Lindy's tea, coffee, or anything else she consumes."

Ricky smiled and reached for Lindy's hand.

"I know my woman....that's all. After all, we practically grew up together. We've been together for more than half a lifetime....right, Babe?"

Even though Lindy smiled and nodded, Ricky could see she was deep in thought and that her nerves were on edge. He studied her for a few moments before he said anything.

"Babe, let's start from the first minute that we discovered Samantha missing…from the first phone call."

"That's where I am right now…..the first phone call. There is nothing in that call that helps. I've gone over it and over it. It's time to move on to the second call. That is when we talked to Samantha for the first time. They were going to have fun, she said. She was on vacation and she called him John."

"Okay….I don't think there was anything significant in those two phone calls, do you?"

Lindy shook her head and then rested it on the kitchen table, enjoying the coolness of it on her cheek. She closed her eyes and tried to get a mental picture of Samantha talking to her on the phone.

"Lindy, it's six-thirty. I'm going to go get a shower. We don't know which of us he wants to make the drop so I think we both should be ready. I'll put a pot of coffee on first."

Lindy nodded without opening her eyes or lifting her head. Ricky quickly got the coffee pot ready and stopped to pat Lindy's head before he ran down the hallway to take his shower. Lindy jumped when Chris spoke to her.

"Try to stay calm and focused, Pumpkin. I know how hard this is for you."

"I just hope he doesn't play any more games with us. Just take the freaking money and return our daughter…. that's what I want him to do. I don't care if they catch him, or if he gets away….I just want Sammie back home."

She got up to get cups out for the coffee that was almost ready and reached into the refrigerator for the cream. When the coffee pot stopped brewing, Lindy poured coffee into a cup for Chris and then for herself, adding cream to hers. She listened to hear if the shower water was still running. Because she could still hear the water running she didn't pour Ricky's coffee, but carried hers and Chris's to the table and sat down with him.

"Nick's right."

"About what?" Lindy asked her brother.

"When you are sad it looks like the lights are out. You are always so full of sunshine and light, but now….all that light is gone."

"Is that that Uncle Nick said?"

"Uh-huh."

Lindy sat there looking amused. She loved Uncle Nick and she knew that he loved her. Remembering the past, she knew that Nick observed her during troubled times. She remembered him watching her closely when Nicholas died, and then again when Ricky was arrested and charged with Carrie's murder. Nick was there for her, always watching her to make sure she was okay. She guessed that if anyone could make a fair assessment of how things affected her, it would be Nick.

She heard the water in the shower go off, and got up to pour Ricky's coffee. He came into the kitchen looking damp from his shower, but he also looked refreshed. Lindy handed him his cup, quickly kissed him, and went down the hall to take her shower. As she passed Michael's room, she heard him singing in his bed.

Dressed in running pants and a tee-shirt, Lindy returned to the kitchen after her shower. In the time she spent in the shower, Ricky had gotten Michael up and he was sitting in his booster seat at the table, eating oatmeal. It was seven-ten AM. Chris went to take a shower in the main bathroom while Ricky and Lindy spent some time with Michael. At seven-twenty-five Liz and Nick showed up, along with Sam and Renee.

"We thought it might be a good idea to be on standby in case you needed someone to watch Michael....or anything." Liz told them.

At exactly seven-thirty the telephone rang. Lindy felt her heart leap to her throat as she stared at Ricky for a fleeting second. They ran to the family room. Morrow was standing there directing Ricky to answer the phone.

"Hello?"

"Got everything ready?"

"Yes."

"Good. Put your wife on."

Ricky handed the telephone receiver to Lindy.

"H-hello?" Lindy spoke breathlessly into the phone.

"Are you ready?"

"Me?"

"Yeah, you. You're going to make the drop."

"W-why me?"

"Because I said so. Now....are you ready for your instructions?"

"Y-yes.....I'm ready."

"The money and the antibiotics should already be in the gym bag....make sure it's all there and all hidden. Got it?"

"Yes."

"Take the bag to Washington High school....go through the side entrance on the south side of the building....it's marked......to the girls' locker room in the gym...put the bag into locker Y-26 and leave the same way you came out. Go straight home right away. You only have twenty minutes to get there and back out again. So go now....don't waste any time. I'll be watching. Come alone. If anyone else comes with you....no deal. Got that?"

"Yes. When will I get Samantha back?"

"As soon as I have the money counted I'll call you to tell you where to find her. You only have nineteen minutes left. Better hurry."

"I'm going now."

Lindy hung up and stared at Morrow.

"I have to go....now. Where is the bag?"

Morrow handed her the gym bag after retrieving it from the closet where he had put it earlier in the morning. She struggled with the weight of it. Five million dollars was a lot heavier than she thought.

"I have to go alone. Please don't follow me. He said the deal would be off if anybody was with me."

"Don't worry, Lindy....he won't see anybody with you. Just go."

Ricky was standing in the doorway, holding Michael. Lindy brushed past him, quickly kissing his cheek and then kissing Michael's cheek.

"Lindy!" Ricky called to her.

She stopped and turned around. Their eyes connected and she felt the strength building inside of her.

"Be careful, Baby....I love you."

"I love you, too....and I *will* be careful."

Ricky watched Lindy start the Toyota and quickly pull out of the driveway. He watched as she sped up the road, accelerating immediately over the speed limit. Chris sidled up to Ricky and watched, too.

"Should we be letting her go alone?" Chris asked Ricky.

"Asshole said if he saw anybody with her the deal would be off. And besides, she's not alone. There goes a car full of Feds right behind her."

40

LINDY ENTERED THE school via the door Nelson had designated. The corridor was still dark. She followed it down until she came to what she knew was the girls' locker room and tried the door. It moved soundlessly and effortlessly as she pulled it outward. Standing there looking into the darkened locker room, Lindy felt the hairs on the back of her neck stand up. She quickly turned around expecting to come face to face with Nelson Sutter. There was nobody there. Expelling the air from her lungs, she turned toward the darkened locker room again and, shifting the heavy gym duffel bag laden with five million dollars, she slipped inside the door, letting it fall closed behind her. The room was black. She pulled her keys out of her pocket and felt for the little penlight flashlight she always kept on the key ring. Nothing happened when she clicked it on. She shook it and out came a yellow beam of light, enough for her to see the numbered lockers. She prayed that the light would stay on until she found the locker she was looking for. Checking the numbers and letters on the sides of the lockers, she quickly found the

Y-section. Moving along she found locker Y-26 and tried the door. It was unlocked. She forced the gym bag into the locker, shut the door, and all but ran toward the exit of the locker room. She quickly slid through the large double doors and ran down the hall out the door she came through. As she exited the south door, she saw the first of the school buses coming up the hill. The lights began to come on inside the school and the teacher's parking lot was filling up. She looked around but saw no other cars. She instinctively knew that the FBI had followed her, but where were they? She also noted that there was no gray Ford Taurus around either.

Lindy eased her car around the newly arrived busses and a couple of cars that were dropping students off at the curb. She immediately left the school grounds, made a left, and drove as fast as the traffic would allow back to her house.

Ricky was holding Michael and pacing the floor when he heard her car pull in. He quickly moved to the door and held it for her. She was trembling as she fell against him. Chris immediately took Michael from him so that Ricky could hold Lindy. It was eight-twenty AM.

"So…now what?"

"We wait, I guess. I don't know what else to do. Where's Morrow and Daily?"

"They're going over the tapes again. The phone calls….. everything."

"We should listen to them too, Ricky."

"They said we could after they hear them all. They're listening for background noises….things like that. The ones they sent to the bureau didn't turn up much to go on. So tell me about the drop off. Did you see anything?"

"No….but I felt something. The hairs on the back of my neck stood up and I thought Nelson was going to be right behind me when I turned around. He wasn't, so I guess it was just jitters. My knees are still quivering. Let's go see Morrow and then go sit with our family. They're still in the kitchen?"

"Yeah, I made them some pancakes for breakfast. Michael ate a couple of them, too, even after the oatmeal. I saved you some if you want them."

"You know I can't eat. Did Chris eat?"

"No….that must be a family thing with you. When you're upset or nervous neither one of you eat. My family has always been just the opposite. Stress makes them all hungry."

"Yeah….I've heard your mother. EAT! EAT! It will calm you down!"

Ricky started sniggering. He knew Lindy was right about that. He followed her into the kitchen and watched as she hugged everyone, and then followed her into the family room.

"Did everything go okay?" Morrow asked her.

"Yeah, but you should know that already. There was a carload of agents following me all the way."

"Yeah….well….the chaos that broke out at the school kind of…..messed things up. They lost him."

"Chaos? What chaos?"

"Well…Sutter is sharper than we gave him credit for."

Lindy stared at Agent Morrow, waiting for him to continue. Ricky and Chris flanked Lindy and Morrow saw them tense up. He began his narration of the events that followed the drop.

331

41

NELSON WATCHED LINDY leave the school from the corner
of the window he had been watching her through. He saw
the light from the door move rather than actually see her
go out through it. As the lights in the corridors came on
and students began making their way to their classrooms
Nelson, wearing a long brunette wig, unlocked the janitor's
door and slipped through it. He slipped across the hall
and into the girls' locker room and made his way to the Y-
section of the lockers. He opened Y-26 and there was the
gym-duffel bag. Lindy had stuffed it into the locker so it
was jammed in there. He tugged and pulled several times
before he got it out. He could hear movement coming
from the far end of the locker room. Feds. He could smell
them. Quickly and noiselessly, he made his way toward the
double doors of the locker room. Just as quickly he pulled
out a smoke bomb from the deep pockets of his jacket.
He lit it and threw it in the direction of the noises he had
heard, and then pulled the fire alarm beside the doors. He
ran out of the locker room and tossed another smoke bomb
into the hallway before slipping back into the janitor's

room. Students were running in all directions, screaming before he went through the janitor's door, clutching the gym bag. He locked it behind him and ran down the stairs toward the tunnel.

The two federal agents ran from behind the gymnasium doors into the locker room and were overcome by smoke. The other two agents were overcome by smoke in the hallway. None of the four actually saw Nelson Sutter or knew which direction he had gone. The students were overcome by smoke and panic and had not paid any attention to the strange looking man in the brunette wig.

Nelson ran down the stairs and into the tunnel. Moving at a reasonable pace, Nelson quickly made his way back through the tunnel and into the daylight at the other end. His car was sitting there waiting, just as he had left it. Throwing the gym bag into the trunk, he jumped into the front seat and quickly, but cautiously, drove away, keeping to the back roads that he had grown to know so well. He was pulling into the driveway at the cottage by eight-thirty-five, just fifteen minutes after Lindy pulled into her driveway. Quickly, he shut the garage and then opened the trunk. He smiled at the gym bag and then lifted it out of the trunk. Dropping it on the kitchen table, he moved toward the living area to check on Samantha. She was sleeping right where he left her.

After pouring himself a cup of coffee, he sat down and opened the bag. There it was. Stacks and stacks of bills. Before he started counting it he looked for the antibiotics. They were there. He read the label and then took out a bottle of juice from the refrigerator. Samantha had to wake up so she could take the tablets, so he poured her a glass of the juice, went to the loveseat and proceeded to wake her up. As usual, Samantha was cooperative, and she quickly took both pills, swallowed them with the juice, and then quickly went back to sleep. The label said every four hours, so he would give her more at twelve-thirty. They had to leave by three o'clock in order to get checked in and ready for the flight to leave at five o'clock. He wanted to leave earlier than that, but the pilot wouldn't budge on the time.

Samantha went back to sleeping peacefully so that left Nelson with the time to count the money. He began counting but soon realized that he would need pencil and paper to help him keep track. He kept forgetting which thousand he was on. He began stacking the bundled money into piles of ten thousands, and then began writing down the figures. He got halfway through it and just gave up. It was more than he could keep track of, so he had to assume it was the right amount. He began counting out the amount to pay for the flight. Twenty thousand seemed like a lot of money, but he wasn't in a position to bargain. If that was what the guy wanted, so be it. That was his ticket out of the country. Twenty thousand didn't even make a dent in the volumes of cash he still had sitting on the table. He counted out another twenty thousand for expenses. That would cover meals and taxis once he got to Brazil. It was all going to work out. He was on his way to freedom and happiness. Happiness like he had never known. He had a daughter that loved him and cared about him. Samantha—his daughter. He liked how it sounded.

To make the time go faster he began cleaning up the kitchen. Once all the dishes were done and put away and the counters were wiped off, he went to the bedroom to get the suitcases together. After zipping them shut he carried them to the garage and put them into the back seat. He returned to the kitchen and got the paperwork out. He tucked the passports and documents into his jacket pocket so that they would be easily reached for when needed. One more thing went into his pocket—a hand gun. All he had to do now was wait. He glanced at the clock and decided to give Samantha another dose of antibiotics. It was twelve-fifteen.

Samantha was awake and staring at the television when he entered the living area. The episode at the school was being shown on the twelve o'clock news.

"Look at all that smoke, John. The school is on fire."

"Yeah, that's really something. How are you feeling?"

"A little better."

"Good….because we're going on the airplane soon."

"Really? Mommy and Daddy and Michael, too?"

"Yep. They'll be there."

Samantha smiled at him, and he couldn't help but smile back at her.

"When are we going?"

"In three hours. So….I made you a sandwich if you want to eat. Do you like ham and cheese sandwiches?"

"Uh-huh."

"Good…I'll get it out for you. You can eat and then take another little nap and maybe feel even better….. okay?"

"Okay."

Nelson got the sandwiches that he had made earlier out of the refrigerator. Carrying the sandwiches into the living area in one hand and two glasses of soda in the other, he set them down on the table in front of Samantha.

"This is like a picnic....right?"

"Yes....but no ants," he responded.

Samantha laughed and then bit into her sandwich. She smiled at him again and then told him the sandwich was good.

"That's because I put potato chips on the sandwich."

"You did?"

"Yeah....that's how I like mine."

"Well....me, too. I like them that way, too."

"So....that's the way we eat them from now on...okay?"

"Yes....okay." Samantha grinned at him.

After eating the entire sandwich, Samantha asked to watch a movie. Nelson was thankful that she seemed to be feeling better. He selected 'Babe' out of the stack of videos and put it in for her. While she was engrossed in the movie he put away the rest of the money and cleaned up the rest of the dishes. He checked on Samantha afterward and found her to be sleeping again. Good. Sleep heals. She seemed to be so much better after the antibiotics were in her.

42

LINDY AND RICKY listened to the story Morrow told them.

"So....he got away? With the money?" Lindy asked.

"That's the size of it."

"And you call *him* a bungler?"

"We didn't foresee the smoke bombs."

"But he foresaw them as something to deter the FBI..... nice work, agents."

Morrow didn't answer her. He knew what she was thinking about the bureau at this moment. Her child's kidnapper has five million dollars and she doesn't have her child, nor does she know where the child is. It looked to her like the FBI flubbed it—and they had—badly.

"I'm going to get some breakfast and then go lie down....to think."

She turned away and walked out toward the kitchen where Liz, Nick, Sam, Renee, and Chris were waiting for her. Ricky followed her, carrying Michael in his arms.

"Want me to make you some breakfast, Babe?"

"Can you just heat up those pancakes, Ricky? We have

to think. The FBI messed up....they messed it up real bad. Ricky.....I think it's going to have to be up to us now."

"Kids....don't do anything foolish," Nick warned, the alarm clear in his voice.

"Uncle Nick....we're Lindy and Ricky.....and together we can do anything. We made a mistake letting the FBI handle this...now it's our turn."

Ricky set the warmed pancakes, butter, and warmed syrup down in front of her.

"That's my girl. Good thinking. Now all we have to do is think about what we know. We know something and we just have to pull it to the surface. It's something obvious.... that's why we missed it."

Lindy ate the pancakes, drank another cup of coffee, and announced that she was going to lie down....to think. Nick saw a look of determination on her face as she got up from the table. They watched her walk toward the bedroom to go lie down. When she was out of earshot, Liz spoke up.

"She's different somehow. She seems.....stronger.... or..."

"Determined?" Nick offered.

"Yes....determined....that's it. I guess she's through playing with the FBI."

"I know I am," Ricky growled.

Chris glanced up at the clock. The hands showed that it was eleven o'clock. 'How long does it take to count five million dollars?' he wondered to himself.

Liz and Renee stood up, both of them having the same thought.

"I think maybe I'll do the dusting and vacuuming while

she's resting. I can't sit here and do nothing any longer." Liz confided.

"I was thinking the same thing. This floor could stand to be cleaned. With everybody congregating in here it hasn't gotten done. Sam, why don't you and Nick take Michael to the park? Keep your cell phones on, just in case."

"Not a bad idea. Michael? Want to go to the park?"

"Yeah! And go on the swings!"

"You bet. Ready, Nick?"

Liz and Renee watched them walk out with Michael in tow. Liz turned to Ricky and Chris.

"You two…..go lie down. You both look like you're going to fall over."

"Yeah, well…..we didn't sleep much last night. I think I'm going to go lie down with Lindy. We need to go over everything together. Chris, you too. I think you need some rest…….I may be needing you later."

"I'll go lie on Sammie's bed."

With everyone out of the way, Liz and Renee got busy cleaning. Ricky stretched out beside Lindy as she stared at the ceiling.

"What are we missing?" She asked him as she continued to stare at the ceiling.

"I don't know. Let's let our minds drift as we think about everything," Ricky answered with a sigh.

They linked their fingers together and dozed off, both still staring at the ceiling before they closed their eyes.

···

Lindy jerked awake and jumped up. She stared at the alarm clock beside the bed. It was two-ten—the exact

341

time she awoke the night that Sammie disappeared, but it was PM—not AM this time. Ricky was stirring as she stood up.

"What time is it?" he asked her.

"Two-ten in the afternoon. My God, Ricky....we slept all day. We have to get moving....but get moving to where? It may be too late to get Sammie back.....Oh, *God*. No phone call either. Oh, *God*, Ricky."

Lindy ran out of the room quickly, and Ricky was right behind her. She stopped and leaned her head against the wall in the hallway. 'Think, Lindy! Think!' she said to herself. She jumped when the front door opened. Sam, Nick, and a laughing Michael came through the door.

"Mommy! We went to yunch!"

Michael ran to Lindy and she automatically picked him up.

"Where did you go to lunch?"

"McDonald's!"

"Yeah? What did you have?"

"A happy meal! I got a toy!"

"Well, let's see it."

Michael showed Lindy the toy he got with his happy meal and Lindy inspected it for any possible danger to him. It appeared safe, so she handed it back. With Michael in her arms, she went into the kitchen and sat down with him.

"We went to the park......and I went on the swing! Uncle Nick and Uncle Sam pushed me!"

"Wow! That sounds like fun. You went on the...... swing.....*swing*.....Ricky! *That's it*! *Swing*! Michael, *thank you*! Thank you, Honey!! **Ricky!!**"

Ricky ran into the kitchen.

"*What? What is it?*" He stared at Lindy.

"*Swing*! I heard Nelson tell Sammie to hang up so she could go on the *swing*! Ricky…..that last house….the one that was supposed to be vacant…..had a *swing* hanging from the tree. How many ninety year old men do you know would swing on a swing?"

"The swing in the front yard of the vacant house….that had smoke coming from the chimney……..*let's go*, Baby…. let's go get our daughter back! Chris! You drive! Your car's the fastest."

"I just hope we're not too late," Lindy whispered to herself. She handed Michael off to Liz as the three of them ran out the door.

Just as Chris swung out of the driveway and headed toward the highway, Morrow's cell phone rang.

"Morrow," he answered.

"This is Jim Heiser."

"Yeah? What's up?"

"Well….look….I don't want to go to jail…or anything….but….I rented that cottage out for the month. I'm not supposed to, according to the estate rules….but I couldn't see leaving it empty all the time. Anyway…. I rented it to a guy named John Nelson. I didn't know anything about a kid. The guy said he was coming away from a bad marriage and a worse divorce and needed a quiet place to think. I couldn't see the harm in renting it to him. He's still there….but he's leaving soon. He called me to tell me he would leave the key under the mat. I wouldn't have even thought anything except I could hear a Disney movie playing in the background. Now….unless the guy is weird…….."

Morrow snapped his cell phone shut, hanging up on

James Heiser. He opened it again to make a call, and then shut it again.

"Jack, let's go! The DeCelli's were right all along. Let's get out there to that cottage. Call the others on the way. We can still salvage this case."

Morrow was not aware that Ricky, Lindy, and Chris were already on their way to the cottage.

43

Nelson waited for Samantha to come out of the bathroom wearing her new outfit. The dress was lilac with a full skirt. Petticoats were attached to the underside of the skirt, making the skirt puff out. Nelson had purchased shoes to match the dress, lilac with faux diamond stones across the tops of the shoes. He thought enough to get a pair of white socks with lace trim. She was going to look adorable! He wasn't even sure why he had purchased the dress and shoes. He had no intention of taking her with him when he formulated his plan to take her out of the DeCelli's house. 'Maybe I planned on taking her with me all along, but just didn't realize it,' he thought with a smile. He heard the bathroom door open and he waited for her to come out. She was favoring the leg that held the scratch. John was still worried about the scratch, because even though her fever seemed to go down, the red line seemed to be getting longer. It was obviously traveling up her leg. He knew he still needed to seek medical attention for her when they landed in Brazil. As for right now she was a vision standing in front of him.

"You look beautiful!" he exclaimed.

Samantha beamed at him.

"This dress is beautiful, John! Thank you!"

"You're welcome! You're going to be the prettiest little girl on the plane."

Again, Samantha beamed.

"And Michael will be the handsomest boy on the plane."

"Uh-huh."

"Did you call them? Are they ready to go?" She wanted to know.

"Sure did. They're getting ready to leave right now.... so we better get going, too....okay?"

Nelson glanced at his watch. It was two-fifty-five—time to go. He looked around for the key, but couldn't find it.

"Where did I put that key?" he muttered to himself. "Samantha, have you seen the key to the house?"

"No, I haven't seen it," She answered.

"Oh, well.....I'll just leave the door unlocked then. Nobody will come in here."

'And if they do, who cares? It's not my house,' he rationalized to himself, but as an afterthought, called Jim Heiser to tell him the key would be under the mat.

He glanced at his watch. Exactly three o'clock.

"Ready, Samantha?"

"Yes, John....I'm ready."

He smiled to himself as he led her out through the garage door and helped her into the backseat with the luggage, strapping her in the seat with the seat belt. He started the car and opened the garage door, and then got behind the wheel. Slowly, he backed out, stopped the car, and got out to close the garage door. He swung the car into the yard in order to turn it around to face out toward the road. The tires spun as he stepped on the gas. He tried it again, and they spun again. He gunned the engine and the tires caught on the gravel on the driveway as the car shot forward. Taking his foot off the gas momentarily, he let the car drift forward until he was sure he was on solid ground. He pulled out of the driveway and made a right to go around the loop to the main road. He checked his watch—three-ten. They were on their way.

44

"Next exit."

Ricky kept his arms around Lindy as he directed Chris. He could feel her body trembling as he held her. He tightened his grip to give her reassurance that everything would be okay, which was something he wasn't so sure of any more.

"Right, and then another right," he instructed.

He remembered the day that he and Lindy came out this way just to look around. They had been right then, but had listened to the FBI. He leaned his head on top of Lindy's to stifle a sob that was threatening to emerge from his throat. Lindy didn't want to go back that day. She knew their daughter was there. She knew, and he should have listened to her. The FBI may have cost them their child.

"Straight, and then slow down."

"There's the house….with the swing," Lindy pointed to the small cottage.

Chris drove past and then parked the car on the side of the road. They jumped out, running toward the house.

Ricky reached the door first. He knocked but got no response. He tried the doorknob and found that the door was unlocked. They rushed into what was obviously the kitchen area. Lindy ran down the short hall.

"Sammie? Sammie! Are you here, Baby? Mommy's here!"

No one responded. Lindy looked into the bathroom and spotted the pajamas Samantha had left behind when she changed into her dress. Lindy was blinded by tears as she stooped to pick them up off of the floor. She turned from the bathroom as she held them.

"Oh…..oh, God!" was all she could say.

A noise very close to a dying kitten escaped her lips as she walked the short walk down the hall. Ricky was rifling through some papers in the trash and Chris was looking through papers on the table in the living room. Ricky looked up when he heard the pained noises coming from Lindy. He was about to reach out for her when the door burst open. The room filled with Federal Agents.

"Don't touch anything!" Morrow shouted at them. "You'll bungle the crime scene!"

"Like the FBI bungled the crime?" Ricky retorted.

"See? This was never a five year old child to you! It was a crime….a crime for you to solve! Like a game of Clue! You never cared about Samantha!" Lindy shrieked at them.

Morrow stopped and stared at Lindy, not knowing how to answer her. He didn't have an answer for her. He glanced at what she held in her hands and realized that she was holding her daughter's pajamas. He felt her pain.

Ricky looked down at the paper he was holding. As his

eyes focused on the writing, he began to comprehend what he was reading. He grabbed Lindy and called to Chris.

"Let's go!"

Both Lindy and Chris immediately understood that Ricky knew something. They started out the door and Morrow called to them.

"Hey! Where are you going?"

"To get our daughter!" Ricky yelled back over his shoulder.

The three of them ran to the car, thankful that they hadn't pulled into the driveway to be blocked by the FBI sedans. They jumped in and Chris started the car.

"Where to?"

"County Airport. He has a flight chartered for five o'clock. What time is it?"

"Three-thirty. We must have just missed him."

Their faces were grim as they rode in silence. Chris pushed his Camaro to the very top of the speed limit, dangerously close to being stopped by a trooper if there were one along the highway. They couldn't take that chance.

•••

The cottage was being turned upside down for clues to the kidnapping. Morrow picked up the paper Ricky had been holding and read it.

"Sutter's on his way to the County Airport….and so are the DeCelli's. Come on…Jack…..you, me, and two more of you….let's go. We need to get there. I don't want to think about what Ricky DeCelli will do to Sutter if he catches up with him."

"Do you blame him?" Jack countered.

"No…but we can't let him break the law either."

The four agents got into the last car in the driveway and Morrow backed it out.

"Which way to the County Airport from here?"

"Make a right….go around the loop and then hit the highway, heading south. It's almost an hour's drive," Jack told him.

"Except Chris Riley drives a Camaro….so you can cut that time down for them."

"Christ…..Jack….give me a cigarette…will ya?"

"Nervous?"

"Yes….Christ, I don't want those two to get hurt."

"You mean you don't want *Lindy* to get hurt."

"What's that supposed to mean?"

"I see how you look at her," Jack chuckled.

"Well….she *is* easy on the eyes," Morrow responded as he lit the cigarette Jack Daily handed to him.

"Yeah…she certainly is."

"Jack…..we didn't handle this one very well. We should have paid attention to her. We should have listened."

"Tom, we can't run an investigation on woman's intuition, for Christ sake."

Well, no…but….mother's instinct is a whole other subject. Lindy is an excellent mother. Very intuitive…..always in tune with the kids. She was right all along, Jack."

"We couldn't have known that though."

"We didn't listen….really listen….to her."

The agents got quiet as Morrow initiated a couple of high-speed turns on the highway. Morrow wondered how far ahead of them the Camaro was.

45

LINDY AND RICKY were holding onto each other for support as Chris maneuvered the turns in the road. Chris checked his watch. It was four o'clock. His jaw tightened as he pushed the pedal a little further down and then relaxed his foot. He was driving too fast. What would be worse than getting stopped by a trooper would be having an accident. He slowed down to just five miles per hour over the speed limit. They were making good time anyway, so he could drive a little more carefully.

"We should be at the airport in about fifteen minutes," Chris told them.

"I just want to get my hands on that piece of shit. Okay, so Chris.....here's what we do. It's up to you to grab Samantha....okay? You have to be fast and efficient. That's why I picked you to be there with me....because of your army training. You may have to grab her out of his arms, or out of his hand. You know how to do that.... right?"

"Yeah....it's my specialty."

"Good. I'll take care of him."

"What do *I* do, Ricky?"

"You will sit out of the way and wait for Chris to bring you our daughter."

"Ricky…"

"Lindy, don't argue about this. He knows you. He probably watched you from somewhere this morning, so he knows very well what you look like now. Besides…you haven't changed since high school. He's only seen me once and he has never seen Chris. I'll be wearing mirrored sunglasses so I'll be harder to recognize. The element of surprise is going to be our best weapon right now…. okay?"

"Okay."

Lindy knew that Ricky was right. If he spotted her at the airport he would run. The three of them were silent for the rest of the drive to the airport. When the airport was in sight Lindy tensed and sat up. Ricky felt as though she were about to jump right out of her skin.

"Remember, Baby….he can't see you. You have to stay behind and wait for Chris to bring you our daughter….. got that? This is our last chance to get her back. Our *only* chance."

Lindy shivered as she agreed. She knew she had to do what Ricky said, but it was going to be hard.

Chris swung the car into the short drive that led to a small parking lot for the patrons of the County Airport. There were only a few cars in the small lot, so Ricky instantly spotted the grey Taurus parked at the far end of the lot.

"There's his car back there."

Lindy and Chris looked in the direction Ricky was pointing, neither of them speaking. Lindy's heart was pounding hard. Chris and Ricky felt the adrenalin start to pump through their veins. Quietly and effortlessly, the three of them got out of the car and approached the main entrance of the airport. Chris peered in through the door while Ricky and Lindy stayed behind it. Nelson was not visible, so Chris stepped inside and looked around. He spotted him—and Samantha—at the vending machines. He was dropping coins into the vending slot and Samantha was retrieving the bounty. Their backs were to him, for which Chris was glad. Maybe Sutter wouldn't know him but Samantha sure would. He backed out of the door and turned around to Ricky and Lindy.

"I see them. They're at the vending machines."

Lindy's heart leaped. Ricky felt the blood rush to his head. They both stood there unable to move. Chris quickly moved to another door and peered through its window. He saw Sutter take Samantha's hand and proceed down the hall toward the terminal. Samantha was limping and she seemed to be having trouble staying up on her feet. He waved Ricky over to the door in which he was staring through the window.

"Let's go in this way. We just follow that hall. It leads to a tunnel that comes out onto the boarding area for the planes. There aren't too many people around so we have to keep a good distance from him at first. We have to be quick to catch him right before he goes through the tunnel. Let's go. Lindy, there is a lounge right inside this door. Go sit there and wait for Samantha. Please, Lindy....don't try to do anything else.....okay?"

Lindy nodded, not trusting herself to speak.

"Ready? Let's go, Rick."

The three of them slid into the inside of the terminal

from the door Chris had been peering through. Ricky waved Lindy toward the small lounge as he and Chris slowly made their way to the hall. They spotted Nelson and Samantha just past the vending machines. Slowly they made their way past the vending machines, following at a safe distance. Samantha was reeling as they proceeded down the hall. Suddenly her knees buckled under her and she slowly slipped to the floor.

"Now!" Chris whispered to Ricky, who caught the signal immediately.

Chris moved like a panther. His long strides quickly covered the distance between him and Nelson. Nelson bent down to help Samantha back up just as Chris struck him just below the elbow, causing him to drop Samantha's hand. Chris shoved him back as he grabbed Samantha around the waist and lifted her into his arms. Nelson took a step toward Chris as he felt the hand bearing down on his shoulder. He turned his head and stared straight into the face of Ricky DeCelli. He gasped.

Chris strode back up the hall with Samantha in his arms. She appeared to be unconscious.

"Come on, Sammie…..Uncle Chris is here. Wake up for me."

He got no response from the little girl he loved so much.

"Mommy is here, Honey. Come on, wake up and see mommy."

There was still no response from her. Lindy, sitting on one of the straight backed chairs in the lounge, was staring at the floor with her fists clutched tightly to the sides of the chair when Chris approached her. She gasped when she saw Samantha.

"Oh…..Sammie…..Baby, wake up. Mommy is here. You're going home with mommy and daddy now. Baby? Please wake up, Sweetheart. Open your eyes."

There was no response from Samantha. Lindy's body was wracked by sobs.

"Ricky? Where's Ricky, Chris?"

"He'll be back. I'm going to go check on him right now. Here, Call Nick and have him alert the hospital that Samantha DeCelli is coming in. Preferential treatment. Wait a minute."

After handing Lindy his cell phone, Chris spied a limo driver standing around looking like he was waiting for something.

"Hey, man….you looking for someone or are you free?"

"I just dropped a guy off….why? Need a limo?"

"We will in about five or ten minutes. See that girl holding the child? That's Missus DeCelli and her daughter Samantha. Watch the news at all?"

Recognition gleamed into the driver's eyes.

"That's the kid that was kidnapped."

"Right. And now she's being returned to the parents. They are going to need a fast ride to the hospital as soon as Mister DeCelli gets back from…..negotiating with the kidnapper. Two hundred dollars be enough for the ride?"

"Yes, sir…..that's plenty."

"Good. Now go help Missus DeCelli."

Chris watched the driver go introduce himself to Lindy and take her hand to help her up. Lindy wouldn't let go of Samantha. He turned and hurried down to see if Ricky needed any help. From the way people were hurrying back up the hall, he figured Ricky was handling things. He spotted them.

•••

When Nelson turned and saw Ricky standing behind him he felt terror go through him. Ricky had gotten a lot bigger than he remembered him, and the boyish look was replaced by a man's face—a man's face showing pure rage. Nelson gasped in surprise. Ricky hit him. Nelson tried to run, but Ricky was fast. He grabbed him by the shirt and hit him again—his fist connecting with Nelson's nose and shattering it. Once more Ricky's fist connected with Nelson's face, only this time his mouth. Nelson felt some of his teeth give way and felt his lip split open. He struggled for air. Ricky hadn't even broken a sweat yet. Nelson felt sheer terror as he began to bargain.

"I didn't hurt Samantha….I swear…..I didn't…"

"*Samantha?* This is for Lindy…..I haven't started on you for Samantha yet."

And with that, Ricky hit him again. He sank to the floor.

"Get up!" Ricky ordered. "Get your ass up off that floor!"

Nelson reached into the inside pocket of his jacket and pulled out the hand gun. Quick as a cat Ricky snatched the gun out of Nelson's hand and threw it.

"This is a fist fight, you moron! Now get *up!*"

He reached for Nelson and pulled him onto his feet and hit him, and hit him, and hit him. All of Ricky's rage was being released. The hall suddenly filled with FBI agents. People were running in the opposite direction and screaming. Ricky tossed Nelson and his body hit the wall and slid to the floor. He went to pull Nelson to his feet when Morrow shouted to him.

"That's enough….Rick…..that's enough."

"No it isn't….I'm not done yet," Ricky retorted.

"Yes, you are….stop…..right now."

Ricky slowly came to his senses and stared down at a bloodied, broken Nelson.

"Don't you *ever* come near any of my family again. Do you hear me?"

Nelson barely nodded but Ricky was satisfied that he got the message. He turned and faced Morrow, staring him square in the eyes.

"There's your kidnapper."

"Rick….I…had to stop you…I hope you know that."

"All I know is that you guys didn't do your jobs. We almost lost our daughter forever because of it. I have to go. Samantha is really sick…..she's unconscious."

"I'll see you at the hospital." Morrow answered.

Ricky nodded as he sprinted back up the hall to where Lindy was waiting, crying.

"Ricky….Uncle Nick and Aunt Liz are meeting us at the hospital. They're bringing Michael with them. Chris has a limo waiting for us to get to the hospital. There are police to give us an escort."

Lindy turned toward the hall and saw the agents leading Nelson up the hall in handcuffs.

"One moment," she uttered to Ricky.

Lindy quickly walked up and stood in front of Nelson. Her hand lashed out and slapped him across the face.

"You *bastard*!"

"I didn't hurt her."

"She's unconscious, you son of a bitch. Let me tell

you this….if Stacey Stockwell were here, she would *loathe* you!"

"Stacey…..what does she have to do with any of this?"

"Stacey Stockwell was my *mother*, you son of a bitch!"

Morrow saw something in Nelson's face when Lindy revealed that. Recognition, regret, and self-pity all fleetingly passed in his eyes.

"I'm sorry," was all he could say.

Ricky came up behind Lindy and took her arm.

"Come on….Baby, I'd stand here and watch you slap him all day long….but we need to get to the hospital. Chris is holding Samantha in the waiting limo."

Lindy nodded and turned. She and Ricky quickly made a beeline for the exit where the limo was waiting. Two motorcycle cops were waiting in front of the car. Lindy and Ricky quickly slipped into the back of the limo, Ricky reaching for Samantha. Chris got out of the limo.

"See you there. I'll drive my own car."

The sirens screamed and the blue and red lights came on as the limo pulled out of the airport parking lot.

"Hear the sirens, Sammie? They're for you. Please open your eyes, Sweetheart." Lindy cried as she brushed hair off of Samantha's forehead.

"Lindy, she's really burning up. Do you think he even gave her the antibiotics?"

"I don't know….all I know is….we could still lose her, Ricky."

Lindy choked on her sobs and leaned her head against Ricky. She felt his body shaking and knew that he was openly crying, too. His voice quivered as he spoke to Samantha.

"Hey, Princess....open your eyes for daddy. Let me see the big baby blues."

They felt the limo slowing down and looked up to see the hospital looming up ahead. It was the very same hospital where Lindy had once fought for her own life. The limo came to a stop and the driver got out and opened their door. Lindy slid out first and took Samantha so Ricky could get out. He took Samantha back into his arms as the driver held the door for them. The two police officers led them through the double doors to the crowded emergency room. A man wearing a doctor's white coat called to them.

"DeCelli's? Over here."

A murmur went around the emergency room waiting area as many of the people waiting recognized the name. They looked up at the couple and the unconscious child. The parents had tears rolling down their faces. Someone yelled to Lindy.

"Missus DeCelli....is there anything I can do?"

"Pray.....just pray....*please*," she answered as a sob caught her words.

Liz and Nick were standing there holding Michael. Lindy reached for Michael and hugged him as he spotted his sister. Michael began to cry as he called to Samantha.

"Sammie! Sammie! Pease wake up! I yuv you!"

"And she loves you, too, Sweetheart. You can see her after she wakes up. Now...stay with Uncle Nick and Aunt Liz so we can help Sammie?"

"Okay," Michael sniffed and nodded. "Tell her to hurry up and wake up, Mommy. I miss her."

As Lindy kissed Michael and handed him off to Liz, she looked beyond Liz's shoulder to the waiting area.

Several people were on their knees praying—praying for Samantha. Lindy swallowed hard and entered the room behind the curtain where doctors and hospital staff were already attending to Samantha. Ricky stood off to the side and she quickly joined him, slipping her arms around his waist. He wrapped his arms around her as they stood there watching—crying—silently praying.

After what seemed like hours a doctor spoke to Lindy and Ricky.

"She's very sick. That scratch on her leg is very infected and it's carrying toxins through her body. We have to get her to intensive care under twenty-four hour observation. We are pumping her with a strong antibiotic right now, but she's dehydrated and her body seems to be breaking down. We've done what we can down here...so we'll get her to the ICU floor. She's young and strong and healthy. Kids are resilient. She has a good chance. We're working on bringing her fever down. That is another worry. So you two go out and get a cup of coffee or something. We'll call you when we get ready to transport her upstairs. We have an excellent pediatric ICU section....she'll be in good hands. And judging from what I've seen in the waiting area she's got other good hands working in her favor."

Ricky looked puzzled by the doctor's last remark.

"You'll see," Lindy whispered to him.

Beyond the separate examining rooms, in the waiting area, several more people had joined the original small group who were on their knees praying.

"It's for Samantha," Lindy whispered to Ricky.

"I'll be...."

Nick and Chris quickly joined them as they stood there in awe. Nick gave them a heads-up.

"There are television cameras and reporters being kept at bay by police. You should probably go address the press….hard as it is. I don't know how they found out."

It had been announced on television that Samantha DeCelli had been found. Every Television station broke into their regular programming with the news that she had been found alive but unconscious. Lindy was staring up at the television in the waiting area, tears streaming down her face. A picture of Samantha was on the screen as the newscaster spoke.

"Let's get it over with," she muttered to Ricky.

They stepped outside the emergency room doors and were bombarded by reporters and flash bulbs. Blinding lights interrupted their vision. Ricky held his hands up to get silence. They all understood and became quiet.

"We have Samantha back. She's very sick and she is unconscious. We ask that you all pray for her recovery. We don't know any more about her condition."

"Mister DeCelli….did he rape her?"

Ricky felt his blood begin to boil. One of the doctors who had been treating Samantha appeared at his side.

"I'll take it. Calm down."

"We have thoroughly examined her and found that there was no sexual assault on the girl. Physically, he had done nothing to hurt her at all. There is a small scratch on her leg that became badly infected and toxic. This is why she is in distress right now."

"What is the prognosis on her?" a woman reporter shouted.

"She's holding her own, and all we can do is watch her closely. She's young and strong so she has a good chance of recovery. That's all for now. We'll keep you all updated."

As he ended the interview, he led Lindy and Ricky back through the doors.

"Is it true that Mister DeCelli beat the kidnapper to near death?"

"Is the kidnapper in custody?"

"Let the FBI handle those questions," Doctor Thomas chuckled. "I knew you needed me to get you out of that last question, Mister DeCelli. I saw the fire coming from your eyes."

"Thanks...people are sick."

"Yeah, you think that until you see these people in here....all praying for your daughter's recovery."

Ricky nodded as he reached for Lindy's hand.

"We have to thank them....somehow."

"They've all been here quite a while. We're short staffed all day today....as usual. They're getting ready to take your daughter up to the ICU. We've made arrangements for you two to spend the night if you want to."

"Yes....I don't want to let her out of my sight," Lindy answered.

Nick and Liz joined them in the waiting area and waited for the gurney transporting Samantha to her ICU bed.

Ricky handed Nick his credit card before he got on the elevator with Lindy, the gurney holding Samantha, and the three caregivers attending to Samantha.

"Uncle Nick, feed these people that are praying for our daughter," he told him.

Lindy and Ricky both kissed Michael and promised

him that he could see Sammie soon. That last thing they heard as the elevator doors shut was Michael calling Samantha.

46

ANGIE AND RON came running into the house, Angie half hysterical. Sam and Renee were sitting in front of the television watching the news. Lindy and Ricky were talking to the press. Angie was gulping air as she tried to ask questions.

"How did they find her? What happened? Where is she now?" Angie was beside herself. "*Oh, God*! Is she going to be okay?"

"We don't know yet. We stayed behind because we figured there would be too much confusion at the hospital. All that really needed to be there was Lindy and Ricky," Renee responded.

"Well...Lindy wanted Michael there thinking that Samantha would hear his voice and respond to it," Sam reminded her.

"So what was that about Ricky beating the kidnapper to death?"

"We don't know. Would you blame him?"

"No....I wouldn't," Ron interjected.

Renee's cell phone rang. She answered and heard Ricky's voice.

"Renee, just thought I'd touch base with you and Sam. Sammie is still unconscious and she's in ICU. She's resting comfortably. Lindy and I are going to stay here tonight. Aunt Liz and Uncle Nick have Michael with them. Michael...he kinda got upset at seeing her like that, but he'll be okay. Did the Feds get their equipment out of the house yet?"

"No...not yet. Your mother is here, Rick."

"Okay....let me talk to her then."

Renee handed Angie the cell phone. Angie dove right in.

"Ricky.....Oh, GOD! *How is she?*"

"We don't know yet, Mom. We're going to stay here tonight."

"Of course you are! That's the only place for you to be. Do you want me to take Michael?"

"He's with Aunt Liz and Uncle Nick. They're coming to the house, so if you want to wait there you can see if they want you to take him. I gotta go. I'll call when we know something."

"Okay, Honey....give Lindy and Samantha my love.... and Ricky....I love you, too."

"I love you, Mom," he responded before he hung up.

He was walking back to Samantha's room when he spied Ray and Diane getting off the elevator.

"Hey," he called softly.

They stopped and waited for him to catch up to them.

"What's going on? How is she?"

"She's still unconscious. They're giving her fluids and antibiotics. We don't know anything else."

"Tell me, is it true that you nearly beat Sutter to death?"

Ricky snorted a laugh. "The press exaggerates."

"Yeah, I know first hand how hard you can hit, and you were seventeen then, before work outs, weights, and Karate. How badly did you hurt him?"

Ricky smiled at Ray.

"Put it this way….I don't think he'll bother anyone in *my* family again. Lindy hit him, too. That was actually kind of funny."

Ricky stopped talking as they entered the ICU room. Samantha was lying on the bed as still as a doll, while Lindy stood beside the bed holding the hand that wasn't hooked up to tubes. Ray looked at Lindy and saw the look of pain and sadness on her face and remembered that same look when Stacey was dying. 'Oh God….don't do it to her twice,' Ray silently prayed. 'Three times,' he corrected himself, remembering that she must have gone through this with Nicholas. He hesitated for a moment and then strode the short distance to the bed and engulfed Lindy in his arms.

"I'm so sorry, Princess. I'm so sorry."

Tears slid down his face as he silently chastised himself for not doing this when she was fourteen and needed him.

"I should have been there for you…when you needed me. I'm so sorry."

"But you're here now, Dad…..and I need you."

Ray held his arms around Lindy as they stared at Samantha, willing her to open her eyes. Nurses came in and suggested that they get a cup of coffee while they attended to Samantha. A nurse looked pointedly at Ray and Diane and announced that ICU visiting hours were over.

"Come back tomorrow, Dad? And Diane?"

"Of course. Try to get some sleep. We'll be back tomorrow."

Lindy and Ricky walked them to the elevator and then went to the ICU lounge to get coffee. Ricky bought Lindy a Mounds Bar and she insisted on sharing it with him. A nurse appeared at the doorway and told them they could go back in. A cot had been set up in the room, she told them, and she apologized that there was only one available.

After checking on Samantha once more, both Lindy and Ricky curled up on the cot. They were exhausted but found it hard to sleep.

"Ricky.....she *has* to make it. All those prayers for her.....God just *has* to listen....doesn't he?"

"I hope so, Babe....I hope so. I've been silently praying...and I know you have. If love and prayers can save her....she'll be fine."

He tightened his arms around Lindy and, exhaustion taking over; they fell into a fitful sleep.

47

LINDY'S EYES SNAPPED open. What was it? A sound?
She glanced up at the big clock on the wall. One thirty-
five. She looked around, trying to remember where she
was. The hospital. Samantha. *Samantha*! Crying? Yes!
Crying!! Lindy swung her legs from the cot to the floor and
in one fluid movement was standing and moving toward
the bed. She moved around to the other side of the bed
to avoid the tubes, IV pole, and monitors. Samantha was
staring at the ceiling crying.

"Hi, Sammie…." Lindy spoke just above a whisper, the
tears already coming.

"Mommy…."

Her voice was raspy and she sounded surprised. The
surprise was followed by a warm smile.

"And Daddy…."

Ricky appeared on the other side of the bed, grinning,
but fighting tears, too.

"Hi, Daddy….are we in Brazil?"

"No, Princess….we're still in Pennsylvania."

"We didn't go?"

"No.....you got real sick and fainted. We had to get you to a hospital."

"Is that where we are now? I was scared when I opened my eyes…"

"Yes, Princess…you're in the hospital. Don't be scared."

"We missed you, Sammie….we missed you so much." Lindy told her as she wiped tears away.

"Where did John go?"

"He's gone, Sweetheart."

Ricky heard the darkness come into Lindy's voice and saw the warmth in her eyes replaced by a fleeting coldness at the very mention of Nelson.

"Babe….we have to tell the nurses that she's awake. Want me to go? Or do you want to?"

"I'll be right back, Sweetheart. You can talk to Daddy for a minute."

Lindy rushed out to the nurses' station to let them know that Samantha was awake. The supervising nurse went to retrieve two more nurses and they went to Samantha's room.

"Okay….Mommy and Daddy will have to go for a walk. We need about a half hour in here."

Lindy and Ricky nodded and walked down to the lounge. Once inside the lounge they wrapped their arms around each other and cried tears of relief. They stood in the middle of the lounge just holding each other until the tears stopped flowing.

"Thank God. And thank *you*, Ricky…for believing me. If we had listened to the FBI we would never have gotten her back."

"I know. They operate by the book….*you* operate by

the heart....and I'll follow *that* any time. We have to call everybody and tell them that she's awake."

"Shouldn't we wait until morning?"

"What....you think anybody is actually sleeping?"

"You're right. Let's call Uncle Nick and Aunt Liz.... Then Renee and Sam will know, too. Have them call your mom. We can call Chris and Cindy, and then they can call my dad and Diane, Luke, Shawna and Ally."

"Okay....that'll work."

Ricky stopped and smiled at Lindy.

"You know....I can remember having to make this kind of call quite a few years ago. When you finally came out of the unconscious state you were in....I called Uncle Nick.... he called everybody......"

Ricky stopped and reached for Lindy and hugged her to him tightly.

"I love you, Lindy.....and I will never stop loving you."

Lindy tried to speak past the lump in her throat, but all she could get out was a whisper.

"Please don't ever stop, Ricky. I couldn't stand it."

With their arms around each other, they walked back to Samantha's room. The nurses had finished up and Samantha was already dozing off into a velvet slumber. Lindy stretched out on the cot while Ricky went to make the phone calls. When he came back, Lindy was sound asleep. He curled up beside her, draped his arm over her, and followed her into a sound sleep.

48

"Mommy?"

Lindy sat up on the cot.

"Sammie? Are you awake?"

"Yes…..I was calling you."

"Are you okay, Honey?"

"Yes….I wanted to make sure I wasn't dreaming that you were here."

Lindy laughed and strode to the bed.

"I'm really here…..and so is Daddy."

"Where's Michael?"

"He's with Aunt Liz and Uncle Nick. They are going to bring him up later. He has really missed you. We all did."

Lindy held Samantha's hand and brushed the hair out of her eyes. Ricky joined them on the other side of the hospital bed and kissed Samantha's forehead.

"Her fever seems to be down, Babe."

"Thank God," Lindy added, as she swallowed hard to keep from crying tears of relief.

"Mommy?"

"What, Sweetheart...."

"John didn't tell me the truth....did he? I wasn't on vacation....was I?"

"No, Sweetheart....you weren't."

"He said you came out to see me one night but I was sleeping so you left me sleep. You didn't....did you?"

"No, Sweetheart."

"And you and Daddy and Michael were not going to be on that airplane like he said....were you?"

"No, Sweetheart...."

"Did John steal me?"

"Oh, Sammie...."

Lindy couldn't hold back the tears any longer. Ricky came around to the other side of the bed and put his arm around Lindy.

"You're safe with us now, Princess. We don't ever have to talk about John again," Ricky assured her.

"I remember now....he came in my room and.....put something over my....nose...I tried to yell for Mommy....but then I went to sleep. When I woke up at John's house I thought it was a dream. He wasn't nice at first....then he was."

"What do you mean he wasn't nice?"

"He told me to shut up and that he hated kids that cried. He talked real *mean*. He told me that if you didn't pay him money you didn't want me back."

"Then what?"

"Well, then he got real nice and gave me presents....and then we watched Disney movies, went for walks and then on the swing. He told me all about cows and sheep...and other animals. Oh....and he let me hear one of Mommy's CD's....I liked that the best."

Samantha's eyes were full of love as she smiled at Lindy. Both Ricky and Lindy were relieved to hear that Nelson had not mistreated her in any way. In all fairness, Ricky as well as Lindy realized that the scratch and the resulting illness from the scratch was really not Nelson's fault. Kidnapping her in the first place was unforgivable and they wanted to see him punished to the full extent of the law.

A nurse brought a breakfast tray in for Samantha and two trays were specially ordered for Lindy and Ricky. They ate breakfast together and had just finished when Liz and Nick, carrying Michael, arrived.

"Sammie! I yuv you!"

Michael was grinning from ear to ear as he reached out to hug Samantha. Her grin was just as big as she wrapped her free arm around him and placed her forehead on his. The reunion was interrupted when Agent Morrow entered the room.

"FBI man!" Michael shouted.

Everyone laughed, including Agent Morrow.

"Sorry to interrupt. So....you're Samantha. I'm so glad you're feeling better...and I'm glad you're back with your mommy and daddy....and brother, of course."

"Did you save me?"

"No....not really, Honey. Your Daddy and your Mommy and your Uncle Chris saved you. They're real heroes."

Samantha looked from Ricky to Lindy, her eyes full of love, as she smiled at them. Morrow cleared his throat.

"Anyway.....I came up here to see her, of course....but to see if I can talk you into a press conference. Reporters are still crawling around outside, obstructing traffic. They all want an update. I'll be there, of course...."

"Okay....press conference....at ten o'clock. Go set it up....we'll be there," Ricky assured him.

Satisfied with their response, Morrow walked out, telling them he'd be back for them at nine-forty-five. He met Chris getting off of the elevator, shook his hand and traded places with him, punching the first floor button. Chris bounded into the room.

"Is my favorite niece in here?"

"Uncle Chris!"

Samantha reached her arm out to Chris as he rounded the bed and swooped down to kiss her cheek. She hugged his neck with her free arm and smiled at him.

"And I didn't come empty-handed either....." he grinned slyly at her.

"What did you bring?" She smiled sweetly at him.

Chris reached into the bag he had carried into the room and produced a pink and white shaggy dog. He handed it to Samantha and reached into the bag again. Out came a stuffed Eyore and he handed it to Michael. Once again, he reached into the bag and emptied it this time, pulling out coloring books and crayons for both of them.

"Now what do you say?" Lindy reminded them.

"Thank you, Uncle Chris!" They replied in unison.

"Folks...this is an ICU room....some of you are going to have to clear out of here."

Doctor Thomas was standing in the doorway glaring at them. He spotted Liz and Nick and smiled.

"Oh...never mind. So....how is my patient? Awake! And looking much better. Okay, I need some space in here so I can assess Samantha's condition. How about everyone except the parents going away for about fifteen minutes?"

Lindy and Ricky stood back as Doctor Thomas examined Samantha. He paid particular attention to the area where she was scratched, and then added a couple of notes to her chart. When he was finished he turned to Lindy and Ricky.

"Well....she's out of the woods. I'm going to keep her two more days just to make sure that infection goes away. I'm ordering some tests, just as a precaution. If the tests come out fine, she can go home on Friday. In the meantime, I'll check in on her tomorrow and be here Friday to sign the release forms. My partner will see her tonight. I want to make sure that infection is well under control before I let her out of here, though."

Relieved, Lindy and Ricky slowly let the air out of their lungs.

"Thank you, Doctor Thomas. Thank you so much."

"You're welcome. Now....you two.....you need a good night's rest. Rumor around the hospital has it that the whole affair took its toll on both of you. Get somebody else to spend the night here tonight. You two go home and sleep in your own bed and get eight hours in. That's doctor's orders."

"Lindy? Let's ask your dad to stay with her."

Lindy nodded in agreement. Doctor Thomas was walking out of the room just as Agent Morrow was walking in. Lindy glanced up at the clock and saw that it was nine-forty-five. Ricky ran down to the lounge to get someone to stay with Samantha so he and Lindy could go down and meet the press.

The front of the hospital was crowded with cameras

and reporters, and of course, the FBI and the police who were trying to control the crowd. Lindy and Ricky walked outside and went to stand behind a podium that had been placed there for them. Microphones from the four major stations had been erected on the podium. Once again flashbulbs went off as they walked up to the podium. It was three minutes to ten. They waited until they were given the sign that they were on the air, and Ricky began.

"First of all my wife and I, as well as our entire family, want to say thank you from the bottom of our hearts to those of you who prayed for our daughter's safe return and then her recovery. We appreciate you. Samantha has regained consciousness and is out of the woods.... the doctor told us that this morning. She is expected to make a full recovery. And be released from the hospital on Friday."

"Does she know what happened to her?" A reporter from a CBS television station asked.

"Yes, she does," Lindy answered. "Our daughter is very bright. Right after she regained consciousness she asked me point blank if he had lied to her. He told her she was on vacation, but she remembers him taking her out of her room and putting something over her nose to make her go to sleep, she said."

"Did he hurt her in any way?" The ABC reporter asked.

"No....he didn't. She said he was mean at first but then he got nice."

"How was he mean?" The NBC reporter piped up.

"He told her to shut up and that he hated crying brats, or something to that affect. She said he was very nice to her after that....taking her to see farm animals, watching Disney movies, bought her presents. I'm very grateful that he wasn't cruel and that he didn't hurt her."

"Mister DeCelli....rumor has it that you and Missus DeCelli are the ones who found her rather than the Federal Bureau of Investigation. How did that come about?" It was the CBS reporter's turn.

Ricky smiled. "My wife's radar. Lindy senses things with the kids. She just knows."

"But actually....Samantha herself provided most of the clues to her whereabouts." Lindy added. "The first clue was when she said the bushes are red. We knew to look in an area that had a lot of red bushes. We found them."

"But why is it you two had to go there to find her rather than let the FBI go?"

"Because we wouldn't listen to her."

Morrow's voice came out of nowhere, and then he was beside Lindy. He introduced himself and then continued.

"She told us that her daughter was there but we didn't listen. Thank God these two were persistent and determined. They wouldn't give up. They are the true heroes in this case. I highly commend them both."

Applause erupted from the reporters and the crowd that had gathered around.

"Thanks....thank you, Agent Morrow. Thanks again to all of you."

"Mister DeCelli....do you have any special plans to celebrate Samantha's homecoming?"

"Well....yes, of course....as soon as we know she is well enough I plan on taking my family to Disney World. We all need some fun in the sun....as a family."

"You have a son, too. How did he take it when Samantha disappeared?" ABC asked.

"He was distraught. They are very close. When he saw the state she was in when we found her he…kind of freaked out a little…..begging her to wake up….but he…. he's okay. Right now, they're together upstairs coloring in coloring books." Lindy answered.

"Missus DeCelli….there has been some speculation as to why he chose your child to kidnap. Is there a history of some sort there?"

The reporter from Fox News asked her first question since the press conference began, and it was certainly a loaded question of high impact. Lindy and Ricky looked at each other before either of them spoke. Lindy took the floor.

"When I was seventeen, I was placed in the Sutters' home as a foster teen. Nelson Sutter raped me…..was prosecuted for it and went to prison. He blamed me for his sentence, and consequently, his financial demise. He felt I owed him since he lost everything when I told….his wife, his home, his job, and eventually his freedom. When he got out of prison he had nothing….so he decided to get revenge and money at the same time by taking one of my children and then demanding a ransom."

"Do you think he'll stay out of your life after this?" Someone asked.

"He better," Ricky retorted.

"Missus DeCelli….how did you get through it….when you were seventeen, I mean?" Another reporter questioned. "I mean…..that had to be traumatic."

Lindy looked up at Ricky before she answered.

"I had Ricky. His love….and his strength….got me through it. He was there for me then and he has been there for me ever since."

"That's all for now….we would like to go back up and be with our children. We'll keep you updated on any further developments," Ricky promised as he began to steer Lindy away from the podium. "Once again…..thank you for your prayers."

Some of the reporters were still trying to get their attention as they entered the front doors to the hospital. Ricky kept his arm around Lindy as they got through the doors and across the lobby to the elevators. He pushed the up-arrow button and they waited.

"Babe, that was brave of you to disclose that….about being raped, I mean."

"Someone would have found it out anyway…so why not just say it and get it over with?" Lindy sighed.

"Yeah, you're probably right. It was a news item and public record at one time. Here comes my mother and Ron."

Angie and Ron met them at the elevator just as the doors opened. Angie hugged them as the elevator car started its ascent.

"I can't wait to see her. I can't wait to give her these."

Angie pulled a pair of Cinderella pajamas out of a bag, and then a pink shorts outfit.

"For Disney World…." Angie told them. "And….for Michael….."

She produced a pair of Mickey Mouse pajamas and a blue shorts set.

"There goes my mother…..spoiling our kids again."

Ricky made a comical face and rolled his eyes toward the ceiling.

"Ricky....I wouldn't want it any other way," Lindy answered with a smile and a wink.

"No....me neither." Ricky answered as he hugged his mother and Lindy, one on each side of him.

Agents Morrow and Daily were standing in front of the lobby elevators waiting for the doors to open. They were going to stop up to see the DeCelli family once more before going to the house to remove the equipment from their family room. The case was over and there was a chance that they would never see the DeCelli's again. If the case went to trial, which he didn't think it would, they would see them in court. They had been more than hospitable to them and in fact, had provided them with some excellent meals. Tom Morrow was both glad and saddened by the thought that he would never see them again. He knew he had feelings that he should not have for Lindy. He needed to get away and go back to his routine, but he also wanted to stay, just to see her again—over and over again. He also knew that was not possible or plausible. Lindy and Ricky were very much in love. He needed to forget her. Agent Jack Daily brought him out of his thoughts.

"I'm sorry, Jack....what did you say?"

"I said....you may take some flack for saying what you did....about us not listening to Lindy.....and that they are the heroes...."

"Don't care, Jack....I just spoke the truth."

"Hey, Tom....we went by the book...."

"Yeah....well....apparently Sutter didn't read the same

book. Admit it....we could have cost the DeCelli's their child."

Jack Daily didn't answer him. He knew that Tom Morrow was right.

49

Lindy and Ricky spent the afternoon and the evening with Samantha and Michael. Shawna and Ally showed up, laden with gifts, after they got off work. Lukas came in right after they left. He apologized that Michelle didn't come up but they didn't know if they could bring little Lukas up. Michelle was waiting downstairs in the lobby so Lukas didn't stay long. He promised that they would be there to see her the next day. Cindy brought Samantha and Michael a tray of fruits and candies. She cried when she hugged Samantha. When Diane and Ray got there, Lindy and Ricky asked them if they could stay for the night. They were delighted and thrilled that they had been asked. Ricky appeased his mother's hurt by telling her she could take Michael home with her. Lindy and Ricky finally left for the night to go home and get a good restful night's sleep. Carrying take-out in with them, they entered the house in time to say their final good-byes to Jack Daily and Tom Morrow.

Ricky held the door as they took the last bit of equipment and belongings out of the family room. Arms around each other, they watched the two agents drive away before they sat down to eat their Chinese take-out.

"You know that Morrow has the hots for you, don't you?"

"No he doesn't!"

"Yes, he does."

"How do you know that?"

"You're not the only one in the family with radar. You think I don't know it when some guy is drooling over my wife? I watched him when he thought I wasn't looking. I would just laugh to myself and think......eat your heart out, dude."

"Ricky! That's terrible!"

"What is? He shouldn't have been having those thoughts about my wife. Hey, I didn't get mad or anything. I knew he wouldn't act on it....but I saw it all the same."

"Agent Morrow? Are you sure?"

"Uh-huh."

They finished eating and Lindy started the cleanup while Ricky wandered into their bedroom and then to their bathroom. He began drawing water for a bath for Lindy. He added scented bubble bath to the tub and left the water running while he went out to get her.

"Oh what a welcome idea!" She exclaimed when she saw the bubble bath waiting for her. "On one condition...."

"What's that?"

"Join me?"

"I was hoping you would ask," Ricky responded with a grin.

They soaked in the tub together and then wrapped

themselves in towels and fell into bed where they made love slowly and passionately. They fell asleep in each other's arms and didn't awaken until dawn.

50

AFTER A LEISURELY breakfast, Lindy and Ricky showered and dressed to get back to the hospital. It was close to ten o'clock when they parked in the parking lot and then walked through the front doors of the hospital. They hurriedly crossed the lobby and hopped on the elevator that arrived promptly after they pushed the button. The elevator stopped on the floor below Samantha's and they endured the wait while two elderly people got on and selected a button for another floor. Finally, the elevator rose to Samantha's floor and they got off and hurried down to her ICU room. They stopped dead. The room was empty. Lindy felt her heart leap to her throat. Ricky felt his muscles tighten as they stood there looking at the empty bed.

"DeCelli's?" A middle-aged nurse came up beside them and smiled.

"Yes."

"Come with me. They moved your little girl about a half hour ago."

"Why? I mean that's good.....isn't it?"

"Oh yes….but you'll see why in a moment."

The nurse led them down the hall and turned to the right into another corridor.

"We had to put her in a private room because of everything coming in."

She stood aside as Lindy and Ricky walked past her into the room. They stared in awe at everything. Samantha was surrounded by flowers, dolls, stuffed animals, and various other toys.

"Where did this stuff come from?" Ricky asked.

"Everywhere. Since last evening things have been arriving. Well-wishers from everywhere have been sending her things. We had to give her a private room to accommodate all of it. There are several boxes of candy, and there are a couple of fruit baskets over there. It's incredible."

"Yeah….it is. Hi, Princess! This is better than Christmas, isn't it?"

"All this stuff! Mommy…can we give some of it to other kids?"

Samantha was sitting up on the bed looking at a book that someone had sent her. She looked much better than she had yesterday. There was color in her cheeks and her eyes were a very clear bright blue.

"Of course we can, Sweetheart. You keep what you want and we can give the rest of it to the other kids in the hospital. That's a wonderful idea, and you're very sweet to think of it."

Lindy went to the bed and hugged Samantha, then sat down and pulled her into her lap. The IV's and the monitors were all gone. That meant she was getting well. Lindy kissed the top of Samantha's head and looked up at

Ricky with tears that were threatening to spill out of her eyes.

"Oh…..to think that I may have never been able to do this again. I'm so….relieved."

"I know…..me, too."

"Mommy? Did you cry when I was gone?"

"Yes, Sweetheart….a lot."

"Daddy didn't…..because he's a grownup man….right, Daddy?"

"Right," Ricky agreed.

He sat down on the bed and lifted her from Lindy's lap to his own.

"Daddy's fibbing. Daddy cried. Daddy cried real hard."

"You did? But I thought men didn't cry…"

"They do when they're sad. You're my little girl….my princess. I was afraid that I might never see you again."

"I'm really your princess?"

"Yep."

"Is mommy your princess, too?"

"Mommy? No….*Mommy* is my *queen*."

"Wow! Then that makes you….."

"That's right, Sweetheart. A king. Daddy is my king. And Michael is our prince."

"The royal DeCelli family, I presume…"

They all turned to see Nick and Liz entering the room. Both of them were awed by all of the gifts and flowers that had been sent.

"So….King Ricky….where did all of this come from?" Nick asked.

"Everywhere…the nurse said. People from all over the country have been sending things."

393

"Samantha wants to give some of it away....to other kids. It was her idea." Lindy told them.

"That's sweet," Liz responded. "Sammie....you're an angel like your mother."

Sam and Renee came in to say their good-byes. "We have a motel to run....so we have to get back. Sammie, give us a hug. And here, you take your family out to dinner."

Sam handed Samantha an envelope which she quickly opened. It was a gift certificate to a local family steakhouse. Samantha recognized the logo on the certificate. She smiled up at Sam.

"Okay, Uncle Sam....I will."

She hugged him and then hugged Renee. Lindy and Ricky hugged them both and thanked them for coming up.

"See you soon?" Renee asked, teary-eyed.

"Try to. Love to you both," Ricky added.

"Next time you come up you can stay with us. There shouldn't be any FBI men in our family room."

They all laughed as Sam and Renee waved and left.

"It's always so hard to say good-bye to them....isn't it, Ricky?"

"Yeah," Ricky agreed and nodded.

Angie and Ron and Michael passed Sam and Renee in the hall, said their good-byes, and then rushed in to see Samantha. Michael was all smiles when he saw that Samantha was sitting up and there was no IV in her arm.

"It looks like Toyland in here," Angie observed. "No wonder they moved her to a private room."

"Mommy? When can I go home?"

"The doctor said tomorrow, Sweetie."

"Good. I miss my room."

"That means you're feeling better, I guess."

Lindy smiled at her and kissed her forehead. Two men entered the room. One was carrying a camera and he introduced himself as a reporter for the local newspaper.

"Can I get a picture of the family for the paper? It will be featured in Sunday's edition."

"Sure....why not?" Ricky allowed.

They posed for the picture and the reporter left happy. The other man remained. He cleared his throat for attention.

"Hi.....my name is Lawrence Furman. I have been sent here by the CEO of Disney Productions, who I work for. Disney Productions would like for you, the DeCelli family, be our guests at Disney World. Airfare, hotel accommodations, transportation to and from the park, meals, and a pass to all theme parks is included."

He handed Ricky a large envelope.

"Really? No kidding?"

"You said in your press conference that you wanted to take your family to Disney World.....and we would love for you to come. All on us."

"Samantha....Michael....want to go to Disney World?"

"Yeah!" They chimed.

"Okay...then we accept. Thank you. How about this, Babe?"

"I'm overwhelmed.....thank you....and tell your boss we said thank you. Can we contact him to say it in person?"

"That will be arranged. Now....I have a plane to catch.

395

Here is my card. Please call me when you get there. And Samantha? I am so glad you are okay. We at Disney love happy endings." He smiled at her and waved at everyone before he left the room.

...

As promised Samantha was released from the hospital the following day. Before she left the hospital, Samantha, Lindy, and Ricky, with the help of a hospital cart, distributed fruits, candies, and toys to every child on the pediatric ward. Samantha seemed to enjoy the smiles she got from giving away her gifts. Ricky planned on returning to work on Monday, so that gave them the weekend together as a family. Life would return to normal.

On Sunday, Lindy and the kids surprised Ricky with a birthday cake. In all the turmoil of the past couple of weeks, Ricky had forgotten that it was his thirty-third birthday. They would be spending Lindy's birthday and their anniversary in Disney World since they were scheduled to leave the following Sunday. Ray and Diane would be going with them. They had a special surprise planned for Lindy's birthday and they hadn't told anyone. Ray had a lot to make up for and he was doing his best to do it.

Lindy had a full week planned. They had shopping to do for her, Ricky and the children. New shoes, clothes, bathing suits, sun screen and sunglasses were on the list. Arrangements had to be made to have the mail picked up and the paper stopped. The alarm would be set but somebody had to have the code in case there was a need to enter the house. Liz and Nick agreed to pick up the mail and asked them not to stop the paper. They would read it and pay for it for two weeks. Everything was coming together and soon they would be off enjoying a wonderful family vacation. It was well-deserved.

Epilogue

LINDY AND RICKY stood smiling with their arms linked loosely around each others' waists as they watched Samantha and Michael sitting in a teacup waiting for it to move. It was their second day in Disney World and the whole family was having a ball. Samantha looked over toward her parents and shouted.

"I love you, Mommy....I love you, Daddy!"

"We love you too, Princess," Ricky answered for both of them.

"I yuv you, Mommy! I yuv you, Daddy!" Michael shouted.

"And we love you, Michael," Lindy answered back.

"Michael......love...love.....la...la...love. Say it," Samantha coached, pressing her tongue against the back of her front teeth and holding her mouth open for Michael to see.

"La....la...love," he mimicked.

"Good! Now say it to Mommy and Daddy. Say I love you."

"Mommy! Daddy! Listen to Michael!" Samantha shouted.

"Go ahead, Michael....say it. La....la....love."

Michael grinned at Samantha and then grinned at Lindy and Ricky.

"La....la....love! I yuv you!" His grin got bigger.

Samantha hit her forehead in frustration and Lindy and Ricky just doubled over with laughter.

"Sammie, he'll get it....eventually. Thank you for trying to teach him, though."

The teacup started to move and both Samantha and Michael had faces full of anticipation as they felt it move. Lindy and Ricky smiled as they watched. The children were wearing the outfits Angie had bought them. Samantha was happy when Lindy dressed in a pink shorts set to match. Ricky wore blue to match Michael's outfit. Michael's grin showed that he was happy about that.

"To think that we might not have ever seen her again..... oh, Ricky."

"I know Babe....it was a nightmare. Thank God it's over....and it turned out the way it did. It has always been one of my biggest fears.....losing one of them or losing you. I hope I never have to face either one of those fears again."

"Do you think Sammie's okay? I mean...do you think she'll have...I don't know...any problems because of the kidnapping?"

Ricky looked at Lindy and then stared at the ground for a moment.

"I don't know. I really don't know. All we can do is hope *not*. Maybe she should see someone....a child psychologist maybe...just in case."

Ray and Diane, hands full with treats for everyone, joined Lindy and Ricky to watch as the teacup spun around and listen to the squeals from Samantha and Michael. The four adults, all grinning, waved every time Samantha and Michael passed them.

"Hey, you two.....how about if we baby-sit tonight so you two can go walk in the moonlight....or something. That hotel complex we're staying in has a lovely pond with a bridge over it. It's a nice romantic walk for you. We went there and walked last night after everybody settled down. Why don't you two go tonight?"

"Want to, Babe?"

"Uh-huh. It sounds nice."

The ride was ending so the adults walked to the exit ramp to wait for Samantha and Michael to come through the gate. The day ended with the parade and two tired children were carried by Ricky and Ray to the bus waiting to take them back to the hotel. After a late supper and baths, Samantha and Michael were ready to be tucked into bed. They knelt alongside the double bed they were sharing and said their prayers, asking God to bless those that they loved, being careful not to leave anyone out.

Lindy and Ricky and Ray and Diane stood back and watched with pride. It was the end of Samantha's prayer that stunned both Ricky and Lindy. As they listened they heard her special request.

"And God....I almost forgot......please look in on John. I think he really needs you. Amen."

Lindy was speechless and close to tears. She stared up at Ricky, her mouth gaping. He put his arm around her shoulders, pulled her close, smiled down at her, and whispered.

"I think Samantha will be just fine."

***

At that moment, almost fifteen hundred miles away, a figure stood peering out through a grated window, staring at just a sliver of moonlit sky. Tears rolled down his face as he cried silently.

"I'm sorry. I'm so sorry," Nelson whispered.

His thoughts ran through his head. Loraine—Lindy—Samantha. Stacey? He hadn't hurt Stacey. Hadn't had the chance. She was already dead. He thought about all four of them. He had loved Stacey—wanted her. She never knew it. He had loved Loraine in his way. She was a classy lady. That made him look good in front of employers and clients. Lindy? She was a kid who needed them. He messed up. He shouldn't have touched her. Samantha? Samantha. Samantha!

"Samantha….I'm so sorry I caused you to be sick, Munchkin," Nelson whispered. "Out of all of them….I loved you most of all. Please forgive me, Little Princess…. please forgive me."

Nelson turned from the window and picked up the newspaper photo of Samantha—one that had appeared in the paper after she was found. He quietly kissed her forehead and set it back down before he stretched out on his cold hard cot in the facility that was to be his home for many years to come.

The end?

About the Author:

Carole McKee is a native Pittsburgher and her love for the city shows in the stories she writes. Although now residing in Clearwater, Florida she still calls Pittsburgh her home. She began writing in 1996 when she wrote a short story about her black Labrador retriever. *Perfect*, her first novel was published in July of 2007. *Choices*, the first book of this trilogy came out in July, 2008. After reading *The Bushes are Red*, don't miss the next one! Please visit Carole at her websites: www.authorcarolemckee.com **or** www.carolemckee.com

Printed in the United States
214794BV00001B/1/P

9 781438 960760